PRAISE FOR *NEW POMPEII*

"An intriguing spin on the *Westworld/Jurassic Park* template,
this marks Godfrey out as an author to watch."
FINANCIAL TIMES (BOOKS OF THE YEAR)

"Full of mind-twisting time paradoxes, this conspiracy thriller
is a remarkably promising debut."
MORNING STAR (BOOKS OF THE YEAR)

"Should fill a void in the hearts of many a Michael Crichton
reader: a story so irresistibly entertaining, it should be
accompanied by a bottomless bucket of popcorn."
BARNES & NOBLE

"A rollicking adventure in the well-researched but
page-turning style of Michael Crichton."
THE SUN

"The historical detail is impressive, the mystery is interesting,
and there's a chewy time-travel puzzle for fans of the genre."
SFX

"Fascinating, cleverly wrought, intelligent and occasionally
brutal. A thrillingly original take on the time travel genre."
TIM LEBBON, *NEW YORK TIMES* BESTSELLER

"A high-concept thriller that brings ancient Rome crashing
into the present day. Smart, inventive and action-packed."
TOM HARPER, BESTSELLING AUTHOR OF *THE LOST TEMPLE*

"An impressive debut. A smart, intriguing thriller in the
tradition of Michael Crichton and Philip K. Dick."
GARETH L. POWELL, BSFA AWARD WINNER

EMPIRE
OF
TIME

DANIEL
GODFREY

TITAN BOOKS

Empire of Time
Print edition ISBN: 9781785653155
E-book edition ISBN: 9781785653162

Published by Titan Books
A division of Titan Publishing Group Ltd
144 Southwark Street, London SE1 0UP

First edition: June 2017
10 9 8 7 6 5 4 3 2 1

A CIP catalogue record for this title is available from the British Library.

Printed in the USA.

What did you think of this book? We love to hear from our readers. Please email us at: readerfeedback@titanemail.com, or write to us at the above address.

To receive advance information, news, competitions, and exclusive offers online, please sign up for the Titan newsletter on our website: www.titanbooks.com

FOR SARAH, DAVID, JAMES AND ROBERT

"Turn thy thoughts now to the consideration of thy life, thy life as a child, as a youth, thy manhood, thy old age, for in these also every change was a death. Is this anything to fear?"

MARCUS AURELIUS, EMPEROR OF ROME

1

NovusPart Research Labs, Cambridge, prior to the
construction of New Pompeii

Mark Whelan leant over the model and eyed the narrow streets. He took in the rough-hewn buildings of cork, plastic and plywood, and flashed a wide grin. Since he'd last seen it, Joe had pushed matchsticks into its surface. Presumably, they were meant to represent Romans. He flicked one and it toppled all too easily. Beside him, Harold McMahon gave a heavy sigh.

"Relax, Harold."

"I'm not his damn slave."

Whelan glanced across to where Joe Arlen sat with his back to them, working at his computer. He hadn't even acknowledged their presence, but he knew they were there. After all, knowing who had crossed his path – and when – was fast becoming Joe's specialism.

"Just be patient," Whelan said, turning back to the model. Nothing was quite at the right scale, but it represented what they'd been working towards for months. Their grand vision of the future, and the way by which they could control it. He noted one of Joe's more obscure dictums had now been chalked around the edge of the model: *The Master of Pompeii will become the Emperor of Time.*

"Joe," said McMahon, his voice heavy, "we've all got things to be doing."

Arlen stiffened in his seat. Whelan hoped he would just go back to his computer. He didn't.

"There was a girl in those lectures with Professor Jackson," Arlen said.

Shit, thought Whelan. *This again*. Professor Jackson. A man so insignificant his telephone number had once been left off the department directory. And yet for Arlen he was suddenly important, because Joe now apparently needed to trace everyone he'd ever met. It was his new obsession. "We've identified all the female students," Whelan said, trying to keep his voice neutral. "There weren't many of them, were there?"

Arlen turned, and Whelan felt an immediate wave of pity. In many ways, Joe remained as when they'd first met. A guy who'd managed to keep hold of his teenage looks, even though he was much older. And yet his eyes were now red-rimmed, and the fresh-faced excitement of youth had been replaced with frustration and anger.

"No, not a student," Arlen said. "An assistant. She was helping Jackson. Maybe a post-grad."

Whelan didn't respond, but McMahon couldn't help

himself. "I think I remember," he said. "Yes, didn't we see them in a restaurant together? You know? That Thai place down by the river?"

Fucking great. Whelan tensed.

Arlen rose from his chair and walked over to them. "The Thai place?"

"Thai *Palace*," said McMahon. He laughed. "Or was it an Indian? After all these years, I'm starting to forget. But she had bright red hair and the biggest…"

"No," said Arlen, suddenly quiet. He put both hands to his temples. "No," he said again. "She was a brunette. Bangles and a perm. Those lectures were part of all this… and we need to record any possible point of intersection. Because if they were dating it means—"

McMahon grunted. "Jesus, Joe. I was kidding…"

"What?"

"I was kidding about seeing them together," McMahon continued. "You think an old guy and a girl that good-looking? He wasn't exactly rich, was he?"

Avoiding Arlen's glare, Whelan again looked down at the table. He waited for the screaming fit that would surely follow. But it didn't come. Instead, he noticed a soft white mist start to mingle around their feet. He kicked at it, but the swirls re-formed until it looked like he was standing in snow.

And then he knew he was going to die.

Strangely he didn't try to fight it. Arlen had once predicted his "transportations" would be accompanied by a change in atmospheric pressure. Just enough to spill the moisture from the air before a person was pulled into the future.

He knew that when he woke up – thirty years from now – he wouldn't have long to live. Maybe he'd get to look Arlen in the face again before a gladiator killed him. Or maybe Arlen would strike the blow personally. After all, that's what he'd talked about. Even though Joe had first said it as a joke. An off-hand remark to win some petty argument with Harold.

Whelan fixed his eyes on the model. He saw the matchstick men, their red bobbled heads, and wondered why he'd agreed to so much madness. Arlen started to hurl abuse at McMahon. But, almost as soon as it started, the shouting stopped. Arlen vanished.

Whelan waited a few long minutes before speaking. "You saw it too?"

McMahon nodded, then started to retch.

The mist had gone, the implications obvious and immediate: Arlen had been stolen from time, and there were now just two of them left. Carefully, Whelan picked up one of the matches from the model. He snapped it between his fingers, relief flooding through him. McMahon broke into hysterical laughter.

"Thirty years," Whelan said, slowly. "Our first paradox. So do you think it was me who did it to him, or you?"

McMahon continued to laugh. He didn't even try to answer.

"So much for New Pompeii."

Slowly bringing himself back under control, McMahon shook his head. He wiped the slightest trace of saliva from his lips. "It may still have its uses."

2

New Pompeii, fifteen years after the fall of NovusPart

"SHE KNOWS I'M here?"

The slave on the door nodded. He remained standing at the side of his cubbyhole, his expression close to a smirk. Two guards flanked him.

Decimus Horatius Pullus hoisted his satchel further onto his shoulder. The sooner he could get this over with, the sooner he could get back to his own villa and be done with it all.

A few female slaves darted past him, heading towards the outer courtyards. Their urgency indicated they must be on their way to their mistress. One carried a towel, so perhaps Calpurnia was swimming. He glanced back at the porter and the two guards. The porter grinned at him.

"I need to speak with her," Pullus said.

"Habitus will be along in a few minutes."

Pullus sighed, his satchel pulling again on his shoulder. Other than the three men at the door, the main atrium of

Calpurnia's villa was empty. Four Corinthian columns jutted up from the corners of the central *impluvium* to support the roof, and each wall was covered with a sequential panoramic view of the forum in Rome.

The fine frescos couldn't hide the fact he'd been given the cold shoulder by Calpurnia. Pullus needed to explain things. But first he'd have to negotiate with Habitus. From somewhere deep in the villa came a metallic sound, almost like the slow drip of water. Which meant young Marcus was getting another lesson in swordplay. Habitus could be some time.

That was all he needed to know. He waited – just long enough for the porter and the two guards to take their collective attention away from him – then ran. Ignoring the porter's shouts, he continued quickly past a small interior grotto, and made his way out into a larger room, the walls of which were covered in a sweeping depiction of Pompeii's old harbour. If this had been a townhouse, then the decor would have marked out a *tablinum*. But this was a room for pleasure, not business.

Calpurnia's son Marcus and his bodyguard, the *frumentarius* Appius Hostilius Habitus, circled each other in the centre of the room. Both their faces were set with concentration, and both held real swords – not wooden training ones – ahead of them and ready.

The porter appeared in pursuit, and Pullus was pleased to see he had lost his smirk.

"I told him to wait!"

Habitus ignored the man, who slunk back to his post, and

broke off from his training. He walked towards Pullus with his eyes narrowed as if trying to work out a puzzle. Behind him, the boy looked disappointed his fun had been interrupted.

"Pullus," Habitus said. "We weren't expecting you for another day or so."

Pullus frowned. Whilst Marcus's tunic was drenched in sweat, Habitus hardly seemed out of breath. Calpurnia's chief bodyguard didn't appear outwardly athletic. The guards at the door easily out-muscled him but, then again, Calpurnia didn't employ him to strike any blows. At least, not personally.

Pullus had found Calpurnia's bodyguard not long after the fall of NovusPart. He hadn't particularly stood out from amongst the other men in the slave market. Being of average height, and slight build, he'd not been highly valued, especially given the focus on getting manpower to the many farms surrounding New Pompeii. Habitus had simply been unlucky. Visiting the town at the time of the eruption and without any friends, it hadn't taken long for him to fall into slavery. Yet when Pullus had asked him what he was doing in Pompeii, the academic centres of his brain had all fired in unison.

Grain. Habitus had been ordered to Pompeii from Rome to check on the supply of grain.

Of course, that wasn't the truth. But the words had caused them both to lock eyes, and it was clear in that moment that they'd both known. And so Pullus had been happy to pay the price. Because keeping watch on the grain supply was often used as a cover for other activities. And

Pullus guessed a *frumentarius* – an Imperial spy – was worth much more over the long term than a simple farm labourer. Unfortunately, Calpurnia and her father had agreed, and taken him for their own household.

"You've progressed from the wooden swords?"

Habitus shrugged. "Skill from wood, weight from metal," he said.

Marcus was sitting in the *tablinum*, gulping down water and wiping his forehead with a rag. The boy looked shattered. But although the sword he held looked that bit too big for him, his shoulders were starting to broaden. He'd soon be able to bear the weight of it for longer sessions.

"It seems risky."

"I'm aware that the gods don't protect us as they do you."

Pullus caught a momentary scowl passing over Marcus's face at Habitus's words. It was clear what the boy was thinking. Pullus had seen it in the eyes of most Romans who'd witnessed the event or heard the story: *The gladiator who tried to kill Decimus Horatius Pullus had simply disappeared as he'd been about to strike the killing blow.*

"And you've finished reading your Beard?" Pullus said to Marcus.

Marcus put down his cup. "Nearly…"

"I take it you haven't started?"

Marcus looked towards Habitus. But the bodyguard knew better than to get involved.

"Well?"

"I can't see the point of learning about our failures,"

Marcus said. "I like Suetonius better. I'm on to the Emperor Tiberius now!"

"Your mother—"

Marcus issued a deep, heartfelt sigh. Pullus quickly suppressed a smile. Being a teenager remained universal. Something about the frustration of being so near independence, and yet so far. For Pullus, that feeling had lasted long into his early twenties. Being a Roman boy, Marcus would at least become his own man much sooner.

"Your mother," Pullus continued, "thinks there are lessons in Mary Beard's work that will help you avoid the mistakes of the past."

"But *you* don't, do you?"

Pullus grimaced. "We'll unpick the detail in our lessons."

"Suetonius—"

"I need to speak with Habitus," Pullus said, aware his tone was a little too sharp. It reminded him of the teachers who'd irritated him as a student. "We can catch up with your studies later."

The boy gave another sigh. But after a further show of procrastination, he left. Habitus chuckled. "He's strong willed," he said. "Like his mother."

"She still won't see me?"

"No."

Pullus pulled at his satchel, dislodging dirt from the folds of his tunic. He desperately needed to wash and remove the residue of his travels. "I need to speak with her. It's important."

"You can speak with me."

Pullus hesitated. After the fall of NovusPart, he'd been seen as a useful gateway between the Romans and the outside world. Their *de facto* ambassador. But now there was less and less for him to do when he flew back and forth between New Pompeii and Naples. Which meant his other role as her son's teacher had become more important, and it remained his one link to Calpurnia.

"Pullus," repeated Habitus, softly. "You can speak with me. But she won't see you."

"She still won't leave the villa?"

Habitus shook his head. "No. She feels safe here."

"The people of Pompeii need to see her. If only occasionally—"

Habitus issued a short barking laugh. "And when was the last time you were in town?" he asked. "You spend almost as much time at your villa as she does here."

The *frumentarius* had a point, and Pullus didn't try to argue. It felt a long time since he'd experienced the excitement of first arriving at New Pompeii. But it was so much more comfortable at his villa, away from the crowds and the increasing numbers of people that appeared to want to worship him down at the Temple of Fortuna Augusta. The man whom the gods had protected from the gladiator. *The man who couldn't be killed.*

Habitus turned away, back in the direction of the main body of the house. Pullus hadn't noticed anything, but the *frumentarius* always seemed to sense things before they happened. Sure enough, a household slave appeared.

"I carry a message from the aediles for Appius Hostilius Habitus."

"Yes?"

"The latest convoy of supplies arrived at the Marine Gate this morning…"

"And?"

"…one of the men with the convoy has gone missing from quarantine."

3

Ancient Rome, temporary amphitheatre, AD 62

T HE CROWD WAS thin. Achillia took a moment to scan the faces but all she really saw were the empty seats. Most of the men who'd come to the amphitheatre for the early show had pushed themselves right up to the edge of the perimeter wall, and it didn't look like anyone was interested in moving them back into the right sections.

She heard her name being called by a group of men hovering close to a drinks stand. It rang out alongside the usual boasting about what they wanted to do with her. Achillia ignored them. She tried to focus on the trap doors set into the arena, to sense when they were about to shift. Tried to work out when the first of the beasts would be released and the slaughter would commence.

The other fighters circling around her would be trying to do the same. Six of them, each armed with just a *gladius* short-sword, and no shield. Achillia looked towards the nearest fighter, checking she was still standing where she'd been told to wait. The animals wouldn't give them much time, and they'd need to move quickly as soon as the traps opened. Although they hadn't been paired, working together would reduce the risk of injury. The fighter closest grinned back at her, indicating she too understood.

They were ready.

But the traps didn't shift.

"We going to fight each other?"

Achillia didn't move. *No*, she thought. *We're not going to fight each other*. That was stupid: they'd all been given the same weapon. There were no nets, pikes, tridents, or shields. There was, in short, no variety. So they'd be fighting animals, but not the big cats she'd once seen being brought into the *ludus*. No, something cheap like a warthog. Something small and nasty – and probably starved.

"We going to fight each other?"

Achillia suppressed her irritation. It was one of the new girls, only on her second or third appearance. Decent against a *palus* training post, but probably not in front of a crowd, no matter how small.

The traps still didn't move.

Achillia squinted. Covered in a fine raking of sand and stone, they were hard to see. But she'd made a point of reminding herself of their positions when they'd been brought in through the lower gates: there'd be no surprises. Except the lack of animals.

The crowd was starting to turn. Soon the *editor* wouldn't have any choice but to start proceedings, whatever was holding things up down in the vaults. Achillia tightened her grip on her sword.

Suddenly she heard panicked shouts heading towards them, people screaming in terror. Achillia closed her eyes. They weren't going to fight each other. And there'd be no animals. Just unfortunate creatures of a different kind.

She turned towards the gate in the perimeter wall. A group of women were being forced through it by armed guards. They wore expensive tunics, their hair not cut short to their heads as Achillia's was, but instead arranged in intricate curls.

These were women who didn't belong in the arena.

No doubt they were here at the command of the Emperor. Probably because their husbands hadn't bowed low enough, or had failed to laugh at a bad joke. Or had been betrayed by someone looking to take their place. Maybe some of the women were here on account of their own actions, but Achillia doubted it. And it didn't matter anyway. Today she wasn't to be a fighter. She was to be an executioner.

The noblewomen were dispersed around the arena at spear-point, the guards throwing swords at their feet. The crowd immediately understood and murmured their approval. Most would no doubt be thanking Jupiter they'd decided to take a chance on the early show. They were going to see their betters brought down to size.

"Pick up the sword!" Achillia yelled at the noblewoman closest to her.

The woman ignored the weapon by her feet and shook

her head, as if trying to deny what was happening. Denying the fact she was about to die, when in fact her only hope rested on taking the decision out of the Emperor's hands, and placing it into the crowd's. She needed to be brave. She needed to fight.

"Pick up the fucking sword!"

Achillia checked that the nearest trap doors were still shut, but knew it was now unlikely that any animals were going to make an appearance. The *editor*'s logic was clear. She and the other fighters all had the same type of weapon, but they hadn't been given any leather pads to protect their arms and legs. She'd assumed this was to increase the chance of blood for the crowd; the frantic kicking of an animal was sometimes hard to control with a sword. But in fact it was because the *editor* didn't expect to see any of his fighters injured.

He'd been paid for slaughter, and had decided to maximise the flesh on show. Simple loincloths were more than enough for his fighting girls. No need for pads or armour or shields to stop the crowd seeing jiggling tits as their swords started to swing.

Achillia grunted. The noblewoman in front of her still hadn't picked up the sword, and she was shaking, her hands clasped, head slightly bowed. The other fighters were not being so patient with their opponents. To Achillia's left one methodically cut past a noblewoman's pathetic swordplay, and buried her *gladius* in the woman's chest, before withdrawing it and hacking at her throat. The crowd roared as blood spattered across the sand, first a torrent, then a fine spray.

Taking two steps towards her opponent, Achillia shoved the woman hard, knocking her off her feet. She collapsed onto her backside and started to scream. Achillia kicked sand into the woman's face, and the scream soon turned into coughing.

"Die like a Roman," Achillia shouted. "Die like a fucking Roman!"

Around them the slaughter was already coming to an end. One noblewoman was dragging herself across the sand, intestines trailing behind her, the novice fighter who'd been so eager before stalking after her, ready to strike the killing blow. But after the initial excitement, the crowd sounded restless. The fights had been too swift. Where was the competition? Where was the fun?

Achillia dropped to her haunches, lifted her blade so that it touched the woman's face and drew it slowly down across her cheek. She hoped the spilled blood would run into her mouth so this noble bitch could taste it. "Do you have children?"

The noblewoman nodded.

"Do you want to see them again?"

There was no answer. Achillia pushed back onto her feet, then used her right foot to flick the sword into the woman's lap. "Don't end your life being a man's plaything!"

The noblewoman slowly got to her feet. She held the sword out loosely, and started to swing. Too far to the right, then too far to the left, leaving her body exposed. The victory would be easy. But it didn't need to be fast. From the crowd came a small cheer.

Achillia smiled and lunged forward with her own weapon, catching the oncoming blade halfway through its arc and knocking it aside. She shoved the woman away with her free hand, not letting this rich whore get too close. She met the oncoming blade as it swung again but didn't knock it from the woman's grip – even though it would have been easy – slapping her own blade against the noblewoman's shoulder.

The crowd seemed to get the joke and began to chant. The other fighters joined in, their opponents finished. Achillia let the swordplay continue until she sensed the crowd growing bored. Then she hit the woman hard in the face, dropping her to the ground, and stepped behind her and held her sword to her opponent's exposed throat.

It was time to give the crowd the decision. Live or die.

4

New Pompeii

PULLUS HEARD THE name clearly, but part of his brain was still trying to dismiss it. Too much time had passed for it to make any sense. And yet his steward stood waiting for his answer, his message dutifully delivered.

"You're sure?"

Galbo nodded, his weight resting on his staff. He didn't repeat the name. Although they'd been granted a few minutes' privacy in the atrium of Calpurnia's villa, there was always the chance someone would be listening. And it wouldn't be long before Marcus came to find his teacher to return him to their lesson, especially if he suspected an interesting message had arrived from town.

"Where did you get this from?"

Galbo raised an eyebrow. His stoop was slightly more pronounced than normal but, then again, the old man had travelled all the way out to Calpurnia's villa from central Pompeii. He hadn't sent a younger member of the household staff, knowing the message was important. But despite his fatigue, Galbo retained enough sense not to blurt his answer so that it could be overheard. Instead, he beckoned his master forward and whispered directly into Pullus's ear. "He came with the convoy, then escaped from the quarantine. The *duumvir* now has him."

"And you know this how?"

Galbo didn't answer, just smiled knowingly. After all, his steward knew most of the key slaves owned by the important households of New Pompeii, and Romans had an unfortunate habit of assuming their human tools wouldn't pass on information.

Turning away, Pullus felt a moment's alarm as he saw Barbatus watching them from the side of the atrium. But whilst the likeness of the bust sitting on its plinth was remarkable, the old *duumvir* was long since dead. After all, fifteen years had passed, and old age was the one thing no man could defeat.

Fifteen years.

Surely that was enough time to allow him to forget?

"And this man – this *Harris* – he asked for me, personally?"

"He asked to speak with 'Nick Houghton'."

Pullus winced. *Nick Houghton*. He looked back at his steward. Galbo's expression remained neutral. Was that how everyone still knew him here? When he wasn't around to hear their whispers?

Nick Houghton? Not "Decimus Horatius Pullus"?

Galbo coughed, gently. "The horses are waiting outside, sir."

* * *

Pullus caught the stench of rotten fish long before he arrived at the Marine Gate. Or rather, he caught the stink of their guts left to putrefy in the late afternoon sun. Despite New Pompeii having no sea port, garum remained an important part of its economy, and a large section of the convoys had been given over to supplying fish for the trade. Even after all this time, demand for genuine Pompeian garum – especially in the east – was enough to make a stomach-turning profit.

Pullus tried to ignore the smell, focusing instead on who he was going to meet. The *duumvir*, certainly, and perhaps the man known as Harris. He grimaced, and felt the tang of garum at the back of his throat. At least the town's chief magistrate was a known quantity. Harris was another matter entirely.

He had to remind himself they'd only met once. And yet, on the slow journey to Pompeii from Calpurnia's villa, passing the tombs that had sprung up along the roads leading toward it, Pullus suddenly realised he'd always been waiting for someone to mention Harris. Even if he'd expected it during one of his trips to Naples, rather than at the centre of the new *Pax Romana*.

"Decimus Horatius Pullus?"

A woman was blocking his path, holding something out towards him. He took the offering – a small clay disc – and let her say a few words before he thanked her and went on his way. The disc had been pressed with the image of a womb. Although they were sold in their dozens outside the forum baths, Pullus was in no doubt he'd been offered it out of personal motives. The lady wanted help conceiving. He slipped it into the pouch hanging from his tunic. He would add to the shingle in his garden, just like all the others he'd be given before the day was over.

Yes, the streets were busy. He wove between groups of Pompeians, the deep recesses of his brain still trying to pick out bits of urban conversation even if they were no longer being stored away for future transcription. No longer a source of academic interest. He felt a pang of regret, and quickly squashed it. That wasn't his task here now.

As he turned the final corner, he found a long queue outside the *duumvir*'s house. Pullus never felt comfortable cutting ahead of people who may have been waiting for hours to bring their concerns to the magistrate's attention, but the Pompeians always waved him through.

"Pullus!"

Lucius Salonius Naso appeared at the ornate wooden screen separating the small atrium from his main room of business. "I didn't realise you were in town," the *duumvir* continued in his nasal tone.

"I've just arrived."

"Huh." Naso didn't hide his annoyance. His network of informants clearly hadn't alerted him that the House of McMahon had its master back in residence. "Good trip?"

"It will be easier when I finally learn to ride a horse."

"I meant the other one. To see *her*." Naso gave a signal to his porter before sliding the *tablinum*'s screen back into position. The *duumvir*'s room of business was dark; instead of leading out onto a garden, as was usual in a Roman townhouse, a solitary stone staircase led downwards. The *duumvir*'s mansion was built into the town's south-western wall, meaning that instead of sprawling like the House of McMahon, the floors were stacked on top of each other like a wedding cake. Atrium and *tablinum* at the top, the more private rooms below until they joined the marina baths – and the tanks filled with fish intestines that made Naso rich. All of which meant it was easy to hide someone to eavesdrop.

"It was okay," Pullus said, not wanting to admit he hadn't been granted an audience. He noted absently that since his last visit Naso had redecorated: the walls were covered in expensive black paint, and a new mosaic floor had been laid out to represent the inky depths of the ocean. The only flashes of colour came from the squid, fish and crabs that swam on the tiles beneath their feet.

"Well, at least you occasionally put in an appearance… unlike her highness."

Pullus didn't respond. Naso probably felt safe in his own house, but he certainly wouldn't let so careless a remark slip out on the streets. After a moment's silence, the *duumvir* perhaps realised he'd overstepped the mark. He nodded in the direction of a panel painting, which had been left propped against the wall leading back into the atrium.

"Theseus and the Minotaur," Naso said. "*Again*." Despite the stink of fish guts, it hadn't taken the *duumvir* long to sniff out more imaginative ways of earning cash from exporting goods to the outside world. Academics had long suspected the frescos lining the walls of Pompeii might be copies of much older Greek works. So Naso had "found" some painters who'd seen these lost Hellenistic masterpieces. But could a Renaissance artist construct the *Mona Lisa* having seen her only once? Probably not. That little detail hadn't stopped the orders rolling in to create replicas in New Pompeii though.

"If it isn't minotaurs, it's Medusa," Naso complained, waving at the panel. "Or that whore Phryne stripping at her trial. That's all your people seem to care about: tits and monsters. Monsters and tits."

"The myths aren't ours," Pullus replied.

"True, but that's Greeks for you." The *duumvir* eyed Pullus suspiciously. "So what can I do for you, Pullus?"

"You're holding one of the men from the convoys."

"I am?"

"Word reached me."

"Did it now?" The *duumvir* smiled. "Because I thought he was trying to contact a dead man. Someone called 'Nick Houghton'?"

Pullus didn't rise to the bait. "You have him then?"

"Yes."

"I want to see him."

"And he wants to see you."

Pullus waited, but the *duumvir* didn't move.

"He arrived with the convoy," Naso said. His meaning was clear. Harris had smuggled himself in with the town's supplies, not used the normal diplomatic channels. And the *duumvir* was very protective of his convoys.

"I didn't arrange it."

"I want to know what's going on."

There was little Pullus could tell him. But he knew the sensitivity. Outsiders sometimes tried to sneak into New Pompeii. Things didn't end well for those that were caught, or for those that Habitus suspected of helping them.

"You didn't meet up on one of your little trips away?" asked Naso.

"No. I barely know him."

"Well he knows you."

"Where is he?"

"Safe." Naso swallowed. The action didn't appear to free up his nasal passages. "The convoys are my responsibility."

"I know."

"Good. Because if Calpurnia found out un-vetted men were simply—"

"Okay, okay." Pullus paused. "At least tell me he went through all the normal procedures?"

"Yes."

"The quarantine and the dips?"

"I just told you: *yes.*"

Pullus considered for a moment. The convoys employed only about two dozen non-Romans, and they'd spent a lot of time together in quarantine. If one disappeared, they'd all know about it. But he also knew Naso would have assigned some of his men to act as chaperones. He'd know where they all were. "And the others?"

Naso laughed. "Soaking in the baths downstairs."

"And they know you're holding one of their own?"

"They couldn't give a fuck. They don't know him, do they? He's not one of the regulars."

"I need to speak with him. To find out what he wants."

The *duumvir* lowered his voice. "No one uses my convoys to get a free pass into town," he said. "And that includes your friends, Pullus. So maybe you should think on that for a few hours, and come back tomorrow."

5

"What do you want me to do?"

"I WANT YOU TO accept the job offer you've been given."

"I already have…"

"Then you'd better impress them," said the guy. "Keep your nose clean, wait for me to contact you, and then maybe we can find out what they're really doing in New Pompeii."

Nick nodded. But the man hadn't finished. "There's one other question," he said. "One I can't believe you haven't asked yourself."

"All the others were transported," said Nick. "Sucked into the future."

"They should have taken you. You were a threat that should have been eliminated."

"So why didn't they?"

"NovusPart can't perform near-past transports. They have to wait thirty years. So the decision is going to be taken in the future, not the present. So at some point between now and then, you must affect the timeline in some way that means you can't be moved."

"Like what?"

"That's the mystery. And the interesting thing is: they probably don't know themselves. Not yet. But it's clear you're no longer a pawn. You have value. And so they pull you close, Mr Houghton. Somewhere where they can keep an eye on you."

Nick hesitated. "You haven't told me your name," he said.

"Everyone just calls me Harris."

Pullus opened his eyes, the dream dissipating. The memory of his first encounter with Harris replayed in his mind. He wasn't even sure he was remembering it correctly.

But that wasn't what had woken him. From somewhere deep in the house came sounds of movement, hushed voices. On any normal morning, the first noises came from the street: wagons making deliveries, shop shutters being swung open. But it was far too early.

There was a soft knock on his bedroom door, and Galbo shuffled inside.

"The boys are back, sir."

"Thank you." Pullus rose and stretched, trying to remove some of the stiffness from his travels. His steward had already retrieved his tunic and sandals and handed them to him. "The *duumvir*?"

Galbo nodded. "The convoy is on the move, heading to the Vesuvius Gate."

"Vesuvius? Not the Marine?"

"No. Vesuvius. Primus is ready to escort you, sir. But I'd prefer it if you took me."

Pullus shook his head, pulling on his clothes. His satchel lay unopened beside his bed. He kicked it out of view. "I'll go alone," he said, waving away Galbo's protests. The *duumvir* had reacted just as he thought he would: waiting until the middle of the night before making a hurried attempt to get the convoys back on the road. All it had taken was to ask his slave boys to watch for any sign of movement at Naso's townhouse and report back to the House of McMahon.

Pullus slipped down into his atrium, and then out onto the street. With the hour so early, it was all but deserted. Too late even for the most committed drunk to be awake, and yet still too early for the first workmen to have started the new day. He flicked on the small torch he'd brought with him.

Primus, one of his crippled boys, watched him from the door, his withered arm held awkwardly at his side. The young slave didn't pass comment on the blue-white light in his hand. The fact he could produce such a strong and permanent light was no longer surprising. It was one of the few things NovusPart had left behind that still functioned.

Pullus headed past homes and shops that remained shuttered. When he'd still been masquerading as an academic – conducting interviews for a PhD he knew he'd never achieve – he'd quickly made a connection between the Roman and modern world. If the authorities wanted to do anything secretly, they did it at night, when the population weren't just asleep, but were in no fit state to be awake. In the modern world, that was at about 4am. Here in New Pompeii, where there was no electric light or late evenings, it was somewhat earlier. Whilst everyone was slumbering, Naso would be seeing off his problem convoy.

And Harris would be taken away with it.

After a few streets, Pullus spotted a group of men, wagons and horses clustered just beyond the Vesuvius Gate. The *duumvir* stood at the centre, his accompanying bodyguards setting him apart from those working to get the convoy moving. Behind Naso were people in modern clothing. He recognised some of them. Many had been working on the convoys for so long they'd become familiar faces around town. And, in New Pompeii, a strange face always aroused suspicion.

Pullus moved closer, letting the torch light up the street, tracing it along the high kerbs and stepping stones, giving warning of his approach. He didn't want any swords drawn in alarm.

"Pullus—"

Pullus let the torch come to rest on the first wagon and eyed Naso. "Don't you normally send them back during the day? And from the Marine Gate?"

The *duumvir* took a long time to respond. The men behind him looked nervous. All that strength, and yet they remained frightened of a man carrying a torch. "I want your word that this will never happen again," Naso said, his voice high and tight. "The convoys are mine, Pullus. And you'll do me the courtesy of keeping your sickle out of my wheat!"

Pullus took a deep breath. The old him might have said he couldn't promise something he couldn't control. But that was back then and, somewhere in the convoy, his past was waiting for him. "You have my word," he said. "I just want to talk to him."

6

THE FIGURE STANDING next to the wagon was almost unrecognisable as James Harris. Yes, they'd only met once, and under difficult circumstances. But Pullus suddenly realised he'd been expecting to meet the same man who'd yanked him off a London street all those years ago. Maybe older and a bit greyer, but the same man nonetheless. As it was, only the horn-rimmed spectacles were the same. He watched as Harris shifted them up past the bridge of his nose. He stood alone – a man withered down to a thin, brittle frame – shivering against an early morning chill that wasn't even all that cold.

The *duumvir* suddenly seemed to understand. "You really didn't know he was coming, did you?"

Pullus couldn't bring himself to respond.

"When he mentioned your name," Naso continued, "we didn't let him leave my house. Habitus already has men looking for him. It's best to get rid of him."

Pullus nodded slowly. "Did he see anyone else whilst he was here?"

"Not that we know of," Naso answered. The *duumvir*

gestured at a guard, who ushered Harris forward.

"You seem to have done well for yourself, Nick."

English. Pullus was frozen by the sound. When was the last time someone had spoken to him in English in New Pompeii? One year ago? Two? Of course, the outsiders working the convoys used it, but that machine was now so well-oiled it no longer needed his direct involvement. He made sure to keep a good distance between himself and Harris, still thinking of their first meeting. The way he'd been pulled off the street and told the truth about New Pompeii and NovusPart.

"Don't worry," continued Harris. "I haven't threatened your biological containment."

Good, thought Pullus. A strict quarantine had been maintained around New Pompeii. One of the few features of NovusPart's control that had been vital, but also something it had been initially hard for the Romans to fathom. Harris himself looked ill though, close to death.

"You can't catch cancer," Harris said, his tone blunt. "Even the new kind." He gestured at the sleeping town. "Some people here think you're a god, don't they?"

"It's not something I encourage."

"But you don't enlighten them either, do you?" He grinned when Pullus didn't respond. "I was unsure if you'd even be here. You left in quite a hurry, if rumour is right. I occasionally read reports of you heading in and out of Naples. I want you to know that I'm sorry you can never truly go home."

Pullus felt his cheeks burn. Most of his business with the outside world was conducted in Naples. An increasing number of European countries had announced he was no longer welcome, the travel bans supposedly imposed because of the Romans' continued use of slavery, and their unwillingness to move to a different economic system. But the reason he couldn't travel to England hadn't been made public: too many trips to Cambridge to poke around in the remnants of NovusPart had started to arouse suspicion. Fortunately, Italy wasn't quite ready to give up on a Roman society it considered its own. But his trips to Naples only provided a link to a world that was becoming less and less familiar with each visit. "This is my home," Pullus said.

"So you're a Roman now, Nick. Is that it?" Harris's voice was strong, and seemed at odds with the sunken flesh of his cheekbones. Pullus took a closer look at the man who'd threatened him all those years ago. He did a few quick calculations in his head. Harris must be in his mid-sixties but he looked much older. His hair was thin. His skin grey. It didn't look like he had much time left.

"My name is Decimus Horatius Pullus."

Harris seemed to consider this. "I've often wondered what living here would do to you," he said. "Has the lustre started to wear thin? Haven't you any trouble with some of the more... problematic parts of Roman life? Slavery? Girls forced to marry in their early teens? Capital punishment?"

Pullus thought back to his last trip to Naples. "Were you sent by the Bureau?"

Harris seemed to find the question amusing, and Pullus quickly regretted asking it. The Bureau of Roman Affairs was ostensibly an administrative organisation: a small group who helped organise the convoys supplying New Pompeii and negotiated prices for its products. And no, Pullus couldn't quite imagine Harris fitting in there.

"I never did find out who you worked for," Pullus said. In truth, he'd long since stopped thinking about it. After the fall of NovusPart, Harris had simply disappeared.

"My organisation became defunct," Harris replied, almost sadly. "Buried under shifting sands and disappearing states. But I hardly think that matters now – I'm here very much on my own business."

Harris nodded in the direction of the Vesuvius Gate. The men loading the wagons had all moved up to the front end of the convoy, ready to leave. "Perhaps there's somewhere where we can talk in private?" he said.

Pullus shook his head. They were well away from the other outsiders manning the convoy. Only Naso and his guards stood close enough to hear. "We're the only ones who can speak English."

Harris nodded at Naso. "You're sure?"

"You know I'm the only one left."

"Ah, that's right," Harris said. "All the remnants of NovusPart were butchered, weren't they?"

Pullus didn't answer.

"You killed McMahon," continued Harris. "Stabbed him several times, I heard. And the Romans took care of Whelan.

But the rest of the NovusPart staff… what happened to them, Nick?"

Pullus felt his throat constrict. "You know."

"Why don't you remind me?"

"They were crucified."

"And you couldn't stop them? I mean, the security staff would have been a threat, certainly. But the translators? The construction teams? The household staff?" A flicker of a smile passed across Harris's face. "So only you survived. The man who can't be killed."

"And is that why you're here? To put the myth to the test?"

"I'm here because I need your help."

Help. Such a simple word, and yet so unexpected.

"You're the closest thing this place has to an ambassador, Nick."

"Call me Pullus."

Harris gave a brief snort. "I need to speak with Calpurnia."

Pullus took a step back to put some distance between him and Harris. From behind, he sensed Naso and at least one of his men draw closer. The *duumvir* had obviously heard the trigger word. "No one gets to see Calpurnia. Least of all you."

Harris leant forward, his voice barely audible. "Why do you think the people back home let this place exist, Pullus?"

"The NovusPart device…"

"Yes," said Harris, his eyes suddenly bright. "The NovusPart device. They think that if they threaten New Pompeii, you'll scrub them from history. But you haven't managed to get it to work yet, have you?"

Pullus raised a hand and waved the *duumvir* back. Ordinarily, Naso would have ignored him, but he must have seen the shock on Pullus's face. Maybe he realised he'd been wrong to assume that Harris was a friend.

"Do you have any idea how frightened people are back home?" Harris continued, almost casually. "They worry about what your Roman chums might do, if your influence slips."

"Calpurnia understands the consequences of altering the timeline."

"And yet we both know she's done nothing irresponsible because she can't," Harris said. "Not because she won't."

Pullus felt a soft prod of guilt. "We had Whelan."

"But he didn't tell you all you needed to know to use the NovusPart device, did he?"

"You didn't see what they did to him."

Harris didn't answer. Behind, the *duumvir* and his guard waited impatiently. Maybe it was time to admit the truth, even if that meant Harris wouldn't be allowed to leave. "How did you know?" asked Nick.

"That your device doesn't work? You claim to have the same power as NovusPart – to be able to reach back and pluck people from time – and yet you've allowed yourself to be penned into a small reservation." Harris glanced at the wagon beside him, and its weathered wooden frame. "Reliant on convoys from the real world, and always getting a fairly poor deal for your exports." Harris paused. "But the most telling thing is Calpurnia. She claims the gods protect her in the same way as they protected you. That she controls the future and will stop anyone from killing her. And yet she hides away in her villa. Relying on her bodyguards, not her precious NovusPart device."

Naso spoke up, clearly frustrated. "What does he want?"

Pullus ignored the *duumvir*. "So you think the NovusPart device doesn't work," he said. "That doesn't explain why you're here."

"I can understand why you did it," continued Harris, wiping at his brow. "Who would attack you openly if they thought you could eliminate them from time?"

"Answer the question."

"I am long since retired, Nick. Replaced with less subtle men. But you may remember that I took a very close interest in NovusPart. And they kept records of everyone they transported." Harris's lip curled. "DNA profiles of the people that got in their way, and who appeared in their paradox chambers."

Of course. Pullus remembered now: Harris had gone up against NovusPart for very personal reasons. He'd admitted as much, fifteen years ago. "Your brother?"

"They took him when he was just a boy," Harris replied. "I saw it. Saw him being sucked from time. But he's not in the NovusPart archives – and Joe Arlen was meticulous in recording everyone they stole from time. Whelan and McMahon continued his procedures, right up until their deaths. Which means I began to question what I'd once assumed was true: did NovusPart really take him? Or did someone else, maybe someone who took control of the device years later and who changed what was meant to happen. You see, if I'm right and your device doesn't work, then no one's been transported since the fall of NovusPart. And that means my brother's still out there somewhere. Moving through time and waiting to land once a device is activated."

Pullus nodded slowly. "Waiting, in short, for someone to make the NovusPart device work," he said.

"Maybe it's because I'm growing old," Harris continued, adjusting his spectacles. "But I've become a firm believer in destiny. The date and location of his transportation are seared into my mind. Only I know that information. Only I can give you the correct coordinates to initiate the device and resolve the paradox. And, as you can see, I'm running out of time. If it's going to happen – and it will – it needs to happen soon."

"But, as you said, our device doesn't work. So I don't see how…?"

"I took a *very* close interest in NovusPart," Harris interrupted. "And I now have a complex alphanumeric code. A failsafe, designed to stop the device from being used by Joe Arlen's enemies. It means I can help make your device work. And then you can bring my brother back home."

7

"I DON'T CARE WHAT he told you," Naso said. "I don't care if he knows it doesn't work. He's leaving with the rest of the convoy."

Pullus clenched his fists. He needed the *duumvir* to see sense; Harris couldn't be allowed to leave. Not when he could put their secret at risk. Not when he could tell the outside world they didn't really have a defensive shield.

Naso turned away and looked towards the horizon. "It's going to get light soon," he said. "We need to make a decision."

"Turn him over to me," Pullus said. "Let me deal with this."

"Ha! And let you take him to Calpurnia?"

"If she finds out, I can say I found him in town. You don't need to be involved."

Naso shook his head. "No. I'm not going to take that risk, Pullus. She'll think the convoys have been compromised."

"This is more important than your convoys."

"Nothing is more important than my fucking convoys!" The *duumvir*'s nasal tone had almost broken into a shriek.

Pullus took a step back. "Relax—"

"This won't look good for me," Naso continued. "She'll

know how he got in. Fucking hell, Pullus! She'll put Habitus in charge! I'd be finished!"

"It won't look good for either of us," Pullus replied, breathing hard. He looked in Harris's direction. He had never admitted the truth to Calpurnia; that he had come to New Pompeii – in part – as Harris's spy. After withholding for fifteen years, that news might not go down well. "Don't worry, I'm not going to take him to Calpurnia, not yet anyway. I don't trust him. There's something else going on here. There always is, with men like him."

"There is, of course, another option."

Pullus felt his stomach tighten. He knew what Naso was thinking, and he was tempted.

"The guy's practically dead already. Why not give him a push?"

Pullus hesitated. Then shook his head. "No."

"It could be seen as a mercy."

"No."

"Calpurnia need never know he was here. No man, no risk, and no problem."

And no code, thought Pullus. He'd been selective in his translation. He'd only told the *duumvir* that Harris knew the Romans didn't know how to make the device work, not that he might be able to show them how. Experience told him information like that needed to be carefully managed. He stared at the wagons. *Was it hidden away amongst the convoy? If it was as "complex" as Harris had suggested, then it was likely written down, but…*

Written down! Pullus felt irritated at himself. His thinking was too Roman, too antiquated. Arlen's code would be stored electronically, not on wax tablets or paper. It had been a long time since he'd used anything electronic within the boundaries of New Pompeii; most of the electronic equipment NovusPart had left behind had long since stopped working. The modern world hadn't been stupid enough to provide everything the Romans had requested on Naso's damn convoys. "We need him alive."

Naso rolled his eyes. "Then where will we keep him?"

"I'm happy for him to stay with you."

"And how long do you think it will be before Calpurnia finds out?"

"He can either go with me, or you can take him. Make up your mind!"

The *duumvir* gave a roar of frustration. Then he froze, staring over Pullus's shoulder towards the Vesuvius Gate, a look of panic on his face.

Pullus turned. Habitus was standing in the shadows, a few metres away. The *frumentarius* was grinning, a sword in his hand.

"Calpurnia will see you now."

8

Ancient Rome, AD 62

"ACHILLIA! YOU HAVE a visitor!"

Achillia took her time walking from the training yard to the gate of the *ludus*. She had little interest in the men who came to visit the female fighters. But the man waiting for her wasn't the usual type. He wore a toga and had several men with him, all of whom stood waiting at a distance which they no doubt thought was discreet, but actually made them stand out from the passing foot traffic. From the look of them they were bodyguards, or at least household slaves who could handle themselves.

"It's man sweat you want," Achillia said. "Not mine."

She stood a few feet from the bars of the gate, not close enough to be grabbed. It was unlikely, but it happened. Even by those wearing such fancy clothes.

The man looked confused by her comment. "What?"

"Male drippings," she continued. "They sell it at the main gate. If you're having trouble with your *gladius*, or need to attract the attention of your mistress."

The man didn't reply, tipping his head back as if trying to get his nose above the stench of the *ludus*. He flicked his eyes over her shoulder towards the training ground. The *clack-clack* of wood was the only hint of the work going on behind them. Most of her fellow fighters were inside, doing chores.

"My name—"

"I don't care. Fuck off." This man didn't interest her. Achillia turned and started to walk away.

"My name is Gaius Asinius Varro!"

Achillia continued to walk.

"Wait! You saved my wife," Varro shouted. He lowered his voice, perhaps afraid of being overheard. "Two days ago in the arena."

Achillia narrowed her eyes and turned back. Varro looked embarrassed. He glanced at his men, who kept their distance.

"You saved my wife," he said again.

"I heard you. She didn't want to say 'thank you' herself?"

"She is safe at my house."

"Safe? Until the Emperor calls again?"

Varro's face turned white. He took a slight step forward. "Careful," he whispered.

Achillia grinned. "Or will it be your turn next?"

"I understand our gracious Emperor was impressed with tales of my wife's performance," Varro said, with some pride. "He's been telling the court how she took on one of the whores of the arena. That's right, isn't it?" He nodded towards the *ludus*. "You whore in there, do you not? Between fights, when those with money come calling?"

"I'm in here," Achillia replied, slowly in order to make her point, "because I killed a man."

Varro smiled, then tapped the metal bars of the gate with the nail of his forefinger. "Then it's lucky I'm on this side." The smile faded. "My wife is concerned the Emperor may ask for a repeat performance."

"Then she'd better start practising."

"She thinks it would be safer to leave town. She's got it into her head that you could go with her."

"I belong to the *ludus*."

"I can afford you. I'm an important man."

"One the Emperor would like to kill?"

Varro blanched again. Achillia glanced at his companions. "Keeping your best men with you?" she asked. "No one to spare to escort your wife out of the city?"

"Perhaps you would prefer to die in the arena?" Varro replied, his voice sour. "Finally meet someone better than you? Or take a goring from a bull?"

Achillia smiled, then tipped her head towards one of the buildings within the *ludus*. "You'll need to talk to—"

"I already have."

"Then why come and ask me?"

"I wanted to see what type of bitch I was buying."

"And where am I and your wife going?"

"A small town on the coast. You may not have heard of it."

"Try me."

"It's called Pompeii."

A covered wagon arrived at the *ludus* before dawn. Pulled by a pair of horses, it had a single driver, but two other men followed on their own mounts behind. None of the men looked as if they could handle themselves, and Achillia realised she'd been right. Her new master was keeping his best men in Rome. Those he was sending with his wife looked like they knew it too.

"Get in," shouted the driver.

Achillia pulled aside the door covering and looked into the wagon. The only occupant was the woman she'd fought in the arena. Her face was bruised, the slope of her nose buckled and raw. The cut down her cheek had only just started to heal.

"I guess I should thank you," Achillia said, taking a seat opposite the door under the small window, its woollen cover rolled down to keep out the morning chill. On the seat beside her was a change of clothes – a clean *stola* and a new pair of sandals. There was also a knife, brand new from the condition of the blade.

"The trip will take a few days," the woman replied as the wagon started to move, ignoring the question. "My husband told you what I'm expecting you to do?"

"He told me everything except your name."

"Trigemina."

Achillia nodded, then turned to the bundle of clothes and picked up the knife. It was a decent weapon, the handle bound in black leather, and it was small enough that she could keep it inside her belt without drawing much attention. Maybe even hide it away in the folds of the *stola*. She looked about her. A short-sword had also been clamped above the wagon's door, just below the roof.

"If you try to run," said Trigemina, "my husband will set the *vigiles* after you."

"I don't intend to run."

Trigemina stared at the knife. Achillia realised the last few days had probably been in stark contrast with the rest of her life. The spouses of high-ranking noblemen didn't normally have to fight in the arena.

"I'm not a fool," Achillia said calmly, but not putting the knife down. "And if we're attacked on the road – or in Pompeii – then they'll need to kill us both. I know what happens to slaves who let their masters die."

"Good." When Trigemina spoke, her thoughts seemed to be elsewhere. "In the arena... I was expecting you to be wearing helmets."

"The crowd like to see our faces," Achillia replied. "With the men, they just want to see death. We give them something extra. A lot of it is theatre."

"Did you train with the male gladiators?"

"No."

Trigemina was silent for a moment. "And the men with us?" Trigemina asked. "The driver and his outriders? Would you be able to kill men like them?"

Achillia smiled. "Oh, I would beat them with a sword. Probably with a knife too, if it came to it."

Trigemina considered this. "Then you'll do fine."

9

New Pompeii

Only Pullus and Habitus were allowed into Calpurnia's villa. For the time being, however, Pullus remained alone whilst the *frumentarius* briefed his mistress. Naso had been told to wait outside on the road with Harris.

Although the *duumvir* had protested, Pullus was glad to be rid of him. Naso hadn't stopped talking on their journey. His precious convoy had been sent on its way from the Vesuvius Gate, but the *duumvir's* only concern seemed to be whether he'd be allowed to keep charge of them in future, rehearsing the arguments he'd use when he next met Calpurnia.

Pullus leant against a chest-high wall. He'd been shown into a small interior garden. He spent a few moments studying the delicate throngs of ferns that had been painted on the plastered surfaces, the effect completed with animals peeping out from amongst the foliage, both real and imagined.

Smoke and mirrors, Pullus thought. He sighed. NovusPart had built much of their power on illusion. The clever placement of cameras and microphones, used to confuse and frighten. But spaces like this proved the Romans had beaten them to the trick by about two thousand years. The garden and a small opening in the roof gave the illusion of being outside even though the space was mainly enclosed. Other frescos around the villa depicted images of grand public spaces that had long since been lost to the past. And Calpurnia used other smoke and mirrors too.

The NovusPart device didn't work. Never had, not even with Whelan's input. NovusPart had left behind two devices: one at its old headquarters in Cambridge and the second in New Pompeii. The Cambridge device hadn't lasted long following the reported fall of NovusPart: destroyed in an ill-considered attempt to close Pandora's Box by inept politicians and academics, desperate to end potential tampering with the timeline. Pullus had been able to confirm its destruction prior to being banned from travelling to England, when MI5 had realised what he was doing. Had the British government realised there was a second device in New Pompeii – put there to feed the amphitheatre and NovusPart's other projects – then they might have thought better of keeping hold of their own device.

"I thought our next lesson wasn't until tomorrow?"

Pullus turned. Marcus stood in the doorway, a book under his arm.

"I'm not here as your teacher."

Relief flashed across the young man's face. He pushed the book further into the cleft of his elbow, hiding the spine from view. Which meant it wasn't by Mary Beard. And it didn't look like Suetonius either.

"What are you reading?"

Marcus didn't answer, shuffling his feet.

"Marcus…"

The boy walked to where Pullus stood, self-consciously examining the frescos. "It's called *The Modern Prometheus*."

Pullus blinked. Had he heard right?

"*Frankenstein*?"

Marcus nodded. "It's about—"

"I know what it's about." Pullus took a few steps forward. "Give it to me."

The boy didn't resist. It was new, not an old edition. Mary Shelley's *Frankenstein*. He flicked through a few of the pages. It was in Latin.

Marcus shuffled. "Some of the writing is a little… difficult."

Pullus read a few sentences and couldn't help but agree. Victorian prose, translated into an ancient language, was never going to be an easy read. "Where did you get this?"

Marcus didn't answer but he didn't need to. It must have come from the town, from a convoy. Another breach. And one far too close to Calpurnia. He'd need to tell Naso, warn the *duumvir* of the problem.

"You have more of these?"

"No."

"You're sure?"

The boy hesitated. "Yes. It's the only one."

"Your mother wouldn't be happy if she knew—"

"Why don't you ask her?"

Calpurnia stood a few feet behind him. Her son must have seen her approaching, but there hadn't been any hint of it in his expression. *Shit.* Pullus held the book towards her. "It must have come in on the convoys," he said.

"Yes, Naso procured it for me whilst you were away."

Beside him, Marcus couldn't stifle his amusement. "It's a difficult text for him to be exploring on his own," Pullus said.

"It's about a man being brought back from the dead. What could be more appropriate?"

"You've read it too?"

"Yes."

Pullus handed the book back to Marcus. "I'll think about how we can incorporate this into your lessons."

The boy smirked.

"I need to speak with Pullus," Calpurnia said. "You can pick this up with him later."

The boy looked like he might object, but then he hurried away. Presumably heading to his room to poison his mind with some more gothic horror. It would no doubt mix in well with what Suetonius would be telling him about the reigns of Tiberius and Caligula.

"He reminds me more and more of his father," Calpurnia said.

"He's becoming a man, certainly. I saw some of his sword work with Habitus."

Calpurnia nodded. She looked different, but it took him a while to figure out why. Then he noticed her fringe had been styled into a line of little ringlets: traditional and conservative. Hints of grey ran through it. "Habitus told me you wanted to see me yesterday?"

"I've been wanting to see you for weeks," Pullus said. "When we last spoke… I didn't think one argument—"

"It's not about what you said to me, Pullus; it's what they're saying about us again in Pompeii. It's not a good idea for us to be seen together. Not even here."

Pullus grimaced. "You were pregnant before you met me."

"And it's too long ago now for people to remember that. You turned up; I had a son. That's the gist of what they're writing on the columns of the forum. In the *tabernae* and brothels."

"And why does it matter?"

Calpurnia drew a deep breath. It could have easily signalled an outburst, but she held back. "Whispers are important," she said, finally. "And we're speaking now. So, tell me: do you know the man in the convoy?"

Pullus hesitated. "I met him only once. A long time ago, and far from here."

"Your friend's name is Harris?"

"He's not my friend."

Calpurnia didn't pass comment. "Whelan used that name."

Pullus closed his eyes. He thought back to Whelan. Remembered the drill. And the molten lead. Most of all, he remembered the screaming. Fuck, he remembered the screaming. "Yes."

"Both McMahon and Whelan hated this… Harris. They were enemies?"

"Yes."

"They wanted him dead."

"Harris tried to stop NovusPart," said Pullus, trying to explain from what little he knew. "In many respects, he failed."

"I'm told Naso wanted to kill him too rather than bring him here?"

I'm told. Pullus just about stopped his derisive snort. Despite her isolation, Calpurnia's network of informants kept her close to the centre of things. Just like the Emperor Tiberius on his island at Capri. At least, that's what the men of the *Ordo* said. Albeit even those men on the town council did so very quietly. "He's not dead."

"And Harris knows our NovusPart device doesn't work?"

"Yes."

"How?"

"A guess, perhaps."

"You haven't said anything?"

"Why would I?"

Now it was Calpurnia's turn to hesitate. She examined him a moment. "And what else did he tell you?"

Pullus thought briefly about Arlen's code. Harris was outside with Naso. But of all those present, only he could speak English. The outsiders had all left with the convoys. Which meant he didn't have to reveal the full truth. Not yet. Not whilst he remained uncertain of what Harris truly intended – or what Calpurnia would do with a device that actually functioned. "Nothing."

"We used to spend many hours debating how the

NovusPart device could be used," Calpurnia said, as if reading his mind. "You always said that it was actually very limited. That the risk of paradox was too great."

Pullus turned away. "Even if you got the device working, what could you do with it? Really?"

"Maybe I could stop Rome from falling."

Calpurnia had made a study of the Empire's fall. There'd been a time when she'd sought answers from him almost on a daily basis, seemingly in a state of shock. It was as if someone had told her the sun had one day failed to rise. It didn't help that there wasn't a singular cause to the calamity, an individual Vesuvius event that could be blamed. And, even if she could claim some satisfaction in the Eastern Empire lasting well into the second millennium, Calpurnia's pride was always tempered by the knowledge that Rome had succumbed.

"That's what you're worried about, isn't it?" continued Calpurnia. "That's what we debated before your last trip home."

"It was more of an argument than a debate."

"Christians, Gauls, Visigoths and vice. Too many problems, I think, for one woman to solve."

"Then what?"

"My husband remains in Herculaneum."

"It would be difficult to bring him back," replied Pullus. "NovusPart failed to transport all the people from Pompeii, and Herculaneum was consumed by rock, not ash. Dense, falling rock that buried the town metres high. The device simply can't reach through it. And we can't pull him much before his death—before the eruption—because that would change the timeline. Your past self would behave differently if he suddenly disappeared, and who knows what the repercussions would be."

"We know when he left Pompeii," Calpurnia said, her voice shaking, but remaining hard. "I remember the day clearly. So we know when he'd likely arrive. All we'd need to do would be to transport everyone in Herculaneum. But we'll do it before the eruption, not during it."

Pullus felt his throat contract.

"There haven't been many bodies found in Herculaneum," Calpurnia continued. "Your books say as much. They ask the question: where is everyone? Where are they? So it might be how things are meant to play out. And it would be no different to what NovusPart did."

"It's completely different."

"Tell me how. Tell me again why I can't use the device to save even one person?"

Pullus thought of Harris, and Arlen's research, knowing without any doubt he was doing the right thing keeping it from her. Even if it meant losing some people to the past. "There are records of close escapes," he said. "People who left the town just before the eruption. And how many children did those people have? And grandchildren? And great-grandchildren? The effects could be catastrophic."

"So, this *Harris*," Calpurnia said, anger rising in her eyes. "All he told you was that he knows our NovusPart device doesn't work, is it?"

"Yes."

Calpurnia glared at him. "I thought I could trust you, Pullus," she said. "And yet you stand there lying to me. You may be the only one here that can speak English, but it seems this Harris has some basic Latin. He's already told Habitus everything he told you. I know about the code. I know he can make our device work."

10

Ancient Roman Empire, the road to Pompeii, AD *62*

T HE SLOW PROGRESS and rising heat inside the wagon allowed Achillia to get more sleep than she'd expected. But when the quality of the road started to give way to a broken track she was bumped awake. Which was odd, given that Trigemina had said that the road to Pompeii was smooth.

The thought brought her sharply awake. Her mistress, Trigemina, sat opposite, seemingly relaxed. Achillia peered out of the window to check her surroundings. They weren't heading along anything resembling a road, but rather seemed to be cutting through a forest and heading up into some hills. The wagon was having a hard time navigating the exposed white rocks that littered the trail.

"We're not going directly to Pompeii," Trigemina said. "Before leaving Rome I consulted the auspices. I was assured we would arrive at our destination safely. But I'd like some clearer guidance for when we arrive in Pompeii."

Achillia stared out of the window again, trying to make

sense of it. Then it struck her and she did her best not to laugh. "You're going to see the Sibyl?"

Trigemina nodded. She hadn't seemed to detect the scepticism in Achillia's voice. "We shall discover what plans the gods have for us."

"I'm not a big believer in fate," Achillia replied, somewhat coldly. "Either the Emperor wants you back in Rome, or he doesn't. If he does, then his men will soon be with us."

"The Emperor doesn't know I've left Rome."

"He would have had men watching your house. They would've seen you leave. And if he didn't, news will still get to him. Because your husband's enemies will surely be keeping tabs on you."

Trigemina didn't say anything.

"You don't agree?"

Trigemina's lips twitched. "Your job is to protect me, not to question me."

"If bandits hit us, then I'll protect you. But if the Emperor sends his men, then we're going back to Rome. Unless they try to kill you." Achillia sat back. "But I suppose the Sibyl will give you fair warning. If you reach her in time."

"The Emperor won't know we've left the city for a good few days."

"How do you figure?"

"We left from the home of a close friend…"

"He would have been watching you wherever you stayed."

"…via a tunnel."

For a second, Achillia didn't respond. And then

she laughed. A long, rolling laugh.

Trigemina glared at her, fear finally giving way to irritation. "Don't question me!"

"Your husband's a dead man," Achillia explained. "He could maybe explain you leaving for Pompeii. Even why you'd set off so early. But to sneak out of the city? Using a fucking tunnel? He may as well have accused the Emperor of plotting to kill you. Everyone in the city will be talking about it."

The anger drained from Trigemina's face, replaced by the fear Achillia remembered from the arena.

"And then he'll come after us," Achillia continued. "And he'll kill your men out there. He'll kill me, and then he'll drag you back to the arena where you will surely die."

"We will consult the Sibyl."

"You don't need a little woman hidden away in a cave to—"

"We will consult the Sibyl!"

Achillia rolled her eyes. She let her head thump against the back of the wagon, and looked up at the short-sword hanging above the door. Next time they stopped, she'd check its weight and its balance. Because when the Emperor's men arrived, she'd need to fight. At least then there'd be a chance she'd be returned to the *ludus*. But it was doubtful. She looked back at Trigemina, at her broken nose. Maybe she should have punched her harder.

Much. Much. Harder.

* * *

"I remain unconvinced."

"She speaks truth. After all, her books adorn the Palatine."

It was at least the fourth time Trigemina had said as much. She and Achillia had left the wagon back down the hill, stuck between a couple of trees and a rock. The men had still been struggling to free it as the women started up towards the entrance of the Sibyl's cave.

The perfectly triangular opening in the rock face led to a tunnel, a string of oil lamps illuminating the entrance. Beyond was only darkness. It appeared they were alone, but Achillia scanned the trees for any hint they were being watched.

"You're telling me that was created by the hand of man?" asked Trigemina, pointing to the entrance. "Do you know how old it is?"

Achillia didn't answer the question. "Somehow, I doubt whoever wrote those books is waiting for us inside."

"Apollo provided the Sibyl with many years of life."

"But not youth," replied Achillia. "That's the story, isn't it? All that's left is a voice. The body long since shrunken away to nothing?"

"It's not just a story."

"Fine," Achillia said, scanning the surrounding woodland. "We should do this quickly. Get back to the wagon, and continue our journey."

Trigemina smiled. "Don't worry, this isn't my first visit."

Achillia waited a moment before following Trigemina into the tunnel. If there was someone ahead of them waiting to attack, there wouldn't be much she could do to stop it. But attackers were more likely to come from behind, waiting until they were in the cave and then coming out of the trees to cut off their escape. There was, after all, at least one person here, someone who kept the oil lamps burning. Achillia checked her knife and swore. Her new mistress had refused permission to take the *gladius* into the cave.

"You've been here before?"

"Just once," replied Trigemina. Her voice was shaking.

"And what did it tell you?"

"The Sibyl's words are private."

"And what do you expect it to say this time?"

"We're not here for me," said Trigemina. "We're here for you. This is your reward for saving my life."

11

PULLUS SCANNED THE occupants of the *tablinum*. As Calpurnia led him into the chamber, he saw Harris standing at its very centre. His hands were tied in front of him and – although Habitus stood closest to him – it was clear he was too frail to pose any sort of threat.

Naso looked deeply uncomfortable. Pullus recognised each of the three heavy-set male slaves who lingered in the background as being Calpurnia's, not the *duumvir*'s. Which meant Pompeii's chief magistrate knew he was vulnerable, now he'd finally been invited inside.

Pullus stared at Harris, hatred welling up. The sick old man had arrived in Pompeii with a potentially dangerous message: to tell the Romans he knew their device didn't work. Such an admission might have been enough to have him killed. To silence him, and stop him telling anyone else the secret. Except Harris had arrived with a strategy; he'd also learnt how to speak Latin.

Pullus glanced at Calpurnia. *I thought I could trust you, Pullus.* Fuck. He'd not even told her how good it was to see her again. Maybe now he wouldn't get the chance.

"You and I both know how you survived the gladiator fifteen years ago," Calpurnia said. "Those who operate the NovusPart device in the future reached back and removed your attacker in order to let you live. But only because you were important to them."

"I know," Pullus replied.

"You're not important anymore," she said. "There's no safety net. I have the device, and the person who will get it working for us is now in my possession. So if you betray me here, today, I will have you killed. Do you understand?"

"I get it."

"Good. And don't forget the Greek knows some English too. He'll be monitoring what you say."

Beside one of the columns painted onto the walls, Calpurnia's Greek slave stood listening. The Greek often stood mute, hidden in the background as he recorded Calpurnia's instructions. Sure enough, he held a thin wax tablet by his side. But Pullus also knew this silent observer had a sharp mind. The Greek had made the most progress with the old NovusPart technology. He'd even got so far as activating the transportation tracking system, scanning back through data representing those occupying particular points in space deep in the past. However, the last step of actually initiating the transportations continued to be elusive. Not that the Greek ever showed his frustration. Not within earshot, anyway.

Today though, he was likely wasting his time. Harris probably knew little about how the NovusPart device actually worked. It would only be when he chose to hand over Arlen's code that the Greek's skills would be really put to the test.

"Ah, at last…" Everyone looked towards Harris when he spoke. Calpurnia tipped her head back slightly to signal she was in charge, but she also took care to keep close to Habitus. "My Latin doesn't exactly sparkle," Harris continued. "So it would probably be best if you could translate, if you wouldn't mind, Nick?"

"You seem to have been more than capable when speaking to Habitus."

"A few phrases learnt by rote," Harris answered. "Not enough to talk about the intricacies of time travel. And trust me, things are going to get complicated."

Pullus nodded, bitterly, and readied himself. He hadn't needed to translate a two-way conversation for some time.

"Ask him for the code," Calpurnia said.

Pullus repeated the question in English. Calpurnia looked at the Greek, who nodded wordlessly in confirmation, though how much he'd really understood wasn't entirely clear. The Greek had spent a long time working through all the material left behind by NovusPart, the handbooks, tablets and computers found in the control villa and the House of McMahon, so presumably had picked up some working knowledge of English. But Pullus had never managed to engage him in anything that could be considered as a conversation. The Greek's natural state was silence.

"First, I need to know her intentions," Harris said.

Pullus didn't translate. Instead, he edged closer to Harris, avoiding a warning stare from Calpurnia. "Don't play games," he said. "She *will* kill you."

"I'm already dead, Pullus. If I wasn't, I wouldn't be here."

"Fine," he said. "For you, it's about your brother. For her, she's never stopped talking about her husband."

"NovusPart failed to transport him from Pompeii?"

"He wasn't in Pompeii," Pullus replied. "He'd travelled to Herculaneum prior to the eruption."

"If NovusPart couldn't transport everyone from Pompeii through simple ash, then there's no chance they could pull him from Herculaneum through that hell storm."

"I know."

"And it's been fifteen years, Nick. I mean, look at her."

Pullus understood. Even if Calpurnia could get the device to work, she'd now be fifteen years older than her husband remembered. Not a massive gap in the modern world, but a chasm in the Roman one. Instead of being much younger than her husband, she'd be about the same age. Maybe older. "It doesn't matter to her."

"But it would to him – it would be a pity to spend fifteen years pining over someone only for them to run off with the nearest slave girl."

To Pullus's right, Habitus bristled. "You shouldn't let them talk to each other in their own language," he said.

Calpurnia turned to the Greek. "What are they saying?"

The Greek didn't reply, but he smiled. The reassurance seemed to be enough. "Tell him to hand over the code," Calpurnia repeated.

Pullus translated. Harris simply responded with a roll of his eyes. "I spent most of my life trying to stop NovusPart from vandalising the timeline. Before I betray myself, I need some level of assurance."

"Yes?"

"If Calpurnia here was to promise not to use the device to transport anyone other than my brother... and her husband?"

Pullus translated.

"Don't put your own words into his mouth," Calpurnia said.

"I'm not."

"The problem is one of paradox," Harris continued, ignoring them. "If the timeline is fixed, then whatever actions you take will be irrelevant. The timeline cannot be changed." Harris paused and nodded towards Calpurnia. "Say she transported her father forwards before she'd been conceived. She finds the timeline hasn't changed. She instead discovers she was adopted – or maybe sired by one of the household slaves."

Calpurnia listened to the translation, but didn't seem impressed.

"But, if the timeline *can* be changed," Harris continued, "the risk of paradox presents itself: the creation of an infinite loop of circumstance."

"The timeline has already proven itself to be durable," Pullus said. "As you should know, McMahon and Whelan didn't seem too concerned about altering history for their own benefit."

"Well, just as long as you remember the central panel of

the NovusPart triptych wasn't there to stop them. Joe Arlen was always quite clear in his warnings: the risks increase exponentially with every alteration. So this is an experiment we can't afford to get wrong."

Pullus tried to lower his voice – to make it as difficult as possible for the Greek to hear. "What do you mean: *Arlen's warnings?*"

Harris's eyes flickered. "You'll find out – and soon."

"Ask him for the code," Calpurnia repeated. "And he'll get to see his brother again before he dies."

Pullus hesitated. "There's an option you've missed," he said, speaking to Harris. "Maybe multiple timelines exist, and paradoxes therefore simply create alternative streams of events. The timeline becomes a self-healing animal. So, whatever you tell us, it simply won't matter."

"I can tell you don't actually believe that."

"No. But do you think I'd allow her to damage the timeline?"

Harris shook his head, almost as if in defeat. "Most standard thinking relies on the theory that events propagate forwards," he said. "Cause and effect. But I've come to think that events actually propagate backwards. And it's the future that's fixed, and those that live there simply take action to protect their own existence."

"Maybe…"

"So tell Calpurnia here to go easy on her threats. It didn't work on Whelan and it won't work on me."

Whelan. The molten lead. The hole drilled into his skull. The sound of his screaming. "You offered us Arlen's code,"

Pullus said, his voice trembling. "In return, I'll make sure she gives you your brother."

Harris nodded. "Then I'll need two things. First, one of the old NovusPart phones."

"We have a few undamaged mobiles. But the batteries now only last a few minutes between charges."

Harris flicked his eyes to Naso. "If you're looking for fresh ones, he has some. At least, that's what the men on the convoys told me."

Pullus looked over at the *duumvir*, and saw the confusion on his face. "I doubt it."

"You don't believe he's controlling the convoys to his own advantage?"

"Okay, okay," said Pullus. "So we need a working phone. What's the second thing?"

"The boy," Harris replied, his attention now firmly on Calpurnia. "I need to see her son. Marcus."

Pullus wasn't sure he wanted to know why. He began to translate, the Greek confirming his words with a silent nod. As soon as he mentioned the batteries, the *duumvir* was quick to deny it.

"It's not true," Naso said. "The convoys are clean."

"You're sure?" asked Calpurnia. She glanced towards Habitus.

"Pullus's friend is lying," Habitus confirmed, almost casually and much to Naso's relief. "He's trying to sow dissent between us." Habitus signalled for one of his men to approach. An order was given for him to go and get one of the old NovusPart phones from the villa's stores. They were only turned on occasionally to check that signals from the outside were still being blocked. But fifteen years of being switched on and off, and being charged and recharged, had taken its toll. Few still worked.

"More importantly," Naso said, interrupting. "Why does he want Marcus?"

"I'm not exposing my son to any danger," Calpurnia said.

Pullus looked toward Harris. He looked like he had played his last hand. He had nowhere left to go. No more space for deception. "Barbatus used to say a predator only comes out into the sun to hunt."

"Yes?"

"Well, that man is no longer a predator. He's a woodlouse, whose stone has been kicked. So we hand him the phone with Marcus in the room, and with a knife at his throat. There will only be one person in danger."

Naso, however, remained unconvinced. "We have time to consult the *Ordo*."

"No," replied Calpurnia. "If I wanted the opinions of tired old men, I'd go and pray at my father's tomb."

"The aediles, then?"

"We're not debating the state of the roads or the sewers."

"But—"

"Calpurnia has given her answer," replied Habitus, as his man arrived back with one of the old mobiles. Everyone turned as the man entered.

Because it was already ringing.

12

A REWARD.

Achillia took a few deep breaths to calm herself. She'd been brought here as a reward.

To see the cocksucking Sibyl.

"Many slaves would be extremely jealous you'd been brought to hear your fortune," Trigemina said. "But I think it's only right to allow you to glimpse your future, after you helped save mine."

"Thank you," Achillia replied, hearing in her voice the sarcasm that her mistress didn't seem to notice. "I don't know what to say."

The small cave was dark and silent. The oil lamps that lit the passageway weren't present in the grotto. A deliberate tactic, no doubt, to keep the secrets of the Sibyl hidden. Achillia grasped the hilt of her knife. She looked over at the thin, dark shape of her mistress. Trigemina stood still, waiting. Within striking range.

She could kill her where she stood. Just reach out and slit her throat. Then all she'd have to do would be to get back to the wagon, and kill the other hired hands. She'd have the choice of four horses and any number of towns.

But she'd be caught. A woman, travelling on her own. An obvious slave to boot. No, she'd be found within days.

The drone started so softly she barely noticed it. Then, a sudden drumbeat broke her concentration. Achillia almost laughed. A voice now wailed from the darkness, joining the background whining sound that was steadily growing in volume. The quality of acting was poor, even for a provincial theatre.

"You hear it, don't you?" whispered Trigemina.

Achillia shook her head. She bit down on her tongue; anything to stop her from laughing. The voice was shrill, echoing about the cave, the words unclear. And all the time the whining noise grew louder – almost turning into a whistle – and quickly reaching the point at which it began to hurt her ears. Not that Trigemina seemed to notice. Her mistress stood close, searching the gloom for a glimpse of the Sibyl.

Achillia glanced back towards the tunnel. The triangular entrance, illuminated by the sunlight beyond, now rolled before her, as if she was suddenly on a spinning top. She was riding its edges, and all the time slowing down. Becoming unstable. The light jerked back and forth as the whistling in her ears turned into a scream.

Then she heard it. A voice in her head, not an actor in the dark. Achillia felt the knife drop from her hand, and it skittered away in the dark. She stumbled backwards and dropped to the floor, then began to retch. The ground continued to roll, and the voice shouted in her mind. Inside her. All around her.

You will go to Pompeii, and you will find Manius Calpurnius Barbatus! You will—

13

New Pompeii

PULLUS PUT THE NovusPart phone to his ear. The voice on the other end of the line was barely recognisable, more of a mumble than speech. The sound seemed to be coming from the back of someone's throat, each word barely pronounced. Perhaps whoever was speaking couldn't fully move their mouth, or they were trying to disguise their voice. Either way, the only thing Pullus could really tell was that the person speaking to him was male. "Who is this?"

"Marcus," the voice answered. "The battery on this phone will only last a few seconds so we don't have much time."

"What are you hearing?" Calpurnia asked. Quickly, Pullus informed her.

"I am talking to you from your future," the voice continued. "The man with you – Harris – has served his purpose. I needed someone who would be enough to attract your attention, but he will be dead within the hour. I told him I would save his brother. You should know this now before events unfold: *I lied to him*."

Pullus glanced at Harris. Despite continuing to smile with some satisfaction, the man who'd once snatched him from the streets of London had never looked so helpless.

"What do you want?" Pullus asked.

"Do you remember that day in the amphitheatre when the gladiator tried to kill you?"

"Yes."

"You took a gamble that day. You decided those in the future were influencing events to secure their position, and to do so they would save your life. This call is being made for the same reason. I'm passing a message down to ensure things work out as they should. I'm speaking to you so that it is me – and nobody else – that gains control of the NovusPart device."

"Okay…"

"*The Master of Pompeii will become the Emperor of Time*."

Silence. Pullus waited, expecting more, but nothing came. "What?"

"You heard me. A little riddle from Joe Arlen's research papers."

Pullus froze. Arlen's research. "You have copies?"

"I have the only copy; the originals were destroyed in Naples." The voice paused. Chuckled. "At the time you're speaking, the copy I hold is in New Pompeii. So don't worry, they're not floating around waiting for someone in the outside world to stumble across them. And Harris hasn't seen them first hand. He just knows what I've told him, including the failsafe code."

"I don't understand," Pullus said. "*The Master of Pompeii...?*"

"You'll recognise the meaning when the time comes. Now, go and get Calpurnia's son and send Habitus to fetch you another battery. The next time I call I'll give you the code for the NovusPart devi—"

The phone clicked off. Pullus looked down and found it dead in his hands. He fiddled for a second with the main switch, but it didn't come back to life. Around him, he felt Calpurnia and Habitus draw closer.

"Well? What did you hear?" Calpurnia said.

Pullus didn't answer. The riddle sounded foolish, but even so he couldn't take his eyes from Harris and the flicker in his eyes. *He'll be dead within an hour.*

"Events propagate backwards not forwards," Harris said. "Time is written; we can't avoid it. Can't defeat it. Like I said to you, I've become a big believer in fate."

"I need another battery," Pullus said, speaking to Habitus, and trying to ignore the chill Harris's words had just given him. He unclipped the back of the phone's case. The battery inside was leaking metallic fluid. The thing was barely functional.

"I've heard that voice for years," Harris continued. "At first I didn't believe what it told me, but he kept on being right about things so I was soon convinced. I had my own private oracle. Speaking to me from the future, telling me what to do. Governing my actions. Although it's been quiet of late, he told me to come here. To provide advice to Marcus, and his mother."

"What's he saying about my son?" Calpurnia said.

Pullus looked down at the phone. "It wasn't your son," he said. "It wasn't that Marcus."

The sparkle hadn't left Harris's eyes. "No?"

Pullus shook his head. "No, I didn't recognise the voice."

"That's because you only know him as the boy," Harris said, sneering. "When he makes that call to you – thirty years from now – he will be a man. The Emperor of Time."

"What you're talking about isn't within the limits of what we know about the NovusPart device," Pullus said. He thought about the voice again. The lack of proof. "This is one of your tricks. So cut to the chase, and tell us what you really want."

Before him, Harris seemed to crumple. "You're going to have to make a decision," he said. "Because once you replace that battery the phone will ring again. And then Marcus will tell you the code and the dots between the present and the future will be joined. So ask yourself, Nick Houghton, what will you do when he gives you the code? Will you keep it to yourself?" Harris glanced at Calpurnia, then Habitus. "Do you think they will let you?"

For a few seconds, Pullus hesitated. "Christians, Gauls, Visigoths and vice," he said, almost to himself. *What if Harris was right? What if the voice really was coming from the future? What would Calpurnia do with all that power?*

Calpurnia stirred. "I don't understand…?"

"We've discussed changing the timeline – argued about it – many times, Calpurnia."

She could suddenly tell what he meant, and smiled. "We've always known the device would be activated eventually... after all, someone saved you from the gladiator."

"Promise me."

"All I want is my husband."

"Then go and get your boy, and let's see if we can introduce him to his father."

14

HE'D ALMOST FORGOTTEN. The traces of the old NovusPart control villa were so well hidden beneath Calpurnia's renovations that it was hard to remember it had once been the centre of it all. But a few twists and turns from the *tablinum* soon led into more modern corridors. Ones that were now only trodden by Calpurnia and her Greek. For everyone else, entrance was strictly forbidden.

Marcus let out a yelp of excitement, but was immediately pulled back by Calpurnia to stop him exploring. It hadn't taken much persuasion to tear him away from his Suetonius. Habitus and Harris made up the remainder of the group. Naso hadn't been invited to join them; the *duumvir* had been escorted from the villa and sent back to the town. The Greek too wasn't in sight, presumably working with the device and starting the tracking system. Harris had carefully explained the circumstances of his brother's transportation: where and when he'd been taken. With that information, the Greek had likely already found the child in the time stream. Now, all they needed was the code...

Habitus set Harris down onto his knees ahead of the

main group. The old spy looked shattered. For him, it all came down to this. But, despite what the voice on the phone had said, it was difficult for Pullus to summon any pity. *He will be dead within an hour*. If the call had been from the future, then it was already written. There was no stopping it.

Harris looked desperately towards the paradox chamber. Its heavy metallic door had been left open, the interior empty aside from a small collection of children's toys scattered across the floor. The two geese at its threshold appeared unable to enter.

The creatures whose honking had once saved Rome from being sacked by the Gauls, were now being used to alert the Romans if anyone appeared after being ripped from the timeline. A less expensive way of keeping watch than using a slave, Pullus thought as he glanced at Marcus. The boy continued to pull against his mother, trying to get a good view.

"He'll appear in there," said Pullus, attracting Marcus's attention and then nodding towards the paradox chamber. "As far as we understand it – as far as Whelan was able to tell us – anyone transported appears inside a chamber. This is the main one attached to our device, with a secondary chamber at the amphitheatre."

There was little light to see by; most of the overhead fluorescent squares were dark. Almost unnoticed, the Greek appeared to close the metal door of the paradox chamber. As soon as it smacked into position, an electronic ringing filled the air.

Pullus looked at the phone in his hand, then lifted it to his ear. It clicked, and connected, and then he heard the same mumbled voice as before. "The boy," it said. "It's important he sees this, and it's important you see what he's destined to become."

Pullus glanced at Calpurnia's son, but he didn't have time to think through what he'd just been told. Instead, the voice started to read out a string of letters and numbers. The pattern was repeated twice. Pullus called the code out clearly for the Greek to record on his little wax tablet, who then scurried away again, deeper into the old control villa.

"During the war," Harris said, "the Allies managed to get hold of the Nazis' Enigma machine. It was a simple set of cogs that translated each input into a coded output. To read the messages, they just needed the initial settings for the device."

Pullus didn't respond.

"Decimus…"

Pullus flinched, reacting to Calpurnia's use of his *praenomen*. "You're going to transport his brother first?"

Calpurnia nodded, seeming distracted. "The voice on the phone," she whispered. "Tell me truthfully: are you sure it wasn't my son?"

Pullus hesitated, and then took her a few steps away from Harris. The old man didn't appear interested; his attention remained firmly on the metal door and the patrolling geese. "Marcus is a common name," he said. "No, I don't think it was your son. At least, I can't be sure…"

"But it was coming from the future?"

Again, Pullus found himself floundering. "It could have been a trick," he said. "Something to disorientate us." Then he glanced at the paradox chamber. "I guess we'll find out soon enough."

"You've always told me that time moved forwards, not back."

Pullus nodded, and gripped the phone a fraction tighter. It had already died, its battery lasting barely as long as the first. He realised one thing that he hoped the others present hadn't. Whoever knew the number of this particular phone had made the call. And whoever had made the call controlled the NovusPart device. Not now, but sometime in the future.

When exactly, though, remained uncertain. For transportations, the horizon was thirty years. But perhaps different rules applied for speaking directly into the past. He simply didn't know. But he needed to find out. And after they'd finished here, he needed to recharge the phone and go into the system settings to find its number.

"Calpurnia!"

Habitus's cry was lost in amongst a storm of noise from the geese. The two birds were honking at the doorway. But then everything seemed to stop.

Pullus felt his head slow. The corridor appeared to expand and contract, like a magnifying glass had passed directly in front of his eyes. The NovusPart device was working. He opened his mouth to speak, but couldn't – he watched as Habitus moved forward and opened the door. Harris rose from his knees, and then fell back.

Blood, flesh and shards of bone lined the floor of the paradox chamber.

Whoever it had transported had been flipped inside out and torn apart. They hadn't come through as a person, simply the remains of one. And whoever it had been, they had been very small. Just a child. Maybe a boy.

Harris started to scream.

He will be dead within the hour.

"The code is useless," Calpurnia said. She turned away, dragging her son with her. "Kill him, Habitus."

Pullus remained focused on the paradox chamber. A small shoe lay amidst the blood and flesh. A tiny shinbone protruded from it – cut off short of what would have been the knee, as if scythed in two by a laser.

He turned away, just as Harris started to struggle – the old man's limbs flailed and slapped against the floor. He didn't make any other sound. The *frumentarius* had him in a chokehold, and the voice on the phone was being proven right. Even if it was some way short of the full hour, Harris was dead.

15

PULLUS FOUND MARCUS in his room. The boy was surrounded by his books, flicking the pages of several different volumes. He didn't bother to look up to see who was disturbing him.

"The Emperor Tiberius used to throw people from the cliffs of Capri," Marcus said, sitting on his bed, his Suetonius in his lap. "Do you think that's true?"

"He *ordered* people thrown off the cliffs, yes."

"And Caligula... he killed his cousin..."

"Caligula did a lot of things."

"And Nero killed his mother, didn't he?"

Pullus took a few steps into the boy's room. He looked around, trying to find some small elements that reflected his own memory of being a teenager. But there was nothing. "There's plenty in these books you'll find to admire. If you take the trouble to find it."

Marcus looked up. "Your favourite is Claudius, yes?"

"He was better than most."

"Suetonius said Emperor Claudius was cruel and bloodthirsty. That he liked ordering gladiators' deaths in the arena, no matter how they performed."

Pullus sighed. Marcus had always been naturally drawn to the more horrific stories of imperial excess, enjoying the crimes of Caligula and Nero as if they were no more than Gothic fantasy. "I guess I liked the fact Claudius was never meant to be emperor. And he did a decent job. The Empire was sustained by such men. Not tyrants like Tiberius, Nero and Commodus."

Marcus pulled a face. *Commodus*. His mother's habit of failing to recognise any emperor after Titus had rubbed off on her son. "That man," the boy said. "The one you were speaking to on the phone…"

"What about him?"

"He wanted me in the room for a reason, didn't he?"

Pullus wasn't sure what to say. A breeze made something on Marcus's desk flutter: a small dead bird, one wing pinned to the wood, the flight feathers exposed.

"Do you know why?" Marcus asked again, now sounding irritated.

"No."

"I think I do," Marcus continued. "When the Emperor Tiberius threw those men off his cliffs at Capri, he had Caligula there watching. So his successor would know what had to be done."

"Marcus…"

"I've heard what they say about me. About you and my mother."

"It's not true."

Marcus slipped off the bed. He picked up a wooden training sword from the floor, and held it out in front of him. "The man who can't be killed, they say. But what about his son?"

Pullus tried to smile as he backed out of the room and closed the door. Perhaps he should have said something. But he didn't yet understand what the voice on the phone had been trying to tell him.

"Pullus!"

He turned. Calpurnia and Habitus were walking towards him, their faces angry. Calpurnia had her hand held out as though she was expecting him to offer something. He looked at her blankly, before realising what she meant. She'd figured it out. He still had the phone, and she now understood the implications.

"Don't make me ask for it."

Pullus reached into his tunic, and took from it the mobile phone. It remained unpowered. He hadn't yet had chance to find its number.

"The Greek explained it to us," Calpurnia said.

Of course, Pullus thought bitterly as he passed across the phone. *The Greek.*

Whoever had called them from the future had known which device to call. They perhaps still owned it. Pullus didn't want to wait for Habitus to compel him. "Funny how the most unexpected thing can become an oracle," he said.

Calpurnia didn't answer. She pressed the power button but nothing happened. It still needed a recharge before she'd get anything useful from it.

"Has the Greek worked out what went wrong?" he asked.

Habitus grunted, which was an answer of sorts.

"Whelan told us enough to get the tracking systems working," Pullus said. "And now Harris brings us information that allows us to transport people."

"It didn't work," Calpurnia said. She glared at him and put the phone away. Pullus felt a prickle across the back of his neck. He'd already been back and forth over his exchanges with Harris, and the man on the phone who'd called himself Marcus, every word of their conversations, whether initially translated or not, looking for any mistake or hidden meaning. And even though the string of numbers and letters was long, he'd called them as he'd heard them. There was no error. It simply hadn't worked.

"We got further than before," Habitus said. "This time, at least something came through."

Pullus grimaced. *Something*. Harris had said he'd lost his brother when they were both still children. *Fuck*.

"We know the device works," Calpurnia said. "And we know *we* make it work. After all, Pullus, you were saved in the amphitheatre."

"We know the device works at some point," Pullus replied, keeping his voice calm. "All the rest is speculation."

"We need it to be for *us*, Pullus." Calpurnia took hold of his arm. "We need the NovusPart device to be in our hands."

Pullus nodded, but pulled his arm away. It may have been only the slightest ghost of affection, but he didn't want it. Not now. Not standing outside her son's bedroom, when inside doubt was beginning to grow.

"The man on the phone," Calpurnia continued. "You said he mentioned Arlen's research. He said it was here, in Pompeii?"

"Yes."

"We should instigate a search," Calpurnia said. "Information like that could be stored on something the size of a thumbnail, yes?"

Habitus snorted, stopping Pullus from answering. "The Greek's already been through all the NovusPart stuff. We've checked all the tablets and datacards."

"Property always goes missing at times of change," Calpurnia replied, calmly. "It's why they call it *looting*. Make the necessary arrangements, Habitus. Tear the place apart if you have to. We need to find what's left of Arlen's work."

16

Ancient Roman Empire, the road to Pompeii, AD 62

"WHERE DID YOU find her? Where the fuck did you find her?!"

Achillia didn't hear Trigemina answer the driver. Her mistress returned to the carriage, seemingly unable to speak. Achillia followed and snapped the short-sword back into position above the door. The blade was now covered in blood. She wiped her hands on her *stola*, and found it already slick and damp.

"She found me in a *ludus*," Achillia said, her brain still whirring as she tried to track back over the events of the last few minutes. She'd been thinking about the voice. Sitting in the carriage thinking about the Sibyl's voice when the men had come out from between the trees. And after that: just a blur.

She could just about remember reaching for the sword. Approaching the first man and killing him. She'd spoken to the second one before thrusting the sword flat through the bridge of his nose.

Had he been on his knees? Maybe. She hadn't truly noticed because by then she'd already started after the third man. The man who'd already given up and was trying to get away. The man who'd stopped to beg her, even though she hadn't listened. Because her ears were still ringing with the sound of the Sibyl's voice.

The wagon moved forward. The sudden jolt brought Achillia back to the present. She blinked, then looked at the blood on the blade and her clothes and her hands. She felt specks of it on her face. She'd stabbed the last man so many times he'd fallen in several pieces.

Fuck, she'd enjoyed that.

"This is what you paid for," Achillia said.

"You didn't even ask them…"

"Bandits," she replied. "They wanted your money. They wanted you."

Trigemina didn't say anything.

"Two men were arguing in a *taberna*," Achillia started, slowly, raking the joke up from her memory, trying to ease the atmosphere. "'I fucked your wife,' said the first. 'I'm her husband and have no choice,' said the second. 'What in Jupiter made you do it?'"

Trigemina didn't even smile. "What did the Sibyl tell you?"

Achillia stared back at her mistress. The words had been so clear, so loud. *You will go to Pompeii, and you will find Manius Calpurnius Barbatus! You will seek his daughter, and you will save her husband Marcus Villius Denter by taking him to meet Balbus in Herculaneum.* "Didn't you hear?"

Trigemina shook her head.

"Well, it doesn't matter," Achillia replied. "As you told me, the Sibyl's words are private."

17

Naples, two weeks prior to the death of Harris

"Whether through incompetence or selfishness, Nick Houghton's insistence on keeping the people of Pompeii confined behind their city walls has wasted the key archaeological event of our lifetime. It is the equivalent of opening the tomb of Tutankhamun, and then simply closing the doors and walking away."

Professor Hayden,
Lead Archaeologist, Herculaneum
World Archaeology News Message Board

SHE WAS LATE.

Nick Houghton surveyed the arrivals lounge of Naples airport. The dirty glass-panel doors leading to the "drop-off" zone remained firmly closed.

He tried to relax his shoulders. He'd attracted no unwelcome attention on the short hop over from Tehran, and most of the other passengers on his flight had already grabbed their bags and departed the arrivals hall. Where was his ride? He glanced at his wrist. He wasn't wearing a watch, but the tic had re-emerged almost as soon as he'd changed back into modern clothing. He pulled at his collar.

A cleaner with a small handcart edged into view at the far side of the hall. A few minutes later, another female figure appeared and propped open a side door and started to sort through a collection of unclaimed baggage. Neither woman paid him much notice.

Chloe hadn't let him down before. And being on time wasn't exactly one of her traits, he reminded himself. Never had been, and he'd known her since university, and she'd no doubt arrive soon enough and full of apologies. Even so, if this had been the old days then his loitering would have already attracted attention from what remained of the press. They'd want to know why he'd come back, and who he was meeting. Want to see if they could discover any more details about what had happened to NovusPart, McMahon and Whelan. Fortunately, the news business now seemed to have other priorities. Maybe if they knew why he was really here, things would be different.

"Decimus Pullus?"

Nick turned. A woman carrying a large holdall was approaching from the direction of baggage claim. At first he was puzzled; the other passengers had long since dispersed. Her bag looked heavy, pulling her right shoulder down into a pronounced, lopsided stoop. Had she been on his flight?

"Decimus Horatius Pullus?"

The woman wasn't wearing a facemask. His own hung limply around his neck. He tugged it back over his nose. Not only did it provide a handy disguise, but it was also a useful defence against the dual airborne threats of pollution and disease. In the fifteen years of travelling back and forth between Naples and New Pompeii, he'd noticed many things change as the outside world continued to slip away from him. The economic depression pushing down on the old states of Europe and the US showed no sign of abating, their economies finding themselves unable to compete with the millions of highly educated graduates from China and India. And for all the technology being displayed on the brightly lit advertising hoardings of the arrivals hall, did any of that matter when the burgeoning middle classes from those same countries could buy up all of life's niceties? It was the inverse of the Crassus brainteaser: *if the richest man in ancient Rome couldn't afford a computer, then was he really rich?* But what if the richest man in modern-day Italy could afford a computer, but not a nice glass of red wine? Would he, in fact, prefer to be Crassus?

"Decimus Pullus…?" The woman stared at him. "It is you, isn't it?"

"No," he said, looking away. Habitus had once told him the best route to anonymity was not to make eye contact. "I think you've made a mistake."

The woman dropped her bag next to his, and beamed at him as she straightened. "No, I don't think so," she said, her voice a little too chirpy. "I noticed you by the conveyors." She pointed at her bag. "Took them a while to get mine off the plane, didn't it? I thought they'd lost the damn thing."

The woman was probably in her mid-thirties, with a bob of black hair that matched her olive skin. She wore a lime-green strappy top and khaki trousers. She clearly recognised him. But that didn't mean he had to encourage her.

"My name's Nick Houghton," he said. "Here it's Nick Houghton, not Decimus Horatius Pullus."

The woman nodded. "Oh, okay." She paused. The silence immediately became awkward, but she kept grinning, like she'd met a celebrity. "I studied classics under Professor Turner at Durham," she said. "That's where you were, wasn't it?"

Nick frowned. *Professor Turner?* He didn't recognise the name, but still nodded. Where was Chloe? "Yes," he said. He thought about mentioning his own tutor, Webster, and asking if he was still there. He silently prayed this woman would go away and not post anything on the boards about meeting him. He needed at least a few days off the radar.

"Well, I just wanted to say hello," she said, her grin starting to crumble. "I think what you've done out there is really great. Not like people are saying…"

It was definitely now awkward. He glanced towards the glass doors and felt a flood of relief; Chloe was hurrying towards him. He'd only have to string this out a few moments longer. "Look," he said, "it's been a long flight."

"Sure. Well, it was nice to meet you."

With some effort the woman lifted her bag onto her

shoulder and walked towards the exit. Nick smiled at Chloe as she reached him.

"Hello, Mr Pax Romana!"

Nick scowled. "Don't you mean Mr Ambassador?"

"Don't push it," Chloe replied, smiling. Then her face became serious. "Do you want to go there straight away?"

Nick nodded. "We might as well get it over with."

18

NICK SHUDDERED. WHAT remained of his dad lay on a bed inside a clear plastic tent. The only other person present was a female nurse. She wasn't wearing a bio-hazard suit, but it was pretty damn close; an almost-invisible muslin covered her face, head and shoulders. The woman's hands and forearms were protected by long latex gloves. The rest of her uniform looked thin and stiff, almost like paper, and was probably designed to be stripped off and thrown away, rather than be put through the laundry. It was a uniform designed to be incinerated rather than cleaned.

Nick watched in silence as the nurse moved around to the other side of the tent. His father's head didn't shift to follow her movement, and he knew it couldn't. The muscles in most of his body were frozen. Immobile. Only his eyes moved. And they were focused upwards and towards the extraction fans as they pulled and pumped the air. Nick found himself following his father's gaze. Maybe the air was being incinerated too.

"The nurses say he's conscious," said Chloe, keeping her voice barely above a whisper. "But you'll need to get closer so he can see you."

Nick didn't move. When Chloe had described the sanatorium to him, he'd pictured something between an old Victorian workhouse and a health spa. Two ends of a spectrum maybe, but this place wasn't even on the same scale. As they'd approached, he'd mistaken it for a business park. It had probably been an office block at some point in the not-too-distant past. He could easily imagine the "ward" filled with open-plan dividers and laminated beige desks, perhaps all sitting under a multitude of meaningless corporate slogans. Now the desks had been replaced by tents.

"It's okay, Nick," Chloe said. "Just take your time."

"The Bureau didn't tell me it was this bad," he said.

Chloe didn't respond. Nick saw she was struggling to find the right words. He waved towards the rest of the floor, to the nurses milling around them. "I meant the rest of it," he said. "Not him."

"Despite what you might think, it's better than it looks."

"Really?"

"The strength of the symptoms seems to relate to several factors: past medical history, genetic make-up... Your father's been unlucky. Most people just become disabled."

"Turned to stone," Nick whispered. The last time he'd been in Naples he'd provided a blood sample. It had classified him into one of the higher risk categories, which was unsurprising given his father's biology had found itself so susceptible, and the Bureau had then insisted on him getting airway filters. Despite the tent and all the other precautions, those same filters were the only reason he'd been allowed inside to visit.

"…it's a small outbreak," Chloe said, finishing a sentence of which Nick hadn't heard the start.

It didn't look small. The nurse seemed to have finished whatever she was doing, and was now leaving the tent. She pushed out through a series of overlapping plastic flaps, but didn't approach them, instead following a thick red line painted on the floor, one that took her to the rear of the ward, away from the orange line on which both Chloe and he were standing.

Nick noted the orange floor paint extended to the other side of his father's tent, away from the entry flap. There was no way he'd be allowed to enter. "I didn't think it was airborne?"

"It isn't," Chloe replied. "Spit and saliva. But with the way things are mutating, no one's willing to take many risks."

"They say it's similar to tetanus."

"Only in the symptoms – it impacts the nervous system in much the same way."

"I had tetanus when I was a child," Nick said. "The treatment was… nothing like this."

He let out a deep, pent-up breath. The economic challenges being faced in Europe were one thing; the emergence of new disease and the strengthening of old illnesses in the face of antibiotic resistance were something else entirely. When he'd first gone to New Pompeii, infections like this were being wiped off the planet. Each time he came home now though, there seemed to be something else to worry about. Bubonic plague in the States, polio in Russia. New types of cancer to replace the ones that had been cured…

He turned to leave. His friend just about got ahead of him before he could start walking away. "You might not get another chance," she said.

Nick stopped. In the early days of the Bureau of Roman Affairs, he hadn't trusted the organisation – especially when rumours and counter-rumours had been circulating about NovusPart and what exactly had happened in New Pompeii. When the travel bans had started to be imposed, he'd had no real choice but to go along with it: to use the Bureau as his channel of communication with the outside world. And yet despite this they'd sensed his discomfort, and offered to employ someone he knew as a go-between and personal contact. He'd chosen Chloe almost at random, remembering their university friendship and her easy personality. And given how few other opportunities there were in England, she'd gratefully accepted.

"I don't have anything to say to him," Nick replied.

"You came a long way."

Nick left a long silence. "He never wanted me to leave, you know. He just wanted me to help pull his academic career out of the quagmire."

"That's not fair, Nick."

"Isn't it? Why do you think he moved to Naples? To get closer to me, or to get closer to the tourist circus outside the gates of the real Pompeii?"

"Your father moved to Naples," Chloe replied, her voice stern now, "because most civilised states don't provide visas to men who own slaves. You appear rarely – and only ever here. What did you expect him to do? Remain in England whilst his son jetted into Naples for the occasional meeting with the Bureau?"

Nick didn't answer. He didn't want to rake over it all again, and certainly didn't want to have to explain. Chloe wouldn't have understood anyway. The individual arguments all seemed petty, never quite expressing the weight of resentment that had built up. Maybe their relationship could have been fixed in the past, but not now.

"The last thing he said to my face was that he was ashamed of me."

"He's very proud of you, Nick."

"He said he'd never forgive me for joining NovusPart."

"You can't leave it like that."

Nick glanced at the tent. His father's eyes stared upwards. His last view on life: a dirty grey extraction fan and a fluorescent tube. "Does he even know I'm here?"

"No."

"Then let's go."

19

New Pompeii

"SO YOU'LL BE staying here at the townhouse? Not heading back to your villa?"

Pullus nodded, unable to hide his disappointment. Galbo stared back at him blankly, although his thoughts must have been similar. With his master now back in permanent residence, his role would revert to one of taking orders, rather than running the townhouse.

"I'd like a snack before I go to bed," Pullus said, waving his hand in the direction of the *tablinum* and the kitchen beyond. The trip into town from Calpurnia's villa had been slow, and he'd had plenty of time to think about what had happened to Harris, and what the voice on the phone had told him. This man who claimed his name was Marcus, calling from the future. "Nothing heavy. And some wine."

Galbo waited – just a few perfectly timed heartbeats to make sure there would be no further instructions – then slowly headed for the kitchen. His staff tapped a steadily weakening path away from the atrium. The noise made Pullus feel guilty, but Galbo could have instructed one of the boys to do it. Primus, one of the three other slaves stationed here, hovered at the side of the atrium.

Though several dozen oil lamps burned around them, the atrium was still dark. Little moonlight seemed able to find its way down through the *compluvium* – the square gap in the atrium's roof – and so there was nothing for the atrium's shallow central pool beneath to scatter. But there was enough light to reflect off the McMahon's fresco of the erupting Vesuvius, which still adorned the atrium's main wall. He'd wanted to paint over it, to wipe out all traces of NovusPart before he'd started his new life here, but it had never seemed the right time. Despite the gloom, the glass beads that made up the tip of the mountain sparkled.

Would Calpurnia really try to change things? Just like NovusPart?

After McMahon's death, the decision for him to stay in New Pompeii had been fairly straightforward. He'd been retained because he was useful. And, more than that, Calpurnia had seemed to trust him. But she didn't anymore. And deep down, he didn't trust her either. Not with the NovusPart device. So, yes, he'd follow her wishes and work with the *duumvir* to re-examine the last remaining traces of NovusPart. But if he found anything would he really tell Calpurnia?

He didn't know. It was late, and he needed to rest. Needed to reset his brain and shake from it the last remaining images of Harris's mangled brother. He headed towards the wooden steps in the corner of the atrium, ignoring the plate of cold meat Galbo had brought for him, but scooping up a glass of wine.

Galbo managed to sense his movement from wherever he'd been waiting. "Would you like me to unpack your things?"

Pullus came to a halt on the bottom step. "No," he said, quietly. *Would he tell Calpurnia?* In some ways, he'd already made his decision. "Leave that to me. And no one but you is to enter my room."

"Of course," replied Galbo. His steward cleared his throat. "Calpurnia's gift arrived a couple of hours ahead of you, sir."

"Gift?"

"I've put her in a room at the back of the house, overlooking the garden. Not with the others. She says she's to help in the search?"

"Don't worry about it," Pullus said. There was an ache in his shoulders that emanated into his lower back. He drained his glass in an attempt to numb it.

"Do you want me to send her to your villa?"

Pullus allowed a quiet chuckle to escape him. "I doubt Calpurnia would allow me to do that." He shook his head. "Everyone in town would recognise it as a snub."

"Then we keep her here?"

"Yes, but tell the rest of the household to watch what they say around her."

"You work for Habitus?"

The girl didn't respond. Probably in her late teens, Galbo

had brought her to Pullus early. She now stood waiting in the low sun that filled his garden. Around them, plants within the central colonnade were dying back for winter. The air was cold, with just enough bite in it to let him know it would soon be the Saturnalia.

"He used to work for me," Pullus continued.

"Yes, he told me you once owned him."

Pullus raised an eyebrow. Galbo looked angry at the girl's cheek. No doubt she'd later receive a lesson in old-fashioned slave etiquette. *Be distrustful of women*, Habitus had told him. *Especially ones you hadn't expected to meet.*

And now he'd been sent one.

He looked at her. Everyone in Pompeii would notice she looked out of place among his slaves, very different from the bunch of elderly and disabled misfits he'd accumulated. Worse, he was attracted to her.

Inside, Pullus felt some itch of annoyance. Did they really think he was so stupid? Perhaps some of the older men on the *Ordo* would be flattered and fooled, but there was no doubt she'd have been told to report everything he did back to her old mistress. He looked at Galbo. His steward rolled his eyes at him, indicating that he too understood.

"Your name?"

"Taedia."

"And you've worked for Calpurnia for how long?"

His "gift" didn't answer. Instead she just looked back at him confused.

"You were bought at the market? Or born in the household?"

"I've been with my mistress for as long as I can remember."

Pullus nodded. Slave born, then. Which was all the information he needed to confirm it: Calpurnia didn't trust him, and she was no "gift". She was too young. Too healthy. Too much effort and too many resources would have gone into her training. But that didn't mean he had to play along with whatever Habitus had planned for her.

His eyes narrowed. Did he recognise her? He didn't. But, then again, Calpurnia had many slaves and if she'd come from her inner circle then perhaps their paths wouldn't have crossed. Or perhaps they had and he simply couldn't remember. Hadn't taken notice.

No, he *would* have noticed.

"Well, Taedia, I have work to do. Galbo here will provide you with some duties."

"Our mistress wishes me to assist you directly."

Our mistress. Those words had been given to her; they'd come out like they'd been spring-loaded.

Galbo took Taedia by the arm. In his other hand, he raised his staff a good foot or two from the ground. The speed of the old man's movement was surprising, and the "gift" yelped. She must have known how some Roman masters would respond to being given orders by a woman. Pullus smiled inwardly. Maybe she'd even heard of how many of the men currently bowing and scraping at Calpurnia's feet would like to respond, if they ever got the chance.

"Habitus told me you're a good man," Taedia said,

whipping her eyes between him and the steward's staff.

Pullus wasn't flattered. The *frumentarius* had probably meant it as a sly insult. "Then we'd best get to work then, hadn't we?"

20

Naples

"We gave antibiotics away for every sniff and cold, pumped our animals full of them just to keep the price of food low, and even used them to protect the frescos of Pompeii from further damage. And now we panic that we're about to lose them? The tragedy could almost be from the Greek or Roman theatre: we had our magic bullet, and we simply fired it into the air."

Dr Lasseter, World Health Organization

"HEY? YOU OKAY?"

Nick blinked. Chloe was standing at the table in front of him, indicating a bowl of porridge. A pity that he wasn't hungry.

Opposite him, Chloe's husband Jack was already eating. The chatter of the radio filled the silence. Nick didn't recognise the music. In a break between songs, a voice told them it would be another sunny day. Temperatures in the low twenties. Which was okay, he guessed, heading into winter.

"So, Nick. Will this be another short visit?"

Nick looked up at Jack. It was nearly the first thing he'd said to him, other than a brief greeting as he'd bustled in with his luggage in the early hours. "I don't know," he said.

Jack seemed to mull this over as he chewed his food. It was reasonably clear what he was thinking: how long would he be taking up space in their house? God forbid – would he be hanging around until his father died? "I've got some business with the Bureau," Nick said, trying to put his mind at rest. "It shouldn't take more than a few days."

"Really?" Jack flicked his eyes towards Chloe. "You weren't here too long ago… I just figured this was more of a personal call. Given, you know? How is he anyway?"

Chloe let her fork drop. "Jack…"

"Dying," Nick said. He took a gulp of water, and then returned his attention to his breakfast. Jack, however, wasn't ready to let it drop.

"I've heard some people talking about how this thing blew up quite recently," he said. "I told them they were talking crap but…"

"Jack—"

"People have a right to know though, don't they?"

Nick stopped eating. "There's nothing like this illness in New Pompeii," he said, bluntly. "Aside from the odd cough and cold, they're fine. And they're behind bio-containment designed to protect them, not you."

"But to have people frozen like that…"

"Jack," Chloe whispered. "Please. His father is dying."

"I'm just repeating what people are saying, that's all."

Nick didn't respond. Chloe took the opportunity to change the subject. "You haven't appeared on *Who's Where*," she said.

A look of confusion spread across her husband's face.

"A woman recognised him at the airport," Chloe explained.

"And would that have been a problem?"

"I'm hoping for a quiet visit."

"Well no one uses that platform anymore, anyway. Just like no one wears facemasks."

Nick glanced upwards. He'd slipped his mask off again, but hadn't removed it completely. It hung round his neck so he didn't forget it when they headed into town.

"You should get yourself some airway filters. They just slide into your throat, and take away most of the risk."

"I already have," Nick replied, pinching at his Adam's apple to make the point. "The mask has other benefits."

Jack swallowed the last of his food and stood up from the table. He wiped his hands on the back of his trousers. "Yeah, well, it's not much of a disguise. Just makes you stand out." He paused, his focus suddenly on Chloe. "I'll leave you two to it."

Nick watched Jack go, then said, "He doesn't seem too happy."

"I'm sorry. He shouldn't have spoken to you like that."

"Don't worry about it," Nick replied. "And I meant what I said: this should only take a few days."

"It's not that," Chloe replied. "I don't think he's ever got used to you coming here. Me being your personal contact and all."

Nick felt a spike of irritation. Chloe's home was located inside a gated cluster of apartment blocks, and included a private guard and complimentary cleaning service. And her job meant she could still get access to many commodities that had once been taken for granted. Unlike many others in this city, her cupboards were full of food, not just the basic state ration. And his friendship meant she also got a share of the imports from New Pompeii. "You've not done too badly babysitting me," he said.

"I know." She paused before continuing. "I've set up the meeting with Fabio. I think you took our esteemed Bureau Chief by surprise. He didn't seem to think you'd be back so soon."

"Great. Thanks."

"He wants to meet you at the archaeological museum."

"Not at the Bureau? Did he say why?"

Chloe shook her head. "Babysitter, remember? The Bureau gives me messages, not reasons." She hesitated, then smiled. "You could, though," she said, letting her voice drop. "If you're not here to visit your father, then why are you here, Mr Pax Romana?"

"We get little snippets of information from the convoys," he said. "We know the popularity of New Pompeii is waning."

"It's complicated," Chloe said, before smiling. "But you can still count on the strange coalition of archaeologists and fascists to support you."

Nick paused. He didn't share his host's amusement. He'd seen plenty of the debates on the boards: the boasting from the Italian far-right. The screams for revenge from fundamental Christians. But the most worrying aspect was the emerging debate over the Pompeii Treaty, particularly the preservation of the so-called Roman bubble. The sustainment of slavery. His current travel ban across much of Western Europe was just part of the rejection of the new Roman state. "I just want to get a better feel for things," he said. "On my own, and away from the Bureau."

Chloe nodded. She seemed to accept it.

"And I may need your help."

21

New Pompeii

PULLUS SLOWED TO allow Taedia to catch up. Since leaving his house, they'd walked first a few blocks south towards the forum, and then taken a left turn in the general direction of the amphitheatre. Taedia had insisted on walking a pace or two behind him, despite him slowing several times so she'd catch up.

"You can walk alongside me, you know."

Taedia nodded, but her attention seemed fully focused on the road. She was picking her route through the detritus in the way he had done in his first few weeks here, trying hard to find the granite slabs that lay hidden under fifteen years of accumulated grime.

"You've been to Pompeii before, surely?"

She looked at him. He wished she hadn't. "This isn't Pompeii," she said.

"You haven't been to *town* before," Pullus corrected. "Have you?"

Taedia shook her head. "I don't think I've ever left the villa, no."

Great.

Pullus scanned the street. They were in election season and, from the looks of it, the sign-writers had been busy. Most of the previous night had probably been spent finding every scrap of space available to scrawl their messages. Important families and professions were clearly lining up behind different candidates, but this time there seemed to be a lot of people vying for the two available posts of aedile. So, unlike in previous years, this wasn't going to be a done deal.

"I think it's this way," Pullus said, heading off again. He started slowly, but again found Taedia dropping behind. Fortunately, their destination wasn't too far away. Just another two blocks and down a side street, if his memory was correct.

New Pompeii was a shifting animal. Every time he visited, he found the streets slightly different. Not only did the sign-writers continually alter the complexion of the street, the owners of the little *tabernae* seemed to keep chopping and changing as they tried to find the best position for their trade. So what was a workshop quickly became a wine seller, and where you could buy pottery suddenly became the best place to get a haircut. Only buildings in which there'd been a substantial cash investment stayed the same, pegs on which the rest of the town seemed to hang.

The street outside the bakery was already busy. Although one of a handful in this part of town, it had a cluster of Pompeians waiting outside. The granary behind was simply laid out, with brick ovens to one side, and three large grinding stones dominating the centre of the space. Each stone was being turned by a couple of mules. The animals walked in a slow circle, their heads bowed, with a wooden pole tied over their backs that jutted through the stones.

Pullus made his way over to one of the private tables at the back. Taedia followed, but remained standing. His shadow looked uneasy, as if he'd taken her to a brothel, rather than somewhere to eat. "What's the matter?"

"I didn't say anything."

"Not with your mouth, no."

"I'm sorry."

"Don't apologise; just tell me what you're thinking."

Taedia shifted on the spot. "I didn't think you'd be eating here," she said. "A man like you, in a place like this."

Pullus paused before replying. True enough, it must have seemed unusual. None of the others here would own property, let alone a *triclinium* where they could have eaten in private. But he'd always enjoyed listening to the back and forth between the freedmen and the slaves. "The place suits me," he said.

Taedia didn't respond. Her attention seemed to have been caught by something behind him. Pullus twisted on his seat. On the back wall of the bakery was a rough fresco of the Pompeian amphitheatre. Dabs of colour represented the cheering crowd, as a handful of figures occupied the middle of the sand. One of the figures was different from the others, however. He was being pulled upwards, and towards a vortex circling above the arena. A second nearby figure had been depicted with a glowing aura.

"I know the owner," Pullus said, not sure why he felt an explanation was required. Embarrassment, maybe. *The man who couldn't be killed.* He turned away from the image. The other patrons of the bakery glanced at him, grinned but passed no comment. Although he was by no means a regular, they were all used to seeing him. They weren't the same as those who kept on pushing votives into his hands. Some of them had even seen him drunk.

"Calpurnia said you would be examining material brought to you by the *duumvir* and his aediles? Looking for a…"

"Datacard," Pullus said, finishing her sentence. "Calpurnia thinks Arlen's research will be stored on a piece of equipment we call a datacard." He pronounced the word carefully, and she mouthed it back at him. *Datacard.*

A woman arrived to take his order. "Just some bread and oil," Pullus said. "No cheese. And I'd like to see your master, if he's around."

The woman nodded and disappeared. Whilst he waited, he tilted his head up towards Taedia. Calpurnia probably hadn't told her everything about their situation. An informant didn't need to know the bigger picture. They only needed to feel out a single piece of the jigsaw and return that information.

Before he could say any more to her, heavy footsteps came from upstairs and Celer appeared at their table, a fat man in an oil-soaked tunic. Under other circumstances, Pullus might have smiled. Made some remark about how it had been too long since his last visit. But Celer looked pale and worried.

"Pullus, thank Aesculapius you're here!"

Pullus glanced at Taedia, but knew their visit had been unannounced. He hadn't even told Galbo where they'd be heading. "I'm here on business," Pullus said. "Calpurnia's business."

Celer looked confused. "But I sent riders. To your villa?"

Pullus stood. "I'm staying at my townhouse for a few days," he said. "But as I'm already here, why don't you tell me what's wrong?"

22

THE BAKERY HAD a single room above containing five beds, where the family slept. The smell of fresh bread failed to penetrate from below. Instead, the dominant odour was of stale sweat. It acted as a reminder that there was only so much cash that could be accumulated from grinding wheat. Although Celer was a free man, he wasn't wealthy.

"She's in that bed."

Pullus squinted into the gloom. If Celer's daughter hadn't been pointed out to him, he wouldn't have noticed her. But then the covers of the bed moved, and he caught the faint sounds of breathing.

"How long has she been like this?"

"A few days. Worse than before."

The girl had pulled her covers high so all he could see was a mop of thick hair. The bedding looked damp. The smell grew much stronger as Pullus approached.

"Is she awake? Can she talk?"

Celer shook his head. Pullus knew it was too late. She would either recover, or she would die. Just like the others.

"She needs some of your pills," Celer said.

"She won't be able to swallow them," Pullus answered, maybe a little too bluntly. "She'll choke."

He knelt by the girl's bed. He tried not to breathe, and lifted the cover only ever so slightly. Her eyes were open, and red. Skin pale and wet. Her body was trembling uncontrollably, and she was only partially conscious. She probably couldn't even see him. He dropped the cover and backed away.

"When was the last time she drank any water?"

Celer muttered something, then said, "Drowning is no better than choking."

Taedia came to stand beside Pullus. "This isn't why you're here," she said, her voice very low. Her eyes flicked across the room towards the far wall. He knew what she'd seen.

The room was decorated with objects stolen from NovusPart. Bits and pieces prised away from the few houses in town that had been reserved for their staff. In the far corner stood the door of a jeep. One wall was graced by a flat-screen TV. And then there were the dozens of bits of bric-a-brac: pens, watches, shoes and belt buckles. But he couldn't see what he'd come for. Celer owned a tablet computer, and it would need to be taken from him before Naso found out that he owned it.

"She needs some of your pills," the baker said again.

Pullus shook his head. Where was the damn tablet? "I'm sorry," he said. "It's too late."

"You gave them to the aedile's boy. Remember?"

Pullus winced. When he'd received his first batch of

antibiotics they'd come with a simple list of instructions describing the illnesses for which they could and couldn't be used. And although he'd mainly stuck to those instructions, sometimes he hadn't. News had quickly got around: Pullus could cure the disease the Romans called the shivers. The truth was that the *aedile*'s boy had simply been lucky.

"Please, Pullus. We can grind them up and get her to swallow."

Pullus looked back at the bed. The girl would likely die, and he was almost out of antibiotics. Why should he waste them? Especially when he knew no more were coming? "Calpurnia has instructed me to gather together all the old NovusPart equipment," he said.

"You can have anything you fucking want, Pullus."

Pullus nodded, and moved towards the stairs. He felt dizzy. He needed to get away from the girl and her father, between himself and a promise the gods might not allow him to keep. "Galbo will bring some medicine later this morning," he said. "Have everything boxed up. Including the tablet."

Celer made a choked sound, as if the mention of his most treasured item was almost too high a price to pay. Pullus hesitated at the top of the stairs.

"You still have it, don't you? The tablet?"

Celer didn't answer. He showed it off only occasionally. It had been found in the House of Astridge, its screen long since cracked, maybe dropped by a careless NovusPart employee. During his visits to eat here, Pullus had paid it no attention other than to explain how it was meant to work to Celer. He hadn't expected the baker to ever give it away. In truth, he'd arrived here today expecting to have to argue with the baker – hoping that he'd be able to persuade Celer to give up the tablet voluntarily rather than have Naso bludgeon it from him.

"You sold it? Really?"

"I didn't sell it, Pullus. The aedile – Popidius – took the damn thing when my daughter became sick."

"I don't…?"

"You weren't here, Pullus. I thought he might have some of your pills left over." The baker laughed bitterly. "You'll be taking his collection as well, I hope?"

Pullus hesitated. "I didn't know he was in that market."

"Over the last few months, he must have built up the single biggest collection in Pompeii."

After walking a few streets back towards the forum, Pullus stopped at another food joint and bought two more pieces of bread, this time with raisins. He chewed slowly, and waited whilst Taedia made up her mind as to whether she was going to accept her breakfast.

"That girl isn't going to live, is she?"

Pullus shrugged, but instantly regretted giving the impression he didn't care. "Maybe," he said. "She has a chance, but it doesn't look good."

"And yet you're still going to give her some of your pills?"

"Yes."

"I heard you were running short of them."

"That's right."

"And I also heard they only work on illness that creates pus?"

"We're going to run out of them anyway," Pullus said, thinking of the problems now facing the outside world. "And at least we haven't become too used to having them."

Taedia nodded. He offered her the bread again. Hesitantly, she took it from him. "So now we go to the aedile? Popidius?"

Pullus considered for a moment. A large part of him wanted to go back to his townhouse. To wait, whilst Naso and the aediles did the hard work of collecting together everything they could that even smelled of NovusPart. But something about what Celer had said about Popidius had puzzled him. Why had he been collecting NovusPart memorabilia before Harris had arrived in town? Before Calpurnia had issued her instructions? "No. We're going to see the *duumvir*."

Taedia looked confused. "I don't understand."

"Naso doesn't like me talking directly to the aediles. He prefers me to go through him."

"But we're working for Calpurnia…"

"We?"

Taedia seemed to shrink back into herself. "You. I meant to say 'you'."

Pullus took a final bite of his breakfast, licking the crumbs off his fingers. "I think you were right the first time, actually."

Taedia looked away down the *via*. "Then we head this way, yes?"

"No," Pullus replied. "We'll skirt around the other side of the Forum Baths, and head to the Marine Gate, via the Temple of Apollo."

"But this way is quicker?"

"The long way round is fine."

Pullus didn't explain further. He'd no intention of walking directly past the Temple of Fortuna Augusta. He could already see its front steps were busy, and there was some sort of ceremony going on inside. Although he didn't mind eating underneath a fresco of *the man who can't be killed* amongst friends, he had no wish to amble past a religious ceremony in which his statue was front and centre.

His shadow kept pace behind him. They passed under the Arch of Germanicus, and he only caught the tail end of someone shouting his name as they reached the aedile's offices. He ignored them; he didn't need any more votives. He turned to Taedia. "There's something you need to understand," he said. "We're dancing to a tune that's already been played."

Taedia was silent, and Pullus suddenly wondered how much she knew about the NovusPart device. Maybe this would be a good time for her to find out. Perhaps the informer could work in two directions.

"Growing up in Calpurnia's service, you must have got to know a lot about the NovusPart device? You must have heard Calpurnia discuss things with her Greek?"

"Yes."

"Then you must know we can't change what happens from

here on in. After Calpurnia's father – Barbatus – defeated NovusPart, I spent a long time thinking about what happened. About my role in events. And I came to one conclusion."

"And what was that?"

"No matter what I did, things would have still worked out the same," Pullus said. "The two sides of the square would have still been joined. Except for one big difference. I would have been crucified along with all the others."

"But you can't be killed…?"

"I couldn't be killed in the arena, no. But only because I was needed to make one particular pathway to the future work. Others existed. They just weren't taken."

Before they reached Naso, he needed to make his shadow understand. That they didn't have to step so much quickly, as carefully. "Maybe there is no tune," he said. "Maybe we're making decisions and doing things that have no bearing on the future. Calpurnia's Greek may suddenly wake up with the answer buzzing in his skull. And what interest would the gods have in us then, eh? Would they rescue me from the amphitheatre again?"

23

Naples

BENEATH HIS FACEMASK, Nick grinned. There was something thrilling about crossing a road in Naples. He waited for the final vehicle in the platoon to pass, then hurried to the relative safety of the opposite pavement. *So much for being the man who can't be killed*, he thought. Perhaps in New Pompeii he believed it. But certainly not here in Italy.

Pausing, Nick lifted his mask a couple of centimetres to get a breath of fresh air. Chloe had dropped him a few blocks south so that he could make his way through the old part of town. On either side of him, small shops spilled out into the narrow confines of the street. Hardly any sold food and drink now; most were just stocked with junk related to both "new" and "old" Pompeii.

The Bureau of Roman Affairs wasn't far from where he was standing. Of course, there'd been other potential hosts for their offices. As the former seat of NovusPart, the British had initially put forward Cambridge, until they'd got cold feet about the associations with Roman slavery. The Turks had then made a bid for Istanbul and, for no clear reason, the French had suggested Paris. But of the remaining candidates nowhere – not even Rome – could match Naples, because no city was closer to Pompeii. The real Pompeii.

It didn't take too long before the narrow, winding streets of the old town gave way to the pastel pink facade of the Naples Archaeological Museum. As ever, a couple of long, sleek coaches were parked at the bottom of its steps. Nick weaved through the clusters of rich tourists and headed towards the ticket booths. On the other side of the turnstiles, his contact at the Bureau gave him a nod of greeting and instructed the guards to let him through. "*Ciao.*"

"*Buongiorno.*"

Fabio was in his mid-forties and putting on weight proportional to that age. But although he spent most of his time cooped up in an office, he did at least know something about the ancient world, which meant he was able to understand the details Nick brought him. Unlike many of his counterparts.

Fabio looked puzzled. "I thought last time we gave you airway filters?"

Nick pulled the facemask down. "You did."

"Good. And… I'm sorry to hear about your father. He's now in the last stage?"

Nick deliberately didn't answer, and instead indicated towards the crowd milling in the foyer. "Busy day?"

"No different from normal," Fabio said, turning into the great hall. Nick followed him. He thought he knew where they'd be heading. With all the relics from Pompeii and Herculaneum filling the upper floors, the warren of displays and side rooms on the ground floor were often left a little quieter, which meant they could talk without being interrupted. Fabio, however, made for the main marble staircase. "Good trip?"

Nick nodded. "Got in last night."

"Any groupies?"

Nick shook his head. "Just one. I seem to have lost my allure. But I don't miss the attention."

"Then good."

Nick initially followed his Bureau contact, but then pulled Fabio to a halt as he reached one of the two massive marble lions guarding the foot of the staircase. "I saw a couple of children die of whooping cough when I got home," Nick said. "Two minor miracles gone because you've stopped sending us penicillin."

Fabio's jaw flexed. "The Bureau is having difficulty securing the necessary supplies."

"We're talking about a common medicine."

"Common since about 1945."

"What's that supposed to mean?"

"The Roman Empire died a long time before antibiotics were invented," Fabio replied. "More and more people are questioning why you should benefit from the advances of the modern world, when your society remains so primitive."

Nick had heard this line of argument before. "The terms have been agreed for years."

"You're not aware of all the facts."

"Which are?"

"It's better that you see for yourself. It's why I asked to meet you here."

Above them, the marble steps led up to the key exhibits from Pompeii and Herculaneum. They walked through the galleries, then stopped ahead of a wrought iron gate at the mouth of the *Gabinetto Segreto*.

Nick peered in at the first exhibit – a giant stone phallus. His first visit to this part of the museum was etched well into his memory: he'd been caught gawping by a female student he'd wanted to ask out. Needless to say, he hadn't got a date.

Nick looked towards Fabio. The Italian didn't appear to be in a hurry. Outside, the sirens of emergency vehicles provided their usual background soundtrack. "Well?"

"There's too many people," Fabio said, switching to Latin, although not the Latin of New Pompeii. It took Nick a while to tune back into the more stilted version used by academics and priests. It was clear the Bureau Chief didn't want anyone to overhear and understand. "I've arranged a private viewing."

"I've been here before."

"We've got some new exhibits. Some things we needed to keep away from academics. Security will soon have cleared the area."

Indeed, a few seconds later a couple of security guards

started to usher the other visitors from the *Gabinetto*. There were a few grumbles, but for any regular visitors what was now happening fitted fairly innocuously with the random way in which the museum opened and closed its galleries.

Fabio turned to him. "The terms of the treaty are clear, yes?"

Nick nodded.

"And you've always assured me that your friends in New Pompeii haven't been using the NovusPart device. Just as per those same terms?"

"That's right," Nick replied. "There have only been a few experiments."

"Two or three, you said."

"Just enough to test the tech."

"Certain matters have come to light that have made us rethink things."

"Such as?"

With the *Gabinetto Segreto* empty, Fabio ushered him forwards. The Bureau Chief swept aside a curtain beside one of the cabinets, and unlocked a door hidden behind it. It led out into a brightly lit laboratory.

"A secret room?" Nick asked. "Inside the *Gabinetto Segreto*?"

"What can I say," Fabio replied, leading the way inside. "The Italians have a distinct sort of humour."

Inside the lab, a collection of Roman frescos were laid out on a workbench. A magnifying glass mounted on an articulated arm was swung over the set. Fabio indicated he should take a look.

The frescos were little neat squares of plaster, all depicting sexual acts. The colours remained vivid, not having been dulled by years spent in display cases, nor damaged by roughshod excavation.

Nick squinted at the label. "From Pompeii?"

"Yes. From the new digs."

Nick wrinkled his nose. "This is what you wanted me to see?"

"Yes."

"Somehow, I figured you'd have something more interesting than porn."

"Forget the label. Look at the damn fresco."

Nick took hold of the magnifying glass, and pulled it over the central fresco. The eyeglass picked up the finest of surface details – and brought into view something that perhaps hadn't been seen by those cutting it from the walls of the dig site.

Underneath the bed on which two young lovers were copulating, a few words had been scratched, but only one was still legible. "Shit," Nick whispered.

NovusPart.

24

Ruins of Ancient Pompeii

"With the passing of so many years and so many men, unfortunately we can now learn more in the sewers of Herculaneum than we can from speaking with Mr Houghton's faux Romans, a growing number of whom were born long after the eruption of Vesuvius."

Professor Hayden,
Lead Archaeologist, Herculaneum
World Archaeology News Message Board

NICK PEERED THROUGH the small opening and let his eyes adjust to the gloom inside. He could just about make out the pool – the reservoir – within the simple brick structure. Once fed by the Serino Aqueduct, all that remained of Pompeii's "header tank" was a nondescript rectangular block situated on the northern edge of the town. The brick and stone exterior hid what had been an ingenious system, delivering through a few slender pipes enough water to serve all the baths, fountains, and private houses lucky enough to have their own supply.

"You can go inside, you know."

Nick turned to Fabio. "I'm fine," he said. After taking a last look into the "water castle", he slipped back along its eastern flank and onto an area of granite block pavement fronting the Vesuvius Gate. From the direction of the forum, a loud, heavy bell started to sound.

Fabio noticed his discomfort. "Time for the ceremonies," the Italian said, chuckling. "Do you want to see?"

"No," replied Nick. His response was automatic. The ruins of Pompeii were attracting a cult following of those now wanting to worship the old gods. From what he'd seen, however, it didn't look like they had any real understanding of what the old Roman religion was like. They'd certainly not read his articles on the subject. They seemed to view the Roman gods as some sort of superheroes, rather than representations of the real world.

"We have time. It can be quite fun."

Nick shook his head. Chloe had already shown him some video footage. They'd be lining up on the steps of the Temple of Jupiter, Juno and Minerva, murmuring about gods none of them knew. "Has there been any more trouble?" he asked.

"Not since we locked down the site."

Nick nodded. The number of visitors was now closely monitored, and they could only visit the forum. The rest of the site was effectively mothballed. This was due to the rise of theft and vandalism; people loved the site so much they wanted to take part of it home with them or they hated it enough to attack it with hammers.

"Don't worry," said Fabio. "I doubt anyone noticed you arrive."

Nick shrugged. It hadn't occurred to him that he might have been spotted. The vehicle Fabio had driven was discreet, and they'd slipped through the security cordon without needing to show a pass.

"It looks like they're making good progress," continued the Italian.

Beyond the edge of the Via Stabiana, the new diggings were well underway. This was the street that had always marked the boundary between the excavated part of the town and the buried portion. But the bank that had once hugged tight against the Via Stabiana was now being slowly peeled back and, about a hundred yards away, a few dozen archaeologists laboured at its surface, clearing away the stone, ash and lapilli to uncover new streets and buildings. The workings were covered with a series of white tents and yellow tape, used to cordon off areas from those without authorised access. All in all, it looked more like an exercise in police forensics than archaeology.

"I've arranged for the dig director to show us where they found the fresco," Fabio said. He paused and nodded in the direction of the dig. "Have you joined the sweepstake? I got a decent tip about them finding a school under there."

Nick remained unconvinced by the case made to unearth

more of the town. When he'd studied it, the authorities hadn't seemed to care about Pompeii unless a building collapsed or a critical piece appeared in the media. Yet Pompeii was now the centre of the world's interest, and nearby Naples was again awash with money.

"Well," continued Fabio. "A school? What do you think?"

Nick finally smiled. The archaeologists working here didn't seem to have had to work very hard to pull money from Fabio's pocket. "There's no school building in New Pompeii."

Over at the dig site, a couple of archaeologists were moving hurriedly back and forth between two of their tents. A third was heading towards Nick and Fabio. Nick squinted. He couldn't quite bring them into focus.

"You okay?" Fabio asked.

"Yeah," Nick said, struggling with the light. The figure heading their way was a young woman. "Headache. I only ever seem to get them here."

"When was the last time you had an eye test?" The Italian had lost his humour, and considered him seriously. "You've been having trouble on your last few visits," he continued.

"You're worried about my eyes now?"

"I'm paid to notice these things. We're your friends here, remember?"

"I'm fine," Nick replied. He rubbed his eyelids with his thumb and forefinger, trying to massage the pain from his head.

"Blurring?"

"Yes."

"Myopia, probably. You should get it checked while

you're here. Get them zapped, if you don't want your friends to see you with spectacles. Non-surgical, you know. No risk of infection."

Nick shrugged. He could see just fine. In front of him, the archaeologist from the dig slid down off the bank. It didn't take long to place her. She was wearing the same style of clothes as when he'd met her at the airport. Except the strappy top was a different shade of green, and the khaki trousers had been replaced by shorts.

"Hi again," he said.

"Hi!" The woman blushed. "I don't think I introduced myself properly when we last met. I'm Amel." She stuck out a hand, which Nick shook. Now he thought about it her accent sounded Dutch, even if her name wasn't. "We've found something we thought you might like to see?"

Beside him, Fabio bristled. "Another fresco?"

The woman shook her head, confused. "No. A void. We've found a cavity."

The news seemed to disappoint Fabio, but it gave Nick a distinct chill. A void. The empty space left by a body that had rotted away long ago. He felt his throat constrict. "Are you going to use plaster?" he asked. "Or resin?"

"Why don't you come and find out?"

Walking onto the dig site turned out to be only marginally more comfortable than taking a mid-afternoon stroll through the forum. Most of the archaeologists had been drawn to Pompeii for the same reason he'd first studied the town. And most would have given their right arm to travel to New Pompeii. They stared at him with a mixture of jealousy and outright resentment. Nick had discovered that by shunning the limelight, most people had forgotten his face, which meant in Naples, with the facemask, he was pretty much anonymous. But not in Pompeii.

Nick tried to avoid catching anyone's eye. Ahead of him, Amel stopped and turned. "Doesn't the Bureau want to see?" she asked.

Nick glanced behind him. Fabio was still prowling by the water castle, his mobile having erupted with an Abba tune just a few steps short of the edge of the *via*.

"I'm sure he'll follow soon enough," Nick replied, turning back to Amel. She was wearing some sort of phallic necklace, similar to the charms and apotropaic symbols that hung outside *tabernae* back in New Pompeii. "I hadn't realised you were an archaeologist."

Amel gave a slight shrug. "Would it have helped if I'd been wearing a leather fedora?"

Nick wasn't quite sure whether she was joking. "Sorry," he said. "I guess when we first met I wasn't ready to be recognised."

"Don't worry about it. So what brings you to Pompeii this time?"

"I like to remind myself."

"Of the reality, rather than the fantasy?"

Nick gave a soft chuckle. "Something like that."

"The others told me you normally visit in the early hours, or just before sundown?"

"Yeah."

"But not today, huh?"

Nick shook his head, eyes scanning the dig site. Sure enough, they'd already uncovered the walls of a few buildings. The functions of some were pretty clear: two boasted mottled green serving counters with deep amphora set into them. Another had been unearthed complete with grinding stones and ovens – all ready to process the next batch of wheat, if it ever arrived.

Unlike the rest of the town, none of it reflected what had been recreated by NovusPart. Where here there were bars, taverns and bakeries, in New Pompeii there were residential houses, workshops and fulleries. Whilst the outline of the rest of New and Old Pompeii was almost a perfect overlap, this was the area where NovusPart had been forced to fill in the gaps, and had got things wrong.

"We've been working here for some time," continued Amel. She stopped to wave at a small girl near one of the tents. The two shared the same dark hair and some of the same facial features. "Haven't you been in the least bit curious about what we found?"

Nick shook his head. He hadn't given it much thought. Although he had known new digs were happening, he hadn't wanted to get involved. He had access to everything he needed back home.

The girl by the tent was staring at them. He squinted. She was maybe about ten or eleven. "You're training them young?" he asked.

Amel beckoned the girl over, but she didn't move.

"Sabine," she said. "My niece. A few days of enlightenment away from school."

"Shy?"

"Bored." Amel started walking again. "Come on. I think they've already started."

Sure enough, a few other members of the dig had assembled in an area that hadn't been fully excavated. A machine was slowly delivering plaster via a long, clear pipe into a hole in the ground. Another hole was letting air escape. The machine didn't sound too healthy. The pump was grating against something, the racket drowning out what the rest of the team were saying as more and more plaster was pumped into the void.

Giuseppe Fiorelli had first developed this technique back in the late 1800s. In concept, it was simple. The plaster would fill the cavity just like any other mould. After it hardened, it would show the shape of a person, right down to the clothes they'd been wearing, and the expression on their face at the point they'd been suffocated. Except no one had done it like this in a long time, and it had the potential to go very wrong.

"You've done the laser scan first, I take it?" Nick asked.

Amel nodded. A little mouse-sized robot would have already worked its way through the space. Somewhere on the site, or possibly back in Naples, a 3D image of the void had already been printed in case things went wrong. Now they were free to use the plaster and not worry about making a total mess of it.

"We're using plaster, not resin," said Amel. "It should give a more traditional effect."

Nick watched the process with a sick feeling brewing in his stomach. For a brief period, resin had overtaken plaster as being the preferred material to preserve the finds. But although it gave better access to the bones, there was something about plaster that resin couldn't quite capture. Perhaps because plaster made the bodies look like sculptures. Or ghosts.

Nick watched the last of the plaster be injected, and then suddenly turned away. He walked back towards the Vesuvius Gate, knowing that when he reached Fabio, there was a good chance he might vomit.

"Do you want us to call you back when he's ready?" Amel called after him.

No, he thought. *No I don't*. Because whoever it had been, they'd been one of the unlucky few. Someone who'd been caught in a pocket of ash and pumice just thick enough to stop them being transported to safety by NovusPart. A few hundred lost souls, out of a population of fifteen thousand. The margin of error McMahon and Whelan had found satisfactory.

Nick doubled over and gave a dry heave. He wondered if he knew the victim's friends or family. Whether – if he took a picture of the plaster cast – he could perhaps find out who they were and finally tell their loved ones what had happened to them.

"I'm sorry," said Amel, running up to him. "I should have realised."

"It's fine," Nick said, trying to swallow. "I didn't expect to react like that."

"Do they ever talk to you about them?"

"All the time," said Nick, gasping for air. "They all know someone who didn't make it." He heaved again. He'd tell Fabio they'd come back another day to see where the fresco had been found. He couldn't stand the thought.

"Strange, then," Amel said quietly, almost to herself.

"Strange, what?"

"That they didn't have another go at rescuing them."

25

New Pompeii

Pullus had expected a long queue outside the *duumvir's* door, but he was wrong. It was more like a mob. Where there should have been an orderly line, instead there was a jostling crowd. He could just about see a single porter standing at the door, a baton held casually over his shoulder. Ready to be brought down, if needed.

"Pullus…?" Taedia sounded scared.

"Don't worry," he said, moving forward. "I've seen this before."

In fact, he'd seen it too often. But whilst those at the back of the mob might be trying to push forward, those at the front were braced and pushing back on their heels. No one wanted to actually breach the *duumvir's* threshold and risk being beaten back by his porter. Everyone, though, wanted to get a sense of what was going on in the atrium beyond.

"We should come back at another time," Taedia said.

Pullus ignored her. They were a few feet away from the

edge of the scrum, close enough to hear the crowd's mockery mixed in with its anger. Taking Taedia's hand, he pulled her towards the crowd.

"There's no way through," she said.

There was. The crowd hushed at Pullus's approach and parted before him. Pullus yanked Taedia forward, past the porter and into the *duumvir*'s atrium.

"What's going on?"

Taedia's question was whispered, but it still carried further than she likely intended. A few of the people in the atrium turned, eyebrows raised, but none spoke. There were about twenty or so waiting in front of the *impluvium*, many members of the town *Ordo*. Most had their attention on the *tablinum*, the bronze-embossed wooden shutters of which were open. Just above the distant murmur of the crowd outside, Pullus could hear two people engaged in a very one-sided conversation.

"So now we come to your children."

The voice was all nose and throat. Naso. The reply, however, was barely audible, and it was hard to tell if it was a man or a woman. Pullus edged forward to get a better look. Sure enough, the *duumvir* was standing with his bodyguards facing a man who looked pale and weak. Scaeva? Had his actions finally caught up with him?

Pullus glanced sideways. Another man was looking in his direction, and he gave a shallow nod. Popidius. The aedile who'd taken the tablet from the bakery. He was young, and by all accounts arrogant. Pullus returned the gesture.

"You have two daughters, and a son?"

"Yes," Scaeva replied.

Pullus felt his stomach tighten. The man was beaten. There was no fight in his voice, even when speaking about his own children. There'd been rumours circulating that a member of the *Ordo* couldn't quite match his spending to his income. If Barbatus had still been around, he would have intervened. But the old *duumvir* was gone, and the economics in New Pompeii were no longer centred on Rome but the prices paid by boutiques in Paris, Milan and Beijing.

"I'll keep the girls," said Naso. "Your son will go to the markets. He'll pay off your debts by ploughing our fields."

Just the smallest ripple of shock moved through the atrium. The children kept at Naso's house would be fine in the short term. But the boy was effectively being sent to his death and everyone knew it. Scaeva said nothing.

Naso glanced behind him. "What's the tally?"

A slave standing at the *duumvir*'s shoulder totted something up on a wax tablet. "With the remaining farmland," he said, "townhouse, slaves and his three children, we're nearly there."

"I have nothing left," Scaeva said. "You've taken everything."

At last, thought Pullus, *a bit of fight*. Too late, though. Everyone knew what was coming: Scaeva would be offered his sword so he could meet a more dignified death than starving on the street.

Naso cleared his throat. "How much are we owed?"

"Two *denarii* should clear the remaining debt."

"Two *denarii*? Is that all? Now then, Scaeva: what do you

still own that could be worth two *denarii*?"

There was only one thing. His tunic. A few giggles broke out in the atrium, but they didn't last long. It was all too easy to imagine any of them standing in front of Naso, and they all knew it. Some would have already taken loans. Others would be praying for a good harvest to allow them to make the repayments.

Scaeva didn't move, and for a second Pullus thought he might be waiting to be stripped. But then he looked up at Naso, with some strength left in his voice. "Swear you'll protect my girls."

"You have my word no harm will come to them. And you don't need to spend the rest of your life on the street, Scaeva. I have made provision for you."

"Where?"

"The forum."

The jeers from the crowd outside seemed to grow louder even if they couldn't have heard what had just been said. The forum was close, but Scaeva would still need to walk naked through the town. By the time he reached it, he'd probably welcome the chance to thrust a sword into his own stomach. Everyone in town would get the message: no one was above paying off their debts. Even Scaeva of the town *Ordo*, former aedile of Pompeii.

Scaeva was stripped and led away, his fellow members of the *Ordo* following to watch the show. Naso spotted Pullus and he raised a hand. "Pullus!"

Naso walked swiftly towards him. A few members of the

Ordo lingered to try and catch a little of the conversation, but the *duumvir* waited for the atrium to clear before he spoke again. "Who's the girl?"

"A gift from Calpurnia."

"Huh." Naso's eyes narrowed. Around them, slaves had begun to tidy the atrium. But they couldn't hide the fact that the *duumvir* had been busy. With the people gone, the accumulation of NovusPart material was more obvious. Stacks of clutter had been positioned around the atrium, all of it presumably the result of the dragnet ordered by Calpurnia.

None of it looked particularly interesting though: more bric-a-brac than actual artefact, just like the scraps in which Celer had taken so much pride. But in amongst it, there were also bits of Roman art, pottery, and paintings. Some of it looked genuinely old, even if most had been knocked together by the *duumvir*'s growing army of artists. It looked like Naso was using Calpurnia's instructions to line his own pocket, and to use it as an excuse to help himself to some of the town's better art.

"Another debt repaid, then?"

"You can bottle it, Pullus. I know you don't approve."

"Seems like a waste. We're few in number as it is."

Naso issued a snide laugh. "He'd have died within a couple of years anyway."

"I was talking about the children."

The *duumvir* didn't respond.

"They're good Romans," Pullus continued.

"The eldest is a spoiled brat. The other two can serve

me here and, if they don't like it, they can always go to the markets. You can be assured I could get a better price for the pair of them than got entered into my ledger."

"A pity then that the price we get for our wine is so low."

Again, Naso didn't say anything. But the smile on his face remained wide. The price paid for Roman wine in the outside world was extraordinarily high, but that didn't mean all that money reached the farms that grew the grapes. Not when the man controlling their loans also managed their exports. "Everyone gets what they're owed."

Pullus thought fondly about the peace he could be enjoying at his villa. "Your business with Scaeva isn't why I'm here," he said. "So you can take my advice, or leave it, as you please."

"Good. I'll leave it."

"I've been to see a friend…"

"Yes, yes. Celer."

"You're having me followed?"

"No, but whenever you pick your nose, some whelp thinks I need to know and hurries here seeking a reward."

"Huh. Well, I understand Popidius is also a collector of NovusPart material."

"As my aedile, he's helping with the search, yes."

"No. I'm talking about a couple of weeks ago. Before this all started."

Naso looked surprised. "Really?"

"According to my source, yes."

"And why would he be doing that?"

"I was going to go ask him." Pullus nodded in the direction of one of the cubicles facing out onto the atrium. It was jammed full of artefacts, presumably taken from the town. A particularly fine vase stared back at him. "Oscan?"

Naso stepped across to block his view. "Never mind that," he said, irritated. "And leave Popidius to me."

26

Ancient Pompeii, AD *62*

ACHILLIA WOKE, AND swung her legs over the edge of the bed. After several days sleeping in a wagon, a night spent on a mattress – even a thin one – had allowed her to drift off into a deep sleep. They'd arrived in Pompeii the previous night. Late, and clearly unexpected. With no messenger sent ahead of them, the slaves stationed at the townhouse during the off-season had all been caught off-guard, playing dice. Fortunately, it hadn't taken long for them to get some food ready and beds prepared.

Achillia glanced at Trigemina, who was still fast asleep. Her more comfortable bed would likely keep her in that state for some time. Achillia would have a bit of time to get used to her new surroundings. Moving to the door, she opened it just enough to slip out and onto a narrow balcony that hung above the atrium.

It was raining, the drops falling through the *compluvium* and down into the pool below. Achillia headed down into the atrium. She hadn't worked in a townhouse for some time, but she could tell the steward hadn't been doing a very good job. The point of an atrium was to impress: everything from the marble table fronting the *impluvium* pool – and its little collection of marble statues – to the heavy metal straps of the money chest placed beside the *tablinum* were meant to signal wealth. And yet it all looked a little tarnished and untidy. A set of tools had been left in one corner, the remains of a meal in another. Even square-framed looms, presumably brought out so that the slaves could generate extra income for the household, hadn't been tidied away. No doubt if they'd known their mistress was coming, the slaves would have put everything back into place. But last night they'd all been taken by surprise; someone was likely to get whipped for it.

Achillia headed to the entrance, automatically checking at her hip but finding no weapon. The sword had been taken from her upon their arrival, and that perfect little knife she'd been given by Trigemina for their trip would no doubt end up being picked up by some vagrant lucky enough to find it on the floor of the Sibyl's cave.

A solitary slave on the door poked his head from his cubbyhole before she reached it. "Where you going?" he asked. He looked tired, hungover and angry. He probably hadn't slept much, and would no doubt still be expected to do a long day's work today to put things right.

"To see the street."

"House ain't open yet," the porter replied.

"Then do your job and open it."

The porter blinked, his brain likely trying to take in an instruction given to him by a woman. "Been told what you did to those men on the road," the porter said. It wasn't clear if the thought amused him. He moved to follow her instructions. "Said I should look out for you. Said you'd be dangerous."

Outside, the rain beat down heavily. Water filled the gulley between the footways, refuse floating in it. Soon it would make it difficult to cross the street to the workshops opposite.

Achillia glanced in both directions, trying to keep under the shelter of the doorway. The porter stood at her shoulder, just a fraction too close. His breath brushed her cheek. She ignored him. Having workshops opposite was good. She could speak to Trigemina about getting a new knife to replace the one she'd dropped, and possibly a better sword, one more suited to her hand. However, the house was positioned mid-block. Getting out would be hard if anyone came at them. She'd need to check the gardens to see if there was any way of scrambling over into a next-door property.

But they were a long way from Rome, and the Emperor had lots of distractions. Maybe he'd already be onto the next amusement. Maybe there'd be nobody coming.

Or perhaps they were already here.

The porter spoke. "My name—"

Achillia lifted her hand to silence him. "I'm not going to be around long enough to care."

27

TRIGEMINA FINALLY ROSE once the fourth hour had passed. Achillia watched her descend into the atrium and could just about smell the stink of relief. She probably thought she was safe. Or maybe not. She hadn't quite re-adopted the normal body language of a mistress in charge of her household. Not yet, anyway.

"My husband has let this place become a sty," Trigemina said.

Achillia didn't reply. She'd spent the morning quietly surveying the house. Unfortunately, like those of many a rich man, it had been designed as a secure box. The walls enclosing the garden were too high to get over, and so the best way in or out was via the front door. Although she'd asked the porter to keep it shut for the day, he'd taken her request as an insult, a challenge of his fitness to be in charge of the house. So the door remained open, with only one man stationed to check people as they came in and out.

"We'll need to find you a role here," Trigemina continued.

"You'll discover I'm not a very good cook."

"I'm sure we'll find you something."

They were no longer on the road, and Trigemina clearly wanted things to get back to normal and to reassert her status. Achillia would probably be given some household work. Her mistress didn't need much protection inside, which meant her skills would only be needed when Trigemina went into town.

"I've been thinking about our encounter with the Sibyl," Trigemina said. "I want you to tell me what she said to you."

"The Sibyl's words are private."

"I'm your mistress; I have a right to know your prophecy."

Achillia took a deep breath. The voice was still very much in her ears, even though the pain and nausea that had accompanied it had long since dissipated. But she wasn't going to tell her mistress – who believed in fate, and that the future was set – the truth. "The Sibyl told me I would keep you safe," Achillia said, "and that I would then gain my freedom."

Trigemina didn't seem ruffled by the statement. "It will be down to my husband when – or *if* – you're given your freedom. But I'll certainly need you for some time yet. I don't intend on spending all my remaining years hiding here."

Achillia frowned. "You're already thinking about heading back to Rome?"

"The last emperor we had like this didn't last long, did he?"

"And what makes you think he'll be replaced by anyone better?"

Trigemina looked irritated that she'd been questioned. Again.

"I need a replacement dagger," Achillia continued. "And the sword from the carriage."

"You can carry a weapon when we leave the house. Only then."

Achillia glanced towards the porter's cubbyhole. "They'll take you in here," she said. "A woman – a noble woman – being attacked in the street is messy. Bystanders tend to get involved, people looking for a reward. If they come, it will be here, where there's no one to see. No one to help."

Some of the nervousness Trigemina had buried seemed to be bubbling back to the surface, but she didn't get a chance to issue a further reprimand, distracted by the noise of heavy footsteps heading from the street and towards the atrium. Beyond them, Achillia could just about hear a horse whinny. So the dismount had been fast. Whoever was coming was in a hurry.

The rider turned out to be a thin young man. Trigemina relaxed as soon as she'd seen his face. Someone from her place in Rome, perhaps.

The messenger stopped at the cubbyhole as the porter moved to block his progress. There was a hushed discussion. Achillia's breathing slowed. She sensed the animals beneath their traps. Just like in the arena.

"Your husband is dead," the porter said, loudly. The messenger only just seemed to have registered Trigemina's presence. Panic and doubt immediately creased his face. Some regret too, and Achillia suddenly realised what was going on. Why he'd been in such a hurry. "The Emperor's men came for him."

Trigemina made an ungodly sound.

"Wants you dead too."

Achillia glanced at the messenger. The man had ridden fast. Probably trying to keep ahead of the Emperor's men. Trying to get here first.

"He wasn't offered a Roman death?"

The messenger shook his head. "No. No sword. And the rest of the household has been killed too."

Trigemina looked indignant. "And how did you survive?" she asked.

The messenger looked back at her blankly. Achillia guessed he'd probably hidden as the other slaves had been killed. Or maybe he'd just run – knowing he needed to warn those living at the seaside getaway of the impending storm.

"No one knows you're here," said the porter.

"No," replied Trigemina, too quickly. Before her brain had engaged. Or maybe she just didn't see it yet. "You could hide me."

The porter laughed. Achillia didn't. "No one knows we're here," Achillia said, including herself in her statement. She knew she was part of the problem now. The Emperor's men would be on their way, and there were a dozen or so slaves in the house, all of whom would be put to death as soon as Trigemina was found. Except that didn't have to happen, as the porter had already worked out. Slow of speech, yet quick of mind. There was a way they could all be sold back onto the slave markets, but it relied on Trigemina not being there when the Emperor's men arrived.

Hence the message.

"Did they know our route here?" asked Achillia. "Do the men coming know Trigemina was going to the Sibyl?"

The messenger nodded. "We all knew. She told her husband before she left."

"So they can't be sure we've arrived yet," Achillia replied. "Our carriage could have got stuck. You could just let us walk out of here."

The porter moved to block the doorway. "No," he said simply. The reply was blunt but not unexpected. The requirement to torture slaves as they were being questioned meant the truth would likely come out sooner or later. And then they'd all be for the crucifix. Achillia really couldn't blame him. He was just doing what she'd have done, if the situation had been reversed.

"But she can have a sword," continued the porter. "Unlike her husband."

28

It's almost funny how many things in a house can kill a man.

Achillia had worked out what she'd use almost as soon as the messenger arrived. But she left him for second; the porter was the bigger threat, although size didn't mean speed.

She made for him, and he started to laugh. She flipped a silver statue of Mercury off the marble table, caught it as it span in the air and pointed the god's outstretched arm at the porter. He smiled, but his body tensed, braced for her attack. Achillia made as if to stab him in the neck with her clumsy weapon, allowing the porter more than enough time to reach up and swat her arm aside. Then there was a knife in her hand; she stabbed him in the stomach. He collapsed to his knees, confusion on his face, blood spreading across his tunic. Achillia didn't wait. She stepped forward and took hold of the messenger, spun him round and kicked out the back of his legs. He didn't get up.

She'd already cut his throat as he fell.

Trigemina hadn't moved, frozen in shock. Achillia showed her the knife, the one she'd been keeping hidden. It had a wooden handle and dulled blade. She'd been intending to take it to the blacksmith to sharpen it up. But it had done its job.

"I got it from the kitchen," she said.

Trigemina finally seemed to come to her senses. "What do we do now?"

Achillia looked at the porter, who continued to breathe as the life drained from him. The messenger was already dead. She thought of the other slaves here at the house. But most of all she thought of her freedom, and the one person who could give it to her. If she could just keep her alive long enough.

"We make our own plans," Achillia said, "rather than waiting for the schemes of others. Your family? They're from Pompeii?"

"No."

"Where then?"

"North of Rome."

"Shit. Then we'll have to stay in town. For the time being, at least."

"There's a horse outside!"

Achillia shook her head. She knelt by the porter and covered his nose and mouth until he felt no more pain. Then she looked to Trigemina. "What do you want to do?"

"My family," she said. "It's my best hope."

"I meant about the others," Achillia replied. "The rest of your slaves. If they're captured, they'll talk. They'll have no choice."

Trigemina nodded, as if she understood, but it was clear

she didn't. Achillia got to her feet and went to secure the door to the street, bolting it from the inside. *It will need to look like a suicide pact*, she thought. Which meant the kills would need to be clean, and ideally somewhere she could easily shift the corpses.

Achillia returned to the atrium, pushing past her mistress who was still staring dumbly at her dead porter. She found the first of the remaining household slaves in the kitchen. A man and a young slave boy, both preparing fish and what looked like octopus. Their distance from the *tablinum* meant they obviously hadn't heard what had happened in the atrium.

The sound of a couple more slaves singing in the garden caused her the briefest of moments' hesitation. But she knew that if she was to survive in the long term, then no one could be left alive. She gripped the kitchen knife tighter, eyeing the much more fearsome-looking blade in the cook's hand. She didn't give him time to use it, moving behind him and slitting his throat smoothly, and then made a grab for the child as he turned to run.

Achillia woke to find Trigemina huddled into the corner of the room, her knees pulled tight to her chest. She'd clearly spent the entire night crying. They were in a small dank apartment in a neighbourhood of Pompeii that Achillia doubted Trigemina had ever visited before. Yet in a matter of hours she'd lost everything, even the signs of her nobility:

the curls in her hair had been shaken out and she was wearing a simple garment taken from a female slave. All so they could get a clear run through the town without being easily spotted.

"A woman was pleading with her dying husband," Achillia said, softly. "She told him that if he left her, she'd kill herself. 'Do me a favour,' said the husband. 'Do it now and put me out of my misery.'"

Trigemina made no sound. Achillia waited a moment and then shifted up onto her haunches. Her mistress looked beaten, just like when they'd first met in the arena. It was time to kick some more sand in her face. Wake her up and get her moving. But first they had to confirm the terms of their agreement.

"The Emperor will be expecting you to run straight to your family," she said. "So, like it or not, we're going to have to stay in Pompeii."

Trigemina lowered her head onto her knees.

"But I should be able to get you to them eventually." Achillia paused and let the offer sink in before naming her price. "In return, I'll want my freedom. And enough to live on. Something to give me a new start."

Trigemina shook her head. "He'll find me."

"You were right before, you know," continued Achillia. "Emperors like this don't last long. And the enemies of one madman… well, they tend to be feted by the next, don't they?"

"I should have taken the sword," Trigemina whispered. "Joined my husband."

"Your husband is dead. Making play with worms, not gods."

"Like my slaves? It's so easy for you, isn't it? The killing, I mean?"

"A mystic," said Achillia, letting the old joke roll around her tongue before spitting it out, "told a woman whose sick boy was dying that her son would soon recover and live a long, fruitful life. 'Come back tomorrow for your fee,' said the woman. The mystic was horrified. 'But what if he should die in the night?'"

"I don't care for your humour."

"And I don't care for your ignorance," Achillia replied. She swept her arm around the small, dirty space. The room she'd found for them teetered on the top of an apartment block that was starting to collapse, the wooded joists half rotten, the plaster on the walls sodden with damp. She breathed in deeply, to make the point that the stink of the previous occupants – and probably the ones before that – still hung around them. "It's so different for you, isn't it? In Rome, in your fine houses and fine clothes. But people die all the time, in wars, having babies, in the street. Who knows – maybe we'll both get a fever tonight and be dead tomorrow? But by the fucking gods, I am not going to go quietly. And if the choice is between me and someone else… that person will end up dead, every time."

"My mother pushed five babies and only two survived," said Trigemina, lifting her head from her knees. "So we're not so different."

"Bullshit."

Trigemina didn't say anything for a moment. She put her hands to her head and momentarily recoiled when her fingertips felt her bedraggled hair. "So we stay here for a while," she said. "We wait, and then we run. Is that it? Is that the plan?"

Achillia shook her head. "There's no plan," she said. "Just like there's no plan for us from the gods. No fate. No fucking Sibylline destiny. We survive today, and then we think about tomorrow."

"We'll need food. And more money than we were able to take from the house."

"Leave that to me. You'll need to stay here. You can't be seen." She glanced about her. "There's a piss pot in the corner. Don't shit in it."

Trigemina nodded, and finally seemed to start taking in her new surroundings. "It's lucky you found this empty."

Achillia rose to her feet, her head just about missing the low ceiling. "If anyone comes looking for a guy called Hermeros," she said, "just tell them he departed."

"And where are you going?"

"The Sibyl told me to find a guy called Manius Calpurnius Barbatus. I think it's time I introduced myself."

29

New Pompeii

Pᴜʟʟᴜꜱ ꜱᴛᴇᴘᴘᴇᴅ ᴏᴜᴛ of Naso's house and onto the street. The mob outside had long since dissipated, no doubt following Scaeva's last journey to the forum. If the former aedile had any friends left, he could at least hope they would help him to his destination. Or bring his sword to meet him.

"So we have to wait before going to see Popidius?" Taedia asked.

Pullus nodded. "Yes. I gave Naso a few hours with him first."

"Then where next?"

Pullus wasn't sure. There were a few other names he suspected might be in the business of collecting NovusPart paraphernalia. But given the number of objects being brought to the *duumvir*'s mansion, maybe it was better to leave that to Naso and just wait to sort through whatever junk was brought to him. And yet there was something nagging at Pullus. A sense there was something else out there. Something he'd missed.

"Scaeva was running for *duumvir*," Taedia said suddenly.

Pullus frowned, irritated that his line of thought had been disturbed. "Hmm?"

"*Duumvir*," Taedia repeated. "Scaeva was standing for *duumvir*."

Pullus shook his head. "No, the elections are only for the aediles."

"I saw the posters," Taedia said slowly. "Most were for the posts of aedile. But Scaeva was definitely campaigning to be *duumvir*."

Pullus grunted. He hadn't taken note of the individual posters. "Then he's an idiot," he said, "trying to depose a man to whom he owes money."

"But there should be two *duumvir*s, shouldn't there? Just like the Empire had two consuls."

"Yes."

"Then they could have shared the position."

Pullus started walking. "That's not how Naso works."

"Calpurnia didn't much like him."

"Who?"

"Scaeva. I think she'll be pleased."

Pullus glanced back at his shadow, then noticed a group of men approaching. To his surprise, he recognised Popidius, surrounded by his slaves and freedmen. The young aedile had clearly been waiting for him to finish with the *duumvir*. However, after promising Naso that he would allow him to speak to Popidius first, this was going to be a tricky conversation to explain.

Beside him, Pullus caught Taedia smirking. "Popidius," he said amiably, then nodded back towards Naso's property. One of the *duumvir*'s doormen was already watching. "An unpleasant business."

Popidius didn't reply until he'd got much closer. "Yes. Scaeva wasn't my favourite member of the *Ordo*, but his children didn't deserve to suffer so."

Pullus nodded, smiling out of politeness and hoping it didn't appear too much like a grimace. He was already hoping Naso's man would report to his master that this meeting had been a result of the aedile's initiative, and not his.

"We are soon to have elections," Popidius continued. "I am again standing for aedile."

"I've seen the posters. You must be confident?"

The aedile flashed an arrogant smile, which was confirmation enough. Although Pullus didn't spend much time in town, he knew the young aedile was popular. He did a decent job of keeping the town clean, and had organised good entertainments at the arena. The ladies seemed to like him too, although unfortunately for him they had no vote. "I wonder if I could tempt you to support my campaign?"

Pullus shook his head. "You know I remain neutral."

"There's nothing to stop a god from choosing a side."

"I'm not a god."

"But you have a lot of followers, and there are a lot of voters at your temple."

"It's not my temple," Pullus corrected, thinking about all the people who went regularly to sacrifice at his statue at the Fortuna Augusta. He glanced again at the *duumvir*'s doorway. A second member of Naso's household was now watching them.

"Most people associate you with Calpurnia and Naso," Popidius continued, seeming to mull the situation out loud. "But, then again, neither of them have to bother being elected." The aedile paused, giving time for a reply that didn't come. "Will you be in town long?"

"Just until I've completed Calpurnia's instructions." Pullus tried to steer the conversation away from politics, and towards a more pertinent subject. "How is your search for NovusPart material going?"

Popidius shrugged. "Fine," he replied. "A strange order to receive from our Augusta, but we will carry out her instructions, as always." He paused. "Let me know if you reconsider endorsing my campaign… or perhaps you will be courteous enough to return to your villa for the election day?"

Pullus blinked, surprised. "Pardon?"

"Naso's told me he's backing another candidate," Popidius said, his tone suddenly lacking in charm. "Sextus Cordus. And now you're here, and Calpurnia has allowed Naso's men free rein in the town."

"You know the two things aren't connected," Pullus replied, a little too defensively.

"But the people don't, and you being here doesn't help. Think on that, Pullus. Think on that."

The aedile gave a short bow and turned back to his men. Pullus waited for a few seconds, just long enough to see the doormen disappear back inside Naso's townhouse, and then continued on his way. Taedia scurried behind him. "Can he talk to you like that?" she asked. "Being just an aedile?"

Just an aedile, thought Pullus. *Just one of the three most important men in town.*

He didn't answer the question. Instead he switched his thoughts to NovusPart and their time in New Pompeii. McMahon and Whelan had used several locations to control the town. Calpurnia had converted their villa into her own private palace. In the town, however, they'd run things from a series of townhouses, the most important of which he now owned himself. But there were others: unfinished townhouses belonging to Whelan and other important NovusPart employees.

"Where are we heading?" Taedia asked.

Her questioning had begun to irritate him. Perhaps he shouldn't have allowed her to talk so freely. He doubted Calpurnia gave her such an opportunity. But if she spotted something he'd missed – like the election posters – it would be worth it. He could go back to his villa and let the world get on without him again. "We're going to take a look at the NovusPart townhouses," he said. "Whelan's to be specific."

"Whelan? One of the two men that ran NovusPart?"

"There were three actually."

"Calpurnia mainly talks about Whelan and McMahon."

"McMahon, Whelan and Arlen," said Pullus, slowly. Maybe Calpurnia had primed Taedia, provided a list of questions to her agent designed to stir the pot, just to see what would come to the surface. "Or Arlen, McMahon and Whelan, as I think it probably really was."

"I've never heard Calpurnia talk about anyone called 'Arlen'."

"He's the reason you're here. He invented the NovusPart device."

"And the other two took it from him?"

Pullus cast a sideways look at her. Quite a leap, if she'd not been told. "In a manner of speaking," he said. "So we were just left with McMahon and Whelan. Things would be so much easier if we could talk to them again."

"I heard you killed McMahon?"

"It's more complicated than that…"

"And Whelan?"

Pullus heard the screaming as the drill tore into the top of Whelan's skull.

"You're going to talk to Whelan?"

Pullus had to remind himself that just because she overheard things didn't mean she understood them. And if Calpurnia had set her up to be a sounding board, then so be it. At least it was cathartic. "We tried that a long time ago," he said. "If he'd been less of a soldier, then he might have seen sense and told us something useful before they killed him."

He looked round, but froze when he saw the confusion on Taedia's face. He didn't even register the next few words as she spoke them. He only saw her lips move as they sought to form the air into a statement. "But Whelan's not dead, is he?"

30

Naples

"It's all too easy to fall in love with the Romans, and all too easy to forget the things that would make any normal person's stomach turn. The executions, the slavery, the sexual grooming of children. What sort of man could continue to turn a blind eye to that level of cruelty? What sort of man is Nick Houghton? Is he really Decimus Horatius Pullus?"

Anonymous posting,
Bureau of Roman Affairs Intranet

NICK WOKE SUDDENLY. It was pitch black. His brain idled for a few moments as he struggled to figure out where he was. Then it came back. Chloe's spare room. He was still in Naples. Not Pompeii.

He let his head fall back into the pillow. No matter the length of his visits, his brain always failed to adjust. And yet there was something odd here. He'd been disturbed by something more than the ambient noises of the modern world.

Nick kicked off his bed covers, and stumbled across to the window. Drawing the curtains, he peered out at the apartment block opposite. Lights were coming on in several rooms.

He thought back to his visit to Pompeii and the *Gabinetto Segreto*.

NovusPart.

A simple word. An anachronistic word – scratched into a fresco two thousand years out of its time, and buried in Pompeii. The answers to the real questions remained elusive: how had it been written? What did it mean? Would they find more?

Nick let out a slow breath. In the apartment block opposite, more lights flicked on. Until that moment in the *Gabinetto* with Fabio, he always thought he understood the NovusPart device. The "rules" of temporal transportation had been the one thing NovusPart had appeared to be open about: *objects and people could only be moved forward in time, and the focal length was thirty years.* The device couldn't move anything from the immediate past into the present. Thirty years had to pass before something or someone could be transported forwards. And there was no going back. Time went in one direction.

Forwards.

Forwards, not back. Had they been lying to him? Nick closed his eyes. He doubted it. Whelan had screamed as he'd been made to talk. And yet he'd still not revealed everything. He'd still held onto the one or two elements that had kept the full potential of the device from them.

Nick turned at a noise from the door. A figure stood framed by the hall light. Chloe. The realisation didn't stop his heart from kicking.

"Shit," he said.

"Sorry…"

Nick looked down. He was in his underwear, and suddenly felt exposed. "You couldn't sleep either, huh?" he said.

"Something… I don't know what it was. Jack's still asleep."

"So we're both having bad dreams," Nick said.

"Did you see the news today? What's doing the rounds again?"

Nick nodded. He lacked a direct connection to the boards but, even so, it was hard to ignore the discussions about New Pompeii. "There was a small demonstration outside the site," he said. "After we'd left. Fabio told me all about it."

"I'm sorry."

"Don't be," Nick said. "Between the timeline conspiracists and the kooks dressed in sheets, it's really no wonder the rest of the world would prefer it if we just disappeared."

Chloe raised an eyebrow. "Kooks dressed in sheets? And when you do it, I suppose those sheets become something else entirely, eh?"

Nick gave a mock scowl. "Of course." He paused, then ploughed ahead. "Fabio took me to the *Gabinetto Segreto*."

Chloe looked at him blankly. "Aren't you a little old for all that? Surely you've seen enough Roman erotica to last a lifetime."

Maybe she hadn't been told. Maybe what she'd said to him was true: she was just a babysitter. But when he wasn't visiting Naples, they had to keep her occupied doing something. He needed to find out just how much she actually knew about the Bureau. "They found a fresco buried in amongst the new digs," he said, carefully. Trying to sense any hint of recognition before he revealed Fabio's secret. "It had the word 'NovusPart' scratched onto its surface."

Chloe froze. Which meant she really didn't know, he was almost certain. "Shit," she said, finally. "Shit. What does that mean?"

For Fabio, it had been a simple conclusion: proof Calpurnia was indeed tampering with the timeline, and a reason to put Nick under pressure. But despite what Fabio thought, it could actually mean any number of things. That was the problem: it was always tempting to draw a conclusion from a single data point.

"It means NovusPart reversed the flow of time," he said.

"You told me things could only be brought forwards. Time moves forward."

Nick shook his head. "It doesn't mean anyone travelled back."

"But then who wrote that word? Who would know what it meant?"

Nick didn't know and he wasn't going to jump to any conclusions. Not yet, anyway.

"It could be a hoax," he said.

Chloe's expression had changed, shock replaced by

confusion. It took him a few moments to realise she was accessing the boards. He waited a few moments, no longer surprised at the speed she was able to pull information, but no longer jealous she was able to do so. It wasn't technology that he particularly wanted or needed. And, given the recent issues of controlling infection, the time for signing up for implants had long since passed.

"What's the matter?"

"I'd put an alert on your *Who's Where* status so I'd know when it got updated," she answered, her eyes still unfocused. "I've just received the ping."

Nick felt mild surprise but nothing more. So someone had located him. "Have you told the security team?"

"No, not here," she said, her eyes suddenly back in the room. "You've not been anywhere without me, have you?"

"Just Pompeii, with Fabio."

"He didn't take you to the Vomero district?"

Nick shook his head.

"Probably someone fooling around then," Chloe said. "We'll talk tomorrow. Goodnight, Nick."

Nick watched her go and then turned back to the window. He took hold of the curtains, ready to pull them back into position. The apartment block opposite him, however, was still coming to life. Lights were being switched on across the building. He wasn't the only one jolted from sleep.

And he suddenly knew what had disturbed him and Chloe.

31

New Pompeii

"MY FATHER SCRAPED a small hole in the ringleader's skull," said Calpurnia. "He did it slowly. Carefully. Kept him alive and screaming. Then he filled his cranium with molten lead until it flowed out through his eyes." For a second, Calpurnia's gaze met his, and Nick felt his entire body shudder. Her voice sounded so cold. So detached. But, of course, she wasn't speaking from memory. Someone must have told her. Let her know Barbatus had allowed her mother to die, and then had gone on to murder his opponents. "The Emperor Gaius once said: 'It's not enough they die; they have to feel themselves dying'."

Pullus tried to leave, but was forced to watch as Barbatus first showed Whelan the tools, then explained how they'd use them.

They cut and shaved Whelan's hair. Then the scalp came away like peeled fruit. Whelan's eyes bulged in their sockets and his limbs strained against the chair to which he'd been tied. The NovusPart security chief didn't talk. He just sat shaking. He tried to break free, until finally – slowly – they started to grind at the bone. Then he started shouting, started screaming. Knowing he was going to die, he was determined to get his message across: *Don't let them alter the timeline!*

Don't let them have the device!

Pullus vomited but he barely noticed. His mind was still in the room with Whelan. Fifteen years ago. Watching Whelan's eyes whirl in their sockets. Then the smell hit his nostrils.

Galbo was with him, pulling him upright and wiping away the vomit from the corners of his mouth. "You're safe," his steward said. "You're safe."

"Shit."

"You're here. At home."

Pullus shifted, suddenly uncomfortable under the hot, damp sheets. He must have been caught in the nightmare for some time, not the few seconds of it he could remember.

"Which one was it?" Galbo asked.

Pullus rubbed his forehead to relieve some of the tension. His neck and shoulders were almost rigid. "Whelan," he said simply. "Shit, it was Whelan."

"That was a long time ago."

"You weren't there."

Galbo nodded, then started to gather the previous day's clothes from the floor and lay out a fresh tunic. Pullus looked towards the bedroom door. Early morning light was already filling the balcony beyond it. It was time to get up. *Fuck.* He barely felt like he'd had any rest. And today he had to head back into his past.

Because Whelan wasn't dead.

That's what Taedia had told him, without meaning to.

"Fuck," he said out loud.

Galbo started to retreat from his room, knowing his master was safe – and having long since grown accustomed to his need for privacy whilst dressing. "Even if your Whelan had talked," he said, "he'd have still learned to fly like all the others."

Pullus didn't appreciate the gallows humour in his slave's words, even though he couldn't fault the logic. The rest of NovusPart's staff had been crucified. Every single one of them. Except him. *The man who couldn't die.* "I'll be down in five minutes," he said. "Tell Taedia to meet me in the atrium."

Galbo nodded, but didn't leave.

"What's on your mind, Galbo?"

"The girl," Galbo said. "Taedia. It would help if I knew why she's here. Why she's really here."

"Leave her to me."

"If you want something unfortunate to happen to her…?"

"No," Pullus said, shaking his head. "Look, I'll be down in a few minutes. Just make sure she gets to the atrium in one piece, eh?"

"As you wish."

Still, Galbo didn't leave. Pullus watched him, surprised again by the old man's ability to read him, to sense when he hadn't quite finished. "Popidius," he said. "Do you know anyone in his household?"

Galbo nodded. "Of course."

"It would be useful to know what his interest is in NovusPart."

Galbo bowed, and finally backed out of the room. Pullus remained in his bed for a few seconds, listening for his steward's staff as it beat its rhythm down the stairs and into the atrium. Only then did he feel his shoulders relax and the last dregs of his nightmare evaporate.

He didn't like it here. Despite clearing out all of McMahon's personal property, the remains of NovusPart were too deeply engrained in the fabric of his townhouse, most obviously in the modern facilities still available to him: an en-suite bathroom to his left, and a small collection of electronic devices scattered about. Most no longer worked. Although almost magical to New Pompeii, the devices would be viewed as antiques in Naples.

When he was dressed, Pullus moved across to his desk. He searched through his field notes, and picked up a small collection of unopened envelopes tied together with string. Letters from his father, received periodically over the years. The latest lay to one side. Unopened, and ready to be bound like all the rest.

He momentarily felt like reading what his father had to say, but he resisted. Just like he'd resisted finishing his long-promised PhD. After all this time, why open those wounds now? Sighing, Pullus briefly checked his satchel, and then headed down into the atrium. As instructed, Taedia stood waiting for him by the *impluvium*.

She looked worried, and the reason was pretty clear. She'd made a mistake telling him about Whelan. Yesterday Pullus hadn't wanted to push the point and she'd not volunteered any further information, simply insisting she didn't know. Maybe she'd misheard; maybe she'd misunderstood something Calpurnia had said to Habitus, or the Greek. But something else was nagging at him. Something buzzing in his memory that he'd only just realised was significant.

He'd been forced to watch. But Barbatus hadn't let him see Whelan's final moments.

He hadn't actually seen Whelan die.

Taedia opened her mouth to say something. Pullus didn't give her the chance. "Where is he?"

"I wasn't meant to tell you," she said. Her eyes grew wide. Maybe she thought his silence the previous day had been the end of the matter.

"You didn't, and you won't," Pullus said, calmly. "If Calpurnia asks you, I'm happy for you to say I worked it out myself."

Taedia hesitated for a good few seconds, stumbling at the precipice. "He's in the town's holding pens," she said, finally. "That's all I know."

The holding pens were next to the amphitheatre, in the same building as the arena's paradox chamber. He knew the place all too well.

"Calpurnia told me to stay with you," Taedia said, following him across the atrium and towards the street. Pullus waved her away. This time she obeyed him.

"Would you prefer to tell her I found Whelan on my own, or that you took me to him?"

32

Modern Pompeii, near the ruins

"Our planning has always been based around one big event, such as an outbreak of a disease like Spanish Influenza or Ebola. But I believe it's now clear that isn't the scenario with which we're dealing. There isn't going to be a big event. We're going to get on with our lives as these things slowly come back to kill us."

Dr Lasseter, World Health Organization

"So did the earth move for you last night?"

Nick had wondered who would be the first to make the joke, but Fabio beat him to it by a fraction as they shook hands. Fabio waved at a nearby waiter, and they settled into a couple of cheap white plastic seats in the back of the restaurant's open-air courtyard.

"How big was it?" Nick asked.

"You'll have to ask my wife."

"Seriously, Fabio?"

"Okay. Just a three or so. Most people slept through it. I didn't even know until this morning."

Nick shifted in his seat, struggling to get comfortable. He couldn't help but think the owner could usefully invest in some new furniture and, more importantly, a few cushions. Still, the food was usually good and, despite its size, the location was relatively private. Above them, a fig tree sprawled out over a rickety frame and covered the whole courtyard. In many respects, they could have been indoors, except for the feeling that the many splints and struts holding up the branches might collapse the entire damn tree on them.

"If it was going to come down," said Fabio, noting where his attention was focused, "it would have done so last night."

Nick grunted. The restaurant's owner was making his way over. The old man always liked to explain what he'd chosen to serve them on any particular visit. All ingredients likely locally grown, outside of the ration, and probably under the blind eye of the Bureau. They'd also be treated to a nice drop of vino. And not from Pompeii either. Maybe one of a few bottles that hadn't quite made it onto the boats to China.

"*Vi preghiamo di portare un giornale...*"

The owner waved to indicate he'd heard Fabio's request, but it was one of his staff that brought the newspaper. Nick recognised it as a conservative-leaning publication, the only ones that seemed to be in business these days. The headline was all about New Pompeii. He pushed it away.

"I don't think you get how serious this is getting," Fabio said.

"It's nothing I haven't read before."

"In socialist rags. Not the papers the government reads." Nick shrugged.

"You don't read much about that Italian pride anymore," continued Fabio. "It turns out we Italians are better Catholics than we are Romans."

Nick issued a heavy sigh as Fabio settled back again. The Italian was probably right. Historians had known for years people living in Pompeii didn't just worship Roman gods, yet his own article about finding a dozen or so Christians amongst the New Pompeians seemed to have caused the biggest ruckus.

"Well, it's too late now."

"If only they hadn't all died, eh?"

Nick sucked in a breath. "It was certainly unfortunate," he said. Beside him, he suddenly noticed their food had arrived. Two glasses of wine had also been poured. He studied them, then turned to find the waiter already in mid-retreat.

"You didn't see him, did you?"

Nick didn't reply.

"There's no slaves here, you know. A word or two of thanks wouldn't go amiss."

"Sorry."

"Forget about it."

Nick made a move for his wine. "Do you have any news about my antibiotics?"

Fabio shook his head. "Your friends are already inside a quarantine zone," he said. "The risks aren't the same as we're experiencing."

"You could just give us a printer and have done with it."

"We're not giving you one of those, Nick. Or telling you where the supplies are located. Or *when*." Fabio flashed him a wide grin, but Nick didn't rise to the bait.

"I could do with a different answer before I leave."

"My grandmother used to say it's better to get a right answer than a fast one."

At the restaurant entrance, a fat man with a neatly trimmed beard was having a discussion with one of the waiters. He seemed to be showing the waiter a card. Finally, the man was pointed in their direction, and a plastic seat was dragged over to their table.

Nick bristled. Fabio didn't introduce the man, but a look between the two suggested they knew each other. "I sense I'm going to get a lecture," Nick said.

"Nothing of the sort, Nick," replied Fabio, his voice momentarily heavy. "This is Professor Waldren. He asked the Bureau for an introduction. Under the circumstances, we agreed it was a good idea."

Nick slowly turned to the new arrival, trying to work out if he knew the name. He didn't but, then again, his knowledge of the academic field wasn't exactly up to date. "Sorry, I'm not familiar…?"

"No reason you should be," Waldren replied. His voice was hoarse, his accent mid-Atlantic. He offered his hand across the table. "Temporal philosophy is a relatively new field."

Nick hesitated. "You're a physicist?"

The professor's grip was tight on Nick's hand as they

shook. "Do you enjoy it?" he asked. "Living out there?"

"It's quite a peaceful life."

"In New Pompeii? I'd always imagined it to be a garish place."

"I spend most of my time in my villa outside town."

"Of course. But this is, what, your second visit to Naples in just a few months?"

Nick nodded. "Just a few days this time, hopefully."

"The Bureau mentioned you were visiting more often," Waldren continued. "More visits in the last two years than at any time since you left."

Nick glanced at Fabio, but the Italian remained expressionless.

"And Calpurnia?" Waldren asked, cocking his head to the side. "Our Empress of Time? How is she?"

"As I said," Nick said, suspicion building, "I'm only going to be here a few days. So why don't you tell me what you want so we can all enjoy our lunch?"

Waldren nodded and then shrugged. "Fabio has shown you the fresco?"

"Yes."

"And what do you conclude?"

The same thing he'd told Chloe. "It's either a very clever hoax—"

"Or?"

"Or someone worked out how to go a step or two beyond NovusPart. Backward transmission of information."

Nick leant back in his chair, popped a cherry tomato into

his mouth and let it burst between his teeth. "If that's what you want to call it."

"Not you, though? Not Calpurnia, or her Greek thinker?"

"Who knows? It may have even been NovusPart themselves. Something they did before they transported everyone to New Pompeii."

"You mean like a painter might add his signature to a painting?"

"Sure. Or maybe it's something they were working on that didn't quite come off before everything went sideways."

"Interesting."

Nick didn't respond, and glanced at Fabio. The Bureau Chief was slumped back in his seat. He seemed to have given up on the conversation as clearly as he'd done his meal. Nick pushed his own plate aside.

"We've been re-examining old finds from Pompeii," Waldren continued. "To see if we can find any more examples of temporal manipulation."

Nick nodded. "I can see where this is going," he said. "But I think you've forgotten it's easy to find patterns when you're looking for them. I've seen Egyptian hieroglyphs showing what look like tablet computers. And I've seen medieval tapestries containing creatures that look suspiciously like Yoda."

"Nothing quite as sharp as a mention of NovusPart though eh, Pullus?"

"No."

The professor smiled, satisfied. "Well, the fresco is the first clear evidence we have that the timeline has been manipulated. It's something of a ground zero for my field."

Nick nodded. When NovusPart played with the timeline, they'd been careful to claim they'd only taken people whose influence on the timeline had effectively ended. People on the verge of death, whose bodies had also been lost, so nothing changed. Not so with the fresco. Someone had scratched that word into it for a reason, and it was clear evidence of tampering—much like when NovusPart had secretly removed children who would grow up to be *inconvenient*. And it might just help him. "We should keep in touch on this," Nick said. "I'm sure this is nothing to do with Calpurnia, but I can see the potential issues."

"Good." Waldren stood and pushed back his chair. "I presume you've heard of the Roman God Janus? The god with two faces?"

Nick nodded.

"I always assumed that meant he was two-faced," the professor continued. "You know, untrustworthy. But that's not it at all, is it? He gazes at both the future and the past. The join in the loop, as it were. The beginning and the end."

"I fail to see your point."

The professor stood and gave the shallowest of bows. "Well, it was good to meet you," he said. "The Bureau will put us in touch again before you leave."

Nick watched him go, irritation burning his cheeks. Beside him, Fabio was also on his feet. "Forgive me, Nick," said the Italian, as he passed across a small card. "I only said I would introduce you."

Nick looked at the card. An appointment card. For an optician.

"Get them checked out," said Fabio. "You shouldn't take chances with your sight. Now, if you've finished eating, should we get you back to the dig? Finally see where they found this damn fresco?"

33

Ancient Pompeii, AD 62

THERE WERE SEVERAL men standing outside Trigemina's
home. Achillia watched them, standing a few doors
down on the opposite side of the street. She occasionally
glanced at passers-by, as if trying to seek out a familiar face.
Not that she needed to have bothered with the pretence.
The men on the door didn't seem interested in searching for
anyone, but instead looked like guards, ordered to rebuff
visitors whilst others worked inside.

What would those others make of what they found?

Hopefully, they'd think it was a suicide pact just as she'd
planned. Achillia had dragged the limp bodies of the slaves
from their hiding places to the atrium and then arranged
them in a rough circle. Some had fought back, and their
deaths had been messy; the bodies had left trails of blood,
but she and Trigemina hadn't had the time to clean up much.
She hoped the men wouldn't notice, distracted by the female
slave dressed in Trigemina's finery.

The rest of the house had been left untouched; Achillia had been in two minds whether to scatter the furniture about to give a suggestion of a robbery gone wrong, but she didn't want to confuse the issue. Better that the Emperor's men left Pompeii thinking Trigemina had killed herself along with her slaves. A robbery would mean involving the local magistrates.

From her vantage point, Achillia noticed that those passing along the street were giving the house a wide berth. Gossip was clearly already circulating about what had taken place. She needed to leave soon – eventually the guards would notice her loitering – but she wanted first to get a sense of who had come for Trigemina before she tried to find this Barbatus. Were these the Emperor's men or locals?

Achillia moved closer, stopping at a fountain to take a drink of water. The stone surrounds of the fountain had unfamiliar writing on them. She peered at it.

"Oscan," said a voice from beside her.

Achillia turned. A man stood a few feet from her. He wasn't particularly young, but his hair was not yet grey. He pointed at the writing. "Oscan," he said again. "There's probably only a few people living here who can still read it."

"And are you one of them?"

"No," replied the man. He flashed a grin at her. "I have trouble enough with Latin."

Achillia tried to look disinterested. She again tried to make it look like she was waiting for someone. The guards outside the townhouse were kicking a stone between them.

"Nasty business," said the man. "Entire household killed, so they say."

"I hadn't heard," Achillia replied.

"They found them this morning. Mistress and her slaves. Throats all cut."

Achillia widened her eyes, imitating surprise. It was time to go; this man would draw attention to her. She bowed slightly and turned to leave.

"I thought you were waiting for someone?"

Achillia turned back to the man, immediately re-evaluating him. He was a little on the short side, if slightly more muscular than most. But the trunks of his arms didn't indicate strength he'd earned through hard work. No, he probably spent each day down at the baths, lifting weights for whoever was watching.

"I apologise," said the man. "I didn't mean to frighten you."

"You didn't." She cocked her head towards Trigemina's house. "So you heard what went on in there?"

"Who hasn't?"

"And what are people saying?"

"Suicide."

"Unfortunate."

"Quite." The man cocked his head. "Odd thing though," he said. "The mistress had marks on her back. Almost like she'd been whipped. A long time ago, but whipped nonetheless. So either she was the sort of wife her husband had need to punish, or else she was a slave stuffed into a rich woman's dress."

Achillia snapped her attention to Trigemina's house. The guards were heading her way, in response to some signal perhaps. One she hadn't detected. Fuck.

"According to my sources, the owner of that house arrived with a female gladiator. That wouldn't be you, would it?"

The man looked strong, but Achillia couldn't see a weapon. The kitchen knife was at her hip. Hidden, yet ready. As she reached for it, one of the approaching men shouted:

"Barbatus! Have you caught her?"

34

Ruins of Ancient Pompeii

"Risk? What risk? Pompeii was a tourist town in the age
of the Grand Tour, when life expectancy was half what it
is today… or maybe a couple of years ago. It will still be
bringing in visitors right up to the apocalypse."

Off-record comments, Campania Tourist Board Officer

"HAS THERE BEEN much damage to the site?"
Nick spun the optician's card around between his
fingers, still thinking about Professor Waldren. He barely
listened as the assembled team of archaeologists talked about
the earthquake. *Minor damage only. A lucky escape. It's been
through worse.* He was glad when Fabio shooed them away.

"The fresco," Nick said. "I'm ready to see where you
found it."

"Yes. But first I need to check if they've uncovered
anything else of interest. The director has a habit of keeping

the best finds to himself for a few days."

Nick nodded and Fabio headed further onto the site. He surveyed the row of white tents and the outlines of the buildings that had once made up this quadrant of the town. In the distance, the yellow tape that marked out the boundary of the dig site fluttered in the breeze. A solitary, scraggy dog ambled about.

About fifty or so yards away, clearing away a mix of soil and ash from the bottom of a stone-block wall, Amel knelt with her niece Sabine. It looked like the kid was undergoing training in some basic digging techniques. They were both working in the full glare of the afternoon sun.

"You'll get sunburn," Nick shouted, heading towards them. "Even this late in the season."

The kid's head spun like an owl's. Amel didn't lift her concentration from the ground. Even when he got within a few feet of her, she didn't look up. "I've worked in hotter climates than this," she replied, sweeping away more of the lapilli.

"North Africa? The Middle East?" he guessed, thinking of her name.

"Tunisia, Libya, Turkey, Spain. But my real interest is in South America."

"And now Campania?"

"Yes. And now Campania." Amel rose and dusted her hands against the sides of her shirt. She waved Sabine towards the shadow of the nearest tent, and the girl grinned in relief. "The geophys has started on the last few parcels of land." Amel pointed into the distance at nothing in particular. "Soon it'll all be uncovered."

"I like to think a few secrets will remain buried," Nick replied.

"If it helps, one of the houses we've found may be a match for the House of the Faun. Once it's all cleaned up."

"But they've got you out here, digging out a tiny section of wall?"

Amel brushed some sweat off her face with her forearm. It didn't hide the fact she'd suddenly turned a little red. And it was nothing to do with the sun. "Well, I guess you could call it academic punishment."

Nick understood. He'd spent most of his fleeting visit the previous day with Fabio near the water castle, or with Amel after she'd been sent to collect him to watch the casting process. No doubt some noses had been put out of joint. So now she was buried under the same old horse shit he'd experienced himself as a post-grad.

"So two visits in two days," she said. "What gives?"

"Fabio showed me some of the new exhibits in the museum in Naples."

Amel laughed. "You mean the sexy fresco they took away to the *Gabinetto*?"

Nick shrugged. She clearly didn't know about the writing. "Sure, amongst other things."

"Well, a lot of people here are a bit – how you say?" She looked at her niece, who was within earshot. "*Miffed* that the museum geeks got to examine the finds from Zone 23 before the rest of us. It would have been good to have had the opportunity to look at them in detail."

Nick smiled inwardly, thinking about the hidden room behind the *Gabinetto*. He glanced over to where Fabio was still in discussion with the dig team. He was making a series of pointing and jabbing gestures. "And you could show me this 'Zone 23'?"

"Sure."

Amel told Sabine to stay where she was, then led the way into a building, the walls of which barely looked capable of standing. Nick paused to consider whether they'd had opportunity to reinforce them since it had been uncovered – but then remembered it had already survived an earthquake.

He followed Amel inside and found himself within the atrium of a modest townhouse. The echoes of the *impluvium* and *tablinum* were just about clear amidst the ruins, but it would take a lot of restoration before it was on the same level as the rest of the site.

"We're still digging out the cubicles surrounding the atrium," said Amel. "You know? The little bedrooms and store cupboards." Amel detected Nick's sigh. "What?"

"It's more complicated than that," he said. "The small spaces around the atrium were used for any number of things."

"I was generalising."

"Sorry," said Nick. "It just bugs me. Some of the interpretation that gets put out there."

"Well," Amel said, more than a little irritation in her voice, "if you'd let some of us in…"

Nick ignored her and walked around the *impluvium*.

The archaeology had been rushed. Rectangular gashes in the wall were all that indicated the spots where frescos had been removed. Other, less well-preserved examples remained intact on the wall. All in all, there was nowhere near the same level of care shown as where Amel had been working to brush away lapilli with her niece. "Shit," said Nick.

"What did you expect? For them to leave the best stuff on the walls to rot away like they have in the rest of the town?"

Nick didn't answer. The removal of artefacts was a double-edged sword. Eighteenth-century paintings and drawings of Pompeii depicted frescos that had faded away after being exposed to the elements. But to simply cart them off to the galleries of Naples created other problems.

He was wasting his time. After finding the *Gabinetto* fresco, the dig director would have likely examined every inch of this zone. They were unlikely to find anything new.

"Come, I'll show you something better," Amel said, leading him out into the road and back in the direction of her dig site. Sabine ran from the tents to join them. When they stopped it was at another building, its original purpose clear from the circular grinding stones and ovens. The stray dog – a dirty, grey Labrador – wandered about, nosing for food two thousand years too late. From the looks of the swollen glands on its chest, the animal had mouths to feed and would likely persist. But it looked harmless enough. So much for *cave canem*.

Amel swept a theatrical arm towards a wall. "See what you've been missing?"

Unlike the townhouse, at least one fresco inside the bakery remained intact: a beautiful image of Venus fishing, the detail dull under a fine layer of dust.

"It looks better after you've thrown a bucket of water over it," Amel said.

Nick spun round in shock, then realised Amel was joking. "Yes," he said, smiling. "Yes, they used to do that, didn't they, for visiting dignitaries on their Grand Tours."

Amel rolled her eyes. "Thanks for explaining my joke."

"Sorry," Nick mumbled. "It's just all so different…"

"…than the stuff you saw when you first came here as a tourist?"

Nick nodded. The sad truth was that, almost as soon as it was discovered, Pompeii had become an illusion. A town destroyed by an earthquake and pyroclastic flow, its statues and relics put back as they were assumed to have been, not how they were. Even discounting the more recent destruction of a fascist government and the Second World War.

"Hey! Watch your feet!"

Nick jumped back and looked down. He didn't see anything at first, just the layer of soil that hadn't yet been excavated from the floor of the bakery. Then he spotted two parallel lines in the earth, a series of shorter lines crossed between them, the area marked out by orange flags a few centimetres high. "A ladder?" he asked, kneeling and tracing the lines with his hands, feeling the indentation.

Amel grinned. "Yeah, pressed into the dirt. The wood's long gone of course, but the impression remains. Maybe they had builders in at the time of the eruption, making repairs after the earlier earthquakes. Just like we are now."

Nick whistled appreciatively. He rose and continued to explore the bakery, careful of the orange flags. He found what he was looking for after about ten minutes. Kneeling low to the ground behind the ovens, he spotted a patch of graffiti. Simple, childlike drawings that were common in every bar and brothel in town. More than likely the work of a barely literate adult.

The words were hard to read, but not impossible. He stared at them, as they came into and out of focus. He didn't even notice Amel had joined him until her bare shoulder bumped into his arm. She swore.

Nick wiped away the remaining surface layer of dust from the wall, revealing the graffiti sharp against the ancient limewash. Suddenly, there were two points on the graph, and they ruled out the possibility that this was something NovusPart had done prior to the creation of New Pompeii. This was a message from the future, transmitted deep into the past.

The writing was eroded and mostly illegible, apart from two words: *Nick Houghton*.

35

Ancient Pompeii, AD 62

ACHILLIA PULLED HARD, but the rope just cut deeper into her wrists. Her hands had been tied behind her back to the upright of the chair and her feet were bound tight to its front two legs. Another rope was fastened round her midriff. In short, she wasn't going anywhere. And they were probably going to torture her.

Despite not wanting to, she let out a small cry. It had taken four of them to tie her into the chair and her struggles seemed to have made them even more determined she wasn't going to get free. "Fuck," she whispered. Again, she tried to move her wrists, tried to find some slack that could let one of her hands slip free. Instead she started to lose the feeling in her right hand. "Fuck. Come on! Come on!"

"You'd be better off waiting."

Achillia stopped. She knew the voice, of course. It was the man from the water fountain, Barbatus. But she thought she'd been left alone, having long since heard the shutter being closed and voices slowly disappearing deeper into the townhouse where she'd been taken. She'd been careful to wait many minutes before starting to try and wriggle free. Had he been standing there all that time, just watching her waiting? Watching to see what she'd do, and when she'd do it?

"How long have you been watching me?"

"Long enough."

The bastard was enjoying himself. "So, ask me then."

"Ask you what?"

"Trigemina. You want to know where she is."

Barbatus came into view, but he stood off to one side. Achillia had to twist her neck to get a good look at him so she didn't bother. Instead, she stared straight ahead at the wall, on which a fresco of Artemis and Actaeon was being replaced with something more modern.

"You must know I can't simply ask you," Barbatus replied. "The law dictates a slave's testimony will only be accepted under word of pain."

Achillia could no longer feel her right hand and the left had begun to tingle. She would need at least one if she was going to fight when they finally moved her from the chair. She forced herself to relax and let the blood again start to flow. "This is no courtroom."

"And I'm no torturer."

A small silver coin fell into her lap. It rested in the folds of her *stola*. The Emperor's face smiled up at her. Gods, she'd love to give that bastard a slap.

"I've seen your type before," said Barbatus. "You spend

your life stumbling from one fight to the next. Flipping a coin and betting it will always fall in your favour."

"It's worked so far."

"And now you're tied to a chair. *My* chair."

Achillia looked Barbatus up and down. "It's in a shit house though, isn't it?"

Barbatus didn't respond for a moment, and then burst out in laughter. "Tell me, how did Trigemina put up with you? I didn't know her very well, but she always seemed so uptight?"

Achillia turned back to the half-completed fresco. *Cocksucker! He knew Trigemina!* All that trouble – killing the slaves, dressing Trigemina up in the dead woman's clothes – and he knew as soon as he looked at their decoy!

"You know her husband is dead, yes? All his property has been seized by the Emperor?"

Achillia remained silent. Fuck.

"That's right," said Barbatus. "You belong to the Emperor. So your calculation was wrong. You should have waited. There was no need for you to toss the coin. No need, in short, for you to butcher them all."

Achillia turned back to the fresco. "Trigemina took me to see the Sibyl," she said. "Before we came here."

"And?"

"I heard a voice."

"Isn't that the point?"

"Inside my head," Achillia replied quickly. "Right inside my head. Trigemina didn't hear it. It told me I'd come to Pompeii and meet a man called Manius Calpurnius Barbatus."

Barbatus didn't respond.

"That's your full name, isn't it?"

"Go on…"

"The Sibyl told me you had a daughter, and that I would – *must* – rescue her husband."

"Daughter? Husband?" Barbatus again roared with laughter. "And you were doing so well…"

"It's the truth."

"Well perhaps you could offer me another truth. One more interesting than something a little woman said to you in a dark, damp cave. Where's your mistress? Where's Trigemina?"

Achillia tried the bindings again, but knew she was beaten. She was going to die. So she did what she'd been trained to do and exposed her throat for this bastard Barbatus to make the killing blow.

"No, that's too easy," Barbatus said. "Why threaten you with something you've faced many times before?"

For only the second or third time in her life, Achillia started to shake. They could do anything to her, beat her, blind her, take her hands, break her legs. Dump her onto the street, unable to fight. Unable to live.

"You are the property of the Emperor," continued Barbatus. His voice was quiet. "And I usually get him what he wants. One way or another." He took a step closer. "She took you to see the Sibyl?" he asked. "People say that oracles mean our future is set. They talk about destiny as if they have no control over their own lives. But there's another way of thinking about the Sibyl's stories. She wrote down her predictions in nine books, and offered them to the last king of Rome. But Tarquinius refused to pay, so she burned three and raised the price of those that remained."

Achillia pulled once more at her bindings. "So?"

"The Sibyl isn't the only one who can burn the future. Life is what we make of it. And if you think your future depends on keeping Trigemina alive, you are mistaken. Now, tell me where she is, before I take your eyeballs."

Achillia let out a frustrated roar. "If you blind me, by the fucking gods I will have my revenge."

Barbatus didn't seem impressed. "Where is she?"

Achillia wanted to scream, to dare him to do as he threatened. But to be blind was worse than losing a limb. And she had no doubt he'd do it. "She's in the fucking tenements; north of the arena. In a place owned by Hermeros."

36

Naples

"Whether we like it or not, Nick Houghton has so far managed to keep the Romans from using the NovusPart device. The danger will come if he ever loses his influence over this Empress of Time."

Anonymous Government Official, COBRA

"DOES IT EVEN work?"

In front of him, the desktop machine continued to click and murmur. A leftover from Nick's days at university, and at one time a machine that had been frighteningly over-specced. Not now though. Today, it was just another forgotten bit of hardware. Something Chloe had found amongst his father's belongings. "Just about," he said. "Or it will do, once it's patched."

"I could get everything you need much quicker from the boards."

Nick didn't doubt she was correct, but that wasn't really the point. He wanted to poke around and find the answers himself, not wait for Chloe to filter them. And as he didn't have direct access to the boards, an old computer was his only point of connection. Just like most of the rest of the population. "This is fine," he said.

The screen went black and continued to load. Nick found himself staring at his own reflection. The plastic sheen of the monitor picked up so much more detail than the polished metal mirrors he used back home. He tipped his head to get a better look at his face.

"I've often wondered," Chloe said quietly, noticing his distraction, "do you see Nick, or Pullus?"

"I see both," Nick replied. He looked at Chloe, smiled, and watched her head to the door of his room. Only on the final step did she hesitate. "Your *Who's Where* status hasn't changed," she said. "It's still saying you're in the Vomero quarter."

Nick looked back at the screen. There were several updates left, which would take a few minutes, even with the speed of the Bureau-provided connection. "Well, today I went to see Fabio and then onto Pompeii. You dropped me off and picked me up, remember?"

"I just think it's odd, that's all."

"Update the entry, if it makes you feel better," he said. "But it's probably better for the cranks to head out to Vomero than come here. Unless you want to move again—"

"No. As I said, I just think it's strange. Anyway, I heard you had an interesting day in Pompeii."

Nick immediately thought about the graffiti. Did Chloe know? He turned to her, and was relieved to see she was grinning. "You've got a date? Fabio said she was a looker."

"Her name's Amel," Nick replied. "And it's just dinner. It'll probably be all classics chat. And anyway, she asked me, in case you're wondering."

Chloe raised her eyebrows.

"It's not like I'm in a relationship with anyone."

"Really?"

"No," said Nick. Chloe didn't seem convinced. "The gossip about me and Calpurnia isn't true, you know. I thought you understood that."

"I know."

"A classic way of undermining a woman in power is to chatter about who she's screwing."

"Thank you for telling me, sir."

Nick let out an exasperated sigh.

"I'll leave you to it," Chloe continued, tapping the side of her head as she left the room. "Call me when you get fed up and want to use my connection."

Nick rubbed his temples. A muscle was starting to twinge and the blue-green light from the monitor wasn't helping. He stared at the screen, waiting for the computer to finish updating, as he thought about a long dead name.

Joe Arlen.

Nick knew very little about the man. One of the three founders of NovusPart, Arlen had arguably been the most important, the man who'd first understood how to pull particles forward along time's arrow from the tail to the tip. He'd written the key algorithms. And he'd also prepared its safeguards.

All of which had been triggered after the fall of New Pompeii.

Joe Arlen. He'd been just a name, not a face. And most of the world thought he'd become a hermit, an eccentric rich man sitting in a darkened room surrounded by bottles of his own piss. Except Arlen hadn't become a hermit. He'd been killed. Stolen from time.

The computer rumbled. If he ever got to meet the diehards providing the fixes and patches for devices like this, he'd kiss them. In many ways, the computer worked a lot better than he remembered, although in others it didn't. Under the desk, the computer's fan was growling.

It immediately warned him what he was doing was archaic. Nick cursed as the computer continued to cycle. Perhaps he should have allowed Chloe to search for him. But she and Jack would be together, sorting through the box of Pompeian wine and garum that smoothed his stay. Jack would no doubt drink the former and sell the latter; the Bureau wouldn't stop him. If everything went to plan, he'd only be staying for a few days anyway, and then he wouldn't be back for a long time. Maybe never.

Just like Joe Arlen.

Nick pushed the thought aside. It wasn't fair on Chloe and, in some respects, it didn't really matter what had happened to Arlen. He was gone. The one man who knew how to get the NovusPart device working simply wasn't around to ask. And yet no one vanished completely without trace. And neither did a company.

The browser loaded and Nick brought up information on former NovusPart employees. A few of them had achieved a limited celebrity directly after what some euphemistically called the "Pompeii incident". A series of archived media articles and defunct blogs gave him a few names for further research, although none looked too promising: low-level staff who likely never had access to the locks and bolts of the NovusPart device.

Most of the blogs concentrated on gossip. There were hints about Arlen's mental state, and mentions of Whelan and McMahon, focusing on salacious rumours about their private lives.

And yet somewhere in amongst all this must be the clue he needed. The fresco in the *Gabinetto* and the graffiti in the bakery both pointed to the NovusPart device being made to work. And yet neither of the messages had made it to him intact. The first had clearly contained the word "NovusPart"; the second his own name. But the sentences around these words were no longer legible; the steady erosion of history had made both pieces of information useless.

Frustration bubbled up within him. His eyes ached and the screen in front of him blurred. The fresco and graffiti were useless. Pointers, yes. But they weren't the answer, and they weren't the only new pieces of information. The professor he'd met at the restaurant – Waldren – what was his field? Temporal philosophy?

Nick tapped the words into the search engine. The machine juddered for a few seconds then displayed a list of bland results. He tried the name "Waldren", but found nothing useful. Certainly nothing that matched the professor's stated field or interests. Which was odd, Nick thought. Because he couldn't have sprung from nowhere.

And neither could Joe Arlen.

Arlen must have had a family. Where were they? Nick started the new search. He quickly found Arlen's mother; like most people over a certain age, Mary Arlen clung to the technology she understood. Her old-style blog was active but hadn't been updated for some time. It would be interesting to talk to her, find out if her son had left anything useful behind. There was an email address. He could send her a message.

But then he saw his own name. *Nick Houghton*. And he understood almost immediately that any attempt to contact her would be pointless. The entry was full of hatred: she openly accused him of wasting Joe Arlen's legacy, keeping the Romans to himself, rather than sharing the wonder with the rest of the world. Any email would likely go unanswered.

He was about to leave the blog when he spotted something else, a short reference mentioned within a longer diatribe.

Mary Arlen had set up an organisation to continue her son's work. Something called the NovusPart Institute.

37

Ancient Pompeii, AD 62

ACHILLIA TRIED TO rest, letting her head fall forwards. She closed her eyes. Barbatus had left and there was no one else in the room with her – this time she was certain – and she likely had at least a little time before they returned. Whether they would have Trigemina with them was another matter. In all likelihood, they'd find her mistress still sitting in that rancid apartment, too scared to leave. Then she'd discover if Barbatus was true to his word; whether she'd be let go or simply executed to tie off a loose end.

Achillia let out a frustrated scream, and stared again at the fresco of Artemis and Actaeon. Her breathing had just returned to its normal rhythm when she felt a deep, low vibration within her skull.

"Shit," Achillia whispered. "Shit. Shit. Shit."

A dark shape forced itself deep into her vision, pushing down hard as a vibration began to build in her ears. Filling her head with noise, before finally a voice emerged.

Manius Calpurnius Barbatus, it said.

"I've found him!" she shouted.

You will go to Pompeii, and you will find Manius Calpurnius Barbatus! You will seek his daughter, and you will save her husband Marcus Villius Denter by taking him to meet Balbus in Herculaneum.

The voice kept repeating the instructions. All of it so close, and yet not quite right. Because as Barbatus had told her, there was no husband to save.

"I've fucking found him!"

The room was now swaying, just as had happened in the Sibyl's cave. Achillia leant forward against her bindings and heaved, vomit dripping down her front and pooling in her lap. Just as suddenly as it started though, the voice stopped. But the room continued to move.

The fresco cracked, scattering plaster and paint across the floor. The vibration in Achillia's ears had been replaced by a loud roar that filled the room as the floor shook. She heard distant screams from within the house and the sound of breaking furniture.

Achillia rocked frantically in the chair until it tumbled, assisted by the rolling of the floor. But still she couldn't get out of the damn thing. "Cocksucking bastard!"

The screams had gone quiet. No doubt the occupants of the house had all run out into the street.

But was that a baby crying?

Finally the back of the chair broke. Her bindings loosened and Achillia scrabbled free. She found a bit of fallen masonry under the wreckage of the chair. *Some small offering of luck from the gods*, she thought. *Maybe even from the Sibyl.*

Achillia didn't pause to think about it too much. She just ran through the empty house and reached the door to the street. Then she stopped. The Sibyl. That tiny bit of luck. The voice in the cave. Manius Calpurnius Barbatus. The daughter. The husband.

How could the daughter ever get married if she died here today?

Achillia hesitated. She could see the street outside. But there was a baby crying. It had been left behind. And somehow, through the terror, Achillia knew it was a girl.

"Fuck!"

There was no one left in the house to hear her. Achillia took a further step towards the street, then turned and ran back into the house. She hurried up the stairs, following the baby's scream to a little wooden cot in one of several small chambers on the first floor.

The child was wrapped in a thick blanket. As Achillia picked it up, the sound of snapping timber momentarily drowned out the infant's crying. They maybe had seconds to get out before the entire house collapsed.

As soon as he arrived, Barbatus took the baby from Achillia and passed it to one of his men, who held the small bundle at arm's length, a confused expression on his face. The party had returned several minutes after the earth shook. In that time, Achillia had waited with the household slaves in the street, surrounded by ruined houses.

"They tell me you brought her out rather than escaping."

Achillia knew she was still Barbatus's captive; his men had already formed a circle around her. They stepped even closer as soon as the baby was clear and out of danger. "Well, these cocksuckers weren't going to do anything," she said.

"Then you have my thanks," Barbatus answered. "And you can be sure that those who ran without her will be punished."

"I'd have killed them."

"I'm going to."

Achillia nodded up the street. Or rather, towards the thin strip that now wound its way through the rubble that had so recently been shops, bars and bakeries. It would take a long time to rebuild. Years, maybe. "Trigemina is dead?" she asked. Barbatus hadn't returned with her, so she already knew the answer. But she still wanted confirmation, just in case the tremor – or the Sibyl – had decided to dole out a little more luck than simply freeing her from a chair.

"She took the sword," Barbatus replied.

Stupid bitch. Why take the sword? Fight. Always fight.

Barbatus smiled. "She cursed your name before she killed herself, you know," he said. "Asked the gods to take their revenge for betraying her. It seems, however, they agreed with you, rather than a woman who was in no position to ever grant your freedom."

Achillia didn't say anything.

"Your plan wouldn't have worked," Barbatus continued.

"When you got to her family, they would have turned you both in. But now what do we do with you?"

"You're going to kill me."

"You would think so, right?"

"Then what the fuck else are you going to do?"

38

New Pompeii

ACTIVITY ON THE route to the amphitheatre rose and fell like the tide. On those rare occasions when the gladiators competed, you could be forgiven for thinking the entire town had become concentrated in one place. The workshops and houses lining the *via* transformed to sell food and drink, and the arches holding up the arena's outer walls suddenly became home to novelties and side-shows, just like any town fair.

But not today. As Pullus walked towards the amphitheatre the streets were quiet, and his slightly hurried walk seemed at odds with the pace of life going on about him.

NovusPart had hoped the arena would generate revenue, but they'd also adapted the structure to accommodate another paradox chamber, linked to the device at the villa, into which they could deliver those people, objects and animals they'd transported forward in time. And if the damn thing looked ugly – jutting from the blind side of the arena like some architectural carbuncle – it was also secure. It was also where Habitus chose to hold outsiders who managed to breach New Pompeii's security cordon, in his damn holding pens.

Pullus stopped. The main gate leading into the amphitheatre had been left open. Inside, he could see the perimeter walls that separated the audience from the show. Pictures of horses, gladiators and slaves had been painted on them in bold primary colours, sadly missing from the grass-covered banks of the original structure in Italy.

This was as far as he usually came. On game days he always headed back home after he'd taken in the atmosphere outside the gates. Maybe that's why Calpurnia had thought this would be a good place to keep Whelan. He'd been so close.

A guard, his face almost obscured by a thick beard, appeared from within the arena. "Back again?"

"I've come to see the cells."

The guard nodded, unsurprised, and then pointed him round the side of the amphitheatre wall towards the annexe containing the holding pens. "No one told me you were coming," the guard said. "I would have waited for you. The others are already inside."

Others? "It's fine," Pullus said, "but if you could take me to them?"

"Sure. Though I told them there was no point hurrying. Dead men don't tend to move very fast, do they?"

Pullus shook his head, and waited for the man to lead

the way. Like the upper floors of the House of McMahon, the annexe wasn't designed to replicate anything in the Roman world. It was wholly modern, and passing through its threshold was like stepping forward in time: from the city of Pompeii, back to the present day. But like so much else, age had wearied it.

Pullus had to walk slowly whilst his eyes got used to the relative darkness. Along the walls, candle-style light bulbs sat dead in their sockets. In their place, someone – probably the guards – had placed a series of oil lamps, although they gave little light.

He heard voices from the corridor ahead. He knew some would belong to the unlucky few who'd been caught trying to breach the New Pompeii boundary, men and women who'd been left in the pens to die of either starvation or the shivers. But he also heard voices that didn't sound like those of prisoners, chatting idly as if passing the time.

Pullus was nearly at the paradox chamber. He passed several holding pens – ignoring the wails from inside – and came to a stop only when he approached two men standing outside one of the cell doors. He immediately recognised their faces. Both were from Calpurnia's household, and both were amongst the strongest muscle retained by Habitus. What the hell were they doing here?

The two men broke off their conversation mid-sentence at the sight of him. The slightly smaller of the pair reached towards the sword at his belt.

Pullus cleared his throat. "You recognise me?"

"Yes," said the smaller man.

"I've come to see Whelan."

Neither of the men spoke. Then, in the silence, another voice could now be heard. A much younger voice.

39

Naples

"Nick Houghton remains silent on one key issue. The Romans killed everyone to do with NovusPart, except one man. So why did they let him live, when they killed everyone who stood with him?"

Mary Arlen, archived blog post

THE BUREAU OF Roman Affairs was a grand name for a dull organisation. It was also significantly smaller than most people assumed. The crest and flag behind the reception desk made a good show of it, but beyond the lobby were no more than fifty people, mainly admin staff dealing with supply issues, liaising with various government offices and – perhaps most importantly – trying to quell rumours circulating on the boards.

Nick waited as the receptionist buzzed through to Fabio's desk. He rubbed the back of his hand across the stubble on his face. The call had come early. He'd been awake but not dressed and certainly not washed. Fabio would just have to put up with his dodgy breath as the main penalty for dragging him out here so early.

"He'll be with you shortly."

The receptionist had only just finished speaking when the door to the main office swung open and Fabio beckoned him inside. "*Ciao!* You eaten?"

Nick shook his head. "A coffee would be good."

Fabio signalled to the receptionist. "I didn't think a good Roman boy like you drank coffee."

"Somehow, I think I'm going to need it."

The Bureau was all open-plan and most of the desks were empty. Nick's Italian contact had a corner bay all to himself, but instead he directed Nick to a circular desk screened by filing cabinets.

"Have you found a third anomaly?"

Nick had meant it as a light-hearted comment, but Fabio didn't look amused. The Italian hadn't said much after he'd been shown the graffiti, instead busying himself making calls. The dig site had then been locked down and the patch of wall carefully removed.

"I wanted to speak with you before we got another visit from Waldren."

Nick nodded. "He's on his way?"

"He will be."

Fabio was about as tense as Nick had ever seen him. Probably more nervous than when they'd first met; the day he'd introduced himself as the head of the newly formed Bureau, an organisation he'd have known would only survive if Nick accepted it. "You're worried about some dusty old professor?"

"He's no academic."

Nick nodded, unsurprised. "Then who exactly is he?"

"Do you really need me to tell you?"

"I'm guessing he's with some sort of security service," Nick said. "It would be nice to know which one."

Fabio almost answered, and then stopped himself. He didn't say anything else until their coffee arrived. Nick took a sip and scowled. He'd probably never get used to the taste of artificial beans. "The graffiti," the Bureau Chief said. "You can see the implications?"

"They're the same as before," replied Nick. "Nothing's changed."

"Everything's changed," said Fabio. "Before we had two options: either this was something NovusPart had done – a signature on a painting, as you put it – or it was something your friends have done out there."

Nick cleared his throat. He could see where this was heading. "No, you're wrong."

"Enlighten me."

"The graffiti used my name, yes, but I crossed NovusPart's path just over fifteen years ago."

"So?"

"So whatever prompted those messages could have been from fifteen years ago to any point in time since that event.

Maybe five years ago. Maybe now. Maybe ten years in the future. Maybe two thousand."

Fabio descended into silence. "Good point," he said, finally. "But I don't think that's going to convince many people. All it's going to do is feed the shit that's going round that you lot are trying to change the timeline."

"They're not stupid, Fabio. Calpurnia knows that alterations to the timeline pose as much threat to the Romans as anyone else. If Whelan succeeded in communicating anything, he got that message across."

"Before they killed him?"

Nick hesitated. "Yes."

Fabio glared at him. From behind the filing cabinets, the receptionist reappeared with a couple of pastries. "Breakfast," she said, and promptly disappeared.

Nick looked at the food, and its plastic sheen. "Is that real chocolate?"

"Of course it isn't."

Nick felt some twinge of disappointment. Chocolate was one of those many luxuries for which demand had outstripped supply. There was, after all, only so much cacao that could be grown, and the crop had also been suffering from different forms of blight for about five years, exacerbating the problem. "They used to sell bars of chocolate when I was a kid, you know. Solid bars of milk chocolate."

"*Delizioso!* It's the thing I miss most."

Nick smiled nostalgically. Like so many simple things, it was now too expensive. "You know, in the 1920s, the only people who could afford jelly were aristocrats."

"Some things stay the same, then."

Nick took a bite of the pastry, but quickly put it down. He was more than aware that Fabio hadn't answered his earlier question, and he wasn't going to let it drop. "I looked up Waldren. Or at least, I tried to—"

Fabio tensed. He brought his voice down into a sharp whisper. "And what did you find?"

"Nothing."

"You won't," Fabio replied. "I doubt it's his real name. Well, would you? Under the circumstances?"

No, thought Nick. He wouldn't. It was clear Waldren wanted something, even if he hadn't yet asked. And in those circumstances, it was probably best to keep your real identity shrouded, especially if you thought the person you were talking to could arrange to have you taken from the timeline.

"Look, Nick. We were asked to introduce you – but if we hadn't… then I guess it would have happened anyway."

"So who is he?" Nick repeated. He thought about the man's mid-Atlantic drawl. "MI5? NSA? CIA? Interpol?"

Fabio grimaced. "NATO," he whispered. "That's all I know. I got a call from the Italian Foreign Ministry. Another from what remains of the UN. Things have changed a lot since you've been gone, Nick. Just trust me on this, okay. The guy is bad news, and I will do my best to keep you from him, but…"

"I've met men like him before," Nick said, trying to sound unconcerned. "And I have diplomatic immunity." He let a few seconds pass. "So what's the NovusPart Institute?"

Fabio's shoulders tensed again.

"There was something on Mary Arlen's blog," Nick explained. "The detail was scant."

"Blog? You've been asking Chloe to read fucking blogs?"

"Chloe wasn't involved."

"Pah! It's just one of any number of crackpot organisations."

"Don't you think you should have told me?"

"Why? They're nutcases!"

"This one's headed up by Joe Arlen's mother," Nick said. "And it employs people who used to work for NovusPart."

"Low-level people."

"Still, have you wondered what they're up to?"

Fabio shrugged. "Not really."

"Because it's not in your remit, right?"

Fabio stabbed a finger onto the desk between them. "Whatever they're doing, it has nothing to do with New Pompeii," he said, his voice quiet. "And the last thing the Bureau wants is you getting mixed up with them. NovusPart is dead, and we want it to stay that way. Do you understand, Nick?"

"Fine."

"Good. So I don't want Chloe telling me you've asked her to take you out to Vomero."

Fabio stood up from the desk, turning to see who was sitting close to the filing cabinets. The action meant he missed Nick's shocked expression. "Okay," the Italian said, turning back. "Let's head out to the dig. Who knows what we might find today, eh?"

Nick heard, but didn't respond. The Vomero quarter. The place that was broadcasting on his *Who's Where* page. His brain struggled to engage with Fabio whilst it tried to process what he did and didn't know about the NovusPart Institute. Maybe he should have drunk the coffee. "I need to be back in Naples by six," he said, slowly.

"For your dinner with Amel?"

"Yes."

Fabio looked embarrassed. "We've changed your dinner date to a quick lunch," he said. "It's why I dragged you out of bed early so we could get started."

"Jesus, I'm getting on for forty, Fabio. I don't need my social life monitored."

"I know, I know. But, you know how gossip circulates. And when you're back in New Pompeii, it'll be her that has to deal with it. Not you."

40

New Pompeii

THE HEAVY WOODEN door swung open, and Pullus found himself looking into a holding cell not more than two metres across. Marcus leant against the left-hand wall. On the floor sat Whelan, his legs splayed out and his arms loose at his sides.

Fifteen years ago they'd made Pullus watch. And he'd done nothing.

He'd just assumed Whelan had died. The last thing he'd seen had been the pot of molten lead being shown to the NovusPart Chief Operating Officer. By that point, Whelan's skull had already been drilled into, revealing the pink membrane covering the brain. His whirling eyes had locked onto the smoking pot as it was brought towards him.

My father scraped a small hole in the ringleader's skull, Calpurnia had said, describing another incident altogether. *He did it slowly. Carefully. Kept him alive and screaming. Then he filled his cranium with molten lead until it flowed out through his eyes.*

Marcus glanced up at Pullus, frozen in the doorway. "My mother thought you'd be upset if you knew."

Pullus didn't reply. Whelan had a mop of thick, greasy black hair, which mostly covered his injuries. Whether they'd managed to repair the skull or had just let the skin grow back over the hole he didn't want to know. It was clear the NovusPart COO wasn't going to recover. A long line of saliva hung down through his beard and onto his tunic. His eyes were open, but there was nothing behind them. No intellect. No humanity.

"'It's not enough they die; they have to feel themselves dying.'"

Pullus turned to the boy. There was anger in his belly but he tried to swallow it. This wasn't Marcus's doing, he reminded himself. Not his responsibility. "What are you doing here?"

Marcus pushed away from the wall and shrugged. "The same as you," he said. "I wanted to know."

"Know what?"

"Whether he could still tell us anything useful. But I don't think even Dr Frankenstein could bring back this one."

Pullus studied the former NovusPart COO. There was nothing left of him. Every last scrap of what had been Mark Whelan had been taken. The student, the soldier, the businessman. Nothing was left.

Marcus stooped and waved a hand past Whelan's unseeing eyes. He then prodded a finger into the NovusPart COO's forehead. Pullus was about to pull him away when the boy returned to his position by the wall and leant back into it, grinning. "He probably retains more intelligence than many of my mother's slaves. Or the *Ordo*."

"Marcus…"

"A weak wrist, I heard," the boy continued. "They were just meant to drop a little of the lead onto his arm or hand. To let him feel the pain, and make him finally talk. When the first drop hit his ear he told my mother enough to get the device operational, but not to work." Marcus paused, considering the shadow of Whelan sitting before him. "And so they tried again, but a few misplaced drops soon stopped him talking. The Greek told me that my grandfather had the idiot slave executed, but I think it would have been better just to have taken his hands."

Pullus wondered how much of Whelan's brain had been destroyed by the molten metal. Wondered if there was anything left that could be coaxed to the surface. Or whether, if he'd been sent straight to a modern hospital, part of Whelan's mind could have been saved. "He didn't deserve this," he said, finally. "He wasn't the worst of them."

Again, the boy shrugged. "Does it matter?"

"Calpurnia – your mother – she knows you're here?"

Marcus shook his head. There was a glimmer of amusement in his eyes. "She thinks I came to town to continue my studies," he said.

Pullus nodded. "We need to get you back to the House of McMahon."

"I didn't come to study, Pullus."

"I don't fucking care." He looked down at Whelan. "We're leaving."

"Your friend Harris got me thinking," Marcus said, ignoring him and leaning back against the wall casually, as if he had all the time in the world. "The NovusPart device works in the future. It may not work now, but we surely find how to make it work at some point."

Whelan's lips were moving, but just barely. A rhythmic opening and closing, a few breaths a minute, keeping him alive. It wouldn't take much to cover his mouth and nose, and finish it.

"Pullus," said Marcus, a little louder. "Listen to me: we know the NovusPart device works in the future, don't we? And we know that I will control it."

"Harris was a manipulative bastard."

"*Marcus*," said the boy, suddenly excited. "Harris said he was getting his instructions from someone called Marcus."

"That's a very common name."

"It's my name."

"And your father's."

"He's not here though, is he?"

"No," Pullus replied. Whelan's mouth was still moving. On each outward breath there was the whisper of a syllable. "Unless your mother's Greek can square the circle." He leant down to Whelan. Yes, it was definitely a whisper.

"He keeps saying it," Marcus said impatiently.

Pullus crouched by Whelan, ignored the smell of stale urine and faeces. It was only after a few breaths that he finally made out what Whelan was trying to say.

Arlen.

41

Modern Pompeii, near the ruins

"The Anti-Christ has risen. He is the son of Nick Houghton and his Roman whore, Calpurnia."

Modern graffiti found on the streets of Naples

"YOU CAME WITH a chaperone?"

Nick coughed, embarrassed, but didn't look in Fabio's direction. The Italian sat near the front of the restaurant rather than at his usual spot at the back. It was the same place they'd so recently met Waldren.

Amel had prepared for the lunch date by putting on a fresh shirt and tying her hair up with a couple of long pins. Otherwise, she remained in her work clothes.

"Downgrading from dinner to lunch wasn't my idea," Nick said.

"They have you on a short leash." Nick grunted at that. "It's fine," Amel continued. "If it hadn't been the Bureau of

Roman Affairs, it would have been my research board. There was a fair amount of finger wagging."

"So will this make them jealous… or just irritate them?"

"Hopefully both."

Nick was silent, searching for something to say. Then he reminded himself this was her idea, and she probably had enough things to ask him. Sure enough, she grinned at him like she'd done at the airport, and then reached into her bag.

What she put onto the table was more than a little unexpected. A small classical statue, about twenty centimetres tall, and in the Greek style of Apollo. A cape covered its shoulders and outstretched arm, but otherwise it was nude. All toned muscle right down to the exaggerated lines of the abdomen.

"I got it from a stall outside the main entrance to Pompeii."

Nick raised an eyebrow. The statue's face looked familiar. So it wasn't only the people of Naples who had chosen to reproduce his face in marble. Or plastic. "Shit," he said.

"I don't think all the proportions can be correct."

Nick flushed. Greek sculptors were conservative about certain areas of the anatomy. "They now have a life-sized version of me at the Fortuna Augusta," he said.

"Life-sized?"

"You know what I mean… and anyway, back then – back there – being well endowed is – was – a sign of being a barbarian."

"Then it would appear you are very civilised, Nick. Very civilised indeed."

Amel started to laugh, but Nick didn't. Fortunately, he was rescued by the arrival of their food. As the waiter placed two plates onto the table he took the opportunity to move the statue to one side and glance over at Fabio. The Italian raised a glass of something in his direction and then he shifted in his seat so that he was turned slightly away from them. At least that was something.

"Shit, this is real lamb!"

Nick turned back to Amel, and took in the smell of seared meat. She looked delighted, already eating but taking her time with each mouthful.

"You can take me out with the Bureau any time you want."

Nick didn't pass comment. Back in New Pompeii the preference of the locals was for pork, but otherwise what they'd been served wasn't anything special. He didn't consider good food and wine a luxury. But he also knew Amel wasn't being facetious. Europe's farms and vineyards had been bought up by a wave of investors – all of whom now shipped the produce east. "The Bureau is good at arranging supplies," he said. "It's basically what they do for us."

"The Chinese would probably buy all you can take at much higher prices."

"I come home to Naples," Nick answered. "Not Beijing."

Amel laughed. "Shit – forget I said that. I'd be lynched if people found out I'd suggested you stop selling exclusively to the Bureau."

"The eastern markets get most of the garum eventually,"

Nick replied. "And, anyway, it's not as if the Bureau are organising charity concerts for Europe yet." Amel winced at his comment. "What?" he asked.

"It's okay," she said. "Just the charity thing. Shaking the tin and sponsored walks. It's a bit dated, that's all. People who can afford to should be giving because a cause is necessary, not just because of some wacky dare."

Nick nodded, embarrassed. Chloe had told him views on fundraising had evolved somewhat. Especially now the shoe was on the other foot and that it was Europe that needed help. He tried to move things on. "So, do your siblings live in the area?"

Amel looked puzzled, then nodded theatrically as she continued to eat. "Oh, my niece? Yeah, my brother lives further up the coast." She paused, then looked at him as if on the verge of an admission. "Look," she said. "Can we talk about Pompeii…?"

Nick nodded, disappointed but unsurprised. "Sure. What do you want to know?"

"The graffiti in the bakery," Amel said. "I mean… *fuck*!"

Nick didn't answer at first. Amel had been told not to talk to anyone about the graffiti find. As Fabio had put it, the story was easy to deny and it would be hard for her to get another job. "It's a surprise, certainly."

"But nothing else has been found like it…"

"Maybe. Maybe not. The rest of the site has been uncovered for too long. Many frescos have faded to nothing. Rain, wind, bomb damage. Even the early tunnellers would have removed a lot we don't know about."

"Excuse me? Tunnellers?"

Nick narrowed his eyes. *Doesn't she know?*

"I'm not a Pompeii – even a Roman – specialist," Amel admitted.

"Then why?"

"This is where it's at," Amel replied. "After New Pompeii, this is where everyone in the field wants to work. It's something I wanted on my CV."

"Oh," Nick replied. "Well Pompeii was never fully buried. And it was just lapilli and ash, not rock. So the Romans came back and tunnelled in, maybe only a few months after the eruption. They took away a lot of the statues and gold, especially from the forum."

Amel nodded, chewing slowly, savouring the food. "But don't you think it's odd that you come to the site and just stumble across it?"

"Not really."

"The odds just seem a little long."

"When the site was first being uncovered, Pompeii attracted kings and aristocrats from all across Europe. On every important visit, something wonderful would be found right at their feet."

"But that was all set up, wasn't it? The guides knew where... oh, shit."

She understood. A message from the future, transmitted into the past. They'd known where he'd be standing on a certain day and put the clue right under his nose, even if they hadn't been able to completely protect it from the damage of the volcano, or the passage of so much time.

"So what else do you want to know?"

Amel looked away. Nick already knew what she wanted to ask. It was inevitable really. Even Chloe sometimes skirted around its edges. "I own about thirty slaves," he said.

Even as he said it, part of him couldn't believe what he'd just admitted. The words didn't belong in a modern restaurant in a modern city full of tourists and traffic jams.

"I don't know if I can justify it to myself, so I'm not going to try and explain," he continued. "I've read what people say about it. And when I'm here, I agree. When I'm there though, it's different."

"How is it different?"

"It's normal."

"How can owning another human being be normal?"

"It's… look, I seem to remember that when the world first found out about New Pompeii, some classicists criticised NovusPart for *not* owning slaves." His observation didn't draw any reprieve. Nick thought about downing his wine to take the edge off. "It's not something I can change," he said finally. "Rome was – *is* – a nation of slaves. Most families had former slaves as part of their ancestry. And I need them to run the house, the villa, the farm. It's just a different time…"

"This is our time," Amel said. "*Ours*. Not theirs."

There was anger in her eyes, and the age gap between them suddenly seemed to widen. She still had the spark of something in her, the mindfulness not to accept the status quo, whereas he suddenly felt part of the problem.

"A few years ago I was lucky enough to go on a trek into the Amazon," she said. "We met up with a tribe who still lived there. On the second night, we found out they were going to kill a baby just because it had been born with a cleft palate. They thought it was a sign of evil spirits or something." She paused. "Would you have done anything? Said anything? Just watched them get on with it?"

Nick shrugged. "I guess there's a principle of not interfering."

"It wasn't a nature documentary," said Amel. "It was a baby."

"Then yes," said Nick. "I would have done something. Maybe. I don't know."

Amel cleared her throat. "Do you... do you use your slaves for sex?"

The expensive lamb provided by Fabio was slowly going cold. "No," he said. He tried to hold her gaze. She seemed to believe him.

"And Calpurnia?"

Nick gave a shallow smile. "We've never been an item," he said. "But if we had been, that would be fine, wouldn't it? I mean, she's a grown woman. Nothing like owning slaves, or sleeping with them."

"I suppose not."

"I'm not Marcus's father, either."

"I didn't ask that."

"But that's where you were heading."

Amel stayed silent for a moment then winced, her expression one of regret. "Shit," she said. "This isn't going how I'd hoped."

4 2

NICK DROPPED INTO the passenger seat of Chloe's vehicle, and watched Amel walk back towards Pompeii's security perimeter. His lunch partner was moving quickly, arms folded in front of her, looking more than a bit annoyed. Perhaps at herself, perhaps at him. Probably a mixture of the two.

Fabio had come to his rescue. A message had come from the office in Naples, and he'd had no choice but to break up their "business" lunch. At first Nick had thought the Italian had sensed the growing tension, but he'd looked truly apologetic. Only afterwards had Fabio realised his timing had been unintentionally perfect. Nick had taken the opportunity to break things up.

"I take it things could have gone better?" Chloe asked.

Nick shrugged. "It probably went as well as could have been expected."

"I'm sorry."

"I'll be gone in a few days anyway."

Chloe didn't respond, and started to programme the vehicle to make a quick loop around the site, and then head back to Naples. No doubt she was keen to avoid the crackpots and kooks on the main drag out of modern Pompeii.

"Fabio sounded rushed," Chloe said, absently. She reached again for the vehicle's controls, ready to guide it out into the traffic. Nick stopped her, taking hold of her forearm and guiding her hand away from the dashboard. He had suddenly realised he had all afternoon, and little to do. And Fabio had been unexpectedly called away.

Chloe twisted towards him. "What?"

Nick paused for a moment, letting his brain tick over. "Can you check my *Who's Where* status again, please?"

Chloe looked annoyed, but the sudden vacantness in her eyes let him know she was complying with his request through her implant. "Still the same," she said. "The Vomero district."

"But have you read the full entry?" Nick asked. "Including the date stamp?"

Chloe's eyes flicked left and right, the automatic reading reflex still there even though it wasn't needed. Just like when Nick kept glancing at his damn wrist. "Shit," she whispered.

"It hasn't been telling us where I've been, has it?"

"No."

"It's saying where I'm going."

Chloe's eyes focused on Nick's. "We've got to tell Fabio."

"No."

"He'll want to know, Nick."

"The NovusPart Institute – the organisation run by Arlen's mother – is based in the Vomero district. And I'm guessing my *Who's Where* status says I go to Vomero now, not wait for Fabio to give his permission. Which won't be forthcoming anyway."

"Just because *Who's Where* says you're going somewhere, doesn't mean you have to comply." Chloe chewed her lip. "Shit, Nick. This is my job we're talking about."

"The risk is small. Fabio won't find out, he won't think to check your *Who's Where* status. And so what if he does? Tell him when you get back, if you want to. Tell him I insisted."

"Do you even know what the NovusPart Institute is?"

Nick hesitated. He didn't. Information about it online had been sparse, with only brief mentions of it on the other NovusPart-related blogs. "No. Fabio didn't exactly want to give me the details."

"It's a hospice. Rich people go there to die."

How does that fit with McMahon, Arlen and Whelan?

"Fabio was probably trying to protect you," Chloe continued. She looked at him sympathetically. "Given your personal situation."

Nick nodded, and stared out of the vehicle towards the ruins of old Pompeii. He could just about see over the wall and towards Vesuvius. "When does *Who's Where* say I arrive?" he asked.

"About 2pm."

"And how long will it take to get there?"

Chloe set a new destination on the dashboard. The computed journey time matched.

"Then I guess you need to make a decision," Nick said. "Which are you more: my friend, or Fabio's?"

* * *

Chloe pulled the vehicle to a halt next to the kerb, but her grip on the wheel didn't loosen. She'd been checking the "self-drive" system for the entire journey, checking the system wasn't engaged. Checking it wasn't tracking their movements.

Nick glanced out of the window and took in the building they'd parked up alongside. The NovusPart Institute had clearly been set up with a healthy budget, and was built in the style of a Roman temple, or at least the frontage was. Behind the marble façade, the architecture transformed into an elongated hall of glass and steel.

"I don't know how long I'll be," Nick said. He kept his eyes fixed on the building. Above the Corinthian-style capitals to the six fronting columns, the words NOVUSPART INSTITUTE had been carved into the stonework of the pediment. Underneath, much smaller but still visible, were the names of Arlen, McMahon and Whelan. And two faces – one at either end – turned in opposite directions.

The faces of Janus.

"They'll recognise you."

Nick tried to smile. He was sure they would, but that wasn't really the point. Chloe wasn't going to change his mind.

"I'm going to have to move," Chloe said, eyeing a parking meter. "I'll be on the first turn up the road."

"No, stay here," Nick replied. He got out of the car and looked back at Chloe. She still had tight hold of the wheel.

"If anyone challenges you, just flash your Bureau card and tell them I'm inside."

Chloe looked as if she wanted to argue, but Nick didn't give her the chance, shutting the car door and striding up the Institute's steps without a backwards glance. Ahead of him, hidden from the road by the shadow of the portico, the building's glass doors slid open.

Nick shivered as he entered the lobby. The building's air conditioning was turned up high, and the shock made him come to an immediate halt. *Who's Where* had told him he would be here, and he'd come, just because someone had updated his status and predicted he would follow it.

"Sir?" The receptionist on the front desk craned her neck to catch his attention. "Do you have an appointment?"

Does she recognise me?

"No," he said, scanning the lobby. The front desk sat squarely in the centre of the space. Down either side were generic statues of various Roman deities. He spotted two depictions of Venus, coyly pulling a towel across her chest and letting it drape between her legs whilst looking back over her shoulder as if being watched. The back of the lobby was dominated by a huge sculpture of Atlas holding the world atop his shoulder. "No," he said again. "I don't have an appointment."

The admission didn't seem to faze the receptionist. Instead, she cocked her head and started speaking, seemingly to someone else in the building. Nick frowned. Her vacant expression meant she had a direct connection to the boards.

A simple receptionist. So it wasn't just show: the NovusPart Institute had plenty of cash.

Another woman appeared through a door in the rear of the lobby, summoned, Nick presumed, by the receptionist. She positively floated towards him. *Kooks in sheets*, was what he'd said to Chloe. But this woman was pulling it off. White robes trailed behind her and delicately offset the darker shade of her skin. The only thing that seemed out of place was her hair, which had been cut into a short, distinctly un-Roman bob.

The woman stopped short of him and waited, her expression a few notches above sombre, just enough to indicate a degree of sympathy. It wasn't clear if she recognised him. Nick swallowed, remembering why most people would visit the institute. He recalled what Habitus had so often told him: *If you're going to lie, at least stir in some truth.* "My father," he said, immediately full of regret and guilt. "He's dying."

The last word caught in his throat as the bluntness of his own words hit home. The full meaning. With his mother already gone, it wouldn't be long before he was left on his own.

The woman nodded delicately. "Perhaps we should discuss your requirements somewhere a little more private?"

43

New Pompeii

PULLUS STOPPED AT his household shrine and stared deep into the recess. The actions he performed there were usually more for show than anything else. Something the rest of his household could observe, and confirm in their minds he was a good Roman.

Not today.

Today he stumbled over his words, and felt his arm steadily shake as he offered the stale bread to the flame. He caught the eye of one of the *lares* guarding its sanctuary. The little thumb-high statue seemed to be mocking him. How many times had he woken in the night thinking about what they'd done to Whelan? How many more times would he now find himself thinking about how he'd been left to rot in that cell?

"You're back."

Pullus turned to find Galbo standing behind him. His steward looked deeply concerned, and was leaning heavily on his staff. "You don't look well. I take it you were right?"

"Yes and no."

"That was pretty much going to be my answer to your question."

"What question?"

"Popidius," Galbo explained. "He's definitely been confiscating things that used to belong to NovusPart. But he's no collector; there's nothing in his house. It goes out almost as soon as it comes in."

"He's giving it straight to Naso?"

"No."

"His slaves told you that, I presume?" Both of them knew information based on slave gossip could be surprisingly accurate, but it only went so far. "What do you think of him?" Pullus asked.

"Popidius?"

"Yes."

"He's young."

"And just finishing his first term as aedile," Pullus said. "He could look forward to many more, if he keeps his nose clean."

Galbo didn't say anything, and Pullus knew his steward couldn't quite place what was wrong in all this. Why had the aedile taken the tablet from the baker but left everything else? And why had he done so days before Calpurnia had issued her order to go through the NovusPart artefacts?

"You'll need to prepare another guest room," Pullus said, changing the subject. "Marcus is here."

Galbo's brow furrowed. "Here in town? In Pompeii?"

"Yes." Pullus allowed himself a smile. "He's gone to the theatre."

"On his own?"

"Habitus gave him a couple of bodyguards. We'll need to get more food in. Send for another pig, or something." He shook his head. "Something's not right here."

"Yes… Calpurnia doesn't normally give him free rein."

"Not Marcus. Something's not right with Popidius."

"Facts are few."

"Celer the baker told me he'd started gathering NovusPart material long before the instruction came from Calpurnia."

"He could have been lying."

Pullus shook his head, thinking about Celer's daughter. Was she dead by now?

He heard laughter from the garden. Pullus turned at the sound, and caught a look of regret on his steward's face.

"What's going on?"

"She was in your room. Going through your things."

"Taedia?"

Pullus took a last look at the *larium*, and then circled past Galbo into the *tablinum*. The garden beyond was arranged around a central colonnade, the columns wrapped in vines. Taedia stood beside one of the columns, her lips moving silently, counting leaves.

It was a relatively minor punishment, torment rather than torture. No doubt Galbo would have told her he already knew the number of leaves, and that she would face a more serious punishment if she didn't reach the same value. Her task was being made that much harder by two other slaves who were calling random numbers at her and laughing. One of them was Primus. The other was a boy with rickets whose name Pullus always struggled to remember. He was carrying a large bag of food, no doubt just back from the market.

"She was in your room," Galbo repeated.

Pullus lowered his voice into a tight whisper. "She's Calpurnia's informer."

"She's your slave."

"Do we know what she found?"

"No," the steward admitted. "When she was found she was staring at your wall oracle. The *tele*-vision. It was hard to tell where she'd been looking, except that she'd been through your clothes."

Pullus nodded. Taedia was still counting, the two slaves behind her trying to put her off. Neither of the boys had noticed him, and at once he was disappointed. All the slaves in his household had been pushed out by other masters: Galbo for being too old, the other two because of their physical deformities. They should have appreciated how lucky they were, rather than taking pleasure in another's punishment.

Galbo cleared his throat. "They're just doing as I instructed."

"But did you tell them to enjoy it so much?"

"No."

Pullus turned to leave. He wanted to get back to his room and count the letters from his father. Check the satchel. Ensure it remained buckled. Who knew what Taedia had seen? "Then have them switch roles," he said. "And see how much they like it."

Galbo nodded, but he had more to say. "There is perhaps another way we could find out what Popidius is up to."

Pullus raised his eyebrows. "And you mention this now?"

"I didn't want you to take on more dead weight at your villa," replied Galbo. He gestured at the two crippled slaves. "Or here."

"Who's Popidius selling?"

"A doorman by the name of Crixus."

Pullus thought back to his most recent visit to the aedile, but it had been months ago, and one man's slaves looked much like all the rest. "The old chap with the sty on his eyelid?"

Galbo nodded, leaning again on his staff. "He fell for a line, and let a stranger into the aedile's private quarters. I've heard they're not expecting anyone to pay much for him. He can't keep upright for any length of time."

Pullus looked again at Taedia, thinking about what she may have found. "Market day's tomorrow, isn't it?"

"Yes."

"Then tomorrow we go buy a slave."

44

Naples

"MY FATHER IS in the city sanatorium," Nick said. "I'm told he's only got a few days left."

It still wasn't clear if he'd been recognised. The NovusPart Institute woman seemed to have mastered the art of keeping her face neutral. "Then he needs to be with us, here," she said.

Nick nodded, but kept quiet. He couldn't have spoken even if he'd wanted to. His throat had clamped shut. For all he knew, his father was already dead. The message could be waiting for him when he got back to Chloe's.

"We can offer a number of options for your father's situation."

Nick nodded again. "I don't fully understand how this all works," he said.

The woman led him through the brushed-steel door and into a corridor that led into the modern section of the building beyond the classical façade. Rather than the glass and chrome presented by the outer building, Nick thought it looked like a hospital, the walls painted in institutional pastel greens and blues. And then he noticed what was missing. There were no wards, just a series of closed doors.

"NovusPart was never limited to New Pompeii," the woman said, her voice unemotional. Either the woman had trained her voice as well as her face, or she was used to repeating the same marketing spiel to a long list of potential customers. "NovusPart sought to save people from death. This institute was set up to continue that work."

"And how exactly is that achieved?" Nick asked.

In front of them, the corridor turned to the left. The woman came to a stop by a door. Nick peered at it. The shiny pale-blue surface was made up of thin horizontal strips, presumably to allow them to roll up and down. Like all the others, there was an electronic lock.

Not a hospital.

A warehouse.

"The doctors caring for your father have the technology to forecast the moment of his death within a few hours. They don't, however, have the technology to save him."

Nick felt cold sweat break out on his brow. What was she trying to tell him? "You have a NovusPart device?"

The woman didn't answer. Instead she gestured at the door. "Your father's last resting place need only be a waiting room."

"So who's in there?"

"We cannot discuss the details; that would be—"

"You brought me here for a reason."

The woman's face didn't flicker. "Thirty years," she said.

"That's how long you will wait but, for your father, the journey will be instantaneous. The NovusPart device cannot be used within that short window leading up to the present. But in thirty years, it will be able to reach back and pull our clients into the future. By that time, two things will have happened."

"Which are?"

"Firstly, the wait for new antibiotics will be over. Disease will once again be under control."

"And the second?"

"The small payment you make to us now will have earned sufficient interest to pay those in the future for completing your contract."

Nick stared at the door. A storage facility. The NovusPart Institute was selling a decades-old dream. Go to sleep in the present, and wake up like nothing has changed in the future. They'd just replaced liquid nitrogen with the NovusPart device. Except there was one big difference.

"So you don't have a NovusPart device?" he repeated.

The woman shook her head, her smile defensive. "We don't need one," she said. Her voice remained friendly and reassuring, as if she'd had this conversation dozens of times. Nick thought of the number of doors they'd passed. Tried to imagine the money that had paid for the receptionist to be linked to the boards. He wondered if this woman could control her expression sufficiently for her to access the boards without him noticing. "We know the NovusPart device functions in the future."

"Because of New Pompeii?"

"No, *Mr Houghton*. Because of you."

Nick blinked. He could hear voices in the distance, coming closer.

"You didn't think you could come here without us recognising you, did you?"

The woman's expression didn't change. Nick looked at the closed door. "So who's inside?"

"For a long time, Mary Arlen blamed you for her son's death."

The woman tapped the keypad of the lock. The door slid upwards slowly and silently. The room beyond was just a few metres square, and was empty except for a steel chair.

The approaching voices were getting louder. There were maybe a dozen or so people heading in their direction.

Nick couldn't take his eyes from the chair. "I'm not going inside."

The woman's expression finally broke. A momentary grin before her solemn expression returned. "No one's asking you to, Mr Houghton."

A group of people came around the corner, led by another Institute woman. She wore the same clothing and short bobbed hairstyle as his guide. The rest of the group were in modern black mourning attire, except for a fragile old man at the centre. He didn't seem to know what was happening. Two ladies in their mid-thirties held onto his hands and led him forward and towards the door of his cell. The rest of the group parted. Some of them looked upset. Others happy. A few relieved.

The old man went to sit in the chair, and the women

leading him backed away. The door slid back down into position. Just as he disappeared from view, he gave a cheery wave, his mouth opening and closing silently, as if he was speaking only to himself.

The lock started to blink. The group let out a sigh, then were silently led away by their guide. All so fast, and so simple.

"This is not a place for mourning," said the woman to Nick. "Or for being joyful. You may never see your father again, but you can be assured that your father will be saved."

Nick felt his cheeks burning. "There was no food in there. No water."

"He won't need any."

"So open the door. Let's check."

"The doors cannot be opened once the unit is sealed."

"Why not?"

"To guarantee the transportation."

Nick strained to hear anything from inside the cell. Because, whether he knew it or not, the confused old man had suddenly become a cat. A very famous one. And there didn't seem to be any way of opening his box.

"I think I've seen enough," he said.

"We have something else to show you."

"I'm not interested. My father's not coming here."

The woman didn't seem to hear him. "Mary Arlen blamed you for her son's death," she repeated. "Until a few days before her own transportation."

Nick froze. The blog hadn't been updated in months. Had he walked past Mary Arlen's own tomb? "What changed?"

* * *

Nick looked at the tiny figure, painted onto a small rectangle of plaster no bigger than a shoebox, and let out an audible gasp.

"You see why she changed her mind?"

Nick didn't respond. Pompeii had first been excavated by the Bourbon kings. Although more pillage than archaeology, their efforts did at least mean the best mosaics and frescos were now safely preserved. But that didn't mean all their finds were in museums. The Bourbon collections themselves had eventually been broken up, sequestered by the state, stolen by organised crime. But none of that had happened to the fresco sitting in front of him.

The figure was of a man, maybe even a *lares*. At regular intervals someone had chipped inch-wide lacerations up and down his arms, legs and the trunk of his body. The damage had probably been inflicted by a chisel. For the first time in years, Nick felt a pang of academic anger. The double-edged sword of eighteenth-century archaeology was right in front of him. Without the gouges, the fresco would have been a fine figure if not an especially noteworthy one. Certainly not the best example. So the Bourbons had damaged it deliberately; if it wasn't worthy of addition to their collections, then they'd made sure no one else could have it either. That's how it worked in the 1700s. Preserve the best, destroy the rest.

Nick glanced up at the Institute woman. After guiding him back out of the warehouse facility, she'd brought him to a small antechamber off the lobby. At least he was near the exit. He'd be on his way back to Chloe and the Bureau soon enough.

"Yes," he said, finally. "I see why she changed her mind."

He looked back at the figure. The fact it was a fairly ordinary illustration wasn't why the Bourbons hadn't added it to their collection. They'd also been beaten to the punch. Despite probably sifting it out of the earth themselves, someone had written something very modern directly underneath the man's feet. Something modern – or entirely futuristic if seen from the point of view of the 1700s.

Nick Houghton, NovusPart

His name alongside that of NovusPart. Maybe the same message that had been scratched into the *Gabinetto*'s fresco and the graffiti from the bakery. But still he couldn't read it all, there were too many words missing.

"Where did you find it?"

"The fresco was part of a private collection, taken from the Villa Maritima. The Institute acquired it for a knocked down price." She smiled. "Given the damage."

Nick didn't say anything. He wasn't familiar with the villa to which she referred but wasn't going to admit it.

"Mary Arlen lived thinking you destroyed her son's legacy. But she died believing you would restore it."

Nick grunted. "NovusPart is dead."

"Its technology lives on in New Pompeii."

It was time to take a chance. This might be the reason he

was here. "Did Mary say anything about having any of her son's research? His data files?"

The woman studied him for a moment, her neutral expression finally slipping. "All those were taken. As well you know, Nick Houghton."

"Who took them?"

"The Bureau of Roman Affairs."

45

New Pompeii

SINCE PULLUS'S LAST visit, the slave market had moved from its traditional location to a small corner near the covered theatre. For anyone who could still remember how the market had once operated – before the eruption and the NovusPart transportations – the meagre collection of human tools couldn't be mistaken for anything other than dregs. Not the prime cuts.

At first, Pullus kept his distance. He waited with Galbo and Taedia beside a water fountain, and hoped to spot Crixus without getting too close to the wares. After all, they'd probably all want to work in his household, given his reputation for gentle treatment. "I can't see him."

"They're not exactly going to put an old man front of shop," replied Galbo. "Do you want me to go in and find him?"

Pullus shook his head, studying the faces of those waiting to be sold. There were about twenty of them, mostly men, in a variety of ages and builds. A few older women were scattered amongst them. He frowned. At this distance, it was difficult to tell who was leading the sales. The owner would no doubt make himself known once they started checking over the merchandise.

He sighed, and started to walk towards the market. It was all so different to his first visit. Hadn't there been something exciting about picking the people who'd form his household staff? *Perhaps*. And yet both Galbo and Habitus had been fortunate acquisitions. None of the others that day had really stuck out in his mind, just the advice he'd received from Calpurnia. *Get a good balance of men and women, and not too many from the same pot.*

She'd been wrong of course. But Calpurnia had based her advice on an economy that had already been blown apart by a volcano. In New Pompeii, the smart money had chosen to invest in female slaves: if their proto-Roman society wasn't going to get fresh slaves from war, then they were going to have to breed them.

As Pullus, Galbo and Taedia approached, one of the men rose to his feet. The rest of the slaves followed his lead, but with the lethargy and enthusiasm of those knowing they were unlikely to be sold. They'd probably been passed over many times.

"We're looking for an experienced porter," Galbo said. Pullus nodded, as if to confirm, but was more than happy for his steward to take the lead. The man in charge of the slave market didn't respond; instead, he pointed at Taedia.

"How much?" he asked.

"She's not for sale," replied Galbo.

"She bleeds though, yes?"

"We're looking for a porter," Pullus said, interrupting. "Do you have anybody suitable? Anyone with experience?"

The man cleared his throat, and swept a bit of crusted food from his tunic. Then he pointed at the nearest woman in his collection. Presumably someone who'd recently lost her fertility, and therefore much of her value. She didn't look particularly healthy. "She could do door work, easy. Knows how to follow an instruction. Speaks some Latin, doesn't eat much."

"We're looking for a man."

The slaver shrugged, and swung his arm in a wide loop to include all of his stock in the conversation. "Feel free to have a look. Most of these are farm hands though. Bit rough even for you, Decimus Horatius Pullus."

The mention of his name had an immediate effect on those waiting to be sold. The lethargy seemed to melt from them. Now they held themselves straight – or as straight as some of their broken bodies would allow. Pullus ignored them, and stuck close to Taedia. He waited as Galbo hobbled back and forth, sometimes pausing at a man about the right age, but none had a sty. Pullus was sure he didn't recognise any of them.

"So is this where I'll end up?" Taedia whispered. "On a market where no one will want me?"

"That's not how I do things."

"But it's how others do things, isn't it?"

"Yes."

Taedia hesitated. "Is it how Calpurnia does things?"

"I don't know… look, things are better than they were."

"How so?"

"You're more valuable," Pullus replied. He frowned, feeling himself lured into the debate he'd had many times when visiting Naples. "When I first came here, I saw a slave thrown from a balcony. His master then rushed downstairs just to break the limbs that hadn't broken in the fall. And all because he'd been served cold cuts rather than a hot meal. I can't remember the last time anyone told me a story like that. Slaves are too valuable now."

Taedia didn't say anything, and Pullus immediately regretted his comment. The lack of a fresh supply of new slaves may have prompted some changes, but all too much had remained the same. And as Galbo sometimes went out of his way to demonstrate, there were always those who could remember the old ways of doing things.

"Maybe people know you don't like hearing those sorts of stories," said Taedia, quietly. "And choose not to tell you…"

Pullus ignored her. Perhaps it was true, but he doubted it. The slave owners of New Pompeii had needed to get used to their new situation quickly. No war or access to the outside world meant fewer slaves. And fewer slaves meant they'd become more valuable. Supply and demand. Those who'd adjusted quickly were now significantly richer than those who hadn't. Men such as Naso and Popidius, for instance.

"Nick Houghton!"

The shout had come from the back of the group, from a

thin man with a mop of curly brown hair. "*Por favor, necesito tu ayuda!*"

Spanish?

Pullus didn't speak it, but he knew enough to recognise it. The speaker's feet had been dabbed in white chalk. The mark of a fresh slave. Something Pompeii hadn't seen for a long time.

"Nick! Nick Houghton! *¡Ayúdame!*"

Pullus made his way across to the man, the slave owner and Taedia following him. "What's your name?" he said, in the only way he knew to communicate with a Spaniard. In English, slowly and loudly.

The man looked back at him, his expression desperate. Like his chance had finally arrived and he didn't know what to do with it. "*No hablo Inglés!*"

"Decent specimen, this one," said the slaver, stepping ahead so he could take up a position beside the Spaniard. The owner waved what looked like a pair of spectacles before slipping them again out of sight. Pullus noticed that both lenses were cracked. "He don't see too well, seems to need these."

"Where are you from?" Pullus asked. The Spaniard just looked confused.

The slaver continued with his sales pitch. "More of a household slave than someone for your estates," he said. "Can't find any cocksucker who understands him though. Feel free to examine his testicles."

"And where did you get him?"

The slaver shrugged. "Swapped him for three others,

didn't I? Thought it was a good deal at the time."

"And now?"

"As I said, no cocksucker knows what he's saying. If you're willing to invest a bit of stick, then no doubt he'd be okay."

Pullus looked back at the Spaniard. "He can't see."

"Then make him work at night!"

"*Nick Houghton! ¡Ayúdame! ¡Ayúdame!*"

Pullus turned away. The Spaniard had probably broken through the biological containment, just like those being held in the amphitheatre pens. He should count himself lucky he'd been picked up by a slaver, rather than Habitus. And yet his desperate cries had excited the others. The nearest slave was telling him to which number he could count; another that she could be put to work in his kitchen. He ignored them all. "You have anything squirrelled away, or is this it?" he asked.

"If you're looking for an Egyptian boy, you're about ten years too late."

Pullus felt a new degree of distaste for the man. Some emperors had once paid a small fortune for a pretty Egyptian boy, and there were rumours some were still being bred. How long that market would last would remain to be seen. He guessed it would probably depend on the genders of the babies being produced.

"*¡Ayúdame! Soy un periodista! ¡Ayúdame!*"

The Spaniard again. Pullus searched for Galbo. His steward had finished his sweep, but had found nothing. Crixus wasn't here.

"I'll take *him*," Pullus said, pointing at the Spaniard. As soon as the opportunity arose, he'd be dispatched back to the outside world. Galbo examined the new recruit as if his master were mad. "Send him to my villa," Pullus continued. "I think it's probably best we keep him somewhere that Habitus won't find him."

4 6

Naples

"The people of New Pompeii have all the protections offered to them by a world shocked at their arrival. And yet, whilst they seek all the rights of minority cultures in the modern world, we have not asked them to pay the price of modernity. When are we going to ask them to give up their slaves?"

Professor Hayden,
Lead Archaeologist, Herculaneum
World Archaeology News Message Board

SMOKE. A THIN line of smoke was rising from the top of Vesuvius, clearly visible against the otherwise crisp blue early winter sky. Nick stumbled, almost missing the last few steps as he hurried away from the NovusPart Institute. He recovered his footing and ran to Chloe's vehicle, still idling at the kerb.

Chloe had shifted over to the passenger seat, probably to get a better view of the mountain. Nick tapped on the window, and then again. Louder. Only on the third attempt did she turn to face him and unlock the door.

"When did it start?" he asked.

"Just after you'd gone inside."

Nick stared at Vesuvius. He'd been up and down the mountain a number of times. He'd found the trick was never to be too proud to take one of the wooden walking sticks from the men renting them out near the bottom. To lean on it, if necessary, like his steward, Galbo. Because what most people thought of as "the bottom" of the mountain wasn't anything of the sort, but rather the very last part of the modern cone. By the time you'd reached it, you were already inside the caldera of the ancient volcano. And only when you recognised those surrounding jagged cliffs as being the teeth of a much larger beast could you truly appreciate how much material had buried Pompeii.

"It's erupted before, you know," Chloe said.

Nick nodded. The smoke was still rising, gaining height, not yet thin enough to be spread by the wind. "Worse than this," he said, distantly.

Chloe pushed him gently on the shoulder, smiling. "You know what I mean." She looked past him to the NovusPart Institute. "So what did you find in there?"

Nick Houghton. Novus Particles. "Nothing," he said, his mind tracking back to the mountain. He suddenly felt as though he was at the bottom of the tourist trail with only an ashen track ahead of him. And there seemed to be only one direction of travel.

NovusPart.

Nick Houghton.

Three messages. Two in Pompeii, one at the Villa Maritima, wherever that was. Two found recently. One found several hundred years ago, but only read by him today.

Two in Pompeii, he thought again. But the last had come from the Villa Maritima. So if the messages had been left by the same person, they must have taken at least one trip outside Pompeii. "What do you know about the Villa Maritima?"

"I thought you were the Roman expert here?"

Nick didn't rise to the bait. "Please," he said. "I need to know where to find it."

"Okay." Chloe's eyes went vacant as she searched the boards. "Okay," she said again. "So references to the villa are pretty sparse."

"Do you have a location?"

"Yes. About halfway between Pompeii and Herculaneum."

"Then let's go."

"We can't."

"We've still got time. The Bureau…"

"The ruins were bombed during the Second World War," said Chloe. "The Villa Maritima no longer exists."

Shit. Nick turned away and rubbed at the sides of his head; for the first time in ages, he felt a migraine threaten.

Chloe suddenly tensed. "Fabio just pinged me," she said. "He wants to know where you are."

The tension in Nick's temples magnified. He felt his sandals slipping on the ashen track. Staring at the classical façade of the Institute, he allowed himself to think about his father, guilt rising in his belly. "How far is it to the sanatorium?"

"Fabio wants me to bring you to the Bureau," Chloe said. "I can't ignore him."

"I want to see my dad," Nick said. "I think it's time to say goodbye."

The gates to the erstwhile business park were closed. Guiding her vehicle in a tight arc, Chloe parked directly in front of them. Nick stared at the small sentry post next to the pedestrian entrance. Beside him, Chloe put her hand on his arm.

Fabio was already standing just inside the gates, his normally jovial demeanour completely absent. Instead, his face was set in a deep frown, as if he'd been waiting there for hours. Somehow, Nick guessed a light-hearted remark wasn't going to help.

"I had to tell him where we were going," Chloe whispered. "And where we'd been." She paused. "This job, Nick. I can't afford to lose this job."

Nick pulled his arm free. He thought she'd zoned out during the trip but hadn't picked up on the fact she'd been using the boards. But, then again, with the vehicle taking care of most of the driving, there was little else that required her full attention. "I'll sort it," he said, getting out of the vehicle. "Stay here and wait for me."

As he approached, the security guard didn't appear from his post, but Fabio's bulk meant he had to stop at the pedestrian gate anyway. "The NovusPart Institute?" the Italian asked.

"It wasn't Chloe's fault," Nick said. He tried his best to look apologetic. "I asked her to take me."

"She should have said no."

"But I didn't let her."

Fabio grunted. "So why did you go?"

"I was curious."

"They're a bunch of shysters."

Nick nodded, not sure how far to dig. Not sure if Fabio knew about the Villa Maritima fresco. "Why didn't you tell me about it?"

"What's there to say? They're just crooks selling tickets to the afterlife."

"Headed up by Mary Arlen."

"Which means they can sell their particular tickets at a premium price. *Fanculo*, Nick! And now they can say you're a patron! It'll be on their adverts by tomorrow!"

"I wanted to see how it worked."

"Well it doesn't," Fabio shot back. "Do you know how many people they've accepted through their doors? Do you know how many units they have inside? Because I can tell you, for the amount of money they charge, I'd want a single room, that's for sure."

Nick was confused. The room he'd seen was empty. The door closed and locked in front of him with only a single occupant. "I'm not sure I understand."

"They've got permits for an industrial grade oven in there," said Fabio. "Do you need me to tell you the rest? Or can you work out how long someone would actually survive in a room without water before they re-use the same room?"

From just inside the business park, there was some activity at the building nearest to the gates. A bed was being wheeled out, turned, and taken deeper into the site. The group of nurses and doctors surrounding the bed were all wearing protective clothing.

"I'm here to see my father," said Nick.

"Visiting hours don't start for another twenty minutes."

"We can talk on the way," Nick said. Visiting hours hadn't applied to him before.

Fabio didn't move, his gaze on something beyond the entrance. Nick turned to see another car drawing up to the gates. Waldren got out and walked towards them.

"Shit." Nick turned back to Fabio. "Why's he here? Because I went to the NovusPart Institute?"

"Fuck that. Because of the latest dig finding at the bakery."

So Fabio didn't know about the Villa Maritima. Not yet, anyway. But, then again, if the Bureau had forced the Institute to give up Arlen's research, why would Arlen's mother have voluntarily revealed what else she knew?

"Despite what you promised," continued Fabio, "your Roman friends are pissing about with the timeline." He nodded at Waldren, who had passed through the pedestrian access and joined them.

"What do you think the full message says?" Waldren asked, not bothering with social niceties. He coughed hoarsely.

"I don't know," said Nick. "But I take it you've already come to a conclusion?"

Waldren grunted, then moved his shoulder so it was positioned fractionally in front of Fabio. Cutting the Italian out. "I think your influence out in New Pompeii is on the wane," he said.

"And you base that on a fresco, and a bit of graffiti?"

"You told us the NovusPart device was active and not being used. Now we find someone is doing a bit of tinkering with the timeline. Perhaps even trying to restore *Pax Romana*."

Nick felt his eyes narrow. "You're worried about the Smale theorem?"

Waldren didn't respond. Fabio saw his opportunity to cut in. "A lot of people are, Nick."

"Professor Smale thought the main point of schism was the botched succession of Septimius Severus," Nick said. "That if Geta had survived, the Roman Empire could have lasted a lot longer. He saw it as a defining moment. A breaking point, if you will."

"There's a lot of people who agree with him," Fabio said.

"I like it too," replied Nick. "But there are also multiple other reasons why the Empire failed. There's no way to extend its life by interfering with a single moment."

"It doesn't matter what you think," said Waldren. "It only matters what Calpurnia believes. Does she, for instance, *believe* she could restore the Empire with a single interaction?"

Nick swallowed. It had once been a frequent topic of conversation between the two of them. He'd transcribed several academic tomes so she could study their main arguments. But every year seemed to carry with it a new theory on why Rome had fallen. And Whelan had made certain she'd understood the dangers. Kept on screaming it, even when the end came. "She couldn't succeed," he said. "The risk would be too great."

"Success is not required. She could destroy the timeline just through experimentation." Waldren paused again. He coughed again. Nick wondered if it was due to smoking or one of the new drug-resistant lung infections he'd heard about. "So tell us, Nick. Are you still at the centre of things out there?"

Nick hesitated. Officially, he was still their ambassador. But he realised the question was loaded. Waldren already knew the answer, as did Fabio. He felt something inside him deflate. "No," he said, quietly.

"When was the last time you spoke privately with Calpurnia?"

"Some weeks."

"Weeks?"

"Okay." Nick took a deep breath. "Okay. Several months." Fabio and Waldren exchanged a glance. "She spends more and more time on her own," he admitted. "With just Marcus and a few household slaves for company."

"The NovusPart device is with her?"

"Yes."

Waldren cocked his head to the side and coughed hard, then wiped his lips. "And is she using it?"

Nick looked towards the sanatorium. His father was dying, and for the first time in a long time, he wanted to be at his bedside. "No."

"Evidence indicates otherwise."

Nick knew where things were heading. "I want to see my father," he said.

"I'm afraid that's not possible," Fabio said.

Nick felt a weight push down on his chest. "He's already dead, isn't he?"

"No. I'm sorry, Nick. But he gave clear instructions that when he reached a certain stage... To be frank, he doesn't want to see you."

Despite their bitter relationship, Nick almost physically bent, shock driving through his system. Fabio put a hand on his shoulder.

"Come on, let's talk about this somewhere quieter."

Fabio led them to the sentry hut by the gates. He spoke quietly to the security guard inside – an old man who looked like he'd need the sanatorium himself before long – who rose and left his post, walking over to where Chloe still stood by her vehicle. Fabio shut the door behind him.

Waldren seemed irritated by the interruption. "Haven't you figured it out, Nick?"

"What?" Nick managed.

"You're not Roman," Waldren answered. "You're not Decimus Horatius Pullus. You're the loose end they didn't quite tie off. And now they don't know what to do with you. Sure, they send you on the odd errand to Naples as their ambassador, but most of what they need is supplied by the convoys. Even the fish for their stinking garum."

Nick tried to turn away but Fabio held his shoulder. His voice remained kind, which was something. "We need your help, Nick."

"What do you want?"

"First let me ask you a question," Waldren said, taking back control. He coughed again. Nick was starting to find it irritating. "You're familiar, I suppose, with the work of Oppenheimer?" Nick nodded. "After he saw the results of the first atomic bomb, he said he'd become the destroyer of worlds," Waldren continued. "I think you have a sense of what he meant, don't you?"

"Yes."

"But what if Dr Oppenheimer had been given the opportunity to put the bomb back in the bottle? Do you think he would?"

Nick shrugged. "It's a moot point. Calpurnia keeps the NovusPart device under armed guard at her villa…"

"You could get to it."

"No," Nick said, shaking his head. "You've already tried, and failed, to take it from her."

Both Waldren and Fabio tensed. Neither spoke.

"NovusPart used to take people from the timeline," Nick said. "People with futures. Dangerous stuff, but they did it. They reached back in time, and pulled them out of existence. Basically put: not all the children in New Pompeii are Roman born."

"That was only ever rumoured," Waldren replied. "Why didn't you tell us this before?"

Nick hesitated. The shock of not being able to see his father again was beginning to dissipate. His brain switched back and forth between New Pompeii and Naples, trying to balance the two.

"Well?"

Nick didn't answer at first. For the time being, it really didn't matter that the NovusPart device didn't actually work. It didn't matter that the outside world's spies had all been left to die in the amphitheatre's holding pens rather than being transported. He just needed to buy himself some time. Above all, he needed to maintain the illusion. He needed to make sure Waldren and Fabio continued to think the NovusPart device worked. "I told you," he said. "Calpurnia has conducted some experiments."

"Fucking hell, Nick!"

Nick took in a deep breath. "You see, removing people from the timeline who've caused you an injury means they're no longer there to cause you a problem. It seems God solves this conundrum by spitting out the paradox, and carrying on regardless."

Waldren mulled this over. "We still need to know, Nick: are you with *us*, or are you with *them*? Does it keep you awake at night? The thought Calpurnia might just decide to rip up all of human history?"

"I've lived there for fifteen years."

"That's not what I asked."

"There's a lot of people here in Naples who'd prefer it if New Pompeii was simply wiped off the map," Nick said.

He turned to Fabio. "The people who blame us for the new diseases. The religious zealots who are scared shitless that our small group of Christians might not agree with what's been made of their religion."

"Your land is protected by a UN treaty," Fabio reminded him.

"Which was only signed because the NovusPart device keeps you awake at night and also keeps New Pompeii safe."

Waldren coughed, then spoke hoarsely. "So it is *Decimus Horatius Pullus*, isn't it, Nick?"

"I'm not going to betray New Pompeii."

"We can offer you guarantees," Fabio said, his tone urgent. "About the safety of the town and its inhabitants."

"Damn it, Nick," Waldren shouted. "How long will it be before Calpurnia puts you in a cell? Before you lose your chance to act? Just like you lost the chance to say goodbye to your father?"

Nick flinched and only just stopped himself lashing out at the man. Instead, he breathed deeply, his fists clenching. He flinched again at a sharp knock on the door to the sentry post. A man in a nurse's uniform stood outside with Chloe and the security guard. He wasn't wearing protective clothing. Fabio swung open the door and beckoned him in.

"Nick Houghton?" The nurse sounded uncertain.

"Yes."

The man handed over an envelope. "Your father left instructions for us to give you this once his condition reached a certain… severity."

Nick looked down. The handwriting was large, and obviously applied by a shaking hand. Still, it was clearly his father's.

"Wait," said Fabio. "Did Mr Houghton senior lick the envelope?"

The nurse shook his head as he left. "It's contaminant free."

Nick folded the letter and put it into his pocket. He'd read it later. He'd seen enough of them. Or maybe he'd just burn this one.

"We want you to think about what we've asked you," Waldren said.

Nick didn't reply.

"We can talk about the details," Waldren continued. "But with what you know, I'm sure we can come up with a workable plan. Something that can save us all."

47

New Pompeii

PULLUS SHIVERED. THE evening was cool. It never truly got cold in New Pompeii, but for the first time this season he felt like he could do with a cloak. In the summer, his garden was full of roses, violets and cypress. Now it smelt simply of wet soil. He swept his hand across the leaves of a pomegranate tree, then took hold of one of its reddish fruits, but didn't pick it. Instead he pulled on it slightly, and let the branch resist.

The slave had spoken Spanish. Pullus could speak some basic Italian, as well as both formal and street Latin. But Spanish had always eluded him. Similar to Italian but infused by invaders who'd brought their own culture, and therefore much like English, a language with its own set of inconsistent rules and etymology. What was a Spaniard doing in New Pompeii?

There'd been a few who'd tested their luck in the early days of New Pompeii. Some had managed to get through the fences erected by NovusPart, and subsequently maintained by Calpurnia's father, Barbatus. But once in, they never left.

No one out. Just the men who staffed the convoys, who then went into their own quarantine. Everyone understood that. And if someone had tried their luck, then they'd tried it too far. It wouldn't be long before an outsider caught the shivers anyway and had to roll the dice to see if they were able to pull through, just like so many others. Just like him.

The man who couldn't die.

Someone cleared their throat behind him in the manner only the servile seemed to adopt. Pullus reached out and picked the pomegranate.

"Some masters have been known to beat a man to death for interrupting their thoughts."

"Some masters do not have your wisdom."

Pullus turned and tossed the fruit to Galbo. They were alone. Marcus and the rest of the household must be inside. He wondered what the boy was up to, but pushed away the thought. For the moment, others living under his roof caused him more concern. "Taedia?"

"I'm keeping her out of mischief."

Pullus nodded. "I counted my father's letters," he said. "None were missing."

"Failure is no excuse," Galbo replied evenly. "My punishment of her was justified. Slaves are kept in order by managing their food, and careful use of the whip. You can't have one without the other." He paused for a moment. "Was there anything else in the room? Anything else she may have been looking for?"

Pullus shook his head, thinking about the satchel and its contents. "No."

"You're sure?"

"I thought *she* was Calpurnia's spy, not you."

"She's either your slave, or she's not." Galbo kept his voice measured. "And if she's yours, you should treat her like the rest of us."

"Even you?"

"She can't be seen to avoid both chores and punishments. You'll just get gripes from the others. I had to threaten Primus this morning to make him sweep the front step."

Pullus stared towards the house. There was some movement in the *tablinum*. "And what would you have me do?"

"Take her back to your room. Let her know you're her master." Pullus knew other slave owners wouldn't have waited to get such advice from their steward. "She's young, she's pretty," Galbo continued. "And her allegiance to Calpurnia needs breaking. So put a baby in her belly, and leave the rest to nature."

"I'm not sure that's wise."

"A good workman oils his tools. All Roman masters dominate their slaves. And in this case, you'll get Taedia's loyalty, and an investment for the future."

Pullus mulled this over. "And your wife, Galbo? How would you respond if I took my privileges with her, I wonder?"

"I doubt she'd be to your taste," Galbo replied, the merest hint of anger in his eyes. "But we're all yours, Pullus. Maybe someday, you'll start to realise that."

Pullus didn't answer. Instead, he looked back to the *tablinum*. Marcus came into view, then disappeared again. The boy was laughing at something. "Have you heard anything more about Popidius?"

Galbo shook his head, suddenly grim. "Not about what he's up to, no. But we were beaten to the slave market. Word is that Crixus is now working on the convoys."

Pullus didn't attempt to hide his incredulity. "Doing what?!"

"Lifting boxes. Moving crates."

"He's surely too old for that."

"He's been sent there to die."

Marcus came back into view through the colonnade, pulling Taedia with him. She followed stiffly, looking uncomfortable. She was clearly not interested in whatever it was the boy was showing her. Pullus watched for a few moments, then realised Galbo's normally stoic features had developed a distinct colour.

"What is it?"

"Nothing."

"Tell me, Galbo."

Galbo hesitated. "I hear rumours about him," he said. "From Calpurnia's slaves, when they come into town to run errands. People in town are beginning to talk."

"What sort of rumours?" Nick asked. Near the house, Marcus continued to tease Taedia. "You mean slave gossip—" Nick stopped himself. He couldn't rely on Galbo's network one moment, and dismiss it the next. "Tell me."

"It's best to manage slaves with *careful* use of the whip,"

Galbo said. "The word from Calpurnia's villa is that the boy has something of an imaginative streak when it comes to both entertainment and punishment."

"I need facts, Galbo."

"You've heard the stories about Emperor Tiberius on his island at Capri? He used to make his slave boys swim beneath his legs, and tickle his genitals. The boy tried to do the same in Calpurnia's swimming pool. One of them drowned."

Pullus glanced at the boy, a little tremor stirring in his belly. Marcus had always been keen on his Suetonius. Always keen to report back to him each gory detail he'd found from the first family of Caesars. And now Pullus realised something else: Marcus and Taedia had, in a way, been brought up together. She'd never left Calpurnia's villa, that's what she'd told him. A female slave, just a few years older than her mistress's son. Someone perhaps to act as a playmate, an older sister. Someone to look after him, until he matured sufficiently that she'd simply become his slave.

Pullus cleared his throat. He needed to separate them. "Marcus!"

The boy turned, and dropped Taedia's hand. "Yes?"

"I hope you aren't getting in the way of our dinner?"

"It would be best to get him back to his mother," Galbo whispered. "Before he takes your prize."

48

"**A**ND YOU EAT like this every night?"

Pullus glanced up from the small pewter dish, and found Marcus staring at him from the couch opposite. The boy looked irritated. Bored. Even a little disappointed. Perhaps he'd been expecting grander fare for his first night away from his mother. But Pullus had long since adopted a simple diet. "There's plenty of food, Marcus."

"But just the two of us," replied the boy, exasperated. He took a couple of small figs. "You could have invited the *duumvir*," he said. "An aedile… as long as it was the interesting one. By Jupiter, even a few members of the *Ordo* would have done! I mean, how hard is it to round up a few people? A mime? A dancing girl? Someone to juggle whilst we ate?"

Pullus raised an eyebrow, resting on one elbow as the length of his body reclined uncomfortably on the couch. He'd not considered organising anything special. Perhaps he should have done. "The healthy stomach should respect all food," he said.

Marcus frowned. "A quote from Seneca, I suppose?"

"No. Emperor…"

"…Aurelius! Aurelius! A man who my mother doesn't even acknowledge as being a true emperor!"

Pullus smiled. He drank some of his wine and felt its effects slowly percolate up into his brain. It wasn't his first glass, and wouldn't be his last. "Well, as she's not here, I guess I can tell you a little about him."

"Don't bother. There were ten emperors. The men who followed – and pissed away our empire – deserve to be forgotten."

"And who's speaking now?" asked Pullus. "You? Or your mother?"

The boy leant back on his elbow. He drained his goblet and held it out for a refill. There were two slaves serving the food and drink, Primus, and Galbo's wife, a short waif called Holconia. "I accept you have a point with Commodus," he said. "He used to fight as a gladiator, executing criminals and clubbing cripples to death."

"There were a number of great and good emperors after the cataclysm," Pullus said, trying to be patient. "You should read about Hadrian, Trajan…"

Marcus reached for some shredded pork. "And? Oh, that's right. You always run out of names pretty quickly after those two, don't you?" The boy chuckled. "By the gods, Pullus! It will soon be the Saturnalia! I've often wondered, does my teacher suddenly throw off his stoic mask, and throw himself into the festivities?"

Pullus flushed. Normally, he spent the festival at his villa where he could hide away. That would be more difficult here at the House of McMahon. He'd be forced to take part, if Marcus was still here. *Shit.* "I'll no doubt be serving a glass of wine and a good feast," he said.

Marcus snorted. He held out his goblet again and looked directly at Holconia. "You should make your master stand on one of these couches and sing to you all naked!"

"Marcus…"

"Slap his buttocks, and… fucking hell!"

Primus, who had been refilling Marcus's goblet, jerked the wine jug away, his crippled arm wobbling. Holconia rushed to dab at Marcus's sleeve. It was just a minor slip – or an unfortunately timed giggle at his master's expense – but it would no doubt leave a deep stain on the off-white linen.

"You fucking cretin!"

"Marcus!"

The boy took a deep breath, his face an angry shade of red. But then he grinned. "Another slave with a weak wrist! The irony! Didn't Emperor Hadrian remove a slave's eye for something like this? My grandfather certainly took the sight of that idiot who maimed Whelan! And you described him as a good emperor, no? Hadrian, and my grandfather?"

Pullus let out a heavy sigh. Now wasn't the time for juvenile arguments. "Let's just finish eating…"

The boy glared at Primus. Pullus motioned for the slave to refill his own goblet and took a large gulp. As the spices hit him, he wondered if he'd already drunk too much.

"Some people at the theatre were laughing at me," Marcus said, suddenly quiet. Still glaring at Primus.

Pullus raised an eyebrow. Marcus hardly ever came to town. "*At* you?"

"They didn't know I was sitting behind them," Marcus replied. "But they were definitely talking about me: 'Calpurnia and her son'. I was so close I could have ordered my men to kill them."

"And what were they saying?"

"That you were my father."

Pullus flicked his eyes towards his two slaves. Neither met his eye. "Well, it's not true," he said.

"You were in love with my mother once though, yes?"

Pullus gave a smile which he hoped was regretful. "You shouldn't read too much into what you read scribbled on toilet walls."

"That's not an answer."

"I care for your mother a great deal," said Pullus, choosing his words carefully. "But I'm not in love with her, and I never have been. And I'm not your father. Is that good enough for you?"

Marcus shrugged. "I don't understand why you fell out…"

"It's complicated."

"She used to talk about you all the time. Now you're just my teacher." He motioned towards Primus. "Some servant, like him. An irritation she just can't be without."

"Huh."

"The man you killed today," Marcus said. "Whelan?"

Pullus suddenly heard Whelan's last gulps before he'd pinched his nose shut. Somehow, it was worse than all the screaming and grinding of bone. He took another mouthful of wine.

"Habitus says it's hard to kill your first man, but that it gets easier and easier. You get to the point where it's just like squashing ants. He once knew someone—"

Pullus grunted. "Habitus is a man of rare knowledge."

"It didn't seem hard for you."

"You're mistaken."

Marcus shrugged. "Some people say my mother can't be killed," he said. "That she's just like you."

Pullus put down his goblet, realising he'd had enough for one night.

"So if my mother and father are both immortal," Marcus whispered, "what does that make me?"

Pullus lay on his couch long after Marcus had retired to his room. He didn't feel able to get up and make his way to his more comfortable bed. He stared out across the atrium. The light outside was failing, and the myriad of oil lamps now lit around and within the *triclinium* were not quite powerful enough to push away the darkness.

Over his left shoulder, he sensed the occasional bob of movement. Primus stood ready to top up his wine. The boy probably wanted to go to bed himself, to rest and prepare for the chores which would no doubt be set for him tomorrow. But he couldn't leave, because his master was still awake.

Pullus reached forward and took another gulp of wine.

All he found in his goblet though were thoughts of Whelan, and what he'd been whispering before he died.

"Pullus?"

Pullus turned his head quickly, but then had to wait for the rest of the room to swim round to meet him. He recognised the voice, though it took a moment or two for his brain to register. He blinked and brought Taedia into focus, and watched as she slipped out of her clothes.

Pullus frowned. "Did Galbo tell you to do this?"

"No."

"Habitus, then?" Pullus twisted on his elbow and turned away. He reached out for his goblet to be refilled, but the vessel slipped from his hand, cracking on the floor. Primus scurried to retrieve it. A weak wrist. Pullus giggled, then realised Taedia was already on top of him, her thighs on either side of his hips, as she searched under his tunic.

"Stop…"

Taedia ignored him. She continued to work with her hands until she was ready to push down on him. He noticed she had a long, pale red scar running across the lower curve of her stomach. "You've had other female slaves?" she asked.

Pullus shook his head, suddenly feeling its weight on his shoulders. He let it loll back on the couch. "I haven't slept with them," he said. His tongue was heavy in his mouth, but he was just about able to hold a picture of Taedia's swaying body. "I haven't slept with any of them," he said again, this time trying to push her away.

She didn't let him. She kept on going until he climaxed. And as the room finally span away and the alcohol took him with it, she pulled his head forward and into her chest. "I've found the satchel," she whispered. "I've found the papers."

49

Naples

"We sometimes refer to Calpurnia as the Empress of Time. It is meant as a joke. But we mustn't forget what Ancient Rome so regularly produced: tyrants sent mad once they were wrapped in the purple dye. Tiberius, Caligula, Nero, Domitian, Commodus, Caracalla, Elagabalus. What if Calpurnia – or maybe even her son – goes the same way? Will Nick Houghton be able to stop them?"

Bureau of Roman Affairs
& NATO liaison meeting notes

"THANK YOU."

Nick didn't acknowledge Chloe's gratitude. He'd spent the last two days since his confrontation with Fabio and Waldren stewing at Chloe's apartment. Today he and Chloe had been summoned to the Bureau, but not to continue the discussion about Calpurnia and the NovusPart device. Instead, he'd found Waldren absent and it had only been Chloe's position on the agenda. Fabio hadn't wasted much time before telling her that she still had a job. *Just*.

"I mean it, Nick," Chloe said again. "Thank you."

"I was hardly going to allow them to sack you," he said.

"For a second there, I didn't think they were going to give you the choice."

"Come on, let's go." The Bureau's stale air and fake coffee had polluted his senses and he wanted to leave, to head back to Chloe's apartment and fire up his old computer again. He'd tried to put the time he'd been forced to spend on his own at Chloe's to good use. Aside from watching the steadily thickening ash streaming up from Vesuvius and visiting an optician, he'd managed to catch up on months and months of research papers, to remove some of the academic rust that had built up on his mental gears. It had been difficult at first, but some of the more interesting finds from the digs at Pompeii had finally got them turning. He'd studied each of the new frescos and mosaics, trying to find anything odd about them. Anything out of place. Once or twice he'd thought he'd seen something. Just tiny marks that might have formed the letters of his name. But none were as clear as the finds that had brought Waldren into his life.

"Hey, what's she doing here?" Chloe said.

A familiar figure stood in the lobby. Amel waved but didn't approach. Chloe stopped and held Nick back. "Jack's still pretty pissed," she said.

"He's always like that," Nick replied. He'd been avoiding

Chloe's husband, but had also been more than aware of the clattering of cupboard doors and the heaviness of his step. Still, Jack's concern about his wife's job was probably well placed. "I thought I'd been doing well keeping out of his way."

"I want you to eat with us tonight. Not tuck yourself away... researching."

"Fine."

"When he was speaking to me on my own," Chloe continued, her voice low, "Fabio seemed pretty keen to know how you were keeping yourself occupied."

"And did you tell him?"

"I think they're monitoring what you're looking at on the boards," she said.

Nick wasn't surprised. He'd anticipated as much, and made sure to keep his research centred on Pompeii, though he'd also started looking more into the work at Herculaneum. Although the two towns had been destroyed by the same event, they'd been preserved in completely different ways, which meant there were things in Herculaneum that had never survived in its more famous cousin. Specifically, the carbonised wood of Roman cabinets, bedframes and doors. Even a handful of scrolls, which were only now able to be read with the latest x-ray machines. But he'd seen no anachronisms. There was no hint of NovusPart or of Nick Houghton. Not that they were admitting, anyway.

"And I take it they soon lost interest in what I was looking at?"

"Yes." Chloe paused. "Somehow, I don't think they know

what game you're playing," she said. "Are you going to tell me?"

Nick didn't want to lie to her. He looked over to where Amel waited awkwardly, examining a painting on the wall. She clearly wanted to talk. "I won't be a minute," he said, starting to walk away.

Chloe reached out and lightly touched his arm. "I'm your friend, Nick."

"I know."

"And I want to help." She looked around nervously. "I checked your *Who's Where* status at the sanatorium."

"And?"

"Someone updated it minutes before we got there," she said. "They knew you were coming, Nick. They knew where you were going before we even arrived."

Nick pulled his arm from Chloe's grasp. "Wait here. I'll see what she wants."

He walked over to Amel, who smiled uncomfortably as he approached. Nick glanced at the painting she'd been examining. It had been placed in a prime spot near the Bureau's entrance, but it wasn't one of Naso's best knock-offs. It depicted a chaotic scene of slaves and masters, drink and food. An image far from the ideal picture of Rome, and a reminder that Christmas hadn't always been Christian. "The Saturnalia," he said. "When slaves become masters, and masters become slaves."

"I've read about it."

"It's not quite as vulgar as many would have you believe."

Amel raised an eyebrow. "Do you join in?"

Nick shook his head, regretting his comment. He didn't want to go back over this ground. "I serve some food for my household," he said, perhaps failing to hide his distaste, "and then I leave them to it."

"Don't only bad emperors dislike the Saturnalia?"

"On this one issue, I agree with Nero," Nick said. The festival wasn't too far away, and he wasn't looking forward to it. "I didn't expect to see you here."

Amel hesitated. "I wanted to apologise."

"For what?"

"My behaviour at our lunch date."

"It really doesn't matter." He didn't want to replay the discussion, even if she only wanted to justify her position.

"We haven't seen you down at the dig site for a couple of days," Amel continued. "I was worried you'd already gone."

"I've been kept busy here…"

Amel didn't look convinced. The grey, drab décor of the Bureau probably never looked so stale, especially for a woman used to spending time outside. "Really?"

"Sort of," Nick replied.

"Well, I'd be pleased to rescue you, if you'd let me? A quick tour of the archaeological museum? Maybe even the *Gabinetto*?"

50

New Pompeii

PULLUS STUMBLED TO a halt just outside the Marine Gate. His head ached and his insides grumbled, but worse was his apparent inability to control his right foot. It caught a paving slab and almost sent him tumbling.

On his way to the gate, he'd noticed another long queue outside Naso's townhouse. It wasn't clear if another member of the *Ordo* was getting a dressing down, but he hoped not.

Rocking back to regain his balance, Pullus belched and started down the ramp that led to New Pompeii's "inland" port, his footing remaining unsteady. Even taking into account the steep gradient and the looseness of his sandals, it was clear he'd drunk too much the previous night. And everyone in his household would now know he'd bedded Calpurnia's "gift", which meant the news would also start circulating in the town by mid-morning. But if Popidius's slave Crixus had been sold to the convoys, this was where he would be.

He stopped to allow a couple of men carrying amphorae

to pass as they headed into town. NovusPart had originally orientated things so all its supplies reached the town from the north, via the Vesuvius Gate. That route had been the most direct from their control villa – Calpurnia's villa – but was also inconvenient because ancient Pompeii had been built around its harbour. The steady ebb and flow of merchant vessels that had once supplied the town with produce and wealth had gone, but the underlying infrastructure had been recreated. The main markets of the forum were positioned to be fed by the port, only the sea was missing.

Pullus glanced up. The *duumvir*'s mansion was located directly above the new "inland" port. Naso seemed to like keeping watch on his cash flow, although to Pullus, the scene always appeared chaotic. If it had been up to him, he would have separated the wagons bringing in supplies from those taking things out. And he would have certainly made sure the operation was kept away from Naso's fermentation pits. The place stank of garum, made even worse down here by the smell of raw fish being unloaded to feed the trade.

"Coming to help us, eh, Pullus?"

Another man carrying goods up from the port had spotted him, and was now heading in his direction. Halfway down the ramp and with nowhere to go, Pullus tensed. It wasn't long before a votive was pushed into his hands. He didn't look at it. Whether the impression on the clay disc was to help with money or the man's wife, Pullus didn't really care. He muttered a few words of thanks and walked into the midst of the many moving carts, horses and men. It would make it harder for him to be spotted in the crowd.

He'd escaped the house early, before Galbo had come to wake him. One of his slaves must have carried him back to his bed during the night. He hadn't slept well, skipping in and out of sleep. Part of him was still thinking about Taedia. If what she'd said was true – that she'd found the papers – then Habitus would surely soon be on his way.

Which meant he was running out of time.

Pullus needed to clear his head. It was unlikely he'd find Crixus on his own, one man he barely knew amongst so much activity, with or without the distinctive sty. But he kept on nonetheless, looking into each face without staring too long to be recognised in return. Or so he thought.

In his search through the wagons, he hadn't been aware of just how much wake he'd created in the crowd, turning heads, the occasional gesture. A path that was easy to follow, once you knew where to look. "It's not safe for you to be out here alone," Galbo said, looking pleased to have finally found his master as he hobbled towards him. "Unless you really believe—"

Pullus shook his head, cutting off his steward. "I just wanted some time before I reported to the *duumvir.*"

"Your shadow's fairly pissed off you left without her."

Pullus shrugged. "Well, you'll be pleased to know I took your advice."

"I heard it wasn't *you* doing the fucking," Galbo replied. "Taedia refused her chores today. Once she'd found you'd gone. She said you'd approve."

Pullus pulled away. *She'd found the papers,* he reminded

himself. So Habitus might indeed be on his way. But he suddenly doubted it. Because there'd been no reason for Taedia to tell him she knew his secret. Other than, of course, to let him know she now had something to use against him. Something to stop whatever punishment Galbo might be tempted to hand her next, or perhaps it would be used as a shield against the unwanted attention of Marcus. Was he now a master who had a reason to keep her rather than hand her back to Calpurnia once the opportunity came? Had she had her own motives for sleeping with him? To put a baby in her belly perhaps?

"What's going on over there?" Galbo pointed into the traffic of wagons and horses. Galbo seemed to have a more instinctive understanding of what system was in place.

"I don't see anything," Pullus said.

"There," Galbo said again, using his staff to point. "I forget your eyes are going bad."

"They're fine," Pullus replied, irritated. Then he saw what Galbo was talking about. In the midst of the large numbers of Pompeians unloading wagons was a small group of people dressed in modern clothing. And they didn't look like they belonged to the convoy team. They seemed confused, huddled together, looking up at the walls of the city like they'd been sent to hell.

New blood, thought Pullus. *New slaves*. About three quarters of the group were young women, perfect for breeding, and the men were all well-muscled, perhaps destined for the estates, where life was hard and short. His hunch was confirmed when a Roman and a regular outsider from the convoys came to examine the group. A male slave said something Pullus couldn't hear and was suddenly beaten to his knees. The others huddled closer, instinctively seeking herd protection.

"Did you know about this?" Galbo asked.

Pullus shook his head, thinking about his new Spanish acquisition. "No."

"Does Calpurnia?"

"I don't think so."

Pullus headed towards the group. The Roman who'd beaten the new "slave" smiled warmly as he approached, but also used the time to usher away the outsider from the convoy.

"Decimus Horatius Pullus! What an unexpected honour!"

Pullus didn't recognise the man addressing him. Had he seen him before? Maybe, but probably not. Pullus eyed the human goods.

"Who are they?" he asked.

The man hesitated, but kept smiling. "Nothing to worry about, Decimus Pullus."

"They breached the bio-containment?"

"No, they've all been through the dips."

So they are slaves, thought Pullus. Imported for a purpose. Perhaps the Spaniard hadn't been caught nosing around. "I'll bring this up with Naso," he said, turning away, intending to return to where Galbo stood waiting for him. Yet something in his peripheral vision made him pause. His eyes tracked from the huddled group, to the passing wagons, to Galbo, and back to the Marine Gate. And the message eventually reached his cranium.

One of the wagons heading out of town was loaded with NovusPart objects. A flat-screen television jutted out of the top of one of them, a large tyre another. Others were filled with clothes. He hesitated. The huddled group, newly arrived, the wagons of NovusPart materials departing. Was one bought with the other?

"We're leaving," he said to Galbo quietly. He forced himself not to turn back; he didn't want the man watching the slaves to realise what he'd seen.

"Naso's doing the right thing," said Galbo, puffing loudly and working his staff as a clear signal he'd like his master to slow his pace. "We need more people."

Pullus shook his head and kept on walking. He only stopped once he'd reached the top of the ramp, just yards away from the gate leading back into Pompeii. His initial thought was to go to Naso – after all, he ran the convoys. But the fact he was in charge of the wagons coming and going also meant he likely knew what was going on. And yet wasn't it Popidius who'd been collecting NovusPart memorabilia days before the instructions had arrived from Calpurnia?

"What is it?" asked Galbo. "What's the issue?"

"Slaves are expensive," Pullus replied.

"That depends on the slave," replied Galbo.

"No," Pullus said. "You don't understand. Where I'm from, people aren't cheap."

"You've also told me that things aren't going well where you come from."

"No. Even now. People aren't cheap."

"So how are they being paid for?"

"With memories of NovusPart," replied Pullus. He looked back down the ramp, the activity of the port continuing unabated. He was just about to turn away again and continue into town when a scrum of movement caught his attention. A small huddle of men had begun pouring out of the marine baths, all shouting and hooting. They were carrying something aloft.

Pullus squinted. No, not something. Someone.

The *duumvir*.

Naso was being carried by the crowd, which was heading towards his garum pits. The *duumvir* was held fast by each limb, but was still writhing and trying to break free.

"Shit," Pullus said. "Shit, shit, shit."

"We should go back to your townhouse," Galbo replied. "And bolt the doors."

51

PULLUS ARRIVED BACK at the House of McMahon to find Marcus gone, and his two bodyguards with him, the only muscle he had to call on. As he paced around the atrium, Galbo waved towards Primus.

"Boy! Bring some water!" His steward's voice was strained and he was breathing hard. "We need to get you to safety," he said, returning his attention to his master. "I'll ready the horses."

Pullus shook his head. "Not without Marcus."

"The boy has his bodyguards."

"No," said Pullus. "We wait for him here."

Primus soon arrived back with a jug of water, walking so quickly he spilled some of it on the atrium floor. The boy offered what remained first to Pullus but he waved him away. Galbo took it gratefully. "I'll take Primus and look for him."

Pullus shook his head. "I don't know where he went, and you're not going to find one boy in a town this size."

"I found you, didn't I?"

"You found me because everyone stares at me wherever I go," Pullus replied, letting his anger show. He thought about Naso's observation. *Whenever you pick your nose, some whelp thinks I need to know.* "But how many recognise the boy? He's just another rich kid with his minders."

"Then we do what?"

"We wait…"

Galbo swallowed, nervously. "If they turned on Naso, they may come for you next."

Yes, Pullus thought, his conversation with Popidius clear in his mind. His absence from town had meant he'd been missing things; subtle changes to the mood of New Pompeii. The humiliation of Scaeva had maybe been too much for some in the *Ordo.* Perhaps they'd decided that if they couldn't remove Naso at the ballot box, they would do so via the mob. But where did that leave him? And where did it leave Calpurnia?

"We wait," he said again, looking about. Suddenly his choice of slaves seemed naïve. There was not one amongst them able to fight. No one to man the barricade. "Hopefully, Marcus will come back soon. News travels fast – his men will understand the situation."

In some respects, there were things occurring in the town more important than local politics. He needed to tell Calpurnia about what he'd seen below the Marine Gate. Because if someone was paying for slaves with NovusPart materials, then it meant that somewhere – somehow – that person was also in direct contact with the outside world. Maybe someone who had a use for the convoys beyond shipping goods. "What if one of those new slaves isn't really here to be a slave," asked Pullus, thinking aloud. "What if they've been sent for another reason? Getting to the NovusPart device, for instance?"

Galbo let his staff clank heavily onto the mosaic floor. "What if the mob arrives here before Marcus?" he said.

"Then I'm sorry," Pullus replied. *The man who can't be killed.* Did he really believe that? Would those ruling the future continue to protect him? "But we're all going to die."

"You look worried."

"I am," Pullus whispered. He gave the *lares* another offering of crumbs and watched the flame in the small oil lamp momentarily fizz. Then he turned to face Taedia. They were alone, Galbo and the rest of his household having taken up positions by the street door, armed with what makeshift weapons they had managed to find. They didn't present much of a barrier. "The research papers," he said. "I had my reasons for keeping them from Calpurnia."

"I'm not interested," Taedia replied. She hesitated. "They're still in the satchel under your bed."

"So you haven't told Habitus? Calpurnia?"

"No. I just didn't want to go back."

Pullus swore inwardly. That was perhaps their last hope. If she'd followed her instructions, then Habitus and the cavalry might be on their way, drawn by the promise of Arlen's research, just in time to protect his household. As it was, they were truly on their own.

"You see him as just a boy, don't you?" Taedia said. "Marcus, I mean."

"He *is* just a boy."

"You shouldn't have waited for him. He wouldn't have done the same for you. If he knows what is happening, he will already be riding back to his mother's villa."

"Galbo told me," Nick said, searching for the right words. "The slave that drowned?"

"He claims it was an accident," Taedia replied. "But other slaves saw it happen. They say he trapped the boy with his knees, and was laughing as he struggled."

Pullus found himself unable to reply. Part of him considered the relationship between Roman masters and their slaves, but he quickly dismissed it. If true, what Marcus had done was murder. Plain and simple. He would need to be punished. But would Calpurnia allow it?

"It wasn't the first *accident* either," Taedia whispered.

Pullus reached towards her, hoping to offer some touch of comfort. He thought back to their encounter the previous night. "Has he ever hurt you?"

"We were very young," she said. "Playing at being married. He told me the game was that I was pregnant, but that I was an adulteress. He sliced my stomach with a pear knife. Some offal from the kitchen served as the 'baby'. Calpurnia was very angry; she even allowed Habitus to beat him."

"I didn't…"

"You were in Naples," Taedia said. "Always either at Naples or your villa."

Pullus was about to ask for more details when there was a sudden hammering at the door to the street. Then came the sound of it opening, a scuffle and a cry. So much for his front line of slaves, ready to protect their master.

"They're coming," Taedia whispered.

But it wasn't a mob. Instead, just two men appeared: the aedile Popidius and a man Pullus didn't know. Both were carrying swords.

Popidius stopped just inside the threshold of the atrium. He gazed at the fresco of Vesuvius, the volcano raining fire down onto Pompeii. Pullus suddenly realised the aedile had never visited the House of McMahon before. Of course, he was too young. He'd have been a small boy when NovusPart fell.

"I don't remember it happening," Popidius said, pointing at the fresco.

Pullus couldn't speak, aware that he wasn't wearing any armour, and that the man with the aedile was clearly part of his personal bodyguard. He would know how to use that sword, and all his attention was on him, the man who couldn't be killed. The man's eyes were wide, his expression one of adrenaline-fuelled fear. The appearance of Galbo and his three other slaves was no comfort. His steward and the cripples looked more like an honour guard than a serious threat.

"I've heard stories, of course," continued the aedile. "How we were saved by the God Emperor Augustus. Before we saved ourselves from you and your friends."

Pullus's throat was tight. He needed to sound confident, not weak. "You've heard what happened in the arena?"

"Everyone has," replied the aedile. "But fifteen summers is a long time. And some of us are wondering if all our parents saw was a clever trick. Just like so much else that NovusPart had to fool us."

The bodyguard momentarily lost his focus. Sweat ran down his cheek and he adjusted his grip on his sword. This man knew. He looked older than Popidius by five years or so. If he'd been in the crowd that day, he might just remember the sight of a gladiator being sucked into a vortex. It might just now be replaying in his head.

"Naso?" Pullus asked.

"Dead," Popidius replied. "We drowned him in his garum pits."

We. Such a simple word, but it confirmed something very important. This was no random mob or spontaneous action. This was a coup driven by the *Ordo*; men who wanted to return to power. And that meant both he and Calpurnia would be in their way.

"I asked you to go back to your villa," Popidius whispered. "And you ignored me."

"But that would only have delayed things, wouldn't it?"

The aedile gave a shallow smile.

"New slaves are being brought into the town," Pullus said. "Whatever happens here today, you need to round them up and send them back."

"I know about the slaves," Popidius said. "The men you saw today work for me."

For a moment, Pullus didn't say anything. "But Naso…?"

"One man can't keep track of everything, can he?" The aedile grinned, again full of arrogant youth. His bodyguard swallowed audibly. He at least feared NovusPart's power. "So why not do a bit of personal business under his nose?"

"Is that why he wouldn't support your re-election?"

"Perhaps."

"And the payment?" Pullus tried not to think about what had happened to the *duumvir*. "Material from the days of NovusPart?"

The aedile nodded. "Anything with their stamp on it." He looked about him. "I'm sure this house contains a fortune."

Pullus stared down at the floor in desperation, looking for any sign of rescue. But there was no mist gathering at his feet, nothing to indicate a coming transportation from the present and into the future. He wasn't going to be saved this time. He wasn't the man who couldn't be killed. Maybe he hadn't been for some considerable time.

"And once we've killed you," the aedile continued, "we'll kill the bitch and her son."

At this signal, the bodyguard lunged forward. Even before Pullus had time to react, Galbo lumbered into his way, swinging his staff weakly. He was the only one who moved. The other slaves simply stood and watched.

The bodyguard shoved Galbo away easily with one shoulder, then pushed his sword into Galbo's gut. The old man slid off the blade and crumpled to the floor, his eyes wide. The bodyguard eyed the other slaves, posed to fend off another attack. He needn't have bothered; they'd already started to back away. Primus turned and ran out of the atrium and towards the street.

"Didn't you save these dregs from the gutter?" asked Popidius, laughing. "But I suppose you get what you pay for, don't you? I'll be sure to teach them some honest Roman values after you've gone. No master should be abandoned by their slaves. Even one who isn't really Roman."

Pullus turned his head to see if Taedia was still behind him, but she was gone. He hoped she'd had the sense to run and hide.

He forced himself to ignore Galbo's body, to instead lock eyes with the bodyguard. The man clearly feared him, or at least what happened to those who threatened him. "Enough of this." Popidius sounded impatient. The aedile waved a hand at his bodyguard. "Finish him."

There was no mist at his feet. Pullus knew he wasn't going to be rescued.

But he didn't need it. The bodyguard made as if to attack, then his sword dropped. And now Pullus didn't doubt that he'd been in the amphitheatre that day fifteen years ago.

"I can't," the man said simply, and lowered his sword.

52

Naples

A MEL OPENED THE door to her apartment, and led him inside. It was small, a lounge just big enough for a TV, compact sofa and kitchenette, with two doors leading off it, presumably to the bedroom and bathroom. It was nothing like the smart complex the Bureau had provided Chloe.

Nick crossed to the window, opened it and stepped out onto the small balcony. Between the other apartment blocks and their lines of fluttering washing, there was a good view of Vesuvius. The volcano had been spewing its cloud of ash for almost a week now, and its tip burned a deep orange against the black mass of the mountain.

"They're saying it's more like '45 than '79," Amel said. She was busying herself in the kitchenette, a modest affair with only a few cupboards, a small cooker and a knee-high refrigerator. She must have sensed his scepticism. "I know, I know," she said. "I promised you the finest chickpea stew you'd ever eaten. Believe me, I don't need fancy equipment."

Nick didn't trust himself to reply. He shrugged off his coat and sat on the sofa whilst Amel quickly began sorting through the fridge.

"So what do you think of the place?"

Nick glanced around the small confines of the flat. There were clothes, clutter and papers strewn around most of the space. All in all, it appeared Amel was all set with regards to vest tops and khaki shorts. "It's nice," he said.

"Yeah," she replied. "I'm pleased with it. I had some help with the costs, but when my niece is here it's better to have the two rooms." She padded across to him, offering a glass of wine. He sipped it and was surprised, immediately tasting Pompeian spices.

"Fabio gave me a couple of bottles," she said, retreating back to the kitchenette. Whatever she was cooking was already starting to simmer on the hob. "An apology for the lunch thing."

Something on the floor at the far side of the lounge caught Nick's attention. It almost looked like an electric steamer, except it was filled with soil and compost, and he thought he could see something wriggling inside. It took him a few moments, then realised he was looking at an insect factory.

"They're nicer than they look raw," Amel said. "You toast them, and they come out nutty. Good source of protein, and very cheap. People have been using them outside Europe for ages…"

Nick just about stopped himself asking her if she was going to put any of them in his dinner. If she was, then that was her choice. After all, he didn't know what she could afford. He'd just need to think of something else if anything was a bit too crunchy…

"We have a sweepstake at work," Amel continued, her voice raised slightly as she pulled out some plates and cutlery.

"Fabio told me," Nick replied. "About whether you'd find a school in the new digs. I told him that there isn't one in New Pompeii, so the chances aren't good."

"No, no. God, not that. We were wondering who your favourite emperor was." She took a sip of wine. "My bet is Claudius."

"Sorry."

"Not Claudius?"

"No."

"But he was a historian, wasn't he?"

"Yes."

"And he was kinder than the others?"

"It's easy to look good after Tiberius and Caligula."

"So who then?"

Nick shrugged. He pointed at a circular, woven textile that was hung on the wall. It didn't look European – the colours were too warm and the patterns unfamiliar – but it didn't look African either. "Did you say you've worked in South America? Did you get that there?"

"Huh? Oh, that. Yeah, I had it made when I was out there." Amel came over and sat on the sofa beside him. "Fascinating people, the Incas," she said. "Very different from Europeans then or now."

Nick took another mouthful of wine. "How so?"

"They thought about time completely differently. In Incan culture, the past, present and future all occur simultaneously, with individual points in time – moments – providing connection and meaning between all three."

Nick raised his eyebrows. "Interesting," he said.

"You don't believe it?"

"I think it will take me a while to get my head around."

Amel pointed to the balcony. "You can think about it just by looking out there."

Vesuvius?

"Ignore the mountain," Amel said. "You see the stars? The deeper you look, the further into the past you're staring. All the light from all those stars is coming at us from different times. All merging into a single picture, from the Big Bang right to the present day. All experienced by us in the same moment."

"I never thought of it that way."

Amel hesitated. "May I ask you about the graffiti we found in the bakery?"

Nick felt as if the apartment had suddenly become smaller.

"It's an alternative timeline, isn't it?" Amel continued. "This. Now. What we're experiencing?"

Nick shook his head. "I don't think so."

"But your name shouldn't have appeared. Things aren't as they should be!"

"It's a relatively small pebble, Amel. A ripple, not a wave. Barely a butterfly beat."

"Still…"

"We don't know why that graffiti was in your dig site. It may have been a hoax."

Amel didn't look convinced. "You believe in alternative realities though, don't you?"

"I don't know." The flat was filling with the smell of cumin and turmeric, but he'd lost his appetite. He didn't want to talk about this, or NovusPart. He got to his feet. "Can I use your bathroom?" Amel pointed wordlessly at one of the doors leading off the lounge.

He took his time before returning, looking into the mirror. Should he leave, or just eat and try to enjoy the evening?

Amel made the decision for him. Nick came back to find her curled up on her sofa, her clothes discarded, everything of interest artfully hidden either by the angle of her thigh, or the curve of her arm.

Nick edged forwards, feeling unbearably awkward. His every movement seemed robotic and unnatural. He eyed the door.

"What's wrong?"

"Nothing," he said.

"It's not as if you're my teacher."

"I know."

Amel rose from the couch. She waited just long enough so he could see she was indeed naked, and then moved towards him to unbutton his shirt. She slid her hands down the front of his trousers. It didn't take long for her to find the scar tissue. He could see the question written on her face.

"An accident," he said, simply.

She kept her hand in place, even though his body was failing to respond.

"What happened?"

"I was attacked. A group of men. I don't want to talk about it."

"So," she said, taking hold of him. "It's a good thing we're not in an alternate timeline, isn't it?"

53

The sickle tore upwards. Nick felt a sudden pain, and then nothing. His head slipped back and cracked against the mosaic floor. And then he was awake again. Coughing and spluttering and gasping in reaction to both the shattering pain in his skull, and the numbness in his groin.

The man with the sickle held his hand out. Nick's eyes widened and he let out a strangled cry. Blood was flowing through the man's fingers. And sitting in the man's palm was a tangle of skin and hair. And two bloody spheres.

Nick woke up shouting, the terror of what could have been drenching him in sweat. He rolled onto his side. The bed was empty. He reached across and felt some of Amel's warmth under the covers. The soft imprint of her body. He buried his head deep in the pillow and breathed deeply.

From somewhere in the room he sensed movement. And then he heard a harsh, scratchy cough. One he recognised.

"You sleep well, Nick?"

The voice wasn't Amel's. It was masculine and hoarse.

Nick scrabbled to sit up, his heart pounding in his chest. Waldren sat in a chair at the foot of the bed.

"What the fuck are you doing here?"

Waldren cocked his head to one side. "When I first went to see him at the Bureau, Fabio told me something interesting," he said. "He told me Rome was founded by criminals. The greatest empire on earth, all emanating from the loins of banished men who found a home together on the Tiber." He wagged a finger. "But how did they breed? Isn't the story that they stole women from a local tribe? Romans are nothing more than the children of murderers and rape victims."

Nick ground his teeth. "What are you doing here?"

"Interesting story, isn't it?" Waldren said, ignoring him. "But Fabio's going to have to work hard to cover this one up."

Nick scanned the room, trying to work out where he'd left his clothes. The bedroom door was closed and there was no sound from the apartment beyond. No sign of Amel.

"Fabio?"

Waldren nodded. The small movement caused something to shift on his lap. A brown folder. "This is probably beyond the Bureau."

Nick felt both confusion and rage bubbling up. He forced them down. "What are you doing here?" he repeated.

"We turn a blind eye to you screwing your slaves in New Pompeii, Nick. But this is Naples. Different standards apply."

Nick let out a short laugh. "I'd hardly call Amel a slave."

"The person I'm talking about wasn't really in a position

to give you her consent, was she?"

Nick looked again to the door. "What are you talking about?"

"The girl in question is with our protection officers—"

"What sort of bullshit is this…?"

"—and being looked after by her aunt."

Nick stopped. *Aunt.* His eyes narrowed on Waldren as the man picked up the brown folder from his lap. It contained a couple of glossy photos, which he tossed onto the bed. Nick on the dig site, with Amel's niece, Sabine. Him in the apartment, Sabine in the apartment. Him on the bed, the person beneath him not quite visible.

Nick glanced up at the ceiling, but couldn't see the camera. Not that he'd be able to; wherever it was, it would be far too small.

"Do you screw twelve-year-olds back in New Pompeii?"

"I didn't sleep with Sabine," Nick said. But his voice was small and he already knew it didn't matter. Insinuations about his lifestyle were already circulating, and conspiracies worked best when they tapped into assumptions. Waldren stared at him blankly. His expression didn't hold any satisfaction as he waited for Nick to feel the edges of the trap. Nick remembered Fabio's quiet observation to which he'd paid no heed: *he's no academic.*

"What do you want?"

Finally a smile, an acknowledgement of victory. "You've been enjoying the best of both worlds for some time now," Waldren said. He gave another harsh cough. "Living in

Pompeii as Decimus Horatius Pullus, but visiting Naples every now and then to remind yourself of what it was to be Nick Houghton."

"That's my job."

"You miss it, Nick," continued Waldren. "Your visits are getting more frequent. You even asked for your old friend Chloe to come and hold your hand, although you still can't pluck up the courage to ask her to hold your dick."

Nick shifted in the bed. "Come on…"

"The cheap shots are often the most accurate," Waldren explained, his smile broadening. He paused, as if mulling something over. "So what would you be doing out there? Say if you'd not decided to take this trip, and had stayed in New Pompeii?"

Nothing as bad as this, that's for sure. "Relaxing at my villa," Nick said, the words heavy in his mouth.

"Hiding you mean," Waldren responded immediately. "Maybe you already sense what you don't want to admit?"

"Which is?"

"You're not Roman, Nick. You're a British bookworm who found the dream turned sour. A Romanophile who can no longer equate his own morals with those of his fellow citizens."

Nick looked again at the photos. He wondered where Amel was, but then suddenly didn't care. He'd never see her again. If this had been a trap arranged by Habitus, then she'd already be dead. But maybe Waldren did things differently; maybe she'd be paid off and set up somewhere nice, with a healthy bank account, a personal connection to the boards, and a fat ration book. Either way, she wasn't coming back. And neither was her niece.

"We wondered if you'd fall for it," Waldren said, unable to hide his satisfaction. "Some wanted to use a woman with blonde hair and bigger breasts. Make her a bit more obvious, given the likely shortness of your visit. But I said you'd want someone more intellectually challenging. You'd be surprised how little money it took to find an archaeologist willing to screw you."

Nick grunted. "I have diplomatic immunity."

"Still, life won't be the same for you if this gets out," Waldren said. "Sure they'll fly you back to New Pompeii. But you won't be allowed back, Nick. You'll sit in your villa and wait for your friends to finally tire of you."

"What do you want?"

Waldren didn't answer. "Get dressed," he said, standing and heading for the door. "And forget the Bureau. You're working for me now."

54

New Pompeii

PULLUS HAD BEEN sitting on his own for what seemed like hours. He let a slow breath escape from between his teeth.

He'd been taken to a small shuttered shop only a few blocks south of the House of McMahon, a disused little hovel built into the side of a townhouse, no doubt owned by an ally of the aedile. It might have once sold pottery; fragments of broken amphorae littered the floor and the remains of a wooden rack reached up to the ceiling on the back wall. Pullus wondered what had happened to the last tenant. Moved on and up? Or pulled down by bad debt, and a bigger fish?

It didn't matter. Galbo was dead. He'd been trying to ignore the fact, but the dead face of his steward hung before his mind's eye. Galbo's constant talk of discipline and duty had often irked Pullus. And yet the man had taken that blade for his master without question.

Duty, thought Pullus with more than a little bitterness.

He'd sacrificed himself out of duty, and a wilful ignorance that they were no longer part of the Empire. At least, not the Roman one. His other, younger slaves may well have understood that, but they were likely already dead anyway. Even if the aedile's bodyguard had disobeyed his master's order to kill Pullus for fear of divine retribution – the fact that the aedile himself hadn't stepped in perhaps meant that he too wasn't completely sure of Pullus's power – it probably only meant the bodyguard had been more willing to spill other men's blood to make amends.

Pullus got to his feet, feeling a little pain in his back as he rose. He could hear little from the street outside, but the shop was situated down an alleyway, a good distance from the thoroughfare. Perhaps that was why it had closed. But it did make the perfect prison cell. Small. Square. And with one heavy wooden door.

He was sure there was at least one guard outside. He'd heard the occasional scrape of sandals, the odd snort and spit. Pullus stood close to the door's panelled shutters and squinted through the narrow slats. The man outside was new, not the bodyguard who'd killed Galbo.

Were they just going to leave him here? Starve him to death rather than risk killing him outright? Turn him into a shell, like they'd done with Whelan?

He turned and leant on the door, scanning the shop for any other exit. The rack against the back wall looked unsteady but he ran his eyes up it anyway. He quickly realised there was no point attempting to climb it; the roof was sealed –

there was no *compluvium* to escape through.

He stooped and picked up a piece of broken pottery from the floor. He'd been wrong before; whoever had been operating this place hadn't been making new amphorae. This fragment was older than that, bearing an Oscan design. Pullus looked back at the rack. Not a pottery but a wine store, which probably explained the strength of the door, and its position away from the street. He was stuck here until someone came for him. He tossed the Oscan fragment, and heard it scatter away.

He'd just resigned himself to more hours of waiting when he heard raised voices outside and the sound of approaching footsteps. Pullus peered through the shutters but could see nothing, the light beyond too bright. He hurried back, pressing his back against the wall, as the door began to open.

Marcus stood silhouetted in the doorway, Habitus at his shoulder. Calpurnia's bodyguard took a few steps forward, the *frumentarius*'s eyes scanning the interior of the shop. His hand rested on the hilt of his sword. Marcus too was armed.

"Pullus!"

For a moment Pullus couldn't speak, his gaze flitting between his rescuers. "How?"

Marcus tugged at the buckle of his belt. "Something from NovusPart," said the boy, amused, and yet also puzzled. "You pull on it and it sends a call for assistance, though I don't know how. I came back to your house and found you gone and that dead slave, so I called Habitus. It wasn't hard to figure out where they'd put you; they didn't have the wit to take you far." He patted the belt buckle. "I thought you'd know about it?"

Pullus nodded slowly. "I didn't think they still worked."

"Well lucky for you they do," Habitus said, cutting in. "Although you might come to wish we hadn't found you." The *frumentarius* stared at him angrily. "When were you going to tell us about the papers?"

55

Naples

NICK STOOD ON Amel's balcony, watching Vesuvius burn and smoke against the steadily brightening horizon. The start of the new day had transformed the forest of apartment blocks into every shade of peeling pastel paint. Many had vegetable and herb boxes hanging from their windows. Buying fresh food was a luxury for many these days.

Behind him, Fabio sat slumped in the same sofa upon which Amel had been curled the previous night. The Italian hadn't said a word to him, not even to pass comment on Nick's attire – he was wearing Amel's dressing gown, his own clothes still strewn on her bedroom floor.

Waldren stood with his back to the front door, cutting off the only route of escape. But Nick wasn't about to run. "Let's talk about the NovusPart device," Waldren said.

Nick didn't acknowledge him. The smoke from the summit of Vesuvius appeared to be thickening. "It's erupted many times, you know," Nick said, absently. "But people just tend to remember the event that buried Pompeii."

"Arlen. McMahon. Whelan. They're all dead." Waldren's voice was cold.

"Charles Dickens visited during one eruption," Nick continued. "He described it as 'the destroyer'."

"Those three men were basically the only ones who knew how the device worked... until your Roman friends managed to gain control."

Nick blinked. He shook away a memory of Whelan's screams. "Another eruption in 1944 buried the small village of San Sebastiano," he said. "It damaged dozens of US Air Force planes too. Remarkable really: to have beaten Hitler and Mussolini, and then be defeated by Vesuvius."

Waldren let out an impatient cough. "Is Calpurnia the only one that knows the secret?" He paused. "Answer me, Nick."

"I guess so."

"Except there's this little place you don't know about. It's called the NovusPart Institute."

Nick flinched. He turned to look at Fabio, but the Italian was avoiding his gaze. Fabio hadn't told him. Waldren didn't know he'd already been. "NovusPart Institute?" he repeated.

"Set up by Arlen's mother," Waldren explained. "If you want to amuse yourself, you might want to look it up. They offer people a quick deal on the afterlife. More interestingly, they had some of Arlen's personal data files, his research. A glimpse into Arlen's mind when he was conceiving his device."

Nick shrugged. "I don't see your point."

"Anything that can be built, can be rebuilt, Mr Houghton."

Nick stared down at Fabio, willing him to meet his gaze, but he continued to stare at the floor. "Arlen's research isn't going to be enough."

"You're right. The Brits may have foolishly dismantled the NovusPart headquarters, but they didn't touch the R&D labs. The prototypes."

Now Fabio did look up at him. The Italian's face was grey, his expression one of regret. "If you have a prototype," asked Nick, "then what do you need me for?"

Waldren didn't answer, and Nick started to chuckle. "It doesn't work, does it? You've had fifteen years, access to the labs and old prototypes, and you still can't figure it out."

"As you well know, Mr Houghton, we need the correct authorisation codes to overcome the safeguards. The ones Whelan gave you."

Nick shook his head. All that screaming. "I don't have them."

"But you can get them. You just need to find the settings we're missing before your next visit to Naples."

Nick thought about Naples. Pompeii. The prospect of never returning to the real world. He turned to Fabio. "I want to talk to 'the professor' alone," he said, his voice starting to crack. "Wait for us downstairs."

56

Nick walked into Amel's kitchenette and poured some of the previous night's wine into a tumbler. "Do you mind?" he said to Waldren. "I suddenly need it."

Waldren shrugged. "Go ahead."

Nick swallowed the contents of the glass in one go. "A few dollars' worth right there," he said, refilling the tumbler. This time, he drank more slowly. "If I do this for you, then what? What happens to me?"

"A nice apartment in Naples," Waldren replied. "Or Rome. Or wherever the hell else you want to live. Maybe even England. You don't need to worry, Mr Houghton."

"And this business with the girl, Amel's niece? Sabine?"

"Forgotten. It will be as if it never happened."

Nick didn't appreciate the joke. *It hadn't happened.* "If the Romans find out I'm a spy, they'll crucify me."

"You've been living amongst them for years," Waldren said. "You'll just need to find a good reason to get to the device. I'm sure a man like you can find a way."

"The biggest problem will be Habitus."

Waldren raised his eyebrow. "I'm sure you can get past

Calpurnia's thug."

"He's a spy," replied Nick, suddenly chuckling. "Don't you know? Not a thug, an Imperial spy. He was in Pompeii at the time of the eruption for reasons he won't reveal. Even now."

"I didn't think Romans went in for spying. Not really their style, was it?"

"True," said Nick. "There wasn't much call for spies when you could simply crush your enemies with a legion or three. Of course, they had state police – Gestapo, Stasi – that sort of thing, to keep watch on their own citizens. But Habitus was – *is* – most definitely a spy. I suppose it's a bit like all those Roman slums that have disappeared over time, whereas we still have the Coliseum. Easier to see evidence of legions than spies."

Waldren looked at him almost pityingly, and Nick wondered how many sad middle-aged men he'd lured with a few kind words from a naked young woman. But he couldn't have counted on it to work, not when the stakes were so high. "If I hadn't said 'yes', there would have been another rung up the ladder, wouldn't there? Another way to apply pressure?"

"People tend not to betray their countries for a singular reason," Waldren said, nodding. "So yes, I've taken out an insurance policy."

"I'm guessing Chloe," Nick went on. "The only person here with whom I have any real connection."

Waldren shrugged and smiled. "You shouldn't worry about Chloe. Not for a while, at least."

Not for a while, at least. He'd taken her to the NovusPart

Institute, Nick guessed. The thought pinged into his brain almost immediately, and he couldn't shake it. Waldren had taken his friend, and put her into one of those godawful cells.

Could he do anything about it? Call the police?

Unlikely. If Fabio's instructions had come from the Italian government, then Waldren's scheme was likely authorised. That didn't mean he had to go along with it, however. All he needed was to give himself a little time. Create a little confusion so he could escape…

Nick looked through a couple of kitchen cupboards and retrieved the second bottle of Pompeian wine. He retrieved a corkscrew from a drawer, then paused and searched for another tumbler. "Do you want some? The way I'm feeling at the moment, I could just about drink the whole bottle."

"Sure," Waldren said. "And don't feel too bad you didn't see this coming. It took a long time to set up. We just needed some way to focus your mind and allow you to see the right course of action."

Nick filled both glasses and handed one to Waldren. "You mentioned Oppenheimer the last time we met," he said. "He created a weapon he thought too powerful."

Waldren nodded, letting out another hacking cough. "Cold War," he said. "Something of a golden era for someone in my business."

"But you're actually asking me to become the other guy. I don't remember his name. The man who took the secrets of the Manhattan Project and gave them to Stalin. There's some that say the Russian spy did the world a service, because it created a balance of power and stopped a nuclear war breaking out."

Waldren cocked his head. "There's a lot of truth in that."

"I just wanted to be clear," said Nick. "Just wanted to fully understand."

"You've made the right decision," Waldren said. He looked at his tumbler of wine and laughed. "And as we're both now agreed you're no Roman, at least I can be sure it's not poisoned." He took a large gulp.

Nick nodded. "But it is heavily spiced."

Waldren doubled over, coughing uncontrollably. He reached for his throat, droplets of wine spraying from his mouth.

"Your Oppenheimer analogy is flawed," Nick said. He lunged forward and stabbed the corkscrew into Waldren's neck. He gave it a sharp twist. "Giving you a NovusPart device doesn't counter the risk, it simply doubles it. So you can go to hell."

57

Nɪᴄᴋ sᴛᴇᴘᴘᴇᴅ ᴏᴜᴛ of the elevator and into the lobby of Amel's apartment block. Fabio was pacing back and forth by the swing doors that led out onto the street.

"You've changed," the Italian said dryly.

Nick didn't respond at first. Then he realised Fabio was just talking about what he was wearing. He'd taken his time before leaving Amel's apartment, carefully washing the blood from his hands and face, stuffing Amel's stained dressing gown under the sofa and putting on his own clothes.

Fabio craned his neck, looking around Nick, presumably expecting Waldren to appear. "I hope you didn't get into a fight," he said. It was clear he was trying to make a joke, but the comment lacked any humour.

Nick suppressed a grimace. "Do I look like the physical type?"

"So are we to wait for the 'professor'?"

"No," Nick replied. He pushed open the swing doors and walked out onto the street. The morning heat was building, but the fresh air on his face was refreshing. "He's clearing up after his whore."

"Look, Nick…"

"You don't have to say it."

"I didn't know."

Nick stopped. He gazed up and down the street, spotting Fabio's vehicle a couple of hundred metres away. The road and the cars lining it were covered in a centimetre of grey ash. A few kids were playing football, each kick lifting clouds of powder into the air. One of them was hobbling crab-like on bowed legs.

You shouldn't worry about Chloe. Not for a while, at least. "You're enabled, aren't you?" he said to Fabio.

Fabio nodded. "I don't like using it."

"Can you connect to *Who's Where* for me?"

Fabio looked confused. "No one bothers using that site anymore, Nick. Not for years. Is it even still active?"

"Yes, and someone's been dicking me around," Nick replied. "Changing my *Who's Where* location ever since I arrived here. So just run a search for Chloe, will you?"

Fabio's eyes glazed. "Nothing," he said. "No messages either. I'll try calling her."

A few seconds passed. Nick felt each one thump through his skull. "Well?"

"No answer." Then: "Huh. There's something on *Who's Where* about you though. Apparently you're in Herculaneum. Which is odd, given that we're in Naples."

Herculaneum. Another dot on the graph. Another point through which he could draw his line. Two findings in Pompeii. One at the Villa Maritima, halfway between the two towns. And one journey, marked out by a line of breadcrumbs dropped over two thousand years ago. There would be another anomaly there, he was almost sure of it.

"We can pass by Chloe's apartment on the way to the Bureau," Fabio said. "She's probably just taking a shower."

But Nick was already shaking his head. "She won't be there," he said. "Waldren took her, to put more pressure on me. You allowed him to do that."

Fabio blanched. "You forget what the Bureau really is, Nick," the Italian replied. "In the end, we're just a few people who administer your supply chain. And the world's been happy to leave us to get on with things. Until that fucking fresco."

"Ignore the fresco," said Nick. "It's unimportant. What matters is Arlen's research."

Fabio stumbled. "I don't understand."

Nick took a deep breath. He'd thought about it as he'd washed Waldren's blood off his hands and down the plughole. He needed some grain of truth. Something Fabio already knew to make him swallow the lie. "Waldren wants me to go back to New Pompeii and obtain the authorisation codes."

Fabio nodded. "Sure."

"He's asked me for five parameters," continued Nick, stirring the pot. "He already knows two of them from Arlen's research, but won't tell me which he already knows."

Fabio frowned. "I don't get it."

"I'm to give him all five settings he's asked for," Nick explained. "And if the two he already knows match, then he can trust the other values as being correct. If not, then he knows I'm lying and things will get worse. For all of us."

Nick knew the story probably wouldn't stand up to much scrutiny – he had no idea if the device needed such parameters. But it was the best he could think of, and he didn't have much time. Waldren wouldn't be working alone and he'd soon be missed. The window of opportunity was closing and all he had to work with was Fabio, who didn't yet know that Waldren was no longer their primary concern.

"Waldren was right," Nick said, slowly. "I'm losing Calpurnia. The risk she'll use the NovusPart device to alter the timeline increases by the day."

"That doesn't make Waldren any less of a bastard," Fabio replied.

"But it does mean he missed what I've been trying to do here," Nick said. "Why I was so interested in Mary Arlen and the NovusPart Institute. Why, when I saw that fresco, I knew what had to happen."

"Which is what?"

"It's time to close Pandora's Box," said Nick. "Not create a new one. You agree that Waldren and whoever he's working for mustn't get hold of a device? A man like that?"

Fabio nodded quickly. "Of course."

"Then we need to get moving," Nick said. "Before he insists I get on a plane back to New Pompeii to get his parameters."

"Fucking hell, Nick! I don't know what you want from me!"

"I need to know which settings Waldren already knows,"

he said. "I need Arlen's research, and we need to get to Herculaneum. We'll find our answer there, I'm sure of it."

"Herculaneum is easy, but Waldren won't give you Arlen's files."

"The NovusPart Institute were quite clear," Nick continued, the semblance of a smile forming on his lips. "The Bureau took Arlen's research files, not Waldren."

"Yes, and I gave them to him. He made me, Nick! I had no choice!"

"And as an office," said Nick. "As a *bureau*. You didn't save a copy?"

58

New Pompeii

ONLY A DAY or so had passed, but news of his imprisonment had already spread through the town. A steady stream of votives were starting to drop into the shop. Each one bore a face on each side of the disc, crude depictions of his own features. *The man who couldn't be killed.* But the man who could evidently be left in a cell to rot.

When Calpurnia finally came, Pullus had completely lost track of time. She arrived at nightfall, when she could no doubt move through the town with only a small retinue of men and draw little attention. There was no sign of Habitus.

Pullus dusted himself down, stood, and looked at her, silhouetted in the doorway. She was holding a small oil lamp. She didn't speak and the flame didn't light her face enough to enable him to sense her mood. Marcus edged into view, grinning.

"I—" Pullus coughed, feeling his lips crack. "I... could do with some water."

"We've taken the papers to my villa," Calpurnia said.

Pullus nodded, unsurprised. He wondered what the Greek would make of them. His work with the NovusPart device had made reading English a necessary skill. And yet, despite his many talents, he wasn't Arlen. Or Whelan. Or even McMahon. "You think he can decipher them?"

Calpurnia didn't answer and Pullus laughed, despite his situation. "They don't give all the answers anyway," he said. "Safeguards upon safeguards. That seems to have been Joe Arlen's style."

The flame of the oil lamp flickered, finally lighting up Calpurnia's face, revealing the anger on her features, despite her calm voice.

"The convoys," continued Pullus. "I take it you've seen what Popidius has been using them for?"

Marcus snorted. "Habitus has dealt with it."

"Stop trying to distract us," Calpurnia interrupted. "All you need know is the men from the convoys are currently aloft and lining the road from New Pompeii."

Pullus didn't say anything. Just felt his tongue heavy in his mouth. The muscles in his back all seemed to twist and set.

"Your friends," Calpurnia continued, "back home, have another NovusPart device, don't they? And yet you told me the original device had been destroyed."

"It was destroyed," Pullus said. "They've found an early

version. A prototype. What information got out on the convoys may not have helped them though. But we don't know what else the aedile—"

"The aedile is dead, Pullus. Popidius was offered his sword and he took it. And now we find you've betrayed us too."

Like a child caught in a lie, Pullus felt his cheeks flush. "I didn't intend—"

"My husband has been trapped in Herculaneum for two thousand years. And you could have brought his suffering to an end when you first got back here." Marcus grinned at his mother's words. He was clearly enjoying his teacher's punishment. "Instead you wait and you watch, just like you always have. All the time knowing outsiders were trying to build their own weapon."

"I made sure that couldn't happen."

"But you still kept us in the dark?"

Pullus swallowed. "I needed to be sure," he said, trying to explain, but knowing he was failing. "I needed to be certain."

"Of what?"

Pullus didn't answer.

"Because that's something only you're able to pass judgement on, isn't it? You and your kind? The only people with the necessary skill to alter the timeline, and to tell us that we mustn't do the same?"

"If you make a mistake…" Pullus tried to organise his thoughts, but he felt lightheaded. "I really need some water…"

"And I really need my husband," Calpurnia replied. "Is

that so hard to understand?" She turned to leave. Pullus didn't try to stop her, or call her back and explain that he didn't trust her. Didn't trust anyone. Not with the NovusPart device.

"I always assumed it would be ours," Marcus said softly. He wasn't grinning anymore. Instead, he looked pensive, and more than a little afraid. He checked that his mother was out of earshot. "I assumed that we controlled the future. But your friends outside. They must be close…"

Pullus shook his head. "Yes," he said. "But they don't have what we have."

"Which is?"

"A device that once worked."

"A device that *will* work," the boy corrected. He surveyed the small cell. "How long has it been since you had anything to drink?"

"Two days."

"So there you sit like Cimon."

Pullus knew the story. Cimon was imprisoned and left to starve, and was only saved by the epitome of Roman charity, his own daughter's breast milk, offered to him on her visits to his prison cell.

"A pity you never married," continued Marcus, as he fiddled with the door's shutter and pushed his little finger through one of the slats. "Although I could probably find someone to act as Pero."

"Please don't."

"Too proud, eh? You'd rather be Julia the Elder, who Tiberius starved to death?"

The man who couldn't be killed. The words had never tasted more sour. He watched as the boy stooped and picked up one of several dozen votives. "Your friends outside are still missing information," Marcus said. "Even with Arlen's research?"

"I think so."

The grin was back, flashing in the dark. But then it faded. "So do you think she'll be able to rescue him?"

Pullus thought back to the test with Harris. The phone call from the future. The way his brother had been destroyed during the transportation, a mess of guts and blood that had been deposited inside the paradox chamber. "I think your mother should do some further tests."

The boy nodded. "And then my father will be here."

Pullus didn't know if that was true. He had no idea if NovusPart had even looked into transporting people from Herculaneum; the profile of the site didn't fit with their business proposition. Whilst most people recognised the name "Pompeii", considerably fewer knew about Herculaneum, even if it was a more interesting site to historians.

Calpurnia had clearly chosen to ignore the fact that many from Pompeii hadn't been saved. Those men, women and children were now displays in the Naples Archaeological Museum, untransported due to minor fluctuations in ash density. And in Herculaneum, the conditions had been a whole lot worse.

"I don't think I want him back," Marcus said.

Pullus stared at him, surprised. The boy checked over his

shoulder, no doubt wondering if he'd been heard.

"As I said, I'm not convinced your mother – or the Greek – will succeed."

"We can't let her." Marcus lowered his voice even further. "He's called Marcus too. And, whoever controls the future, it needs to be me, not him."

59

Ruins of Ancient Herculaneum

"There is no need to panic. We have a robust evacuation plan. Naples is not the new Pompeii."

Italian Official,
Naples Emergency Control Centre

NICK LEANT FORWARD on the railings and stared down over Herculaneum. The ancient Roman town sat inside an excavated bowl of rock, with apartment blocks tottering along many of its edges, all lit up against a rapidly darkening sky. Where there had once been a shoreline there were now just cliffs some twenty metres high.

At the time of its burial, the town had been used to the shifting position of the coastline. The buildings at the water's edge included some fine houses whose lower floors had once been abandoned to rising tides. But now the coastline was some distance away and much of the town remained buried under the modern town and only accessible via tunnels.

The path that led down through the cliff to the foot of Herculaneum should have been bustling with tourists. But there was no one here; the site was deserted. Nick leant further forwards, feeling the weight of Arlen's research in the bag slung across his shoulder, all printed out on crisp, white paper from a printer that was on the verge of running out of ink. Joe Arlen would probably have been amused to find everything he'd saved transferred onto more tangible, archaic sheets. But with so little computer equipment still functioning in New Pompeii, he'd requested them in a format he'd be able to later examine.

Nick felt a twist of guilt and tried to push it away. He and Fabio had travelled directly to Herculaneum, and not stopped at Chloe's apartment. *We didn't have time*, he said again to himself, trying to justify it. Not enough time, when they'd barely made it here before the roads had been closed. And she wouldn't have been there anyway.

You shouldn't worry about Chloe, Waldren had said. *Not for a while, at least.*

Nick shifted his stance against the railings, dislodging some of the rust-coloured ash that had settled on it. He shook more ash from his hair. The authorities had instructed residents to stay indoors and off the roads. He imagined the Italians were keeping their fingers crossed that this was a replay of the eruption of 1944, and not a prelude to another catastrophic event. Those staffing the Vesuvius Observatory were no doubt being kept very busy, but not just with the mountain that had buried Pompeii and Herculaneum. Whilst everyone's attention would be naturally focused on Vesuvius, what perhaps fewer people knew was that the Bay of Naples was also home to a super volcano. The Campi Flegrei, and its massive magma chamber.

Even though the Italian authorities sometimes made a great play on how well prepared Naples was for another eruption, there was no real way of moving millions of people out of the potential blast zone. Everyone understood that. They were doing what the citizens of Pompeii had done all those years ago: sitting tight and seeing if it stopped. Praying it wouldn't get any worse.

Standing in Pompeii's forum, with the site long since cleared and partially restored, you could be forgiven for forgetting the town had once been buried. Not so in Herculaneum. And down there in its streets would be his answer, the thing that would make sense of the fresco in the *Gabinetto* and the graffiti in the Pompeian bakery. He was sure of it.

"We've got to go," Fabio said behind him.

Nick didn't turn round. He stared down to the boat sheds marking the former shoreline. When the end had come in AD 79, many Romans had taken shelter together in those structures. The skeletons had been found where they'd fallen. Nick let his eyes drift upwards to the plateau upon which most of Herculaneum had been built. A marble statue of a man on a horse stood out from the brick buildings. "We just need a few moments of their time," he said.

"They're not interested," said Fabio. "Everyone's leaving."

"They have carbonised scrolls here," Nick explained. "Carbonised, but still readable with the correct equipment. They must say something useful. There must be some mention of me or NovusPart."

"Well, if that's true, they're denying it."

"Can't you use your influence? Flash your Bureau badge?"

Fabio snorted. "You think they care more about that than a volcano?"

"They must have found a fresco," Nick continued. "Some piece of graffiti or even something carved into a beam or something—"

"Nick, we're at a dead end."

"No. There must be something that mentions my name and NovusPart and links everything together." Nick stopped. He stared at the statue of the horse and rider. The white marble now seemed blinding against the ash-filled sky. "They have carbonised scrolls here," he said again.

"They're not going to tell us, Nick. They're not going to admit their site is contaminated by paradox too."

Nick turned to face Fabio. There were two men standing with the Italian. Both wore dark suits, and were thick-set. Little devices snaked out of their collars and into their ears. He felt his next words catch in his throat. "You've brought company."

Fabio winced. He tipped his head, indicating the two men. "It seems Waldren anticipated you'd run," he said.

You shouldn't worry about Chloe. Not for a while, at least.

"And Chloe?" Nick asked.

"She's safe, Nick."

Nick blinked. *What?* "You're sure?"

"I've spoken to her. She's at the Bureau. She went to find Jack when the eruption started to get worse. She ran to her husband, Nick."

Nick nodded, relieved but also suddenly uncertain. *You shouldn't worry about Chloe.* Not a threat against her then, but what? He tracked back over their conversation. What was Waldren's insurance policy?

"Have they heard from him recently?" asked Nick, grimly. "Waldren? Do they know where he is?"

Although Fabio's mouth moved, Nick didn't hear the Italian's answer. He had a sudden and urgent sense that something was out of place. He looked down and saw that a soft white mist had started to gather around his feet.

His feet. Not Fabio's, or those of the two men with him. At first it was barely noticeable above the layer of ash but Nick watched it slowly creep up and swallow his ankles. He looked back to the marble statue of the man on his horse. The one thing seen and photographed by everyone who visited Herculaneum. A beacon. And suddenly he understood where the breadcrumbs led, and the graph had been plotted.

"What's happening?" Fabio said, panic in his voice.

From somewhere in the distance came a deep boom, a loud roll of thunder that seemed to fill the sky and made the ground shake. The men behind Fabio were reaching into their jackets – perhaps for weapons – but they were already too late. Far too late. Nick smiled as he wondered at the future. Thirty years from now. He took in a deep breath as he started to lose sight of Fabio.

"I think I'm becoming a god," he said.

60

New Pompeii

NICK FELL, FEELING as if he was on the edge of sleep. Then he hit the ground hard, landing on his back, the air knocked from his lungs by the satchel that was still slung across his shoulders.

He lay for a few seconds, breathing hard, staring up at the ceiling. It was vaulted in the early Imperial style. He got to his feet and stared around the small, cold room. The only light came in through a small barred window in a wooden door. Outside, he could already hear what sounded like geese honking.

"Hello!"

Nick listened to his voice echo away, and swore at himself. He'd used English as if he was still in Naples. But this wasn't Naples. He was back in New Pompeii, transported by the NovusPart device. Which meant it now worked. Whenever he'd arrived, it now worked.

And New Pompeii still existed.

It still existed, even though thirty years had passed. Thirty years *must* have passed. And yet he'd been talking to Fabio just a few seconds ago.

There was a small collection of children's toys on the floor. An action figure, a small car, a doll. "Hello!" he called again, this time in Latin. "Hello!"

There was the shuffling of movement from behind the door and more honking from the geese. Then a man's head was silhouetted at the window, the features indistinct in the darkness.

"My name is Decimus Horatius Pullus," Nick shouted. He took a couple of steps forward, but couldn't make out the face, only the wide eyes, frightened or shocked, he couldn't quite tell.

"My name is Decimus Horatius Pullus," Nick repeated. "Do you know who I am? Do you *remember* who I am?"

There was the sound of grating bolts being drawn back. The wood cracked and shifted, as if the door hadn't opened in a long time. Perhaps not since the last paradox, when the NovusPart device had interfered with the timeline and pulled someone out of their present and into the future. But someone must have known he was coming. Someone must have reached back to Herculaneum and taken him. So why hadn't this man been expecting him?

"My name is Decimus Horatius Pullus."

The man stepped through the door. Nick looked past him and realised he was in the paradox chamber adjacent to the amphitheatre. He recognised the man or, rather, he recognised the thick beard. He was one of Habitus's men. And he didn't look old, certainly not thirty years older.

"Course I know who you are," the man said, grinning. "Who could forget the cocksucker who can't fucking die?"

Nick stood mute, failing to understand.

"What are you doing in there?" the man continued. "You should have told me you wanted to look round!"

"How long have I been gone?" Nick asked. The guard seemed about to answer but then paused, his expression suddenly confused. Nick realised the man was staring at his head. He ran his fingers through his hair and felt ash drop down the collar of his shirt. "How long?"

"You've been back there," said the guard, quietly. "Haven't you? That day? The day we were all taken?"

Nick ignored the question. "How long have I been gone?"

The guard blinked. "About three weeks."

"I need to see Calpurnia."

"Of course," the guard said, smiling. "She put out word that you were to be brought to her villa as soon as you arrived." He paused, then laughed. "But I think we've got time to get you out of those funny clothes."

61

"She knows I'm here?"

THE SLAVE ON the door nodded. He remained standing at the side of his cubbyhole, his expression close to a smirk. Two guards flanked him.

Decimus Horatius Pullus hoisted his satchel further onto his shoulder. The sooner he could get this over with, the sooner he could get back to his own villa and be done with it all...

The figure standing next to the wagon was almost unrecognisable as James Harris...

Blood, flesh and shards of bone lined the floor of the paradox chamber...

Tear the place apart if you have to. We need to find what's left of Arlen's work...

Calpurnia's gift arrived a couple of hours ahead of you...

Why had he been collecting NovusPart memorabilia before Harris arrived?

Now then, Scaeva: what do you still own that could be worth two denarii?

Pullus finally made out what Whelan was trying to say…

Naso was being carried by the crowd, which was heading towards his garum pits…

He claims it was an accident, but other slaves saw it happen…

When were you going to tell us about the papers?

A steady stream of votives…

62

New Pompeii

THE CLAY DISCS dropping through the shop shutters were now being accompanied by whispered prayers. Pullus listened, both amused and uncomfortable. He wanted them to stop, and yet was grateful for the distraction. It helped pass the time inside his cell.

The days had long since morphed into weeks. Neither Calpurnia nor Marcus had been back to see him, but at least he was being provided with saucers of water and a few thin slices of bread and meat. Often it was delivered at night, when the streets were empty. Just sufficient to keep him from dying. Just sufficient to keep him wondering if each serving would also be his last.

Roman charity.

At least Marcus hadn't arranged any equivalent of Pero to visit him. He soon banished the thought, not wanting to consider what he would do if a wet nurse offered to keep him alive.

Outside it was daylight, and he could hear a crowd gathering, the barking of the guards attempting to corral the worshippers outside. Pullus didn't bother rising from the floor, let alone walk over to the shutters. He didn't have the strength, the muscles in his limbs and back knotted into one interminable ache. Instead, he waited for the first votive. Sure enough, it soon dropped and bounced amongst all the others. Then the prayers started.

He ignored them and rested his head against the wall. He felt a little dry plaster crumble and fall onto his neck.

He'd come so close. After all, he'd rushed straight to Calpurnia, only to be put off by her continued talk of her husband and her empire – and then finally stymied by the appearance of Harris and his brother.

He let out a growl. Tried to move his thoughts back to his current situation, but only found himself again thinking about the trail of breadcrumbs he'd been following in Naples: the fresco in the *Gabinetto Segreto*, the graffiti hidden at the back of the excavated bakery, the partial message from the Villa Maritima. Each had seemed a tiny piece of a puzzle, but what they'd been saying was still uncertain. None had provided him with enough information to understand the full message. Whoever had passed the words into the past, perhaps hadn't understood one crucial aspect of their plan: as years pass, things rot and decay. It wasn't as simple as hiding away a message inside a time capsule – as good a time capsule as Pompeii was – and waiting for a key piece of information to be uncovered. The meaning of the message had been lost.

"Pullus?"

One voice amongst many, but one he recognised. Pullus turned his head slowly, feeling his neck crack.

"Pullus! Quickly!"

He lolled forwards, struggling up off the floor. He went to the shutters and squinted through a gap. Taedia stood outside, buffeted by those waiting behind her in the queue.

So she was still alive. Part of him was glad her life hadn't been wasted. Another wished she had died like all the others.

"We need you, Pullus."

He sighed in irritation. "I'm locked in a cell," he said.

"There are men in town," Taedia continued. "Strange men. Some people are saying NovusPart has returned to punish us."

They're all dead, Pullus thought. Whelan. McMahon. Arlen. "Calpurnia knows about Popidius's convoys. She's dealt with it."

Taedia grunted as she was shoved from behind. Her fingers pushed through the shutters. She held on tight. "But she's not stopping them."

"Stopping them doing what?"

"They're taking the names of all the people in town," Taedia said, just as her fingers slipped.

"What?"

"They're making a list of everyone called Marcus and—"

63

*B*READCRUMBS, THOUGHT PULLUS again. Little tiny breadcrumbs scattered in the past. The fresco and the graffiti in the bakery. Whoever had left them for him to find either hadn't been transported, or had failed to make themselves known to him here in New Pompeii. If they had done, then he could have simply asked. Demanded to know the full message.

There was little light coming through the shutters, and those outside had long since returned to their homes. The solitary shuffle of feet indicated his only company was a guard. He didn't really care. They'd provided him with the day's meagre supply of food and water and were now probably just waiting for the new day to break just like him.

His mind wandered back to the graffiti, and the person who might have written it. Of course, the answer was that they hadn't been transported. The fragment left at the Villa Maritima indicated they'd left before the eruption; assuming the last breadcrumb had been dropped by the same person who'd left the first two. Or maybe it was all just a hoax. A fake. Just like Naso's phoney artworks.

His brow furrowed. Naso. There was a small anomaly he hadn't registered before. He started to scrabble about on the floor, searching through the fragments of broken amphorae. Naso had been pulling a scam: selling fake Roman copies of lost Greek masterpieces. But not Oscan.

There was no demand for fake Oscan art.

So why the fuck was there a piece of broken Oscan pottery in his cell?

He found it moments later. Cradling it in his hand, he took it to the shutters and let what little light they offered shine on its surface. It wasn't a fake. It was a real piece of Oscan pottery. So highly decorated, it was probably a prized ornament before its demise. And it had probably been at least a couple of hundred years old prior to Pompeii's destruction.

In the darkness, he smiled and turned the fragment between his fingers. Pompeii. The Roman town swallowed by a volcano. And yet in some ways, it wasn't Roman at all. Sure, the Empire had stamped its authority on it, given it a forum and an amphitheatre. Integrated men from the army into the population, and bolstered the colony with their wives and children. But at its heart this was a town of many peoples: Oscans, Etruscans, Samnites, Greeks.

Wave after wave of people, with the Romans just being the last of many.

And what he held in his hand proved something. NovusPart hadn't just transported people, they'd also taken objects. Some of the statues missing from the forum perhaps, the gold that had never been found in the temples during the

excavations. Pottery and furniture. McMahon and Whelan
had probably thought the thefts would be attributed to the
post-eruption tunnelling by the Romans themselves. Yet it
also provided the possibility of an unintended consequence.
After all, how do you get a message sent from the future
deep into the past, and back into the present?

Pullus suddenly knew the answer. You don't wait, and
hope against the ravages of time. You don't take the slow
path, not when you know your message could be zapped
into the future along with the people. Somewhere in town
there was written his answer. All he had to do was find it.

64

Ancient Pompeii, AD 79

"Hey! Old woman! Are you going to pay for that?"

Achillia glared at the owner of the *taberna*, then flicked a couple of coins in his direction. He caught the first, but the second bounced out of his palm and rolled onto the floor. As soon as he ducked down to retrieve it, she put another bread roll into her *stola*. *A small price for rudeness*, she thought, waiting for the trader to lift the coin to acknowledge payment. As soon as he'd done so, she continued down the street.

Pompeii was just as much of a shithole as she remembered. How long had it been since she was last here? Fifteen years? Maybe longer. And they were still making repairs. When she'd left, half the town had been little more than rubble. Not just the tenements or the townhouses, either. Temples had fallen, even Jupiter's had been damaged. Work was clearly still needed to clean up the mess, even after all this time.

Achillia stopped near a street shrine, trying to find her

bearings. She tried to remember what she could of her few days here, protecting some silly bitch whose name she couldn't even remember. Hadn't there been some offer of freedom?

"Hey! Old woman!"

"The next person who says that to me," Achillia said, "is going to end up holding their own stomach."

She turned to see a man of average height, lithe, if not muscular. He smiled at her, which was as close to a greeting as she was going to get. Achillia reached into her *stola* and tossed the second roll to him. He started eating without any word of thanks.

"I'm not exactly thrilled to be back here," she said.

"I hadn't realised you'd been before."

"When the earth shook."

The man shrugged and continued to eat. "The earth is always moving here. You get used to it. Keeps the fresco painters in business, anyway."

They started walking side by side in the direction of the forum. Achillia wasn't heading anywhere in particular, but walking made it harder for anyone to overhear them. That was useful in their line of work. "So are you going to let me in on the secret then?"

"What do you know?" asked the man.

"Virtually nothing. When your summons came, I was in Africa."

"Huh."

"And now I'm in Pompeii," Achillia continued. "And you know how much I hate sailing, so…?"

"You're here for the same reason you were over there," said the man.

"Really?"

"We have a new emperor, Achillia. Not long on the throne. He's nervous. Our job is what it's always been: to gently slip knives between the ribs of those who aren't cheering loudly enough." He grinned at her expression. "I thought you'd be happy. We're still just about in games season, and there's at least one session left."

"The games were banned the last time I was here."

"Well, they're not anymore. So it won't all be work."

Achillia raised an eyebrow. She was about to ask for more details of her target when a screeching from overhead made her look up. Birds were flocking, making a hellish noise as they did so. Something ran over her foot. She looked down, and kicked away a rat.

Then the earth shook.

Not for long. And nowhere near as strongly as when she'd last been in Pompeii. Just enough to knock some vegetables from a nearby stall, and topple a ladder propped against the front of a *taberna*.

The man with her grinned. "As I said, you get used to it."

"They come a lot worse than that," replied Achillia, taking a deep breath. Her heart was racing. Despite everything she'd done, and was trained to do, the shaking of the ground disturbed her. "So my target, where does he live?"

"With his father-in-law. Some man on the local *Ordo* who used to be close to Vespasian."

"Odd then, that his son…?"

"Who knows with these provincial families? Anyway, Barbatus is waiting for another turn as *duumvir* here. So, for the moment, he's out of the picture."

"Wait? Barbatus?"

"Sure. You know him?"

"*Manius Calpurnius Barbatus?*"

"That's him. Titus doesn't want the old man harmed though. Remember that. Our new emperor thinks it's useful to have someone here who can put a bit of stick about. As long as he's reminded who he's waving the stick for, of course."

65

New Pompeii

FROM THE OTHER side of the shutters came a cough, then the clink of another votive. Pullus tried to peer through the slats; the street outside was only slightly more lit than his cell. Outside, the guard was staring back at him. A man placed by Habitus, but not one he recognised.

Pullus tried to decipher the man's expression. The old saying about actions and words prompted him. The votive. "You worship at the Fortuna Augusta?"

"It isn't called that anymore."

No, thought Pullus. *No, it isn't.* And yet he couldn't quite shake that label from his head. He thought about the water and the small offerings of food. Always brought at night, but not every day. Perhaps not given under instruction by Calpurnia then, but for other reasons entirely. "You want my help?"

Outside, the guard slowly nodded. "Wife has the shivers."

Pullus felt like a hypocrite. But maybe his reluctance to

accept his position here had blinded him to what he was meant to know. Maybe he'd not seen what had been put in plain view. "Will you pray with me?" asked Pullus, his throat tightening. "At my temple?"

"They'd kill me."

"We have time. You can still bring me back before dawn."

There was no answer. Then the scrape of boots as the guard checked the street.

The door opened. Pullus felt enormous relief, but as he stepped out into the dark street he stumbled and almost fell. The guard caught him and pulled him close. "Don't try and run."

Pullus almost laughed. There was no risk of him fleeing; his legs were too weak and it didn't seem like he could remember how to control them. They headed towards the forum, the guard at his side, a firm hand gripping his shoulder.

The streets were nearly empty. They passed only two sign-writers who were applying fresh paint to their notices. Neither turned from their work to acknowledge them. Both seemed to be erasing electoral slogans supporting Popidius.

"We're not alone."

At first Pullus thought they were being followed. He soon realised though that the guard had probably been selected because he had eyes for night work: he had spotted what Pullus could not. Ahead of them, just coming into view in front of the Arch of Tiberius, stood the Temple of Fortuna Augusta.

Pullus remembered how it had looked when he'd first arrived in New Pompeii. A temple that had been immaculately restored and refined as part of the cover story that the town had been saved by the God Emperor Augustus. And yet back then it had always been empty, shunned by the Roman population who never quite believed NovusPart's smoke and mirrors. Now it had become a centre of religious activity. A multitude stood vigil at the foot of the steps, holding small oil lamps. More stood between the columns.

"You don't come here, do you?" asked the guard.

"No."

The guard let his restraining hand fall away. Pullus reached the foot of the steps leading up to the temple's portico. The waiting crowd stared at him. Were they expecting a miracle? The expression of hope on their faces caused a tug of doubt in his stomach. Pullus ignored it. It was too late now. He headed up the steps, past the colonnade, and into the depths of the temple.

He found the spot he'd first met Calpurnia. She'd been pregnant with Marcus then. He paused for a second, thinking about their conversation, all those years ago. Their secret meeting. Her whispered suspicions. Despite almost seeing through NovusPart's lies, she'd still been transfixed by one thing: the statue of Augustus.

The statue remained in place, although it now wore a different face. His face. Another little Roman tradition. After all, what was the point in wasting a statue when one could simply carve the latest god on top of the last?

He stared into its eyes. His eyes.

Looking into the past, whilst staring into the future.

"What is it I'm meant to see?"

No one answered him. He was quite alone. There was no pregnant girl to help him. He walked closer, peered at his own face. Then he saw it, transcribed onto the wall behind the statue. It was all there: the fragment from the *Gabinetto Segreto*. The graffiti from the real Pompeii. The short inscription from the Villa Maritima.

All in English. Combined and joined together with large parts of the message that hadn't survived the two-thousand-year slow road from the past.

Pullus read the words several times. Felt the implications and regret. He collapsed to the floor, sobbing.

All he'd heard about was the statue. He'd not come to the temple before in order to avoid having to stare into his own face. But it was all here waiting for him, in a language his worshippers didn't even understand. Giving the inscription a final glance, he returned to the portico. The guard was waiting for him. "They found it written on the side of a pot," he said, "left in one of the NovusPart townhouses. They thought it was important so they wrote it here."

Pullus nodded, unable to speak. A pot. A genuine Roman pot, transported out of ancient Pompeii along with its people.

"You're going to have to go back," the guard continued. "They'll kill me if you go missing."

"Fine," said Pullus, his throat tight and suddenly raw. "But I want you to take a message to Calpurnia. Tell her I'm still alive. And that I'm ready to save her husband."

66

Ancient Pompeii, AD 79

ACHILLIA TRIED HARD to push the Sibyl's voice away, but she could still hear it. Still feel the pressure in her ears like her skull might crack and hear its shouted instructions as she had in that fucking cave.

Sometimes it came to her during the day; other times, it disturbed her at night. And it was becoming more frequent, the initial instruction being supplemented with more information. More things she didn't really understand.

Was it because she was back in Pompeii? So close to the Sibyl's cave?

Achillia sat alone in a booth at the back of a small bakery. She was eating the cheapest bread on the menu, taken from loaves that were probably sent to feed rich households' slaves. It tasted fine once toasted and covered in beans and sauce.

She thought about Marcus Villius Denter. Her target. The same as always, the skill wasn't so much in the killing, but the escape. In her youth, she might have just walked up to

someone in the street and slipped a dagger through his chest.
But now her legs didn't carry her away quite as quickly, and
she'd had to become more subtle. She grunted. Wasn't that
what Barbatus had said to her, back in the day? Not just to flip
the coin but to also consider where it might land?

"Hey!"

Achillia glanced up. The owner of the bakery – a fat man
who wore most of the ingredients for his shitty loaves down the
front of his tunic – had stopped clearing another table and was
now glaring at her. She raised her eyebrows at him, took another
bite of her food, and then realised what he was going on about.

Without thinking, she'd scratched something into his
wall. She'd been absentmindedly eating with one hand, and
using her knife to carve a message with the other. Achillia
looked at her handiwork for a second, and then shrugged at
the baker. So much for not attracting attention. "Sorry," she
said. It wasn't the first time she'd found herself doing such
a thing. At first it had terrified her. Now it was just another
thing to bear, like the Sibyl's voice.

The baker went on his way, muttering, his words lost
amongst the noise of the ovens and the sound of mules
slowly turning their stones. His shape was immediately
replaced by her contact, the noticeably thinner Habitus. He
sat in the booth and shook his head.

"This town is a shithole," he said.

Achillia laughed. "I told you."

"I'd pictured somewhere nicer. Given the sorts of people
who come here."

"They mean their villas out in the hills, not the town itself."

"Huh."

"And have you been to *Baiae*?"

Habitus narrowed his eyes. "The bathing resort?"

"Yes."

"Then no, I haven't." He lowered his voice, not that there was anyone to hear. "Don't tell me you've killed someone there too?"

"Bathhouse prostitute," she said. "My cover, I mean."

Habitus laughed. "Never trust a woman," he said, leaning back. The fat baker was heading in their direction, carrying more base bread and, with it, a block of cheese. He set the food in front of Habitus, and then made a show of looking at his damn wall. "And what does that say?"

Achillia looked at her carving. She peered closer and moved her lips as if she were reading. Then she turned slowly back to the baker. "I think it says '*fuck off, cocksucker*'."

The baker took a step forward, seemingly ready to hit her. Then he glanced at Habitus and clearly decided to leave them to it. That irritated her. She was much more likely to use her knife than her current handler.

Habitus smiled at her. "I guess this is where I let you know I've rented a couple of mattresses upstairs?"

Achillia didn't say anything. He better not have fucking done.

"So, have you found the house?" he asked.

"It wasn't hard," she replied.

"How are you going to do it?"

"I haven't decided," she said. This was close to the truth. Although nearly seventeen years had passed, there was a good chance Barbatus would recognise her. And if he did, then even if he didn't know why she was there, he'd suspect trouble. That pretty much ruled out doing the job at the house. Ideally, she'd have hung around outside one of the shops by the front door and knifed Denter as he stepped inside, then pulled the door closed behind him and let him die in the corridor leading to the atrium. With a bit of luck, it sometimes took porters some time to realise their masters had been murdered. *With a bit of luck.*

"You're worried about Barbatus?"

Habitus had misunderstood her. She hadn't decided. After all, the Sibyl had told her she'd rescue this Denter, not kill him. Could she really outrun that voice? She shuddered. A voice that seemed like it could kill her?

Habitus didn't seem to notice her doubt. He reached into his tunic and took out a coin. He rolled it across the table, and it landed imperial side up. The profile was of the Emperor Titus, freshly minted. "I don't really care how you do it," he said. "But leave this by the body, ideally in his mouth. Somewhere Barbatus will find it."

Achillia took the coin and rotated it between her fingers. "He's just a provincial thug…"

"True," Habitus replied. "But now he's a rich one. And he's a clever bastard. So leave the coin; he'll get the message."

67

ACHILLIA FOUND THE trail the following afternoon when Marcus Villius Denter headed past where she'd been waiting on the *via*, walking south towards the forum. She started to follow slowly, letting one leg drag slowly behind her, restricted by the sword tied to her thigh and hidden under her *stola*. It didn't matter though. This Denter walked quickly, but he frequently stopped to talk to shopkeepers and their patrons, as well as seemingly random people in the street.

Maybe he was thinking about a political career. Achillia didn't particularly care. She kept her pace steady and herself hidden amongst the other pedestrians. The crowd thickened as they got closer to the forum, which meant it was too busy. She was either going to have to kill him in a crowd, or wait for another time.

She decided to wait, slowing her pace still further. What if Barbatus saw her at the house and recognised her? Perhaps even realised why she was there?

Fuck.

Denter had stopped again, and now she found herself

a bit too close. She continued past him, and then moved to the side of the street to get a better view. He was talking to a rough-looking man. At first their conversation seemed friendly, but when Denter tried to continue on his way, the other man took hold of his wrist to stop him from leaving. The two men began to argue, getting louder by the second, but only insults were exchanged. She could hear nothing that told her what they were arguing about, or how they knew each other.

A slight pressure started to build in her head. The ground swayed slightly, but she knew this was no tremor. The voice was coming back to her again. *The Sibyl.* "I know," she whispered. "I fucking know."

She shook her head. Across the street, the argument was over. Denter and the other man headed away together, off the main *via* and down a side street. Achillia waited a moment and then followed, her senses prickling. The side street was much quieter. Far fewer witnesses.

The metal blade at her thigh started to bite. She upped her pace and closed the gap. Both men had their backs to her; she could kill them both. The only issue was that they were now approaching a brothel where a pimp and a girl waited outside. The whore had already started to call towards Denter and his friend. She would be no problem. But the pimp? Anyone left to guard the entrance to a brothel would probably be the sort of man who could take care of himself. Sure enough, the pimp eyed Denter and his friend and crossed his arms to show that, yes, the two men could have a good time, but they were going to have to behave themselves. And they were going to have to pay.

Denter and his friend headed inside. Achillia was surprised. Denter would have his own slaves to mount. Why the hell did he want to risk his prick in a brothel? She shook her head and carried on along the street, searching for a new spot to wait and observe. It wasn't easy. A scarcity of people made an assassination easier, but it made surveillance more obvious. She'd soon be noticed, if she hadn't been already.

"Hey," shouted the pimp after her. "You don't need to struggle with that leg in here! Come work for me!"

Achillia ignored him. She'd need to double round the block and head back to the main *via* to take up a new position. Somewhere close to the side street so she could watch for Denter once he'd finished his rutting. Then she'd most likely follow him home and give up for the day. Report back to Habitus and maybe come up with a new plan. Something that might involve the *frumentarius* himself.

"Hey, old woman! No one will mind your wrinkles!"

Achillia stopped and slowly turned. The pimp was laughing at her, but his girl had gone inside. He held his arms loose by his side, his stance relaxed. Which meant he'd also lost his physical advantage. *Old woman.*

She turned and started walking towards him. Feeling the metal first bite then loosen as she flipped the sword into her hand and rammed it into the man just above his waist. She wrenched it to the side, pulled it out, watched him fall. Then she reached down and tore something wet and hot and quivering from his belly. He probably caught sight of it just before his eyes fluttered closed. "Here it is," she whispered.

It was too late to stop now. She stepped over the body and into the brothel. There were two booths on the left and three on the right. Curtains had been pulled across all five of them, although they drowned out none of the noises. Achillia lifted the first curtain and quickly dropped it. The old man and whore inside didn't notice her intrusion. She moved to the next curtain. A woman was riding a man who didn't look like he was really enjoying it. The girl was made up to look Egyptian, and kept speaking what sounded Greek, even if she was probably neither.

Behind the next curtain was Denter's friend. The girl who'd been outside with the pimp lay on the bed, the man standing by her, naked, with a stiff cock that was bent and curled at an angle that seemed to have the whore's full attention, as if she didn't know what she was going to do with it.

Achillia moved to the next curtain but found the space beyond empty. She tensed, her sword up, as she swept inside the final cubicle. But Denter wasn't there. Instead she saw an old man on top of a woman who looked dead behind the eyes.

"Shit," she whispered. Turning back into the corridor, Achillia found Denter's friend had already stumbled from his booth. Still naked, but this time with a knife in his hand. It was only now that he seemed to notice her sword – and the pimp's blood that was still running down its blade.

"Wait," he shouted, dropping the knife and holding up his hands, his dick drooping. "For fuck's sake, wait!"

"Marcus Villius Denter," Achillia said.

The ground started to shake. The building jolted. From behind the curtains came cries of surprise and fright, the sound of men and women scrabbling for their clothes. Plaster fell from the ceiling. Achillia looked up, and wondered about the structure. How much could it endure?

"Upstairs! Fucking hell, he's upstairs!"

The building lurched and rolled. Achillia heard footsteps from above, then hammering downwards. She went further down the corridor and felt a breath of air to her left. There was a second exit, back onto the street. Beyond that, another whore sat on a toilet behind a privacy screen.

Achillia ignored her and headed up the stairs just as two men tried to get down past her. They were moving so quickly they didn't notice her sword. Neither of them were Marcus Villius Denter, and he wasn't in the dank upstairs apartment either.

The second exit. He'd already fled. Maybe ran as soon as the earth had started shaking. Achillia scurried back downstairs. All the curtains had been tossed aside and the cubicles were empty. She looked to the entrance of the brothel. A cluster of people were standing outside, still trying to pull on their clothes. Some were screaming and pointing at the dead pimp.

Fuck.

Habitus would not be pleased.

68

New Pompeii

"I HEARD YOU WERE here…"

It had been another day before they'd come for him. The door to his cell had been flung open in the early morning and they'd hauled him onto the back of a wagon. Pullus now stood inside another small, square room. But at least this one had a clear and definite use. Right down to the small collection of toys by his feet, intended to entertain the children NovusPart had pulled through time. Wiped clean of the blood left behind by Harris's brother.

"Paradox," said the voice behind him. Pullus turned to face Calpurnia. "We keep it set out just as NovusPart had it."

Pullus kicked away a small, wheeled car and walked out of the paradox chamber and back into a corridor of Calpurnia's villa. "Though I take it you haven't had any unexpected arrivals?"

"Not yet. Just you, at the amphitheatre."

Pullus curled his lip. So she now knew about that too. No doubt her network of informers had been poring over recent days to try and work out how he'd been able to deceive her. "I don't know what happened," he said.

"You were transported."

"But not thirty years into the future."

"No. Just a day or so." Pullus thought about their still inactive NovusPart device. "And not by us."

"By who then?"

Someone in the future, thought Pullus. Someone who had a NovusPart device, and who had simply picked him up from their past, and dropped him again. Closer to their present but not a full transportation. Not the full thirty years. Again, something that he hadn't considered possible: just like the messages that had been hidden in Pompeii. "By whoever finally gets our device working," Pullus said. "And by the looks of it, they find a way to improve it."

They were quite alone. This part of her villa still had the smell of NovusPart. Their equipment meant it couldn't be Romanised, so the walls remained covered in a drab terracotta gloss, and the only additions to the bare concrete floor were a few small piles of goose shit.

The NovusPart device sat only a few rooms distant, close to the paradox chamber. Pullus realised he'd never seen it. Not once in fifteen years of living in New Pompeii. He opened his mouth to say something, but found his jaw suddenly locked. It cracked free seconds later, causing him to grimace in pain.

Calpurnia seemed concerned. "Are you alright?"

Pullus didn't know. "Yes… I think so."

Calpurnia looked at him sympathetically. "It can be difficult to decipher what the gods – those in the future – want from us," she said. "You once told me that it sometimes only takes a thought, an off-hand remark, to trigger the solution. And more often than not, it happens inside *your* head."

Pullus looked about him. The only other person in this part of the building would be the Greek. He was likely with the device now, along with Arlen's research papers, trying to entice its secrets. "I didn't hide Arlen's research to stop you from saving your husband," he said, trying to explain. "I just don't trust anyone with the timeline. I thought that if I could somehow stop it, somehow keep the device from becoming active, whilst maintaining the illusion to the outside world that you had the power to use it, then—"

"But we know it does become active."

Fate. Maybe it was just as Harris had told him; that events propagate backwards and not forwards. So the device would become active.

But that was the future. Now it was time to change tack, to show Calpurnia one thing about who really did rule the future. "You must know about the men in the town taking names?"

Calpurnia nodded. "Habitus is dealing with it," she said.

"Why do you think they have a specific interest in finding people called Marcus? The name of your husband and your son?"

"Habitus is dealing with it," Calpurnia said again. "And next time you go to Naples, you can tell them they failed again."

"We heard a voice from the future," continued Pullus, feeling at his jaw. "A man calling himself Marcus. And now we have men making a list of names of men with that name."

"This isn't why you're here."

"But why? Surely we know who Marcus is? It's your son, isn't it? That's what everyone thinks. That's certainly what *he* thinks."

"This isn't why I brought you here," Calpurnia said again. "You told the guard you knew how to transport my husband."

"I told the guard what you needed to hear. But I need you to consider something…"

"I don't have time for your games, Pullus!"

"Your husband and your son both share the same name. And now there's men in town making lists."

Calpurnia shook her head. "I have the cellphone, Pullus. The phone that called us from the future. You said so yourself."

"But you never get to use it," Pullus replied. "It's not your name or your voice. Which means that at some point someone takes the NovusPart device from you, or you die of natural causes before it is made to work."

For a long time, Calpurnia didn't say anything. Then she sighed. "Women just aren't allowed to rule, are we?"

Pullus shook his head.

"My son. That's why you're here, isn't it?"

"All we really know is that whoever has been playing with the timeline does so several years from now… and they go by the name of Marcus."

"Marcus is a very common name."

"Your son certainly thinks it should be him. But what if it's not?"

Calpurnia looked like she was going to cry. At first, Pullus assumed she was thinking about her husband. Then it struck him. She'd had Arlen's research for days and the Greek must have had the opportunity to scan Herculaneum multiple times. But it couldn't have worked, because Calpurnia's husband still wasn't here. And then they would have tried another plan.

Another option.

"I think I've made a mistake," she said, her voice shaking. "But Whelan was whispering it. Always whispering it."

Pullus felt his throat tighten. Whelan's face came to mind, his slack jaw, the blackness of his eye sockets. And the single name he'd been whispering over and over. Arlen. "What have you done?"

"He wouldn't stop. It's why we kept him alive for all these years."

"Calpurnia…"

"You only told us gradually, Pullus. About NovusPart. About how Whelan and McMahon eliminated their business partner…" She let out a small sob. "But how could they have done so, Pullus? How could Whelan and McMahon have transported him into the future when they're both already dead?"

"Please tell me you haven't…?"

"It made sense, Pullus. Safeguards upon safeguards, you said so yourself. And it made me think: what if the inventor became the target of his own device? Why would he risk an incorrect setting ripping him apart like Harris's brother? The answer is simple: he made sure it wouldn't. He designed the device so that if he became the target, he would be transported safely."

"Calpurnia—"

"It was the only choice I had, a gamble. Whelan told us where and when he'd been transported. And who better to help me find my husband than Joe Arlen?"

69

HABITUS STARED ACROSS the booth at the back of the bakery, his face set like it couldn't quite express what his brain was telling him. Achillia was glad there were no other customers. It was nearly nightfall and the baker and his staff were clearing up. Soon they'd be heading upstairs to their flea-infested mattresses. "So you killed a pimp," he said, slowly. Flexing his jaw like he wanted to shout but knew that he couldn't, not with the baker and his staff so close by. "And then you ran amok through the brothel. But you didn't manage to kill a man who was busy fucking some whore?"

Achillia didn't flinch. "He wasn't there for sex."

"So you say."

"Why would he be? He'd have enough slaves at home."

"New wife. Funny creatures." Habitus shook his head. "A brothel," he repeated, like he still couldn't believe it. "I'm beginning to see why they don't let you off the leash in Rome."

Achillia shrugged. "There was an incident."

"Huh. I'm sure there was." Habitus paused. "So, Denter's friend. Would you recognise him again if you saw him?"

Achillia thought for a moment. "I'd recognise his cock."

"This isn't funny."

"You didn't see it."

Habitus glared across the table. Achillia ignored him. "So this Abderite was cremating his dead father," she said. "As the flames started to go out, he rushed home to his sick, penny-pinching mother. To see if she wanted to save some money, and get cremated at the same time."

Habitus was unamused. "Always the laughter lover."

The fat baker approached the booth, a small boy by his side. A cripple by the looks of him, dressed in little more than rags. The baker took hold of the back of his neck and pushed him forward.

"He says he's here to see you."

Habitus nodded, and waved away the baker. The fat man didn't move. "I don't want to see him here again," the baker said, looking down at the boy. "And we'll soon be dowsing the lights, so make this quick."

"Fine," Habitus replied. He held the baker's gaze until he backed away. The boy took a couple of steps closer. He seemed frightened, his one good eye flicking between the two of them. The other remained quite still in its socket.

"You have news?" Habitus asked.

The boy nodded. "He's gone."

Achillia leant forward. "Who?"

The beggar boy's eye switched back to Habitus. "Marcus Villius Denter."

Achillia slapped the table with the flat of her hand. "Where?"

Habitus waited for her anger to subside. "What did you see?"

"Some men came to the house looking for him," the boy whispered. "There was a lot of shouting. The big man was there. He waved them away."

"Barbatus?"

The boy nodded. "Denter had already gone though. He left on a horse like he was in a big hurry."

"Do you know where he went?"

The boy shook his head, his body rigid as if expecting a blow.

"The men at the door," Habitus continued. "Could you hear what they were saying?"

The boy nodded.

"Well?"

"Said Denter had tricked them." The boy's good eye switched to Achillia. "Said he'd brought someone with him to kill them. Some woman."

Habitus leant back in the booth and started to laugh. He reached into his tunic for a few coins, which he passed to the boy. Then he pushed the remains of his food to him. "Eat it," he said.

Achillia couldn't hide her confusion. "I don't get it."

"If you cut Barbatus in half," Habitus explained, "you'd probably find him filled with purple dye. He's the emperor's man here."

"But his son-in-law's a republican."

"And what would you think if you invited a man into your group and some butcher turned up to slay your friends? They don't know Denter was the target."

"I'd think I was betrayed."

"They wanted revenge, but Denter has already run away."

"But not Barbatus."

"Barbatus doesn't run," the boy said, scooping the last of the food into his hands. "Barbatus runs from nothing."

Achillia thumbed towards the door. She was about to tell him to fuck off, but the beggar boy was already on his way. "Smart lad," she said.

"You can always find them," Habitus replied. "Easier money than playing on people's sympathies. Especially in a town like this. You should make more use of them, now you're getting on a bit…"

"Careful…"

Achillia thought of the Sibyl's voice and what it had told her. "Maybe you have another cripple who can find out where he's gone?"

"No, I think it's obvious."

"Really?"

"Denter's family comes from a town called Herculaneum. Just north of here, on the other side of the bay."

Beneath them, the ground shifted slightly. Just a small tremor, but it was enough to make Achillia grip the edge of the table. "Shit," she whispered.

Habitus ignored her. "You think you'll miss again?" he asked.

Achillia felt her grip tighten. The carving she'd made the night before was still fresh on the wall beside her. She still didn't understand it. "I can promise you this," she said. "Marcus Villius Denter is never coming back to Pompeii."

70

New Pompeii

"THE MAN'S DANGEROUS."

"We have him contained."

"Where?"

Calpurnia took a deep breath. At the far end of the corridor from where they stood outside the paradox chamber, several geese came into view where NovusPart's old control villa met the newer, Roman buildings. The birds hissed. "I'm not a fool, Pullus."

"McMahon and Whelan acted for a very good reason…"

"They didn't act at all," Calpurnia reminded him. "You call this Arlen mad, like Caligula or Nero?"

"So you have been listening."

"All men corrupted by power, Pullus. *Power.* A madman is only dangerous if he has a sword or an army. Arlen has neither. We have him contained. He doesn't have access to the device. Everything is done via the Greek."

"And so Arlen is now working to save your husband?"

Calpurnia nodded.

And what else is he working on?

Communication with the past. Backwards transmission of information. NovusPart hadn't been able to achieve it, but what if their boy genius was back behind the controls? Working away with a fully functional device?

Footsteps echoed into the corridor, cutting off his thoughts. Nick turned to find Marcus and Habitus heading towards them. Although the *frumentarius's* face was set like thunder, the boy wore his usual grin. He seemed victorious.

"Marcus," said Calpurnia. "Go back to your room. Wait for me there."

The boy didn't stop, Habitus suddenly looking more like muscle hired for aggression than for protection.

"Marcus—"

"Show her, Habitus."

Habitus reached into the folds of his tunic and slipped out the NovusPart cellphone. The one that Harris had asked them to get from the stores. The one that had rung with the message from the future. The signpost to who controlled the NovusPart device. Calpurnia lurched forward, but Habitus tucked it back out of reach.

"It will be me, Mother," Marcus said. "So now you'll go and call off the Greek. Your husband—"

"Your father," Calpurnia interrupted, her voice cold.

Marcus jabbed his finger at Pullus. "*He's my father!*"

Pullus ignored the angry gesture, his concentration locked on Habitus. As usual, the bodyguard was armed, a sword at his waist. And yet he appeared quite calm, like he was waiting for matters to play out. "The men in town making lists," Pullus said. "They're working for you, aren't they?"

Marcus just rolled his eyes like a teenager would at a parent who'd only just started to understand.

"So are you going to kill them all?"

The boy nodded. "I've already started! I executed the first five myself. It will be me, Pullus. When my mother dies, it has to be me. All the great emperors of Rome eliminated their enemies. I'm going to make sure the future won't have a choice."

"*When Calpurnia dies*," Pullus repeated, "New Pompeii will be ruled by two *duumviri*. The change is already happening, and the *Ordo* is not going to follow a teenage boy."

"Caligula—"

"Caligula was loved by his people," Pullus replied quickly, knowing Marcus was well versed in his Suetonius. "A descendant of Augustus and the son of a war hero. But the people of New Pompeii barely know who you are. And whilst your grandfather was respected, he wasn't loved. So no, they won't follow you. And if you start killing everyone you think may be in your way, it won't be long before you end up dead yourself."

"No," Marcus said, shaking his head. "I'm just like you and Mother. I can't be killed. I have the NovusPart device."

"Really? Because from where I'm standing, it looks like Habitus is the one actually holding the phone."

For a few seconds, no one said anything. The grin froze on Marcus's lips, and then he turned slowly, hand out as if asking for something that he knew wouldn't be given.

Habitus's calm expression finally broke. "Always Pullus, isn't it? Always Pullus who works things out?"

The bodyguard shoved Marcus to the floor. Almost immediately, Calpurnia ran forward. Habitus moved so fast Pullus barely saw the sword suddenly in his hand. "We can't change the future," Habitus said, his sword suddenly glistening crimson.

Calpurnia crumpled. The Empress of Time. Dead. Gone. And no one had intervened. No one had reached back in time to stop the assassin from killing the person he was meant to protect. Habitus the bodyguard.

The Imperial spy.

Frumentarius.

"We've already heard their voices," Habitus said, walking over to where Marcus sat shaking on the floor. Pullus tried to move but the muscles in his back suddenly tightened, and he knew he wouldn't make it in time. Habitus slammed his sword into the youngster's throat, freezing a look of impotent rage on the boy's face. "They've already demonstrated they exist. And there's nothing we can do to stop them from speaking."

Pullus snapped his attention back to Calpurnia. He half expected her to rise again, phoenix-like. "So you fancy yourself as the new Sejanus?"

Habitus smiled. The comparison seemed to amuse him. "The Emperor Tiberius cut himself off from Rome, just as Calpurnia did from Pompeii... but really, Pullus? Sejanus was a simple thug. He would have been far wiser to kill the Emperor and keep a pliable heir under his will at Capri."

Pullus tilted his head towards Calpurnia and her son. "The people won't follow you without them," he said. "Despite everything, they still owe her for saving them from NovusPart. What do they owe you?"

"What did the people of Rome owe Sejanus? Nothing. So let me ask you this: who has seen Calpurnia these last few years, other than a handful of people? And who has seen her son? Virtually no one. So to all intents and purposes, they can remain alive in her villa. Maybe I could even use one of your crippled boys as a stand-in puppet. And the best bit? All it took was a handful of men with no loyalty to the old regime."

Pullus sneered. "Waldren?"

"A fair trade," replied Habitus. "In exchange for useless bits and pieces left over from NovusPart, he sent me some of his best men. Of course, he thinks he'll use one of them to get to the NovusPart device, but that's the game, isn't it? And it's one I've always been good at playing. Maybe I'll up the stakes by skipping them through quarantine and sending one of them home with the shivers. I take it your friends back home don't fully realise the fences protect them just as much as they protect us?"

Pullus blinked. Didn't move. Spy. An Imperial spy. And then he remembered something from his first visit to the old slave market. Just seconds after he'd spotted Habitus and asked about his former occupation. Habitus had hesitated before giving his name. Maybe still confused by the transportation and fall of NovusPart, but a spy nonetheless. He'd given a false identity. He could have been called anything.

Anything at all.

Habitus's smile grew broader. "It's a very common name," he said, perhaps realising. "And soon there'll only be one person in this town called Marcus. And they'll be holding an old NovusPart cellphone. Ready to make calls into the past, whilst controlling the future."

"You really think so?"

Habitus let out a snort. His grip seemed to tighten on his sword, the muscles in his arm bulging. "I've always been told you're the man who can't be killed."

Pullus again looked at Calpurnia and Marcus. A small pool of blood had already formed to cover the concrete around them.

"Except I think I've figured out how to kill you, Pullus."

There was no mist. Just like when he'd faced down Popidius's man, there wasn't anything to indicate a transportation into the future. But the big difference between now and then was that there was no fear in Habitus's eyes. The *frumentarius* had already taken a chance on Calpurnia and Marcus, already proven to himself that he really did control the future. Still, even if it only bought him some time, it would be worth it. A few moments to think about the words written in the Temple of Fortuna Augusta.

"I'd be surprised if you had the courage to kill me yourself."

Habitus didn't respond. Instead he just tossed his sword onto the floor. It scattered across to Pullus and came to rest by his feet.

Pullus looked down at the blade, confused. "You want me to fight you?"

"You've lost, Pullus. Your household is butchered, and you've allowed Calpurnia and her son to be killed. Now it's time to answer your own question. That thing you've been struggling with for the last fifteen years. Are you a Roman, or are you a coward?"

The sword lay there, covered in Calpurnia's blood. Marcus's blood.

There was no mist surrounding it. He was alone. And maybe Habitus was right.

"It's the Roman way. You've lost here. And you've lost at home as well, *Nick Houghton*."

Pullus stared at the sword. Even with it, he wouldn't be able to beat Habitus. The *frumentarius* was too strong. Too fast. Too used to killing people.

"The new men from the convoys have told me some interesting things about you," Habitus said. "They say you've been accused of doing something disgusting. I must admit, I don't fully understand – but I do know you can't go home. But maybe if I was just to bundle you on a wagon and let them take you? How would you like to live the rest of your life under that cloud?" Habitus smiled. "But no doubt your family would help you? Or your friends?"

Pullus remained silent. He no longer had any friends. Any family. He thought of his father, and felt something inside of him crumble. But most of all he thought of the words in the Temple of Fortuna Augusta.

"Not that your remaining life will be very comfortable," Habitus continued. "Waldren told me he'd found a way to ensure your compliance. Something to do with your father? Something he said he could slip into your food, some sort of new disease?"

Pullus felt his limbs tighten, and his jaw lock. It crunched free again seconds later, but by that time he knew it was already too late. *Insurance policy*. Waldren had told him he had an insurance policy, but then he'd made his careless remark: *You shouldn't worry about Chloe. Not for a while, at least.*

Waldren hadn't meant to imply he'd taken her to the Novus Institute – he'd simply been revelling in the fact that he'd soon have more serious concerns. *Because you have the same disease that's warping your father's body*, the spy should have said. But he'd simply not had the chance to apply the real pressure. Nick hadn't given him the time.

"Waldren described it as something that would cripple, but not kill you," Habitus continued. "Which would give you time to think and finally betray Pompeii."

"I don't quite…"

"He was going to tell you he had a cure," Habitus said, clearly taking pleasure in the explanation. "A man who's desperate will do just about anything. Especially when he's seen someone close to him killed by the same disease. But you should know now that there isn't one. Waldren was just going to dangle the idea in front of you and make you grasp for it."

Pullus remembered the sanatorium. All those people suffering from a new illness that turned people to stone.

And the blade was right there in front of him.

There was nowhere left for him to go.

71

Road to Ancient Herculaneum, AD *79*

You will find the daughter of Manius Calpurnius Barbatus.

You will save her husband Marcus Villius Denter by taking him to meet Balbus in Herculaneum.

ACHILLIA WOKE. FOR a few seconds her head spun. The words of the Sibyl thumped inside her brain, the force of the instruction sudden and heavy. But the spinning of the earth hadn't been caused by the Sibyl. And it hadn't been what had toppled her from her horse.

Horse.

Achillia got to her feet and dusted herself down. The damn thing had bolted, taking with it her saddle bags and her sword. She'd have to continue her journey on foot, and kill Denter using nothing more than the dagger at her belt. Which was doable, but she preferred entering unfamiliar towns carrying something with a greater range of thrust.

She took a few steps, trying to sense if any bones had been broken. She felt sore, but her limbs seemed to move freely. She rolled her shoulders, tested her sword arm. She lunged, arm out, as if to stab someone.

Yes, they'd still die. Damn horse.

Damn noise.

Achillia stopped. Yes, that had been what had spooked the horse and made it rear up. Thunder. A great crack of the gods' anger – bellowing out from an otherwise clear blue sky.

Achillia stumbled forward along the track towards Herculaneum. Hercules would likely not be impressed. If Pompeii was the armpit of Italy then Herculaneum was its navel. By all accounts, home to just a few thousand people. Insignificant. Probably not even a good place to hide, unless you had a lot of family living there. Which Denter did, and he'd be surrounded by them. A good idea then to find her horse, or at the very least jump someone with a sword.

The fall from the horse – the voice of the Sibyl – had made her groggy. Achillia swayed. She wondered if the earth was moving again but doubted it. No, she just needed a few seconds to allow her head to stop swimming. She moved to the side of the path and leant against a sturdy-looking tree. Until being thrown, she'd been making good time, had left Pompeii at first light. And yet…

It was dark.

She'd been aiming to arrive in Herculaneum by late morning. Maybe early afternoon. But it was already getting dark. She looked up at the sky, towards the distant Vesuvius. Her stomach turned.

Most of the mountain appeared to have been lifted into the air. A great, thick torrent of smoke was rising into the sky. Higher than even the bravest gods might venture – and then spreading out like a tree, the top of the cloud expanding to form branches above the main trunk. The smoke was completely black, blocking out the sun, but also lighting up every few seconds with brief jagged flashes.

You will save Marcus Villius Denter.

"Shit," she whispered. She turned and started to walk quickly. After only a few steps, a stone landed in front of her. Automatically, Achillia stooped to pick it up. She yelped and dropped it. The stone was scorching hot, and more followed in its wake, pattering all around her. "Shit," she said again, this time louder.

You will save her husband Marcus Villius Denter by taking him to meet Balbus in Herculaneum.

72

New Pompeii

NICK FELL TO his knees. He lifted the sword in both
hands so he could feel the tip of the weapon against his
stomach. He just needed to pull it towards him. Hard and
fast. The blade would do the rest. There would be no more
Nick Houghton. No more Decimus Horatius Pullus.

No more pain.

"All I ever wanted to be was a Roman," Nick said, quietly.
"Ever since I was a small boy, visiting Hadrian's Wall. Waving
my fist at the barbarian hordes as they descended south." He
knew his words meant nothing to Habitus. "He was a fine
emperor. And born in Spain. Imagine that, one of Rome's
greatest emperors, and he wasn't even born in Italy."

"Do you really want these to be your last words?"

"Neither was Trajan," continued Nick. "Or Claudius.
You know him, don't you? Claudius, the historian? The
stuttering fool? Found hiding by the Praetorian Guard after
Caligula had been killed? The most unlikely of emperors. He

was born in Gaul, not Italy. Not Rome. So I guess I've always been wrong about what made a Roman."

Nick shifted his grip on the sword, and started to breathe fast. He looked up at Habitus. "You have the cellphone?" he asked, his voice breaking.

"Yes," replied Habitus.

"And you think that means you control the future?"

"You said so yourself, Pullus. Someone spoke to you from the future. They called this phone. And to do so, they needed to know its number. Its unique identifier. And with the phone, I'm the only person who's going to know it. And I'll be the only man left in this town called Marcus. Why, you think my logic flawed? You think I'm wrong?"

Pullus didn't answer. But he already knew the *frumentarius* was wrong. Because he'd read a clear message from the future, transmitted deep into the past. And he'd heard the voice on the phone. All he needed to do was hold his nerve. The off-hand remark. The one additional piece of information that had allowed him to make sense of all this.

I have a bunch of letters from my father.

Pullus screwed his eyes shut, screaming inside his own head. Because if this didn't work anyone could find those letters. Even Habitus. And then they would all know. Because he couldn't protect a thought that had already been written down.

The *frumentarius* took a few steps forward. "It's time, Pullus," he said. "It's time for the man who can't be killed to die."

"I heard a voice on the phone," Pullus whispered, almost to himself. "A voice I didn't recognise." His words were barely audible, and Habitus leant forwards.

Instinct. Even for a spy, it was instinct.

Something he shouldn't have really done.

"But have you ever heard a recording of your own voice, Habitus?" Pullus turned the sword and thrust it upwards. Straight into the *frumentarius*'s gut. "Because if you have you'll know it's hard to recognise it. Especially if you're going to develop a locked jaw."

73

Ancient Herculaneum, AD 79

A CHILLIA HAD LONG stopped being scared of the ground moving beneath her feet. She stumbled into the streets of Herculaneum, not really knowing where she was going but knowing she needed to be there.

The town was no coastal navel. The buildings looked expensive, the streets well maintained. She could see a theatre in the distance. There was money here, more so than further around the bay in Pompeii.

A brief shower of hot rock and pebbles scattered around her. She looked upwards at the cloud above Vesuvius. It looked heavy. The branches of the smoke-laden tree now looked more and more like a hammer about to fall.

Just as soon as the trunk snapped.

She ignored it and concentrated on the words of the Sibyl. She saw a woman in the distance, covering her head with a pillow and hurrying across the street. Achillia followed her down an alley, felt a moment's panic as a building beside her started to crack, and then caught the woman by the arm.

"Marcus Villius Denter!"

The woman looked back at her, confused.

"Marcus Villius Denter! Where is he? Where can I find him?"

The woman didn't answer. She looked feeble, but still managed to wriggle her arm free and scramble away. Achillia let her go. Another load of hot rock and ash fell around her, singeing her hair, gathering on her shoulders. She headed back to the open street and stumbled onwards, heading through the town until she managed to reach its very edge. A thin promenade that looked down over a wall and deep into the town's harbour.

And then she laughed. Because the sea had gone.

There was no water. No sea. Just a long, wide expanse of sand covered in nothing but a myriad of small pools, fish and stranded boats. It looked odd, desperately funny. Lined up against the boathouses along the shore stood what must have been most of the town's inhabitants, staring mute into the bay. Seemingly stranded between the shore and the town's walls.

Slaves, free men and the rich, Achillia thought bitterly. All suddenly the same, staring at the catastrophe unfolding in front of them, when all they had to do was to look up to see what was going to happen next. The hammer above them.

You will save her husband Marcus Villius Denter by taking him to meet Balbus in Herculaneum.

Achillia felt anger rise in her belly. All this time, the Sibyl had been toying with her. Marking her path, and trying to influence her future. But she didn't want it. *There's no such thing as fate*, she reminded herself. No such thing as destiny.

"Why? Why the fuck should I?"

There was no answer from the Sibyl. And what had Barbatus once told her? Hadn't the Sibyl once burned her own prophecies? Hadn't she burned the future?

Behind her, buildings fell. Each one filled the air with more dust. She wanted to shout at the Sibyl. But she didn't.

Because she'd found Balbus.

She stumbled towards him. A man riding a white horse, looking out over the harbour. Perhaps signalling to those arriving by boat that this had once been his town. *Once*. A man who was already dead. A man who'd already been given his statue.

M. Nonius Balbus.

The inscription was clear.

Achillia blinked, again laughing. A senator. He'd been dead for years. The Sibyl had been fucking with her. Telling her to rescue some man by taking him to see another who was already dead.

She turned away from the statue. Another woman was now heading past her, down towards the harbour. She took a step forward to block her, but the woman swerved just out of reach. "Marcus Villius Denter!" she shouted, but got no response. Perhaps she didn't hear. Perhaps she didn't know who she was talking about. Not that it mattered. Denter would be down in the harbour, along with all the rest. But to find him down there? Amongst all the others? No, it suddenly seemed impossible. And that was perhaps something even the Sibyl hadn't foreseen.

"It's just me," Achillia shouted into the air. "I'm the only one here!"

The ground moved again. From below her, in the harbour, came a wave of noise. A collective scream that signalled they all now understood. Achillia turned back to the mountain. The trunk of the tree looked to have finally snapped, the cloud of ash and smoke falling, tumbling down the mountain.

"It's just me," Achillia shouted again. She leapt forward and began to climb the statue, as a thin mist started to envelop its base. "It's just me," she said again, this time more quietly. She grasped the statue's head with both hands. "Fuck your fate! So make your choice, Sibyl! Make your choice!"

74

New Pompeii

To Nick Houghton, NovusPart

Son,

    By the time you read this, I may very well be dead. I know it is too late for us to reconcile our differences, but I still want you to know that I am very proud of you. I keep reading about you and the Empress of Time, Calpurnia. I can't believe that you were once my Nick, now my Pullus — master of Pompeii. I hope you know that your mother would have been very proud too, and I only wish she could have seen it.

    If we don't see each other again, I can only wish you every success on your onward journey. Who knows? Perhaps the Master of Pompeii will become the Emperor of Time?

Love, Dad

Joe Arlen.

The figure standing beside the statue in the Fortuna Augusta wasn't what he was expecting. He looked young. Almost a kid, not quite an adult. And he stood examining the detail of the inscription on the rear wall like a tourist might survey the finest frescos of Campania, showing more interest than either McMahon or Whelan ever had. Then again, New Pompeii was Arlen's idea. It was his baby, something he must have been thinking about for a long time before he'd finally had the opportunity and technology to put it into action.

"It was written for you," Arlen said, sounding at once both bewildered and relieved. "This is what started it all. At Cambridge, I was shown a fragment of a fresco by a friend studying ancient history. *The Master of Pompeii will become the Emperor of Time.* It was close to when I made my breakthrough with the temporal technology, and more than enough to trigger my obsession with this place. To focus what I wanted to do with the NovusPart device. I thought it was my destiny."

"And is it everything you hoped for?" Pullus asked, suddenly uncertain. This wasn't the man he'd been warned about. Not the man who'd lost his mind before being transported into the future. Maybe that had all happened later. But there was a spark there. Clear in his eyes. Some hint of genius. Maybe madness too.

"It is more than I thought I could possibly achieve."

Pullus walked forward. His limbs remained stiff, and he

knew the path to disability he would eventually follow. But he also knew that he still had time, and that diseases could be cured. Or at the very least slowed down, and relieved. Especially if pressure could be placed on those investigating the illness. What would it do to him though? Whilst he waited? How bad would it get?

Arlen continued to stare at the inscription. "So your father is dead, I presume?"

"Yes," Nick replied. "His letters are at my townhouse. Unopened." Pullus pointed at the rear wall of the Fortuna Augusta. "I assume the last one I received must say something like that."

"And so we know what we must do," said Arlen. The young man's eyes were moving back and forth, as if working at a puzzle. "We'd need some way to communicate with the past, and get someone to write all this down for you."

Pullus's throat pinched. "They had no cellphones back then," he said, thinking about how his future self would soon start communicating with Harris and directing his actions.

"You wouldn't need one," replied Arlen. He laughed as if something had suddenly occurred to him. "There'd be no signal. But I wonder if it would be possible to create a small perturbation using the existing tracking systems. A vibration, if you will. Deep inside the ear, by moving particles a fraction. Bumping them about. It would still be difficult of course, the message perhaps not clear. You may even be able to transmit images, if you could do the same thing in the eye."

"Then why a phone? Why use a phone at all?"

"Oh, a phone would be useful. It would stop someone thinking they were going mad. Voices in the head, and all that." Arlen stopped, his eyes still flicking around. He started chuckling to himself. "Less risk of that in the past," he said. "More gods to whom we could attribute our voices. But still, it wouldn't be pleasant for whoever we chose."

Pullus remained nervous. The power Arlen had once held over all of time had quickly corrupted him. But as Calpurnia had said, that power had now been taken away. *A madman is only dangerous if he has a sword or an army*. That didn't mean, however, that Arlen could be allowed a free hand.

Behind him, some movement caught Nick's attention. Taedia hovered on the portico of the temple, a handful of men with her. As soon as he'd dealt with the bodies at Calpurnia's villa, he'd come back to town to speak with the *Ordo*, to put in motion new elections for the posts of *duumvir* and aedile. The men of the town council had listened to him patiently, aware no doubt that outside in the forum was a large gathering of his temple followers. Not just those that had already considered him to be a god, but all the men, women and children who were now grateful that he'd stopped Calpurnia's son before he could travel down the path of Caligula, Nero or Commodus.

Pullus swallowed. "Tell me about Herculaneum," he said.

"Why do you want to know?"

"Let's just say I made a promise," Pullus replied. "Calpurnia wanted to rescue her husband from Herculaneum. She'd been trying for years…"

"We can only get momentary glimpses through the ash cloud," Arlen replied. "The pull wouldn't be clean... you might not get everything coming through."

"And what if we could get Calpurnia's husband to wait in a specific part of the town? Somewhere we could get a lock? Maybe somewhere easy to find, like at the foot of a statue?"

"Then, yes: it would be possible. You want to bring someone here?"

Pullus kept silent for a moment. No, he didn't want to bring Marcus, Calpurnia's husband, here. But that didn't mean he had to die in agony. He thought momentarily about how he himself had been snatched from the modern ruins of Herculaneum. Brought forward through time, but not all the way to their present. "I just want to skip him forward a few hours. Drop him back into the timeline after the eruption. Do you think that would be possible?"

"No, not yet," Arlen replied. "But communication with the past? Skipping people forwards? Everything is possible with the NovusPart device, given enough time..."

75

"You're sure this time?"

"Yes. The readings remain unclear, but there was one person standing near the statue, exactly as we instructed."

"Then we've finally saved him. I kept my promise."

NovusPart Device transcript, New Roman Empire

Pompeii, AD 79, post-eruption

"AN ASTROLOGER CAST a young boy's horoscope," whispered Achillia, stretching out on her back. Her body felt like it was tucked into a soft warm bed. But she knew she was outside, resting in ash. Not quite alive, and not yet buried either. "'He will be a lawyer, then a town official, then a governor.' And yet the young boy died. 'Ah, well,' the astrologer said to his mourning mother. 'He would have been all those things, if he'd lived.'"

Achillia chuckled. Around her, the plain of pebble, rock and ash continued to steam and smoke.

She was quite alone. And in some ways, she knew she

wasn't. She could see buildings, their upper floors just bobbing out of the ground, as if gasping for air. The largest looked like a temple. She stared at it for a good few seconds. There'd been nothing like it in Herculaneum. At least, not that she'd seen in her brief time there.

She was back in Pompeii. Yet she still couldn't quite place it. The horizon looked different. Vesuvius was half its size. The town was gone, buried. The people all probably entombed beneath her. Habitus. Barbatus. The baker, and the crippled boy.

All gone.

She got to her feet and dusted herself down. Ran a hand through her hair, and rubbed at her scalp. The resulting cloud of dust caused her to cough.

She stared at the top of the Temple of Jupiter. She'd failed. Failed to kill Denter. Failed to save him. And yet somehow she didn't care. The pressure in her ears – something she'd got used to since first visiting the Sibyl's cave – was suddenly gone.

She smiled. Her failure didn't matter because she was alive. She'd beaten them all. She could go back to Rome. And then she stopped.

She was the only one here. The only one alive for miles.

And she was standing above what had been the Temple of Jupiter, Juno and Minerva. Pompeii's reserves of gold and silver were probably only ten or so metres beneath her feet. Completely unattended.

All she needed was something to dig with, and she'd be very rich indeed.

So where the fuck could she get a shovel?

76

"Everyone wants to be them. To emulate them: from the Holy Roman Emperors, to tsars and kaisers, to despots like Mussolini. And yet the main weapon of the Roman Empire is often ignored; the way they included and incorporated populations in the ancient world was a revolutionary approach to conquest. They were, in some respects, an empire of multiculturalism... and yet the way in which their influence still affects us today, also an Empire of Time."

Nick Houghton,
Ambassador of New Pompeii

THE LIGHT IN the Fortuna Augusta was beginning to wane. Behind him, a voice called his name. Pullus turned, then walked towards Taedia. She indicated downwards.

His men – his new household staff – had been sent to find one of the outsiders manning the convoys, one of those who'd been helping to make lists of those called Marcus. Pullus eyed the outsider coldly. The man's face was bruised. Clearly, he hadn't been taken easily. "You work for Waldren?"

The man nodded. "Do you know he's dead? I killed him…"

The man looked upwards, defiance clear on his face. "You didn't transport him though, did you?"

Pullus signalled for the captive to be dragged away, a flash of anger in his eyes. Now he knew he controlled the NovusPart device, the solution to his illness should have been simple. He could simply snuff Waldren out as soon as they'd first met, wait thirty years and then steal him from time. And yet his muscles continued to complain, which meant that action hadn't been taken. His future self had been left with no choice but to suffer.

Insurance policy. Waldren's words came back to him. He must have known he might fail. Fabio had indicated he was using a false name, a false identity. A spy who'd made his personal history hard to find, and maybe had been watching and waiting for a long time too.

Carefully preparing to set him up. Maybe even infecting him on a different Naples visit to his last, so that his insurance policy was in place long before the pressure was applied. After all, his symptoms appeared to be coming on fast. Maybe he'd had the early signs for a long time and simply not recognised them. Either way, it would now be hard to find the point in time at which he could stop it from happening.

"They told me you killed McMahon," Arlen whispered at his shoulder. "I must admit, there were some occasions when I felt like stabbing that bastard…"

"It's complicated," Nick said, bitterly.

"That's the nature of time," replied Arlen. "But I wonder,

are you going to be a good emperor, or bad?"

Nick hesitated, again thinking of how Arlen had lost leave of his senses. All it had taken was control of the NovusPart device, and the simple thought that he was at the centre of it all.

"Calpurnia is dead," continued Arlen. "As is Marcus. And from where I'm standing, you're the man quivering behind the curtain." Arlen's smile slipped. He rubbed his temples. "I wonder: was Crassus really rich, if he couldn't afford a computer?"

Nick stopped. "What?"

"The Roman emperors went insane," Arlen said. "But ultimate power in the past is nothing compared to what the NovusPart device can offer."

"I am nothing like you."

"No? Do you think yourself immune to the drip of the purple dye? Aren't you already responsible for the death of a child?"

Nick found himself thinking again of Marcus. Calpurnia's son had drowned a slave, he reminded himself. And, along with Habitus, he'd been engineering mass murder, preparing to kill everyone who'd shared his name. Which was also likely why his future self had waited until now to interfere in the past. The only possible reason was that he'd been waiting for Marcus to reveal his true nature, to both him and the other Romans.

Just like Arlen, Marcus had been removed before he could become a madman.

I'm going to be a good emperor.

"I'm not talking about Calpurnia's son," Arlen said, seeming to read his thoughts. "The Greek told me what happened. The man called Harris. His *brother*."

Nick felt a stab of guilt deep in his stomach. It had been *his* voice on the cellphone. He had been the one masquerading as "Marcus". And yet everything he'd heard during that call had sounded so alien.

"You did it on purpose," Arlen continued. "You could have provided the correct codes and transported Harris's brother safely into the present. And yet you didn't. If you had done, of course, then Calpurnia or Habitus would probably be standing where you are now. You wouldn't be in charge because they wouldn't have let you take it from them. You were too weak. But that doesn't alter the fact you killed that boy. You lied. What sort of man does that? Nick Houghton? Or Decimus Horatius Pullus?"

Nick didn't want to listen anymore. He walked away, his limbs stiff.

"The man who can't be killed," Arlen shouted. "Do you really think you can resist power better than me? Better than Marcus or Caligula or Nero?"

ACKNOWLEDGEMENTS

It was something of a dream to get my first book published, so I'm delighted to have been given the opportunity to write a second novel.

My continued thanks go to my agent, Ian Drury (Sheil Land Associates), for offering me representation and securing a home for my work with Titan Books.

Miranda Jewess, my wonderful editor, shaped this sequel into its final form, and is responsible for these continuing temporal shenanigans. Thank you for your support, Miranda!

Also, thanks to Ella Chappell for taking a first read, and to Titan's publicity and marketing team who worked tirelessly to get the word out on *New Pompeii* and supported me at various events: Lydia Gittins, Chris Young, Philippa Ward, Hannah Scudamore and Chris McLane. Martin Stiff (Amazing15) has again designed a great cover to mirror that of the original. I was also very grateful for the support from all those who took the time to read and post reviews of *New Pompeii* – to get some space as a debut writer in what is a crowded market was very much appreciated.

Finally, I recently had the privilege of a detailed tour

of Pompeii and Herculaneum, including some fascinating "behind the scenes" access, led by Tony O'Connor. Tony's enthusiasm really did make the sites come alive – both in the past and the present. (Of course, any mistakes – deliberate or not! – are entirely my own.)

ABOUT THE AUTHOR

DANIEL GODFREY LIVES and works in Derbyshire, but tries his best to hold on to his Yorkshire roots. He studied geography at Cambridge University, before gaining an MSc in transport planning at Leeds. He enjoys reading history, science and SFF. His first novel, *New Pompeii*, was chosen as one of both the *Financial Times'* and the *Morning Star's* books of the year, and was described as "irresistibly entertaining" by Barnes & Noble. Dan's next novel, *The Synapse Sequence*, will be published in June 2018.

THE RIG
Roger Levy

Humanity has spread across the depths of space but is connected by AfterLife – a vote made by every member of humanity on the worth of a life. Bale, a disillusioned policeman on the planet Bleak, is brutally attacked, leading writer Raisa on to a story spanning centuries of corruption. On Gehenna, the last religious planet, a hyperintelligent boy, Alef, meets psychopath Pellon Hoq, and so begins a rivalry and friendship to last an epoch.

"Levy is a writer of great talent and originality."
SF Site

"Levy's writing is well-measured and thoughtful, multi-faceted and often totally gripping."
Strange Horizons

AVAILABLE MAY 2018

TITANBOOKS.COM